Texas Treasure

BY VICTORIA THOMPSON

D1454009

ZEBRA BOOKS
KENSINGTON PUBLISHING CORP.

ZEBRA BOOKS

are published by

Kensington Publishing Corp.
475 Park Avenue South
New York, N.Y. 10016

First printing: March 1985

Printed in the United States of America

To Jim and Dad, my two heroes

AUTHOR'S NOTE

Many of the historical events mentioned in this story actually happened. The Centennial Exposition was held in Philadelphia in 1876 to celebrate one hundred years of American progress and many Texas cattlemen attended it. Among them was W. S. Ikard who took an immediate liking to Hereford cattle and later had some brought to his ranch in Henrietta, Texas. They did not catch on, however, until two ranchers named Lee and Reynolds brought in seven carloads of the cattle in 1880 and proved that they would thrive in Texas. Dusty Rhoades would have been very forward thinking indeed to purchase Herefords when he did.

James S. Brisbin's book, *The Beef Bonanza or How to Get Rich on the Plains*, was published in 1881 and prompted many easterners and even Europeans to invest in western cattle operations. Unfortunately, most of them were wiped out in the terrible winter of 1886-87 which changed the entire procedure for raising cattle, ushering in the era of the barbed-wire fence.

The treasure that Jason Vance sought in Rainbow is as fictional as the town itself, but the fact is that Spanish payrolls were transported up the old Spanish Trail and many were lost while crossing streams or rivers and others were buried during Indian attacks or other hardships and never recovered. For more information on the subject, J. Frank Dobie's book, *Coronado's Children*, is an excellent explanation of why such treasures are almost impossible to locate and why Jason Vance was lucky to even find a *wrong* place to dig.

Chapter One

Priscilla looked down the barrel of the rifle. It seemed to stare at her like one large, black eye. She knew little about guns, but she knew enough to sit very still on the settee. Of course, a gun was only as dangerous as the person holding it. Cautiously, Priscilla looked up into the face of the man behind the rifle. Two cold gray eyes stared down at her. Cold, yes, she had always thought so. The eyes of a gambler. But were they dangerous? Few men would shoot a woman. Fewer still a woman who was . . .

Instinctively, her hand went to her still-flat tummy. No, he would have no way of knowing that. Afraid he might have read her thoughts, she glanced up at him again, but he had turned to watch the woman who stalked cat-like to and fro, across the room, from the front door to the window and back, eyes searching the empty road.

The woman turned fierce eyes on Priscilla. With certainty, Priscilla decided the danger lay not with the

9

man, though he was dangerous enough, but with the woman. She could see quite plainly that this woman hated her, and Priscilla had to admit that she had good reason.

"Where is he?" the woman demanded.

"I don't know," answered Priscilla. That much was true.

"When's he comin' back?"

"I don't know that either," Priscilla said, although she had a pretty good idea that it would not be long.

"Don't worry, my dear," said the man. "He won't be gone long."

"What makes you so sure?" snapped the woman, her green eyes flashing.

"Because," he replied, turning his gaze on Priscilla, and looking at her in a way that made her turn away, "he won't stay away from her too long."

The woman cursed violently. Priscilla was shocked but did not show it. After a long, awkward silence, she decided to speak.

"Please, if you will just tell me what it is you want. Whatever it is, simply tell me. It's yours. Take it and go."

The woman laughed scornfully and resumed her vigil at the window. The man simply smiled sardonically. "If only it were that easy, my dear lady, but alas, I am afraid we must wait. He"—he gestured toward the empty road—"is the only one who knows where it is."

"That's right," agreed the woman. "We'll wait for him. I been waitin' for him for a long time." The tone in her voice sent a cold chill over Priscilla.

The man stared at the green-eyed woman, a look of frank wonder on his face. "I'd almost give my share to know why it is that you hate him so much," he murmured.

When the woman did not reply, he turned curious eyes to Priscilla. "You know, don't you, ma'am?"

Priscilla simply met his gaze with unblinking eyes. He sighed in defeat. All of them turned once more to look out the open window at the still-empty road.

Priscilla looked again at the rifle, no longer pointed directly at her but certainly close enough. Well, she had come west for adventure. For a while she had been afraid that she would find the West just as tame as the Philadelphia of her youth. That fear seemed ludicrous now. She suddenly longed for her peaceful classroom, and for once, as she looked again at the winding road, she had no desire to see the man she loved. What would he say, what would he do, when he saw her captors? Odd, too, that the four of them—four people whose paths had crossed in such unusual ways—should soon all come together. In the deadly silence that remained, she thought back to the very beginning.

Priscilla's first view of Rainbow, Texas, had been through a cloud of dust outside the tiny window of a jolting stagecoach. The town seemed to spring from nowhere, a single street of unsightly buildings with a few houses scattered along the outskirts. That long street was virtually deserted in the early afternoon hour, and in place of the curious crowd of welcomers she had expected stood one lone cowboy.

The cowboy rubbed his chin thoughtfully. The new schoolteacher was not quite what he had expected. Not that he could see too much of her. He had caught a glimpse of a face when she had stepped off the stage but she was wearing one of those bonnets that stuck out in front and now she had turned away from him. What he had seen was all right, though. She wasn't quite pretty, but then few women really looked good after fifty miles on that stagecoach. Maybe she would clean up to look better. She was a little on the small side, too—maybe not even up to his chin—and she was wearing one of those consarn dusters that covered her from neck to knees and effectively concealed whatever feminine charms she might possess. But still, he liked what he saw, even if there *was* something about her that didn't sit quite right with him. Stella had said, "Meet the stage this afternoon and look for the new schoolma'am. Look for a young woman, says she's twenty-four. Now she'll be real scared and nervous just comin' into town, so you mind yourself and be real kind to her."

That was the part that didn't fit. She did not look twenty-four, but then maybe women didn't dry up as fast back East as they did in Texas. But it was more than that. She did not look one bit scared or nervous, either. In fact, she looked downright confident, standing there with those little shoulders squared, looking up and down the street to see who was going to meet her, just like she was some kind of queen come to pay a royal visit or something. Confident, that was it. Too damn confident, he decided, leaning back against the front of the hotel and taking a deep drag from the cigarette he had rolled a short while ago. He liked a woman to be a little off guard, a little vulnerable. Suppose he waited a minute or two, let her think no one had come to meet her, that she was all alone in a strange town in the middle of Texas. She would get a little worried. Those big, dark eyes—he could see they were dark now that she'd turned this way again—would get all soft and misty. Then he would come to her rescue. He liked that idea. How grateful she would be. He smiled slightly at the thought, crossed his arms over his chest, and shifted his weight from one booted foot to the other, to wait.

Priscilla Bedford looked around for someone who might be Ben Steele, come to meet her. She saw no one who looked like a successful, middle-aged rancher. No one, in fact, who seemed to be looking for her at all. The only person around was that cowboy. She had seen him as the stage had driven up. Leaning indolently against the front wall of the hotel, he presented a striking picture in the western clothes she had not yet become accustomed to. He was tall, over six feet she guessed, in those high-heeled boots, and whipcord lean, although he had a pair of shoulders that any man would envy. He was wearing the usual plaid shirt with a red silk bandana knotted at his throat, and a pair of the faded blue Levis, that seemed to be *de rigueur* for men in this part of the world, covered the impossible length of his slender legs. Bench-made boots, Priscilla noted, adorned his feet, and on his head he wore a large Stetson that had once been white pushed carelessly back to reveal a shock of hair that was the strangest color she had ever seen. Not exactly red or blond, or any other color she could name, it waved gently across his broad forehead in an untameable tangle. All this she had noticed in the time it took for the stage to draw up and stop before the Rainbow Hotel. She had managed only a glance at his face, hastily averting her eyes when she found him staring back, and was left with the impression that he possessed the bluest eyes she had ever seen. He was clean shaven. That much she had noticed and it was noteworthy, since almost every man she had met sported either a beard, long side whiskers, or at the very least, a mustache. That hair, she thought, would make a remarkable beard. What color *was* it? Just about the color, she decided, of the Texas dust she had been living with for the past two days on the stage. She hazarded another glance in his direction, and found he was still watching her, so she kept her eyes moving, scanning the sidewalk in both directions for someone coming to meet her. Still no one in sight, except the cowboy, and he was obviously not looking *for* her, just *at* her, so she deliberately avoided looking back at him.

Her only fellow passenger had gotten his bag and was ready to go on his way. He approached her and asked, "Anything more I can do for you, Miss Bedford?" Priscilla looked up into a well-chiseled face. He was definitely handsome, she had long since decided, almost aristocratic with his aquiline nose and molded chin. The thin, well-trimmed black mustache and his carefully oiled and combed hair completed the well-ordered impression created by his black frock coat and white silk shirt. The only thing that prevented her from thinking he was a traveling minister was the brightly flowered vest he wore. New to the West, Priscilla could not know that the gaudy vest was a trademark for a certain type of man, but she did know that he wasn't a preacher by the vest . . . and by his eyes. What was it about those eyes? So light gray as to be almost colorless, they stared back at her like two mirrors, reflecting her own image but allowing her no glimpse of the person behind them. Ignoring the small shiver that danced up her spine, she smiled politely at the man who had shared the stage with her for the last thirty miles. He had been a pleasant companion since a lame horse had forced him to flag down the stage, entertaining her with talk of literature and poetry. Pleasant, yes, but cold, and Priscilla wondered idly if anything ever cracked that cool, emotionless veneer.

"Thank you, Mr. Vance, but no. Someone will be meeting me very soon, I'm sure. I would not think of detaining you," she said. He returned her courteous smile, or at least the corners of his mouth turned up, as he expressed his pleasure at having met her. Raising one long, slender, and very white hand, he tipped his hat to her and disappeared into the hotel.

"Miss, what'll I do with your trunk?" It was the driver.

"Just set it there for now. Someone will be meeting me," she replied. From the corner of her eye she could see the cowboy staring at her with a smirk on his face. It wasn't the first time a young man had stared at her, and she could ordinarily handle it with aplomb, but this particular young man unaccountably annoyed her. She had half a mind to turn around and ask him what he thought he was staring at, but fearing that such an approach might only encourage someone so ill-mannered, she decided to ignore him.

Still no one to meet her. Well, perhaps the stage was early, she speculated. Deciding she would like to get a better look at the town, she walked a short distance down the wooden sidewalk in the opposite direction from where the cowboy was standing, passed the stagecoach, and looked across the street.

The street itself was more like a field than the tree-lined boulevards she was used to, large enough for four wagons to ride abreast. On the other side of the street was a row of unpainted buildings, sporting pretentious false fronts. Beginning at one end, she identified among others a Sheriff's office, a lawyers' office, a telegraph office, a saddle shop, and dwarfing them all was the only truly

15

two-storied building in town, which even to Priscilla's inexperienced eye, appeared to be a saloon. A large, ornate sign graced the front of the second story, on which was painted the word "Rita's." Intertwined in the letters was the stem of a yellow rose. "Rita's Yellow Rose," Priscilla said to herself. She smiled because it reminded her of the pubs in England whose signs were pictures because the populace could not read. "Well," she thought, "that's why I'm here."

Was the cowboy still there? The question came unbidden to her mind, and she realized with a slight shock that she would be gravely disappointed if he had given up so easily. But no, she would not be disappointed. A funny little prickle along the back of her neck told her he was still keeping his vigil. Slowly, she turned toward where he was standing. He was indeed still watching, a look of admiration plain across his face, a small smirk twisting his well-formed mouth. He had just made a move to straighten up from his casual posture and for one awful moment Priscilla thought he would actually approach her. She forced her face into its most haughty expression, raising her eyebrows in a way that could only be described as disdainful, ignoring the strange impact those startlingly blue eyes seemed to be having on her senses. Their eyes locked in a silent struggle and slowly the cowboy's smirk disappeared.

Yes, the cowboy liked what he had seen of the new schoolteacher so far. The way she walked, head up, looking around as if she owned the place, like a queen. Yes, regal was the word for her, all right. She did not look worried, though, and she didn't look like the kind of woman who was likely to become distressed, now or at any other time. And that won his respect, however it might have ruined his plans. He found himself thinking how neatly she would tuck in just under his chin, just how cosy it would be to have her there. He was trying to decide if those huge brown eyes would be shy or bold in such an instance, when suddenly those huge brown eyes turned on him full force in all their frosty splendor. A joke was a joke, but Dusty suddenly realized that he had let this one drag out just a little too long. This was his last chance to speak up and explain himself, but as he roused himself to do just that, she gave him a look that could have stopped an elephant dead in its tracks. The words of explanation died on his lips.

A sudden noise across the street jarred her attention away and she saw a man coming out of the law office and hurrying across the street toward her, pulling on his suitcoat as he came. He was too young to be Ben Steele, but from the way he was approaching, she felt certain she was about to be met at last.

"Miss Bedford?" he inquired breathlessly. He was what was called a fine looking man, about thirty, medium height, with light brown hair and a matching mustache, and friendly eyes that seemed would always hold a smile. He had no particularly striking feature, but everything came together very nicely, right down to his tailored suit which, she noted with approval, lacked the tell-tale crease that said "store-bought."

Priscilla put on her best "new schoolteacher" smile. "Yes," she replied.

"How do you do, ma'am, I am George Wilson, Ben Steele's son-in-law. He was unable to meet you personally. His health makes it difficult for him to get into town." Priscilla murmured something sympathetic, and he continued, "I was instructed to meet you and here

I've left you standing in the street. I hope you can forgive me."

Priscilla was smiling for real, now. All the warnings she had received about the uncouth men she would have to endure out here seemed humorous as she looked at George Wilson, so obviously a man of good breeding. "Of course, Mr. Wilson. I haven't been here more than a moment, at any rate."

"You are very kind. We certainly don't want you to get a bad impression on your first day here. My wife, Stella, is Mr. Steele's eldest. She thought that you'd prefer to go directly to your room at the schoolhouse and freshen up a bit before being presented to the entire family."

"Oh, how very kind. That sounds like a wonderful idea to me," Priscilla said happily. She was going to like Stella Steele Wilson.

"Good," George Wilson said. "My wife was going to send someone with a wagon out from the ranch to take you in. Let's see." He was looking past her for that someone. "Yes, there's our foreman now."

A sixth sense and a tiny little flutter in her stomach told Priscilla that she was about to meet her cowboy face to face. Turning expectantly, she watched her admirer sheepishly step forward. Well, she thought with an irritation way out of proportion to the event, maybe he had his reasons for letting me stand here on the sidewalk like a fool, gawking at me, but they cannot be very good ones. Ignoring the small voice that urged caution and following the demon who encouraged revenge, she turned back to George Wilson and asked in a very loud whisper behind her hand, "Can he speak?"

Puzzled, George Wilson looked at his foreman, at her, and then at his foreman again. Now George Wilson was a clever man, clever enough to know when he had come in in the middle of a game, and from his friend's bleak expression and the twinkle in the schoolteacher's eye, he knew who was holding the high card. Never liking to pick a loser, he chose to back the little lady. "Why, of course he can speak," he replied innocently.

"I only ask," she continued in her stage whisper, "because he's been standing there ever since I got off the stage, and he never gave any indication he was here to meet me. I thought perhaps he was deaf and dumb." She lowered her hand and smiled guilelessly at the cowboy.

His bleak expression was turning thunderous now. The worst part was not being embarrassed in front of George, but the fact that *he* had decided to play a game with *her*, and she had beaten him at it. It did not sit well, not well at all.

"Miss Bedford"—it was Wilson remembering his manners and enjoying his friend's discomfort—"this is our foreman, Dusty Rhoades."

Priscilla almost laughed out loud. She had never heard a name like that before. Surely, it must be a joke. But no, neither man was laughing, least of all Dusty Rhoades. And a more perfect name she could not have chosen for him. "How do you do, Mr. Rhoades?" she said and smiled a smile that she hoped made her look very attractive.

It did, and that made Dusty even madder, if that were possible. "Howdy, ma'am," he mumbled, and tipped his hat slightly. To Wilson he said, "I got a wagon down at the livery. I'll load up her trunk."

"Fine, thank you, Dusty. We'll be waiting inside," Wilson said, but Dusty had already gone to get the wagon. With a small shrug and an amused smile, he turned to Priscilla. "Perhaps you would like some refreshment before you continue your journey. It's a long, thirsty drive to the Steele place."

"Thank you. I'd love a cup of tea at least," she agreed.

"There's a very nice restaurant here at the hotel, if you will allow me," George Wilson said, offering his arm. With a short backward glance to where her cowboy had disappeared, she took Wilson's arm and entered the hotel.

Priscilla's private opinion was that the hotel would have been more correctly described as a restaurant that rented rooms. In any case, they could not have had more than four or five rooms down the short hall that led off the lobby, and no one could be seen manning the desk. The restaurant, however, which opened off the lobby, obviously did a brisk business during mealtimes. Even though the large room was deserted now, most of the tables bore evidence of having been used for the noon meal. Wilson's call brought a large, officious-looking woman bustling from the kitchen. In spite of her plain clothes and stained apron, she proved to be the owner of the Rainbow Hotel, and she made Priscilla welcome in a distracted way.

"You'll want to wash up, I expect," Mrs. Siddons said, and without bothering to wait for an answer, propelled Priscilla through the kitchen to an enclosed porch where she found a pump and a wooden bench on which were such items as were deemed necessary for personal hygiene: a dingy tin basin and a bar of homemade soap so covered with dirt as to be barely recognizable. Above the bench hanging from a string was a comb with most of its teeth missing and a roller towel which Priscilla estimated had not been laundered in her lifetime.

Seeing Priscilla's dismay, Mrs. Siddons erupted into a

fit of laughter that shook her ample frame from top to bottom. "S-sorry, miss," she managed at last, wiping her streaming eyes with the corner of her apron. "We don't get many ladies here. I reckon I'm just so used to the place, I don't see it the way a stranger does. Just wait right here. I'll fix you right up." As good as her word, she returned shortly with a porcelain basin, a brand new bar of soap and a spanking white towel, for which Priscilla expressed undying gratitude.

With her face and hands washed and most of the loose dirt brushed out of her duster, Priscilla made her way back to the dining room, where she found George Wilson seated at one of the tables. In another moment, Mrs. Siddons, who was not only the owner of the restaurant but also the cook and waitress, served them a pot of tea and a plate of donuts, which Wilson assured Priscilla were the specialty of the house. Specialty or not, Priscilla found them delicious after the beef and beans regimen of the stage stops for the past two days, and she ate two greedily.

Surprisingly, at least to Priscilla, George Wilson made no mention of the scene outside with Dusty Rhoades, although she could tell by the twinkle in his eyes that he was remembering it with amusement. Instead he made polite inquiries about her trip, and told her a little about the town. Priscilla could not help glancing up from time to time to see if Dusty Rhoades would come in to join them, and she was aware of a vague sense of disappointment when he did not appear.

When she had finished her second cup of tea, Wilson asked, "Are you ready to go? I'm sure Dusty has your trunk loaded up by now."

"Yes, I'm ready," she replied, rising from the table.

The flutter in her stomach, she told herself sternly, was excitement over starting a new life and quite definitely *not* over the prospect of seeing Dusty Rhoades again.

They encountered the cowboy in the lobby where he sat sprawled on one of the horsehair sofas, apparently engrossed in a rather yellowed newspaper. When he heard their footsteps, Dusty allowed himself to steal a glance over the top of the paper. Why, she was no bigger than a minute, he told himself. For sure, nothing to be scared of. Not that he was scared. It was just that, well, she put a man off balance. Nothing he couldn't handle, though. Never met a woman yet who couldn't be handled, if you were just careful, he mused. Dusty heaved a weary sigh. Something told him this one would need a lot of care, though. He put down the paper and rose to his feet with elaborate casualness, his face expressionless, careful to avoid looking at the new schoolteacher. "All set to go?" he asked George, as if Priscilla were not able to speak for herself.

More courteous, George cast an inquiring look at Priscilla before replying in the affirmative.

"Wagon's out front," Dusty informed them and stood aside as George escorted her outside and helped her up onto the wagon seat.

Priscilla was still adjusting her skirts when Dusty Rhoades levered his long form up onto the seat beside her. Only then did the truth begin to dawn on her, and as she turned back to where George still stood beside the wagon, some of her dismay must have shown on her face, because George had the grace to look a little sympathetic as he confirmed her worst fears. "Dusty will take you out to the ranch. I have some business here in town, but I'll see you at supper later. You'll be quite safe in Dusty's capable hands, I assure you," he added as if in answer to her silent plea. She could not be certain, but she thought his lip twitched under his mustache. Priscilla thanked him prettily for his kindness while her eyes condemned him for his betrayal, and as he backed away, he was openly chuckling at her dilemma.

Determined to make the best of an unpleasant situation, Priscilla pulled her lips into a polite little smile and turned to Dusty Rhoades to make a conciliatory remark, but just as she opened her mouth, he slapped the reins and let loose a resounding "Gee-up," and the wagon lurched into motion so quickly she was forced to grab hold of the seat to keep from falling over, all friendly overtures forgotten.

Unknown to either of them, from across the street, two green eyes watched their departure from a window above the painted yellow rose—two green eyes in which the hint of malice was unmistakable.

Rita Jordan watched Dusty and Priscilla from her window above the saloon with great personal interest. "Dusty with a woman," she said to herself and the thought gave her great pleasure. And great pain. For years she had waited for her chance. She had been very patient, like a spider spinning a web. It had taken courage and ingenuity to even get to the place where she could spin it, and that had been accomplished long ago. Then she had had to wait because although the web was ready she had no bait for it, nothing with which to attract her victim to his destruction, and for so very long not even a hope of any. Now for the first time, she had seen Dusty with a woman. Perhaps this woman could be the bait. Who was she? No matter. By sundown tonight, Rita would know all there was to know about her and if she could possibly be useful.

As she thought about these things, she saw someone else come out of the hotel who interested her. A stranger, a man, very handsome and from her perspective at least, he seemed well-dressed. Who was he? That information Rita would also know by this evening and probably would also have met the man himself. Not many men came to town without visiting Rita's Yellow Rose.

The object of Rita's curiosity was Jason Vance, Priscilla's fellow passenger. Having obtained a room for the night, Vance made his way to the livery stable, the one place in town where he was sure to obtain the only two other things he needed: a horse and some information. A man of the world, Vance knew that the livery was usually kept by a nondescript character whom everyone knew and to whom no one paid any attention. Consequently, this character was likely to overhear many conversations in the course of his job and to know everything of importance going on in the town, and quite a bit of unimportance.

In Rainbow the character was an old man, probably not as old as he looked, but too old to punch cows anymore. He sat dozing in a chair leaning back against the wall of the stable.

"Excuse me, sir," said Vance, waking the old man with a start. "I am new in town and in great need of a horse. Would you possibly know of one I might purchase?"

Not used to being addressed as "sir" or treated with any sort of respect, the man sat blinking for a moment, as if not quite certain he was awake. At last he said, "Sure, mister. I think I kin hep ya out."

"I would appreciate it very much. Jason Vance is my name." Vance extended his hand for the old man to shake. For a moment he just stared at it in disbelief and then finally, he wiped his own hand on his dirty jeans and shook hands with Vance.

"Potter's my name. Zeke Potter. Folks jist call me Ol' Zeke," he sputtered.

"Happy to meet you, Mr. Potter. Perhaps you would do me the favor of advising me about the horses you have for sale here." Naturally Ol' Zeke was only too happy to oblige his new friend and for a long time they discussed the merits of the horses whose owners Zeke was sure would be willing to strike a bargain with Vance. Vance listened respectfully, asking questions, allowing Potter to show off his knowledge of horse flesh. Finally, he allowed himself to be persuaded to buy the horse he had long since decided on, a black gelding with white stockings. Not a fine horse, but it would serve his purpose. Vance asked Potter to serve as his agent in the sale, giving him his commission in advance.

Having won the old man's confidence, Vance proceeded to his next order of business. "You wouldn't have anything to drink around here, would you?" he asked conspiratorially.

"Shore do," he chortled and produced a bottle of whisky and a tin cup. Pouring for Vance, he drank straight from the bottle.

"Nice little town you got here," Vance ventured, seating himself on a three-legged stool.

"Yep, it shore is," Potter agreed and launched into a history of Rainbow and how it had been settled by a few big ranchers: Steele, Old Man Rhoades who was dead now, and a few others.

"I notice you've only got one saloon. That the only place a man can get a drink—besides the Livery Stable?"

Vance asked, winking.

Potter chuckled. "Well, thar's a barroom at the hotel, but that's jist fer a se-lect few who don't wanna be seen cavortin' over ta Rita's."

"Rita's," Vance mused. "You don't see many saloons owned by women."

"Nope," Potter agreed. "Don't see many women like Rita Jordan, neither."

"I guess her husband helps run the place," Vance suggested.

"No, Rita's a widow woman. That's a right funny story in itself." Potter chuckled again. The whisky and the audience were making him very talkative. Vance leaned forward with interest to encourage him.

"Seems about five, six years back, Rita, she was workin' the Kansas cattle towns. One day this ol' miner, Sam Jordan was his name, comes inta this town where she was, claims he struck it rich and has the gold to prove it. Says he's got a secret strike somewheres and it's worth millions. He feels like celebratin' and claims he's gonna marry him the prettiest whore in town and build her a castle. Well, he commences to tryin' out every cat house in town to pick him a bride an' he finally settles when he gets to Rita. He shore nuff married her—lasted three days 'til they found him dead in his bed. Doc said his heart give out, but folks all reckoned that Rita was jist too much woman fer him. Anyhow, it took the undertaker two days to git the smile off his face!" Potter dissolved in drunken laughter at his own joke.

Vance smiled politely. He had heard the story before, but like the careful man he was, he was checking his facts. "So she got the mine," he suggested.

"Hell, no," said Potter when he recovered himself.

26

"Prob'ly weren't no mine at all, prob'ly jist stole the gold offin some pore old soul. But she did git what gold he had left an' that was a heap."

"Set her up for life, I guess. Strange she'd choose a one-horse town like this when she could have gone anywhere," Vance said.

"Yeah, even funnier, when she come here, there's already a saloon here. She wants to buy it, but Ol' Franklin, he won't sell. So she waits around. Then, one day, Franklin up an' dies. Doc says it was his heart. Me, I always figured ol' Rita give him a dose of what killed Sam Jordan." He chuckled again.

"She must be a dried up old woman by now," Vance sighed.

"Well, she ain't as young as she once was but she ain't so old neither. An' she ain't too hard to look at, if ya know what I mean." Potter's eyes were a little glazed now, thinking of the lovely Rita through a whisky fog.

"My friend, I thank you for a very enjoyable afternoon, but I am afraid I must be going as I have other business to attend to." Vance rose to leave, setting his untouched cup of whisky on the floor.

Potter leaned his chair back against the wall again. "You're a gambler," he said. It was not a question. Vance stopped. "Be kerful. Miss Rita's mighty particular who gambles in her place." Potter's eyes were closed now and the next moment he was snoring. Vance smiled to himself and moved on. He would be careful. A gambler had to be.

While Vance was horsetrading, Dusty's wagon made its way slowly to the Steele ranch. When they had been gone but five minutes from town, Priscilla began to

27

seriously regret her earlier cleverness. It was one thing to put a man in his place if you never had to see him again, and quite another if you were going to quite soon be thrust into his company for a considerable length of time. If she had known, she would have been more careful. Well, that had always been her trouble, never thinking of the consequences. This was not the first time she had had to get herself out of a sticky situation and she guessed she should know how by now. The first thing she had to do was break the oppressive silence that lay between them. She darted a quick glance at her companion. Something about the tight set of his jaw told her she would get little help from him. She had to think of some safe, neutral topic with which to begin a conversation. At that moment, the breeze caught her bonnet, and as she made the necessary adjustments, she decided. The weather is always a safe topic.

Feeling Priscilla's eyes on him, Dusty looked over just as she looked away. Now what does she think she's looking at? he wondered, taking an extra second to examine her profile. Funny, he hadn't noticed before how her nose turned up on the end. Kind of pert. Yeah, that was it, he thought, with a flash of annoyance. Pert. Described her perfectly. His glance slid over and touched her again briefly. A piece of her hair had come loose from under her bonnet and was hanging down her back. He had thought her hair was dark, brown or black or something like that, but in the sunlight that one piece looked almost red. It sort of glittered. He shifted uneasily on the seat, fighting the urge to reach over and tuck that stray lock of hair back where it belonged. Or better still, have a look at what the rest of her hair was like. Reminding himself of the way she had injured his pride—

in front of George, no less—he brought himself up short. You owe her, pardner, he told himself, stifling any more tender feelings, and smiled grimly.

Readjusting her bonnet against the onslaught of the Texas breeze, Priscilla inquired quite sincerely, "Does the wind blow this way all the time?"

Dusty only hesitated for a moment before answering in his best deadpan, "No, ma'am, it blows the other way about half the time."

It took Priscilla a full thirty seconds to realize she had been had. Her initial reaction was that the poor, ignorant cowboy had misunderstood her, but one glance at his face had convinced her otherwise. He was actually grinning! It was such an engaging grin, too, so boyish and innocent looking. How could a face like that cover such a black heart? Suddenly that face turned toward her, those improbably blue eyes, brimming with laughter, seeking out her reaction to his thrust. Those eyes clashed with hers for one brief instant before she lifted her chin and turned away to watch the Texas scenery go by.

Dusty had waited a full minute before turning to see if he had scored a hit, but when he glanced over, he almost forgot his triumph. Good Lord, her eyes were dark! So brown they were almost black and flashing fire, too, or he was damned. Then she'd poked that little chin out at him and turned away—snubbed him, or tried to, but it was no good. He knew he'd won that round. He stifled a chuckle as he stole another look at his adversary. Those smooth, white cheeks had turned mighty pink and he didn't think it was from the sun, either. And the way her lips were thinned out and pressed together, she must be really fuming. Not that she could really thin that bottom lip. It was still pretty full. And soft looking. A man could catch

29

it between his teeth and . . . he jerked himself back from such reflection, swearing under his breath. This woman had made a fool of him. He had to keep that in mind. Never mind how she looked. A rattler could be mighty pretty, too, until it bit you. With that in mind, he turned back to his driving.

Priscilla *was* fuming, but at the same time she was trying to be sensible. After all, she had made a fool of the man, and in front of George Wilson, too. That was a serious blow, and he had certainly been justified in striking back. It was only fair. Now they were even. And, she reminded herself, it behooved her to be generous since this man was someone she was bound to come in contact with day after day. Peace must be made, and she would be the one to do it. Show him there were no hard feelings. Begin again. She cast about in her mind for another safe topic with which to begin a conversation. What man does not like to talk about himself?

Priscilla let another mile fall behind them and then said, as pleasantly as she could, "Mr. Wilson said you were the foreman. Exactly what does a foreman do?"

Dusty had almost jumped when she had spoken, so shocked was he at the mildness of her voice. She sounded so sweet, like butter wouldn't melt in her mouth. Looked sweet, too, he decided, turning wary eyes in her direction. Anyone would think she was really interested, but he knew better. Trying to get him to talk, was she? Looking for a weak spot where she could stick him. Well, she'd have to do a lot more than flutter those long eyelashes to get to Dusty Rhoades. He was immune to her charms. "Oh, a little bit of everything, ma'am," he replied with a studied lack of enthusiasm.

Only slightly daunted—she had expected a little

resistance—she continued. "Is it like a cowboy?" she inquired ignorantly with a small encouraging smile.

It was wasted on him because he chose not to look up. She'd get no encouragement from him. Determined was she? Well, he'd dealt with nosey easterners before. None of them were any match for a westerner determined not to talk. "Yes, ma'am," he replied blandly, without even so much as a glance in her direction.

Priscilla fought down a wave of annoyance. Stubborn was he? Well, she could be just as stubborn as he. Fortunately, she had read enough about cattle ranching to know exactly what a ranch foreman was and did. She doubted very much whether he could long withstand the temptation to admit that he did indeed almost single-handedly run Ben Steele's ranch with its thousands of cattle. Pretending she was unconcerned by his monosyllabic answers, she continued to question him, phrasing her queries in such a way that he could answer to show himself to advantage, but he foiled her. To each question she received either a "Yes, ma'am" or a "No, ma'am," delivered in an extremely bored monotone, until at last she felt like screaming in frustration. Finally, in exasperation, she snapped, "You needn't keep calling me 'ma'am.' I doubt that anyone over the age of twelve has ever called me 'ma'am.'"

Dusty pursed his lips a moment to keep from grinning at the opening she had given him at last and schooled his features into innocence. Turning to her with what might have passed for total sincerity, he informed her, "Well, *ma'am*"—he put great emphasis on the word—"I reckon you better get used to hearin' it around her. See, folks in Texas are different from folks back east. Folks in Texas are *polite*." He allowed himself the luxury of watching his words sink in, watching those large, dark eyes grow larger still and that pretty little Cupid's bow of a mouth drop open, and those soft round cheeks turn pink and then pinker still, until that little jaw snapped shut, eyes flashing fire again, and the whole face turned away. She was the picture of outrage, and he had to bite his tongue to keep from laughing right out.

Priscilla was so angry, she could scarcely breathe. She was afraid she might start puffing like an enraged old lady at any moment. Polite, indeed! A fine nerve he had, talking about "polite," the rudest man in creation! She'd bent over backward trying to reconcile with him and this was her reward. Several miles rolled by before she could even think rationally and several more before she could be reasonable. No man had ever succeeded in making her this angry, and she had traded witticisms with many men. Educated men. Cultured men. Boring men. The thought startled her. Had they been boring? Of course they had, she told herself ruthlessly. Why else would she have fled the East when the opportunity presented itself? She had wanted excitement. Excitement, yes, but not this! she argued with herself. This cowboy was so, so, what was the word? Relentless! Yes, that was it. Relentless. With a small jolt, she suddenly realized that the same might have been said about her. Indeed, probably *had* been said about her by all those men who had surrendered so graciously to her in those battles of wit. No one had ever been able to best her. Until today. She had simply never met her match before. Her match! The thought was strangely disturbing. And exciting. She stole a sidelong glance at Dusty Rhoades.

He was leaning forward, elbows on his knees, reins held loosely in his large, sun-darkened hands. His hat was pulled low over his eyes, so she could not see much of his face, but she noticed the way his jaw squared away before it curved up to meet his ear and the way that ridiculous red-gold hair curled along the back of his neck. His shirt was pulled taut across his shoulders, and she watched the play of muscles under the material. She had thought him thin when she had first seen him standing by the hotel, with his long legs and narrow hips, but now she realized that she had been mistaken. While not one ounce of fat graced his large frame, he was well padded with a solid layer of muscle that molded his shoulders, his arms, his thighs, his whole body into a thing of beauty. Well, not beauty, exactly, Priscilla chided herself. After all, women were beautiful and men were . . . well, manly. Dusty Rhoades was certainly that. All bone and muscle, his body was probably rock hard to the touch. Priscilla felt a flutter in her stomach and looked quickly away. Such thoughts! A lady never considered how a man's body would feel, for heaven's sake. Still . . . she glanced over to him again. He was engrossed in driving the wagon, and she watched the way his brown hands worked the reins, holding them almost carelessly between his long, thin fingers. She compared her own small, smooth hands to his, dark, work-roughened, calloused, and hard. For a moment she imagined how those hands would feel moving across her bare skin. Horrified, she jerked her eyes and her thoughts away, blushing at her own boldness. What had gotten into her? A lady did not think such things. Especially about a man who had treated her so shabbily. Why, he had never even spoken a civil word to her and here she was thinking about . . . Her face burned even hotter as she tried to concentrate on watching the passing countryside. She tried to be reasonable. A man like that was hardly worthy of her attention. He was rude, uncultured, ill-bred, and probably already had a girl, anyway. Priscilla stiffened at the thought. Now where had that come from? No matter. It was probably true, she insisted. Why, he might even be married, for all she knew. Married! Of their own accord her eyes darted back to his hands. No wedding ring, of course. Men did not wear wedding rings. Well, he didn't act married, but then how did married men act? Well, polite, like George Wilson. No, that wasn't right. Single men acted polite like that, too, usually. But not Dusty Rhoades. Oh, no. That proved nothing. But was he married? Priscilla knew an irrational desire to find out. Later she would realize that she might have waited and found out from anyone in a very casual way, but that was later. At this moment she was only aware of a burning desire to know. Now how could she find out? She could certainly not simply ask, "Are you married?" She cringed at the thought of what his answer to that might be. No, it would have to be subtle. Discreet.

Dusty straightened to ease his back. He did not care much for wagons, but he was still smiling. Almost to the ranch and not a peep out of her for the last five miles. He guessed he knew how to put her in her place. She'd met her match in him, all right. He hazarded a glance in her direction. That chin was still sticking out a mile. It was a struggle not to laugh out loud when he remembered how her mouth had dropped right open. Well, a woman had to learn proper respect, and this one had been taught by a master. He savored the feeling of accomplishment. Yes, the schoolteacher had learned something today, and he was satisfied. And smug.

Suddenly, she spoke. "Will you have any children in

the school, Mr. Rhoades?"

"None that I know of." The words were out before he could stop them. It had seemed so natural, and he hadn't been thinking and now he'd done it. A little friendly banter was one thing, but he'd just made an off-color remark to a lady, and a total stranger at that. A man had to be mighty careful around a decent woman. Hell, he'd known women to faint, or at least pretend to, from just hearing the word "leg." And wait 'til Stella found out. She'd murder him. What a fool he was! He silently cursed himself, not daring to look at his companion while he tried to figure out what to do.

Priscilla was in shock. Well, that was what she deserved for lusting in her heart. Your sins will find you out, she remembered her grandmother warning her. She had thought him uncouth and ill-mannered and so he had proven himself. Heaven only knew to what depravity a man like that would stoop! Horrified, she realized he was stopping the wagon. All the veiled warnings she had received about the dangers of a woman traveling alone started ringing in her ears. What should she do? What *could* she do? She was alone in the middle of nowhere. She had no idea which way to run, if she *could* have outrun the long-legged cowboy, and this she doubted very much. Well, whatever happened, she would brazen it out. She would not betray fear, no matter what happened. Stiffening her spine along with her resolve, she turned her large and over-bright eyes toward Dusty Rhoades.

Dusty was sitting very still, studying the reins that he held with great care. He had quickly, very quickly indeed, considered all his options and come to the very discomforting conclusion that he must apologize. As

35

much as it rankled, he knew he had no other choice if he ever wanted to show his face at the Steele ranch again. He could only hope that she would forgive him, because if she didn't . . . well, it didn't bear thinking of. Gathering his courage along with the strength of will it took to swallow his pride, he took a deep breath.

"Ma'am, I mean, Miss Bedford, you must think I'm the lowest, meanest polecat you ever met." Priscilla blinked in astonishment. Could this be an apology? She had no idea what a "polecat" was, but the repentant tone in his voice was unmistakable. She listened raptly as he continued. "Fact is, you're prob'ly right, but I'm not usually so low and mean to a lady as I have been to you. It ain't no excuse, but I just got a burr under my saddle 'cause of the way you treated me back in town. I'm mighty sorry for offendin' you. If you could forgive me, I'd be much obliged." He forced himself to meet her eyes, as much to judge her reaction as to let her see he was sincere.

Priscilla looked deep into those bluest-of-blue eyes, and saw no dancing devils. For whatever reason, he truly regretted having offended her. And well he should! she reasoned. There was no excuse . . . well, maybe there was an excuse, she admitted as her own conscience pricked her. She had not considered apologizing as a way of clearing the air between them, but since he had started it . . . "Mr. Rhoades, if you offended me, it was no more than I deserved. I was unspeakably rude to you, and *I* must beg *your* pardon for that."

Dusty's eyebrows lifted in surprise. Well, now, that was a lot more than he'd bargained for. Maybe she wasn't such a shrew after all. But he knew the rules. A gentleman never let a lady take the blame. Not if he really wanted to hear the end of it. He swallowed the last remnant of his pride and said, "You were right in that, though. I did leave you standin' and for no good reason." It had been a bad day all around, he decided.

He certainly was a stubborn man, Priscilla concluded with amusement. Now that he had decided to reconcile, he would not even let her share the burden of guilt. Well, she could be as magnanimous as he. "It seems we have both been entirely at fault," she declared, letting her amusement show in her voice. "Perhaps we should call this a draw and declare a truce. Does that seem fair?" The surprise and uncertainty on his face made her smile. She had caught him off guard. Maybe she had managed to maintain some advantage after all.

She sure was a hard woman to figure, he decided, as he watched her lips shape themselves into a smile. Had mighty pretty teeth, too, he noticed. In fact, her whole face looked kind of pretty when she smiled. He smiled back. "More than fair, ma—Miss Bedford," he agreed.

He looked so appealing when he smiled. Impulsively, Priscilla held out her hand. "Shall we shake on it?"

Dusty did not think he had ever shaken hands with a woman, but he surely did not want to offend her again, so he wiped his palm on his pant leg and took her hand. It felt awfully small and very soft and terribly fragile, except that she was gripping back, shaking hands the way a man would, only with that tiny little hand. It gave him the funniest feeling in the pit of his stomach, and a little lower . . .

His hand was so large and warm. It seemed to swallow hers as he gingerly took possession of it. Still, she could sense his strength, the power he was holding back, a force that could overwhelm her if he ever let it go. It gave her the funniest feeling in the pit of her stomach, and a little lower . . .

As blue eyes looked into brown ones, the large hand continued to hold the small one for long seconds after a normal handshake would have ceased, until they both realized the impropriety of just sitting there holding hands. Priscilla gave an embarrassed little laugh as she drew her hand away in the same instant that Dusty blinked and shook his head and released his grip. Both looked quickly away, Priscilla acutely aware of her heightened color, Dusty wondering why his collar felt so tight when he wasn't even wearing one.

"How far . . ."

"We're almost . . ."

They both looked up and began speaking at the same time, and this time they both laughed, each enjoying the other's embarrassment.

"You first," Dusty said, studying the way her eyes sparkled as if they had tiny little stars in them.

"I was just going to ask how far it was to the ranch," she said, liking the way the corners of his eyes crinkled up when he smiled.

He chuckled. "I was just going to say we're not too far from the ranch now. The road forks up ahead here a ways, and then you'll see the ranch over to your left. The school's about a half-mile further after that."

Priscilla nodded her understanding, and after watching her with inordinate interest for another moment, Dusty took up the reins again and chucked the team into motion.

"There'll be a gate before we get to the school. Ben— Mr. Steele—fenced it in with bobwire so the cows wouldn't bother you none." He cut his eyes in her direction to find she was listening raptly. For a moment he almost forgot what he had been saying. "They—the cows—might rub up against the house in the middle of the night," he continued after a second's hesitation. "Not bein' used to it, it might scare you."

"I'm certain it would," she agreed cheerfully, finding herself abnormally interested in the nocturnal habits of domesticated cattle.

"Also the kids ride horses to school and they can just turn them loose in the yard without having to worry about them strayin'," he explained.

Priscilla agreed it was very sensible, and Dusty went on to explain the relative merits of barbed-wire fencing as opposed to the unreasonable prejudices ranchers had always had against it, and Priscilla discovered a hitherto unsuspected interest in the subject. She managed to agree and disagree at the appropriate times as he rattled on, and before she knew it, Dusty was jumping down to open the gate that led to the schoolyard. Soon, just as he had said, the school appeared, and standing in the yard was a plump fair-haired woman watching their approach: Stella Steele Wilson.

Chapter Two

The schoolhouse sat sheltered on the north side by a small hill and the ground fell away gently on the south side to a small creek, a branch of the larger creek which ran over by the ranch house. The building itself was logs, tightly fitted and well chinked. The west side was the front door to the school, and Priscilla could see that the school even had a bell tower. Ancient oak trees grew along the creek bank and provided shade for the schoolyard.

Dusty pulled the wagon up and stopped. "Well, this is it," he informed Priscilla, and she wondered if she had imagined the relief in his voice. She watched in admiration as he jumped lithely to the ground, and then Priscilla turned her attention to the woman standing in the yard while she waited for Dusty to come around and assist her down from the wagon.

Stella Wilson waited expectantly, resting one hand on her rather ample hip and using the other to shade her eyes from the afternoon sun. Silently, and in a very lady-like manner, she cursed the fashion of the day. Poke bonnets had their purpose, she supposed, and that was, of course, protecting delicate female complexions from the ravages of the sun, but they certainly could be a hindrance when you wanted to see what somebody looked like, and she certainly *did* want to see what the new arrival looked like. Not that she was nosy, but she had a vested interest in this young woman, an interest that might prove very interesting indeed if the girl was pretty. It would also help if she had a good figure, but that too, was impossible to know at the moment, what with that very practical duster covering her almost from head to toe. Why, a body would need a pretty vivid imagination just to guess that she was a female at all, from what was showing. Well, time will tell, she decided philosophically, her sharp blue eyes studying Dusty's expression as he reached up to help Priscilla to the ground.

Priscilla actually needed no help in alighting from the wagon, but mindful of her new position, she very demurely accepted the large male hand that was offered. Once again she noted its strength as it briefly gripped her own. She glanced up with a small smile of gratitude and caught him looking strangely ill-at-ease. His gaze touched hers briefly and skittered nervously away toward Stella Wilson, and in that moment Priscilla understood, or thought she understood, that Dusty was worried about his employer finding out how he had treated her. Well, she had no intention of getting him into trouble, but neither had she any intention of reassuring him. Let him worry about it for a while. It served him right.

"Well, here she is, safe and sound," Dusty announced

a little too heartily, almost as if he thought Stella might have expected him to deliver the new schoolteacher in more than one piece. He realized that he had betrayed himself at once as he watched Stella's finely arched eyebrows lift speculatively and her light blue eyes search his darker ones for a moment before turning to greet Miss Bedford.

"Welcome to Texas, Miss Bedford, I'm Stella Wilson." Stella Wilson was, Priscilla judged, in her middle twenties. She had once been a very pretty girl with hair the color of cornsilk and eyes the color of cornflowers, but motherhood had filled in her previously generous curves, turning her into an attractive, if somewhat plump, matron. When she smiled, as she was doing now, a dimple peeped out of her smooth, round cheek, and her eyes turned warm and friendly. Comparing her with her husband George, Priscilla thought they made a perfect couple and decided that the Wilson household must be a happy one.

"I'm glad to meet you, Mrs. Wilson," Priscilla said in perfect sincerity, extending her hand. "Your husband met me at the stage and was very kind to me. He told me it was your idea to bring me here first so I could freshen up before meeting Mr. Steele. I can't thank you enough." She had carefully refrained from making any mention of how Dusty had treated her, an omission that Stella did not let pass.

"I hope Dusty kept you entertained on your way out here," Stella said, grasping Priscilla's hand warmly, the speculative gleam back in her eyes as she cast a mildly accusing glance at Dusty. Priscilla did not miss the way Stella's lips twitched in amusement or the way Dusty took a deep breath as if bracing himself, and suddenly she realized the true relationship between these two. It wasn't a relationship between employer and employee. Rather, they were friends, close friends, and if Stella even suspected what had passed between Dusty and Priscilla that day, she would have teased him unmercifully, a prospect he obviously found unpleasant. Stella was apparently already a little suspicious, and while Priscilla was no tale-bearer, she was a little too wicked to let him off the hook completely.

"Oh, yes," Priscilla assured her, "he kept me very . . . entertained the entire way. I don't know *when* I've had such an interesting or informative trip. Why, did you know that barbed wire is perfectly safe for use with cattle?" she added with just the proper degree of amazement.

Stella stared a moment in mild surprise at the strange topic Dusty had chosen for conversation before shifting her gaze to Dusty, who shrugged in such wide-eyed innocence that she was more suspicious than ever.

"Reckon I'll unload her trunk," he mumbled before Stella could think of any accusations to make, and he turned quickly for the rear of the wagon.

Stella watched his studied nonchalance for a long moment before turning back to Priscilla who was, finally, removing that accursed bonnet. Stella had decided that Priscilla was a more than passably attractive girl, and seeing her without the bonnet confirmed her opinion. The girl's hair was the color of chestnuts, a deep, rich brown but with more than a hint of red glittering in the sunlight.

Priscilla put a hand to the remains of her coiffure. "I must look a fright," she whispered to Stella.

"Why no, honey. You look as pretty as a picture. Ain't

that right, Dusty?" she added, casting a wicked grin in Dusty's direction. She had not missed the way he had stopped his unloading to stare at Priscilla's newly bared head. "What's keepin' that trunk?" she added innocently, as he suddenly got very busy again. Turning back to Priscilla who was grinning appreciatively, she said, "Come on inside and make yourself at home. We'll soon have you feeling yourself again." With that, she took Priscilla by the arm and led her around to the back of the schoolhouse where they found another, smaller door with a step built out from it to form a small porch. "This is your private entrance so you don't have to traipse through the school every time," Stella explained, leading her inside to her private quarters.

As the two disappeared, Dusty muttered a curse on all women. A woman didn't have any right to look good with her hair all in a mess like that. It was irritating. And the way she'd let Stella think he'd done something to her. He had, of course, but a real lady would never have mentioned it. He was sure of that. Not that she *had* mentioned it, of course, but she'd said just enough to make Stella suspicious. If Stella ever *really* found out what had happened, she'd skin him alive. He'd never hear the end of it. Why had he ever let Stella talk him into going to town today anyway? Muttering another imprecation on the female sex, he shouldered Priscilla's trunk and made his way reluctantly to the schoolhouse door.

Stella had escorted Priscilla inside and was somewhat anxiously awaiting her reaction to her new quarters. About one third of the rather large building had been partitioned off to form a living area for the schoolteacher. On one side of the room was a small, round table with two straight-backed chairs for eating and beyond them in a corner by the window was a large, overstuffed chair for which someone had very lovingly made a flowered slipcover. Straight ahead was a small stove that could be used for heating or cooking, and above it, hanging on the wall, was a set of shelves, made from an old packing crate, that held an assortment of eating and cooking utensils of rather mixed heritage and some canned goods and staple foods. The other half of the room had been curtained off into a sleeping area and contained an iron bedstead, a washstand with a slightly chipped bowl and pitcher, and an enormous, and very ancient, wardrobe cabinet. Obviously, the furniture had been gleaned from people's castoffs, but the "used" appearance only added to the room's appeal, and Priscilla noted the care that had been put into making frilly curtains for the windows and a very cheerful quilt to cover the bed. The room seemed to radiate the warmth and good will of those who had prepared it for her, and Priscilla's face reflected that warmth as she turned to Stella. "It's beautiful," she declared.

Stella could not help feeling a small measure of relief and a large measure of pride. "Some of the ladies helped me fix it up. You came so far, we wanted you to have a nice place to stay."

"And I do," Priscilla assured her. "I'm sure I'll be very happy here." She then noticed that a bathtub had been placed in the bedroom area and that Stella had a large kettle of water heating on the stove. "A bath!" she cried. "Mrs. Wilson, I shall be in your debt until my dying day. How can I ever repay you?"

Stella laughed an easy, throaty laugh. "Figured that's the first thing you'd want. I been on that stage a time or two myself."

At that moment Dusty entered with the trunk. He paused in the doorway, awaiting instructions, his face carefully expressionless so as not to arouse Stella's interest. Priscilla could not help staring for a moment, marveling at how he held what she knew to be a tremendously heavy trunk with such ease. "Where do you want this?" he asked when it seemed neither of the women were going to volunteer anything. What were they staring at, anyway?

"Oh," said Priscilla, jogged from her reverie, "put it down here by the bed for now," she instructed him, conscious of the oddity of having a man enter her bedroom. Dusty carried the trunk in and swung it off his shoulder and onto the floor, a small grunt the only indication that he found the process at all difficult. He straightened up to find her staring at him again, a circumstance he found very disconcerting.

Wondering if he might have done something wrong, he glanced around and asked, "That all right?" indicating where he had placed the trunk.

Priscilla blinked, thinking how big he looked in the small room, much larger than he had seemed outside. He seemed to fill the room. And he looked so blatantly masculine surrounded by the feminine decor. She gave an odd little laugh. "Yes, that's fine," she said in response to his question. "It's just that, well, I thought that trunk was heavy," she explained inanely.

Now what did that have to do with anything? he wondered. "It is," he replied, frankly puzzled. He just wanted to get out of there before Stella could start asking him questions, and before he started wondering how Miss Bedford would look stretched out on that bed, with all that hair spread across the pillow. He waited a second, and when she did not seem inclined to reply to his last statement, he nodded politely to both women and made for the door.

He was through it before Priscilla realized his intent. Telling herself it was good manners and not a desire to get in the last word that prompted her, she stepped quickly to the door and called out, "Oh, Mr. Rhoades!" Something in her voice, an excess of cheerfulness, he thought, stopped him dead in his tracks, and he turned warily back to face her. "Thank you very much for looking after me," she called brightly, her face wreathed in a totally mischievous smile.

Dusty studied her face for a moment. She wasn't going to tell Stella anything, of that he was certain, but she wasn't going to forget it, either. And he had been worried about Stella! Something told him the new schoolteacher had Stella completely outclassed when it came to causing trouble. Yes sir, he'd been right when he'd guessed that this one would take some mighty careful handling. He reached for the brim of his hat, raised it slightly, and said, "You're welcome, ma'am." Damn! He'd said it again. Had she laughed? Well, maybe just a small giggle. Frowning bleakly, he turned on his heel and headed for the wagon.

Stella had watched this exchange with marked interest. She had the distinct feeling that much was being left unsaid but nevertheless communicated between the two. It was a very interesting feeling. Maybe she should do some checking. "Honey," she said to Priscilla, "you go ahead and start finding things. I'll be back in a minute. Gotta tell Dusty something," she lied as she moved quickly out the door. "Dusty, wait a minute," she called, and noted with satisfaction the way his shoulders had hunched defensively at the sound of her voice.

Dusty winced. He should have known he wouldn't get off that easily. Trying his best to look nonchalant, he turned back once again and waited for Stella's approach.

She studied his face a moment. "Well, what do you think of her?" she asked.

He shrugged noncommittally. "She'll do, I reckon," he said and then looked away, just a little too unconcernedly.

Stella reached up and grabbed his chin, turning his face toward hers. "You didn't do anything ornery to her, did you?" she demanded, her pale blue eyes suddenly fiercely accusing.

Dusty assumed his most outraged expression. "Stella! You know me better'n that!"

Indeed she did. A man had few secrets from a woman whose earliest childhood memory was being "scalped" by Wild Injun Dusty Rhoades. He had carried her yellow pigtails on his belt for years. He still had them packed away somewhere, probably saving them to show to her grandchildren. It would be just like him. She shook her head in disgust, and they both laughed. Stella let go of his chin, made a fist, and threw a playful punch, which he just as playfully dodged.

"George'll be comin' in for supper," he reported, glad to be able to change the subject.

"Good. Send the wagon back for us in about two hours. That'll give our new schoolteacher time to get prettied up." Stella thought she would test the waters. "Although she don't look like she needs much time to do that."

Dusty was wise to her tricks and did not bite. "See you in two hours," he called as he climbed up onto the wagon seat.

"My lands!" she exclaimed in mock surprise. "You comin' back to fetch us your own self? Yes, I reckon she'll do, all right."

He cast one disapproving look back at her laughing face before calling a final farewell and slapping the team into motion. Only when he had closed the gate to the schoolyard behind him did he heave a sigh of relief. That had not been so bad. Stella would razz him for a few days but with no facts at her command, she would be easily distracted. Then all he'd have to worry about would be Miss Priscilla Bedford. All! He snorted at the thought. She would be a handful, all right. If only she wasn't so consarn pretty. Well, maybe she'd be flat-chested and hippy underneath that coat. Yeah, he thought sarcastically, and maybe she'd be hunchbacked and have a third arm growing out of her chest, too. But a man could always hope, even if it was a lot to hope for that she'd be a little less than perfect in every way. No, not every way. Her manners could do with some improving. He entertained himself for the rest of the drive with possible ways he might teach her better manners. That way, he reasoned, he would not be thinking that right about now she would be stepping into that bathtub without a stitch on, and he would not be wondering how she looked.

As Stella had watched him drive away, her smile had faded. That same feeling of unease that had been bothering her for weeks stole over her. She was worried about Dusty. Mighty worried. He would be leaving soon, leaving the ranch, leaving Rainbow, maybe even leaving Texas if she could not stop him. Not that he had said anything and if anyone else suspected, he was keeping it to himself, but she knew it just as surely as she knew he'd kept her pigtails. It was instinct, she guessed, woman's intuition or something like that. Or maybe just because she loved him and knew his dreams. She'd seen the way he stared off into the distance sometimes, and he was restless. Too restless. He wanted a different kind of life, as Stella knew only too well, and he would be leaving to find it unless something got hold of him first. Stella's gaze drifted over to the schoolhouse window through which she could see Priscilla moving about inside. Yes, unless something got hold of him first.

Priscilla was busy unpacking her trunk when Stella returned. "This is really very thoughtful of you, Mrs. Wilson. I was dreading meeting Mr. Steele looking like a ragamuffin."

"I doubt you ever looked like a ragamuffin in your life," Stella chided. "And would it be polite if we call each other by our first names? I hope we'll be good friends, and if you're twenty-four, I'm only one year older'n you are." Her tone was almost accusing, and Priscilla managed to look a little ashamed.

"Actually, I'm only twenty-one, Stella," she confessed. "I lied about my age because I was afraid your father wouldn't hire me if I were too young."

Stella laughed her easy laugh. "Glory, child, he would have hired you if you were seventeen!" At that, Priscilla's laugh joined hers.

"Seventeen! Is it that difficult to get a schoolteacher here?" Priscilla asked, amazed.

"It's hard, all right. Most girls marry young. That's what happens when there're ten men for every woman, and although we've had some men to teach school, most of 'em would rather punch cows. It pays better, and some say the cows are easier to get along with than the younguns." Priscilla threw her a look of mock horror.

51

"It's prob'ly true, too," Stella assured her.

"I wondered why you had to advertise in an Eastern paper and pay my expenses all the way out here. Why don't you teach the school yourself?" Priscilla inquired.

Now it was Stella's turn to look horrified. "Me? I hardly had any schoolin' myself, and even if I had, I've got three younguns of my own to keep me busy."

"Three?" Priscilla asked in amazement.

"That's right," Stella assured her. "Three and number four on the way," she added, patting her slightly rounded stomach. "So we import teachers when we can and hope they last through the term before somebody marries them."

"Well, you can relax. I'm not planning on getting married for a good long time," Priscilla assured her, pausing in the process of hanging her dresses in the wardrobe, a process Stella had been observing closely. Now Stella did not spend much time reading *Godey's Ladies' Book* to discover the latest fashion, but even she could see that Priscilla's clothes were not those of a penniless orphan girl who had sought a teaching job to support herself. And she had so many! Stella counted ten outfits, not including the simple skirt and shirtwaist she was wearing under her traveling coat. Stella herself owned only five dresses and she was well-to-do.

"Tell me which dress you're going to wear and I'll try to get the wrinkles out of it for you," Stella offered.

"That's very nice of you," Priscilla said, stepping back from the cabinet and surveying her wardrobe thoughtfully. Shrugging in despair, she turned to Stella. "You choose something. You know how formal the dinner is going to be."

"Nothin' around here is ever very formal, and it's

supper, not dinner. Dinner is at noon. See, school-teacher, you learned something today." As they both laughed good-naturedly at Stella's teasing, Stella stepped forward and examined Priscilla's dresses. "Mmmm, such pretty things, it's hard to decide. I think this brown one," she said, pulling out the garment. "Bet it sets off your hair real nice." It would, too, Stella decided, holding it up to Priscilla's chestnut locks to achieve a perfect match. Someone had made that dress especially for Priscilla, someone who knew just what she was doing. Now wasn't that interesting? "It's not too fancy and it'll be just the family tonight. Oh, I think I hear the water boiling."

A few minutes later, Stella had filled the tub, adding a generous handful of her own rose-scented bath salts, and drawn the curtain so Priscilla could luxuriate in private. She put another kettle of water on to boil and then sat down in the easy chair to wait for some steam to develop, smiling when she heard Priscilla's contented "Ahhh" as she lowered herself into the tub.

Priscilla had to pull her knees up to her chin in order to fit in the round, galvanized tub, but when she closed her eyes and inhaled the fragrance of roses, she could easily imagine herself in a porcelain tub, surrounded by luxury. Regretfully deciding that she did not have time to wash and dry her hair before dinner—no, it was supper—she began to lather her travel-grimed body with the piece of store-bought soap that Stella had provided. It didn't take long to wash away the effects of her trip, and when she had rinsed off, she leaned back, letting the steam rise around her and enjoying the blessed idleness. She wasn't surprised a little while later to hear Stella's voice coming through the curtain.

"Bet it was hard leavin' your family to come way out

here," Stella suggested.

"Oh, I don't have any close family left—just a few cousins. I guess you know my father died a few months ago."

"Yes, I read your letters to Daddy. Your mother died a while back, didn't she?" Stella asked.

"Yes, when I was very young. My father raised me alone. Some thought he made me a tomboy. I'm afraid they were right," Priscilla lamented.

Stella laughed at that. "Don't know anyone would call you a tomboy. You're too pretty for that, but if they meant you think like a man, that should help you get along out here." Seeing that the water was again boiling on the stove, Stella rose, and taking up the very interesting brown dress, she held it up to the cloud of steam emanating from the spout of the kettle to help eliminate some of the creases caused from its having been folded up in the trunk.

"I think they meant my unbridled tongue which continually gets me in trouble!" Priscilla informed her.

Stella thought this over for a moment and then suggested, "It got you in trouble with Dusty." She was fishing again and Priscilla jumped at the bait. Stella could hear her very audible gasp.

"He *told* you?" she asked incredulously.

Stella allowed herself a small, triumphant grin. "No, but you just did," she replied. Priscilla was silent behind the curtain, mortified that she had told on Dusty. The fact that Stella had tricked her was small comfort. Hearing no response, Stella added, "I reckon he held his own, though."

"That he did! That he did!" Priscilla assured her, rising from the tub. Her bath did not seem so relaxing any more. She told herself that it was definitely *not* the mention of Dusty Rhoades that had caused her sudden restlessness, but she did not waste any time trying to figure out what else it might have been. Reaching for a towel, she dried herself briskly and hurriedly slipped into her silk pantalettes and chemise. When she was decently covered, she opened the curtain for easier conversation. Stella was still holding her dress up to the steam and achieving remarkable results with her labor.

Hearing the curtain open, Stella glanced over and her eyes widened and then narrowed speculatively at the sight of Priscilla in her underwear. *Silk* underwear, or she was a wild Indian, and Irish lace into the bargain. "Mighty pretty pantalettes," Stella remarked, thinking of her own plain cotton drawers.

"Thank you," Priscilla answered absently, taking up her corset and examining it thoughtfully.

"It must be hard to be a young girl left alone and penniless in the world," Stella remarked, bringing the conversation back to the original subject.

Priscilla laughed at such a bleak prospect. "I'm not exactly penniless. My father provided for me," Priscilla assured her as she wrapped the corset around her body and began to fasten it. "I'm afraid you'll have to tighten these laces for me. That dress fits very closely."

Stella nodded, carefully laying the brown dress across the back of a chair and taking hold of the laces on Priscilla's offered back. Giving a sharp pull, she commented, "Seems strange some eastern dude didn't up and marry you. I don't think much of eastern men, but they can't all be blind and stupid," she added, giving the laces another series of tugs.

Priscilla laughed again, between grunts. "One thing

really bothers me about the West, Stella."

"What's that?" Stella asked as she carefully tied the now-tightened laces.

"The way no one out here ever asks a direct question," she replied, turning accusing brown eyes on her helper.

Stella scowled. "Meanin'?"

"Meaning, you're getting me to tell you my life history, but you have yet to ask me a single question," Priscilla informed her.

Stella shrugged sheepishly and then grinned. "It's just a habit, I reckon. See, there're lots of men out here that are GTT."

"I know what that is," Priscilla said eagerly. "That's 'Gone to Texas.'"

"Right," Stella said, a little surprised that she would know such a thing, "and some of 'em left in such a hurry, they forgot to take their names with 'em."

"You mean they're wanted?" Priscilla asked in amazement.

"Not necessarily. Some are, of course, but most just have somethin' they want to forget, or ain't too proud of, or are ashamed for folks to know. Anyhow, you don't want to go askin' a lot of fool questions, 'cause you never know when you might meet a GTT with a short temper. Course, they'd never shoot a pretty girl like you."

"Shoot!" Priscilla's large eyes flew wide.

"You're in the Wild West, honey," she teased. "Better get used to it!" Seeing that Priscilla was genuinely alarmed, she added, "Don't worry. I'm just funnin'. You'll prob'ly never even hear a gun fired in Rainbow. This part of the Wild West is pretty tame."

"I'm glad to hear that," Priscilla said with relief.

"Well," she added with a laugh, "is there anything else

you'd like to know about me? I promise I won't shoot!"

Stella smiled, shaking her head, and then her face grew grave. "Yes, as a matter of fact. I did wonder why a rich, pretty, educated girl like you come thousands of miles to Rainbow, Texas, to teach lessons to a bunch of snotty-nosed brats."

Priscilla's face grew grave also. "That's a difficult question, Stella. A lot of others have asked it, too." She thought for a moment. "Maybe it's because my father wanted to come west. If he'd been young and strong, he would have been a GTT. When he died, it seemed like I just didn't have a life in Philadelphia any more." She gave Stella a sad little smile. "You were right. I could have married an eastern dude, but somehow, there just weren't any that I cared to marry." Stella nodded her understanding. "I could have become a spinster, but the idea of being 'silly old cousin Priscilla' and being visited by my relatives' cast-off children for the rest of my life just did not appeal to me either. I wanted to do something different. I wanted to be a GTT. When I saw your father's advertisement, it seemed like the perfect opportunity to go west respectably."

Stella nodded in perfect understanding. She had known those feelings, too. She had almost forgotten. Suddenly, she grinned to lighten the mood and cast a censuring eye at Priscilla's scantily-clad figure. "Ain't you gettin' cold?" she asked.

With an answering giggle, Priscilla shivered dramatically, scurried back into her curtained bedroom, and donned her petticoats and stockings. When she was ready, Stella helped her put the brown dress over her head and then stood back as Priscilla buttoned the many, tiny, covered buttons that went from her neck to well below her waist. When she was finished, she smoothed the rich material over her hips, then extended her arms and made a charming pirouette. "Do you see any bulges?" she asked Stella.

Stella stood staring incredulously. She had already noticed that Priscilla had a very nice figure, but seeing it in this dress . . . Stella could not know, of course, that having been raised without a mother, Priscilla had neglected many regimens considered essential for a young woman of good breeding. For instance, she had never considered it necessary to sleep in her corsets, a process that had to be followed if one were to attain the desired waist measurement of 16 inches. Some even managed to go beyond that and 13-inch waists were not unheard of. But Priscilla had rebelled against such strictures and consequently her waist was an enormous 18 inches. In that particular dress, however, no one, least of all Stella Wilson, would have noticed Priscilla's deficiencies. The dress fit like a second skin from the high neckline to almost the knees, faithfully and lovingly tracing the gentle curves of her high, full bosom, narrow waist, and pleasingly rounded hips. A body wouldn't need any imagination at all to tell she was a female, now, Stella concluded. "Not a single wrinkle," Stella judged. "I don't think I ever saw a dress made like that," she added, pointing to the narrow skirt. A piece of material had been draped across the front and gathered in the back but that gather was much too low and much too small to be considered a bustle. No, it was like nothing Stella had ever seen before.

"It's the latest style," Priscilla explained. "In Paris they decreed that a woman should look like a pencil. Unfortunately, pencils don't do much walking, and that can be a real challenge in these skirts," she said, taking a few mincing steps to demonstrate.

"I can see that," Stella laughed, "but you don't want to be walking around in a dress like that anyway. You just want to stand still and be admired!"

"Well, thank you, ma'am," Priscilla jested in a perfect imitation of Dusty's drawl and sketched a small curtsy, sending Stella into gales of laughter.

While Stella slowly recovered, Priscilla went over to the wash stand where someone had very thoughtfully hung a mirror and began to remove the pins from her mane of hair. As it fell past her shoulders in a tangled mass, she groaned, and taking up her brush, began to ruthlessly attack the mess. "Now tell me about the last schoolteacher. What happened to her?" Priscilla ordered a still-shaking Stella.

"Now, let's see," Stella said, consciously sobering. "The last teacher we had run off with a troupe of traveling actors that came through town."

"What!"

Stella shook her head sadly. "It's true. That poor girl never had a lick of sense. Let a no-good actor turn her head. Have to give him his due, though, he was a handsome devil, but I'll bet you money he's got more wives than a hen's got chicks. He's prob'ly left a whole string of 'em from here to Montana. Now don't you go takin' off after no actors," Stella admonished, wagging her finger.

Priscilla raised her right hand and solemnly vowed she would not.

"Now the teacher before that was a fella. He joined up with some drovers heading for Kansas with a herd of cattle. Don't reckon that kind of life would appeal to you, either." Priscilla assured her that it would not as she deftly twisted up the length of her hair and pinned it in place. "The three before that," Stella continued, "all married local boys, though. Showed good sense in that, at least. I expect you'll meet them all, sooner or later. You all ready now?" she asked as Priscilla turned to face her.

Cut short in front, Priscilla's hair curled stylishly—and naturally—around her face. The rest had been tamed into a demure chignon, revealing the very delicate curve of her long, slender neck. "How do I look?"

"Like I said before, pretty as a picture. No," she amended. "Even prettier now. And just in time," she added as they both heard the sound of a wagon drawing up in the yard.

"Hello, the house!" It was Dusty Rhoades, back again, and Priscilla ignored the flutter of excitement she felt. It was only natural. She was going to meet Mr. Steele.

"Don't forget your shoes," Stella admonished and Priscilla hastily rummaged through what was left in the trunk to produce a pair of brown pumps with small, tapered heels which she quickly slipped on her feet. Draping a paisley silk shawl over her arm, she pronounced herself ready.

Stella suddenly felt very dowdy in her simple calico dress. "Be right out," she called to Dusty. "You go ahead, honey. I just need to gather my things."

Priscilla started for the door, pausing only a moment to give her hair a final pat before stepping out onto the porch. She told herself it was just her female vanity that hoped to get a reaction from her cowboy. She was not disappointed. He had been leaning lazily against the side of the wagon, and she noted that he had changed his shirt and put on a fresh neck scarf, and if she were not mistaken, he had even combed his hair, although because of his hat, it was difficult to be sure. He glanced up when he heard her step, and she almost laughed at the comical look of surprise that passed over his face before he caught himself. Straightening up quickly, he self-consciously adjusted his vest and managed a small smile and a nod of greeting.

It was the dress, he decided. Any woman would look good in a dress like that. No, that wasn't right. Not just any woman could wear a dress like that. In fact, hardly any woman could. He had wondered what feminine charms she had been hiding and now he knew: she'd been hiding every one there was! No hunchback here and definitely no third arm growing out of her chest, although what *was* growing out of her chest was mighty nice. Mighty nice, indeed. The rest of her was all right, too. Yes, sir, quite a little armful if he'd ever seen one. It was only natural that he felt like he'd been kicked in the stomach by a mule. A man didn't see a sight like that every day. All he had to worry about was not letting it show. There was, after all, still her tongue to contend with, regardless of how she looked. That was a flaw that outweighed whatever physical charms she might possess. Made a woman unfeminine. At least he thought so. He was sure of it.

"You're very prompt," commented Priscilla with an approving grin.

"Just one of my good qualities," he drawled, grinning back.

Stella, having watched everything from the doorway and feeling satisfied at Dusty's reaction, came out closing the door behind her. "Well, let's get going. Supper's waitin'. Priscilla, you're so tiny, you sit in the middle."

61

Priscilla's grin faded as she stepped to the wagon. Dusty was waiting to hand her up, but instead of accepting his offered assistance, she just stood there looking very ill-at-ease.

"Somethin' wrong?" Dusty inquired after a moment.

"Uh, well," stammered Priscilla, "you see, whoever designed this dress had never seen a western wagon."

"Huh?" Dusty looked to Stella for interpretation, but she was as puzzled as he.

"You see, the skirt, I can't . . ." Priscilla gestured helplessly at her dress. Suddenly, both Stella and Dusty understood. The skirt that restricted her to short, almost mincing steps made it impossible for her to step high enough to climb into the wagon.

"Don't it give none?" Dusty inquired.

Feeling more foolish than anything else, Priscilla responded, "There's a chain sewn inside to keep the material from tearing."

Dusty thumbed back his Stetson and grinned broadly, revealing two rows of even teeth. "Well, I'll be da . . . don't that beat all." He looked to Stella who was struggling not to laugh at her new friend's discomfort.

"I guess I could change," Priscilla offered, struggling to maintain her dignity. The last person before whom she wanted to appear ridiculous was Dusty Rhoades.

"No need for that," said Dusty who had been studying the situation with great amusement. He bent down to Priscilla and putting one arm under her knees and one behind her back, he lifted her swiftly and plunked her down on the wagon seat before she had time to utter more than a startled squeak.

Of all the rude, uncouth . . . Priscilla's brain could hardly find words to express her outrage for a few moments until her sense of humor overcame her anger. It was, after all, a logical solution to the problem, she thought as she adjusted her skirts and moved over to make room for Stella. But he could have warned her! It was very disconcerting to be so suddenly taken into a man's arms, pressed so intimately against his chest. Very disconcerting indeed. That explained why she felt all quivery inside, as if she had just received a fright. Well, it was foolish to be so upset by such a trivial incident, and it would never do to let him know she was. Pulling the remnants of her pride together, she managed to say, "Thank you, Mr. Rhoades," with creditable coolness.

"Just part of the job, ma'am," he allowed, generously, as he heaved Stella up into the seat with an unnecessary show of strain, for which he earned a black look. Ignoring that, he sauntered around the wagon and added, "A foreman's got to be able to figure things out fast. Besides, I'm hungry." He hopped up beside her and took hold of the reins. "A man could starve to death waitin' for a woman to change her clothes," he commented to no one in particular as he slapped the horses into motion, earning another black look from both of his passengers. Was that she who smelled like flowers? he could not help wondering as the wagon rattled down the rough road. He could tell she was trying very hard not to bump against him but without much luck. Not that he minded, of course. She could get just as close as she wanted. He had made the very pleasant discovery that she *was* quite a little armful, just as he had predicted. Didn't weigh any more than a flea, either. There was still that razor-edged tongue, of course, but a smart man should be able to take care of that, and Dusty Rhoades could think of several very agreeable ways to keep the uppity Miss Bedford from saying a single word.

Priscilla forced herself to sit erect and not brush against Dusty Rhoades at every bump. It was nerve-wrackingly difficult work, and she was not always successful in her endeavors. The wagon lurched so unpredictably that sometimes she was caught shifting her weight the wrong way and fell smack against him. She wondered if it bothered him as much as it bothered her. She could not help noticing that their hips and thighs kept brushing each other, a contact she could not avoid, no matter how hard she tried. That, combined with the memory of how it felt to be cradled, however briefly, in those strong arms, made her feel a trifle breathless, which was absurd. Taking a deep breath and letting it out slowly, she at last felt capable of normal speech.

"Stella, is there a dressmaker in town?" she asked.

"No, not exactly. There's a lady used to be one. She's wife to one of the ranchers. You'll have some of her younguns in school. You think you need more clothes?"

"I think I'd better have some of my clothes altered to suit my new . . . responsibilities. I can't go troubling . . . some gentleman every time I need to go somewhere."

"No trouble at all, miss. Glad to oblige," Dusty assured her, enjoying her obvious discomfort.

"Nevertheless," Priscilla went on determinedly, "do you think this lady could help me?"

"Oh, sure. Hazel'd be glad for the work. You can prob'ly go out and spend a few days at her place. I'm sure we can get someone to take you." Stella glanced sidelong at Dusty who said not a word.

"What a lovely stream," commented Priscilla about the water that ran past the ranch buildings. "What's it called?"

"That's the Clear Fork *River*," said Dusty significantly, taking great delight in her ignorance.

Irritated, Priscilla pressed her lips together to prevent herself from replying with an air of superiority that such a small trickle of water would hardly qualify as a *creek* in Pennsylvania. After all, Stella was sitting right next to her, and she had no desire to hurt Stella's feelings. Had she been alone with him, however . . . well, there would be another time, although it rankled to let him have the last word. First the wind and now the rivers. She would remember that for the future.

Just then the ranch came into view and Priscilla momentarily forgot her vengeful desires. The cluster of buildings was rather unimpressive to an easterner's eye. A few of the buildings, obviously the older ones, were made of logs, as was the schoolhouse. The newer ones were made of sawed lumber or clapboard, a sure sign of the owner's acquired affluence. Priscilla recognized a barn and extensive corrals beyond it. The other buildings she judged to be the quarters of the hired men. The ranch house itself was a sprawling clapboard affair that had begun with a rather simple, box-like house to which additions had been made as the need arose. One section was separated from the rest by an open breezeway which Priscilla would later learn was called a "dogtrot" and was sometimes used for sleeping in the heat of summer. This separate section provided private living space for the Wilson family, although they rarely used it for anything other than sleeping, preferring to share the activities taking place in the parlor and around the huge dining table in the main house. Running the entire length of the ranch house was a deep, covered porch, on which, Priscilla saw as the wagon pulled up into the yard, were gathered all the many members of the Steele family, scrubbed and primped for the occasion.

Priscilla knew a moment's qualm as the time came for her to leave the wagon, but after brief consideration, Dusty simply reached up, fastened his large hands around her waist, and lifted her to the ground. Priscilla used the excuse of smoothing her dress to wipe the sensation of warmth from her hands caused by the brief and very light contact they had had with Dusty's shoulders. Dusty, meanwhile, was busy furtively examining his own hands, marveling that they had practically spanned Priscilla's tiny waist.

Her composure recovered, Priscilla turned her attention to the ranch house porch. Ben Steele stood at the top of the short flight of steps to meet her. She would have known him anywhere as Stella's father. He possessed the same pale yellow hair, still thick and wavy after fifty-some-odd years, and the same cornflower blue eyes filled with the laughter that was such a part of life at the Steele ranch. While Stella was pleasingly plump, Ben was enormous—not fat, Priscilla decided, but simply large, with a barrel chest and massive limbs. "Miss Bedford, it's good to have you here at last. Welcome to Texas," he boomed in a voice that seemed to echo in the giant cavern of his chest.

"Thank you, Mr. Steele. It's very nice to be here, at last," said Priscilla, ascending the stairs to shake his outstretched hand. She noticed as he turned to lead her toward the rest of the assembled family that he walked heavily, using a cane.

"Sorry I couldn't meet you myself," he was saying. "Doc won't let me ride any more, not even in a wagon." He gestured toward his legs.

"Oh, Mr. Wilson and Mr. Rhoades took good care of me. You needn't be sorry," Priscilla replied blithely. Dusty made a great show of adjusting his hat in case anyone had happened to notice how he winced at her remark.

With obvious pride, Ben began his introductions. "May I present my family. You know George, of course." Priscilla and George exchanged greetings, his eyes silently inquiring how she had fared after being left in Dusty's clutches; her eyes responding coolly that she had done just fine, thank you very much. "And my other children," Ben continued, indicating a row of thinner and progressively smaller Stella-look-alikes who stood like stairsteps awaiting her inspection. "This is Ruth. She's seventeen, my fourth child. Her two older sisters are both married and gone." Ruth possessed all the charm and loveliness that Stella had once had, having just blossomed into womanhood, and carried her new maturity with a shy grace. She blushed rosily as she greeted Priscilla. Then came Katie, the twins, Alice and Annie, and last of all, Ben junior. Names and faces were beginning to blur. "You'll have all but Ruthie in your school. That's why we built the school on my ranch—I raised the most younguns," Ben chuckled and then went on. "These three little ones are Stella's. This one's Joe," he said tousling the blond curls of the sturdy six-year-old. "You'll have him in school, too. Then there's Molly and our baby, Matthew." Two-year-old Matthew grinned impishly up at Priscilla, his china blue eyes wary but fascinated. Impulsively, Priscilla reached for him and amazingly, he allowed her to pick him up.

"My goodness," Priscilla exclaimed. "Only here a day and already I have a beau!" Everyone's stiff, polite smiles gave way to genuine laughter as Matthew, showing off for his audience, hugged her tightly.

Stella, who had followed Priscilla up onto the porch, observed her normally shy child with surprise and could not resist a glance to see how Dusty was reacting to Priscilla's success.

That little traitor! he was thinking, his disgust plain across his handsome face. Matthew Wilson never let a stranger within ten feet of him. The woman was positively unnatural, the way she just charmed the socks off everybody. Lucky for him he was immune. "Dusty!" He jumped when he heard Ben call his name. "Dusty, you introduce Miss Bedford to the boys."

Priscilla's eyes flew open. "You have more sons?" she asked, amazed.

"Oh, no," he assured her. "These are the boys that work for me." Priscilla's gaze followed the gesture of his hand out into the yard where she saw that a group of half a dozen young men had gathered. Ben leaned over and whispered conspiratorially, "They don't see many pretty girls, so they're all in a lather to meet you." Priscilla nodded knowingly. This was a situation she knew exactly how to handle. Saying a few comforting words to Matthew, she passed the child to Stella and, fixing her most dazzling smile upon her face, she glided down the stairs into the yard where a very reluctant Dusty Rhoades awaited her.

Now what was she up to? he wondered as he watched her coming toward him. Irritated, he turned to the men who were huddling together like a bunch of naked sheep. "Well, come on up," he ordered the men. "She don't bite." Now that was a bold-faced lie, if ever he'd told one, but no use scaring them more than they already were.

Bashfully, the men approached, awkwardly dragging off their hats as they came. "This here's my segundo, Curly Yates," he said, indicating a tall young man with a mop of brown curls any girl would have envied. He was as tall as Dusty but much thinner, as if he needed a good, square meal, and his boyish grin appealed to the maternal instincts in every woman, young or old. Priscilla guessed him to be about her own age and also reasoned, quite correctly, that his shyness had frustrated the hopes of many young girls.

"Pleased to meet you, Mr. Yates," said Priscilla sweetly. She did not offer to shake hands, remembering Dusty's awkwardness in the matter and justifiably afraid that the boys might faint dead away if she actually offered them physical contact. As it was, they looked ready to bolt at any provocation. "What in the world is a segundo?" she asked with unfeigned interest before Dusty could move her along to meet the next man.

Abashed, but immensely pleased that she had noticed him, Curly replied, "That just means that I'm second man in charge, after Dusty."

Priscilla allowed him to see how impressed she was, but before she could pursue her interest, Dusty introduced the next man in line, who bore the unlikely name of "Tucking Comb." "Is that your given name?" Priscilla asked, amazed.

"N-No, ma'am," he replied, flushing to the roots of his hair. "It's just a handle, I mean, a nickname, like," he gulped nervously.

"How did you get it?" she asked, fascinated, and he turned even redder and began to mumble something incomprehensible.

"Save it for another time," snapped Dusty, using her

elbow to propel her to the next man in line. This was getting out of hand. He sure didn't need a bunch of moon-eyed lovers moping around the ranch all the time. That damn dress wasn't helping any either. Why, the love-sick fools were practically drooling. It was disgusting.

"This here is Fatty," he said belligerently, indicating one of the thinnest men Priscilla had ever seen. If Curly needed a good square meal, then Fatty needed a dozen. A gangling scarecrow of a man whose clothes hung on him, the only thing that stuck out on him anywhere from his sunken cheeks to his sunken chest was his Adam's apple, which bobbed convulsively whenever he swallowed, something he did quite often while Priscilla was looking at him.

"I take it that 'Fatty' is a 'handle,' too," Priscilla giggled. Fatty grinned and nodded and then swallowed two more times. "What you need is a good woman to fatten you up," Priscilla declared.

"Are you a good cook, miss?" Fatty asked hopefully.

Priscilla laughed. "Oh, no, I'm a terrible cook. I can't boil water without burning it!"

"Maybe you could learn," he suggested as the men bit their lips and shuffled their feet to keep from laughing out loud.

Before she could reply, Dusty was presenting her to a cowboy named Ed. "Just plain Ed?" she asked in disbelief.

"Yes, ma'am," Ed affirmed quite seriously. He was really a very nice-looking boy, or would have been if he hadn't been missing a few teeth. "Well, we can't have that!" Priscilla declared. "Let's see, Fatty is very thin so they call him Fatty. That means we should call you," she considered for a moment, "ugly!" she announced triumphantly. She watched his forehead crease a moment while her implied compliment sunk in, and then his face broke into a happy smile.

Dusty was seething. He'd never get another day's work out of any of these men. They'd all be finding excuses to ride by the schoolhouse or fix the fence or check on Miss Bedford. He had a notion to take her out into the woods and throttle her—put everybody out of their misery. Giving her elbow an unnecessarily forceful push which earned him a sharp look, he indicated the next man, a very dour-looking individual. "This here's Happy," he said and not pausing for breath went on. "No, he ain't happy and that's why we call him Happy." And pushing her relentlessly onward to meet the last man, he added, "And this here's our cook, Aunt Sally."

Priscilla stood face to face, or rather nose to nose, since the man was no taller than she, with a grizzled old man. His face had been burned by years in the sun until it was as tough and as lined as old leather, and from the direction the lines took, she guessed that that hawklike face was not used to smiling. He did not look as if he were going to smile now, either. Could his name really be Aunt Sally? No one was snickering, so it must be. Priscilla leaned conspiratorially close to him and said, "I'll bet they call you 'Aunt Sally, sir.'"

The gray head reared back on its scrawny neck for a moment in shocked surprise and then the leathery face cracked—there was no other word for it—into a crooked smile. "They do if they know what's good for 'em," he asserted, relishing her tribute.

"They say," confided Priscilla, "that in Europe, all the best chefs are men. I see that's true in the West, also."

Before the old man could respond, Dusty interrupted.

"You ain't et his cookin'," he said, breaking one of the cardinal rules of ranch life: never insult the cook. Aunt Sally scrinched up his face and shot Dusty a look that would have curdled milk—*in* the cow—but that look paled in comparison to the withering glance Priscilla treated him to, her arched eyebrows and snapping dark eyes speaking eloquently of the disdain she had for him. The impact of those eyes was so great he actually backed up a step as if to escape it. If before the men were smiling at Priscilla, they were now laughing at Dusty, at least inwardly.

Turning back to Aunt Sally, she lavished on him her most charming smile and said, "Perhaps you will give me some pointers. I really am hopeless in the kitchen."

"Be pleased to, ma'am. Nothin' I'd like better," replied Aunt Sally with a comic little bow and a very meaningful look at Dusty.

Priscilla turned back to Dusty, clearly allowing all her former warmth to evaporate, and asked coldly, "Have I met everyone?"

"Yeah, that's the lot," he replied bleakly, wondering how she'd managed to get the upper hand again. He sent a silent appeal to Ben who was only too happy to relieve him of his charge.

"Well, now," Ben boomed, "let's not keep our supper waiting any longer. Come on in and set."

The men retired to the cookhouse where they ate the meal that had been prepared for them by Aunt Sally and teased each other relentlessly about the flirtatious remarks Priscilla had made to them. Priscilla and the family dined in the main house, around the largest table Priscilla had ever seen, served by their Mexican girl, Maria. Priscilla answered the usual inquiries about her trip and how she found the school and assorted other topics. She found the Steeles to be a cheerful group, obviously glad to welcome her. At length, Ben Steele announced with mock seriousness, "Well, guess we'll have to call off our little shindig on Saturday."

This statement was met by a chorus of protest from his younger daughters until Stella silenced them. "Hush. Can't you see he's teasin'?"

"Not a bit of it," he protested. "Miss Bedford, we'd planned a little party—nothing fancy, just invited the folks close by—to meet you and get acquainted, but now I'm not sure."

"Why not, Ben?" asked George, playing along to get another rise out of the girls.

"Well, if Miss Bedford starts charmin' all the fellows around here like she just charmed ours out there, why some cowpoke is gonna have her married off before we can even get school started."

General laughter followed and Priscilla's was the loudest. "Don't worry about me, Mr. Steele," she assured him. "I have no intention of marrying anyone for quite some time, and believe me, I'm just as capable of *dis*couraging young men as I am of *en*couraging them, probably better."

"That may well be true," Ben said, "but what you intend and what some Texas boy intends might differ, and I'm not too sure you'd stick to your guns if one of 'em tried to sweet talk you." Ruth Steele gave her father a reproving look, while the other girls giggled. "Yes, ma'am," he continued, reveling in his role of fatherly advisor, "you be mighty choosy when you do decide to marry. Don't settle for no thirty-a-month cowboy. There's too many well-fixed cattlemen around, just beggin' for a woman like you. That's right, we sure don't see your kind of woman around here much. You're a rare thing, Miss Bedford. Why, if I were ten years younger . . ."

"Daddy!" Stella remonstrated, "you're embarrassing the poor girl." Actually, Priscilla was flushing with pleasure at his compliments.

"Oh, I'm sorry, Miss Bedford. Didn't mean to go on so," he blustered.

"Quite all right," Priscilla assured him, laughing a little. "I appreciate your concern."

"Daddy," Ruth interjected, "if you're giving advice, you left out the most important thing."

"What's that, child?"

"What you always tell me—to marry the man I love, no matter what."

"That's true, but it's just as easy to love a rich man as it is to love a poor one; some say easier," he philosophized, but seeing the concensus was going against him, he decided to shift to another tack. "Yes," he said thoughtfully, "we'll have to find a suitable young man for Miss Bedford. Stella, you speak to Dusty about it."

Priscilla started at the thought that they had already paired her with Dusty, but while everyone else enjoyed the private joke, Stella explained, "Don't get scared, honey. Daddy's not fixin' to marry you off to Dusty. What he means is, Dusty's the one found husbands for my two married sisters and now it's a standing joke around here about him bein' a matchmaker."

"Actually," George explained further, "he was inspired to the action by the fact that everyone fully expected him to marry one of them himself, so he did the only manly thing." Now George fell under attack from the Steele women while Ben thoroughly enjoyed the scene.

Priscilla decided to add to his enjoyment. When the tumult died down she asked, "Ruth, has Dusty found someone for you yet?" Poor Ruth blushed furiously as her sisters giggled anew, and replied that no, he had not.

At this point Stella decided to break up the party, and instructing Ruth to see the children got ready for bed, and sending the men off to smoke, she offered to show Priscilla around the place before it got too dark.

Stella showed her Ben's office, a room lined with full bookshelves, much to Priscilla's delight. Ben, having chosen this room in which to enjoy his after-dinner cigar, explained how his wife had longed for some culture in the wilderness that Texas had been in the early days, and when they had finally made good, she had filled her house with books.

"She always tried to get everyone to read, even the hands. They all borry books, time to time, so you come in and take whatever you want, any time," he offered.

After a quick tour through the rest of the house, Stella led her outside where they strolled the grounds, Stella pointing out each building as they passed, the bunkhouse, the cookhouse, a large barn, corrals, and finally a small cabin.

"This," Stella said leading Priscilla inside, "we just call 'The Cabin.' It was the original homestead. That is, the house Mama and Daddy built when they settled here. When Daddy started making money after the war, he built the new house. Now if our foreman was married— and there don't seem much danger of that—this would be his place." They were standing in a large room, comfortably if simply furnished. The large fireplace showed that the room had once served as kitchen and dining room, but no cooking utensils hung there now and the room was furnished as a parlor. Stella led her into the other, smaller, room which was furnished as a bedroom with a large iron bedstead, similar to the one in her own room. "Actually, he ought to live here anyways, but he won't. So whenever you've got a mind to, you can stay here, like when school's not in session. It'll save you the walk up for meals and such."

Priscilla wanted to know why Dusty would not live here and felt certain Stella was dying to tell her, so she did not hesitate to ask, "Why won't he stay here?" and added after a slight pause, "It's not haunted or anything, is it?"

"It prob'ly is for him," Stella supposed, "'cause his mother lived here."

"His mother!" said Priscilla in amazement.

"Most folks have one," Stella teased. "Even Dusty."

Priscilla laughed self-consciously. "It just seemed strange. Why did his mother live here, if it's not a deep, dark, family secret."

"No, it ain't. Well, you see, when Dusty's mother . . . no, before that, when his Daddy, no, back before the war . . . Well, it's a long story." She looked questioningly at Priscilla.

"I'm not going anywhere," Priscilla said encouragingly.

"All right. Set a spell." They sat down in the front room of the cabin. "Back before the war, Dusty's folks and my folks, they all came to Texas right around the same time and settled here. There was nothin' here then, and after the war there was even less. Daddy and Mr. Rhoades was great friends, of course. Anyway, after the war, nobody had any money or any hopes of gettin' any, and then somebody started saying how if you could gather up some cows and drive 'em north, folks would buy 'em and pay cash money. That sounded pretty good so Daddy and Mr. Rhoades and some others each got up a herd and started north. Back then there was no cattle towns nor any real place to take 'em. They were desperate men and they were willin' to take their chances. Daddy was lucky. He got to Missouri and found a buyer an' we was in the cattle business for shore." She paused and sighed. "Dusty's Daddy wasn't so lucky. All he found was the Jayhawkers," she went on gravely. "They killed him and most of his men and stole the cattle."

"How awful!" cried Priscilla. She tried to imagine Dusty as a grief-stricken child. It was difficult.

"That left Aunt Ellen—that's what we always called Dusty's mama—with nothin', no husband, no money, no cattle to sell, and no way to round up any more to drive north, plus a little boy to care for. Well, of course Daddy swore no Rhoades would starve while he was alive so he offered to take them in. Aunt Ellen wouldn't have none of it. She'd die before she'd take charity, so Mama asked—my Mama was really sick the last years of her life. Too many babies, I reckon, but she wanted so to have a son, and that's what finally did it. She didn't live too much longer after Ben junior was born. Anyway, Mama asked Aunt Ellen would she come and be our house-keeper and look after us younguns, raise us up proper and such. Daddy fixed the cabin up for her and Dusty and that's how they came to live here."

"So Dusty grew up here," Priscilla summarized, "and that's how he came to be foreman. His mother never remarried?"

Stella gave a little chuckle. "No, I guess Daddy must've asked her a hundred times after Mama died but she just wouldn't." To Priscilla's questioning look she replied, "She knew Daddy didn't love her and she didn't love him. She'd had a good marriage and didn't want one that was . . . what do they call it in the books? A marriage of convenience. So she just stayed on as our housekeeper."

Stella nodded thoughtfully, looking around the room. "I reckon you *could* say it's haunted here. I can't look around without seein' her. I still miss her, even though she's been gone more'n three years. She was a grand lady."

They sat silent for a moment, and suddenly Priscilla yawned.

"Lordy, girl, you must be dead on your feet!" Stella cried. "An' me runnin' on. We gotta get you to bed. It's been a long day for you." Priscilla made a half-hearted protest, but Stella ignored it and took her outside where she called to Dusty who was lounging outside the bunkhouse with the other men. As he came closer, she told him, "Go hitch up the wagon and take Priscilla back to the school, will you?"

Priscilla hated to be so much bother. "You don't need to go to all that trouble. It's so close. Can't we just walk?" His scornful look told her that once again she had said something wrong, and she had only been trying to be considerate.

Stella intervened. "No, no, you're much too tuckered out to walk anywheres. Dusty don't mind, do you?"

Dusty did not say, but he stalked off to get the wagon.

"What did I say that time?" asked Priscilla in dismay.

"Honey," said Stella patiently, "there's only two things a cowboy's scared of: a decent woman and bein' left afoot. You just threatened him with both in the same breath!"

Priscilla could not resist laughing with Stella as they walked arm in arm to the house to say goodnight to the others. Ben and George saw them approach and met them on the porch.

"Say, Miss Bedford," Ben asked as they waited for the wagon, "do you ride?"

"Yes, I do, at least by eastern standards, I do," she answered.

"We'll have to find you a nice, gentle horse to use, then. Can't have you livin' in Texas and not ridin'," Ben decided.

"The gentlest horse on the place is that chestnut mare," Stella offered innocently, and both men turned suspicious eyes to her.

"That's Dusty's horse," Ben said. "He's mighty particular about that mare."

Sensing that Stella might be getting her into another tangle with Dusty, Priscilla tried to protest. "Oh, it's not necessary . . . ," she began.

"Won't hurt to ask him," interrupted Stella.

"That's a wonderful idea, my dear," said George sarcastically. "Why don't *you* ask him?"

"I'll do that," she replied sweetly, leaving Priscilla wondering where she fit into all this apparent maneuvering. Just then the wagon rattled up, and goodnights were said, Stella instructing her to lie abed as late as she wished, to join them for dinner if she liked or eat some of the food at the school, whichever suited her. At last the dreaded moment came when she must be lifted into the wagon again, but Dusty was as swift and business-like as he had been before, never altering his bland expression, and in a few moments they were alone in the gathering shadows of evening.

Priscilla tried to think what he might do to repay her for the incident with Aunt Sally. She never doubted for a moment that he would do something. Drawing on her vast experience with men and under the present circumstances, she felt certain he would try to frighten her with some outlandish story or warning since she would be sleeping alone in a strange place for the first time. She would be ready for him.

Dusty was struggling with himself. It was mean, but not too mean, he decided. Besides, suppose he didn't warn her and something happened? Then she'd really be mad at him. "Might be a good idea to make sure you keep your doors always shut tight," he suggested blandly.

Here it comes, she thought, and fought to keep her rising anger out of her voice. "Why is that?" she asked just as blandly.

"There's all kinds of critters might like to pay you a visit an' . . ."

"Why is it that men find it so amusing to try to terrorize women?" Priscilla interrupted furiously. "Mr. Rhoades, I came here to live and teach school and if I get eaten by a . . . a . . . a bear in the process, I shall consider it merely part of my job." Closing her mouth with a snap and giving her head a nod that said "so there," she awaited his apology.

Somewhat taken back by her outburst, Dusty remained silent a moment, and then he said with a sly grin, "Well, ma'am, I don't know nothin' about no bears.

What I was talkin' about was skunks."

"Skunks!" cried Priscilla, horrified.

"Yes, ma'am. I can't guarantee they'd eat you, but they'd make you pretty unpopular." Even in the darkness she could see the victorious glitter in his eye.

"Oh, yes," mumbled Priscilla, completely disconcerted. He had won that round, hands down, and she would be a gracious loser. She was too tired to match wits right now anyway.

The schoolhouse looked very isolated when the wagon drew up in the yard. Priscilla shivered involuntarily. She was not a nervous person ordinarily, but something about the way the shadows fell under the trees made her feel very lonely, and for some reason, having Dusty Rhoades with her only accentuated how alone she was.

Wrapping the reins around the brake handle, he jumped down and then reached up for Priscilla. It was silly, she knew, to feel so skittish. After all, what could happen? Quashing her fears, she reached out her hands to rest them on his shoulders as he took hold of her waist to lift her down. Had it taken this long before? she wondered as it seemed everything shifted into slow motion. She was floating from the seat and then sliding very slowly until her feet touched the ground, her face passing within inches of his, her hands gripping his shoulders much more tightly than before, so tightly she could feel the muscles shift as he lowered her. Rock-hard muscles, just as she had thought. She tried to read his expression and even in the dark she could see he was no longer grinning. Her heart gave a funny little lurch and her breath stopped completely as she felt his hands tighten on her waist.

It *had* been mean, he decided, to tell her about the

skunks. She'd looked so crestfallen when she couldn't think up a retort. Sort of took the fun out of it. Made him feel like a bully, especially when he felt how tiny she was, so small and defenseless. She felt like a feather when he lifted her, and yes, his hands *could* span her waist if he squeezed just a little . . . Good God! What was he doing? he demanded of himself as he jerked his hands away. Another minute and he might have . . . well, a man just didn't kiss a woman he'd known less than a day. For sure not a woman who would blacken his eye if he even tried it and then give him a tongue-lashing he'd never forget. He took a cautious step back. "I'll walk you to the door," he offered to cover the awkward silence, more to get her moving away from him than because he wanted to accompany her.

Priscilla stared at him blankly for a moment. She had been almost certain he was going to kiss her, and she felt the oddest sense of disappointment that he had not tried. Not that she would have let him, of course. A woman—a lady, at least—did not kiss a man she had known less than a day. It simply wasn't done. At least not by Priscilla Bedford. "Thank you," she murmured when her breathing started again and turned toward the door.

It wasn't dark enough yet, he thought, following her to the door. He could still make out her shape all too well, even in that brown dress, and the way her hips swayed gently as she walked. Maybe she couldn't help it, having to walk so funny in that skirt and all, but it was almighty tempting the way her little bottom swung back and forth. With a resigned sigh and an iron will, Dusty forced his eyes up to a spot some inches above Priscilla's head and consciously checked his long stride as he followed her.

Priscilla forced herself to think of something else

82

besides the nearness of Dusty Rhoades. Attractive he might be, but he was not the sort of man she wanted to encourage. A man who would mention skunks! she thought hotly as she stepped up onto the small stoop, and then she recalled something she had neglected to ask. Stopping abruptly, she turned. "How do I . . ." she began but paused as the massive bulk of the man collided with her slender form.

Still watching the spot over her head, Dusty had not realized that she had stopped until it was too late. Instinctively, his hands reached out to catch her as he felt her small body rebound from the impact. Her hands had reached out, too, and were clinging to the lapels of his vest. With her standing on the step, their faces were almost even, and he could see every detail of her face as she glanced up, startled—the way those dark eyes sparkled from the shock, the way her soft, pink lips curved into an enticing O, the small gasp when his mouth moved to touch hers.

Priscilla had only a moment to recover her balance, to realize his arms were around her, before she saw his face coming toward hers. Unable to move and oddly unwilling to resist, she received the touch of his lips passively at first, but the gentle contact only lasted for a heartbeat before his arms tightened around her, pulling her unresisting against his chest, his lips moving on hers in a kiss that seemed to draw some essence from the very depths of her being, an essence that left in its wake a burning emptiness, an emptiness she knew instinctively that only he could fill. Of their own accord, her hands had slipped around to his back and she clung to him in that timeless moment with a need she could not begin to understand.

Dusty could not believe the violence of his own response to her. He had kissed dozens of girls, good and bad, but never had he wanted one with the urgency he now felt. He could not get enough of her, could not touch her fast enough, he decided as his hands traced her curves, down her back, into that tiny waist and over that sweet little bottom, grateful for the dress that hugged those curves so faithfully and cursing the corset that kept her softness from him.

Priscilla knew she should pull away, and she would, in one more minute, just one more minute, she thought, wondering if it were at all proper for a man to put his hands in such a private spot or for her to like it quite so much. Before she could decide, those hands were gone, moving up and up, one sliding across her shoulders, bending her backward, while the other came up to touch her cheek and trace her ear and glide down her throat with such exquisite tenderness that she melted against him, her thighs molding against the hard, lean length of his, her hands tightening along the muscled smoothness of his back, pulling him closer against the fire that was burning deep in her loins.

His wandering fingers slid down her throat, their roughness causing the tingling excitement she had earlier imagined as they caressed her delicate skin and then moved lower, slipping over her collarbone and the swell of her breast to find the sensitive tip that rose under his touch to a stiff peak. Priscilla gasped against his still-ravenous mouth as his teasing fingers caused a thrill that convulsed her entire body.

Her parted lips were more than Dusty could resist, and he slipped his tongue into the honeyed cavern of her mouth in imitation of the possession which he craved as his hand closed around the swollen mound of her breast.

Priscilla's initial surprise at his intimate invasion turned to something else entirely as she began to savor the taste of him and the feel of him. Tentatively, she began to move her own tongue in response while his kneading hand sent fuel to stoke the blaze that now threatened to rage out of control. Hazily, Priscilla realized that that should not happen, but before she could analyze that thought, a terrifying sound split the nighttime silence, ending their kiss with cruel abruptness. They jerked guiltily apart, each as startled as the other over what had just happened, and each shaken to the core by the violent feelings that had been unleashed.

"Wh . . . What was that?" Priscilla stammered, her hand going instinctively to her throat where a pulse was pounding wildly.

"A . . . A calf, prob'ly got separated from its mother," Dusty replied shakily, taking one careful step backward, and then another. "I reckon you'll hear a lot of strange noises out here, but don't be scared. Ain't nothin' round here to hurt you," he rambled on, continuing to back away, his mind on a different subject altogether. Why had she let him kiss her? And why had she let him get away with it? Walking sideways now, still facing her but moving inexorably toward the wagon, he kept up a steady stream of talk. "I wasn't teasing about the skunks, though. Be mighty careful about leavin' your door hangin' open."

"I will," she promised faintly, only half-hearing what he was saying. Why on earth had he kissed her? And why had she let him? And why wasn't she angry?

"To tell the truth," he went on, not even noticing her reply, "there ain't nothin' around here to be scared of."

He hopped up in the wagon and took up the reins, slightly awkward in his hurry to get away, adding just before slapping the team into motion, "This is about the most peaceful place you'd ever want to find."

At that very moment, although they could not hear it, a gunshot shattered the evening stillness that had settled over the town of Rainbow.

Chapter Three

At first the men in the saloon could not figure where the shot had come from, and they stood, stupified, as one of the men who had been playing poker at a corner table clutched a large red stain on his right arm. Finally, someone shouted, "A sleeve gun! He had a gun up his sleeve!" and pointed to Jason Vance, another of the poker players, who held in his hand a derringer.

"Slickest thing I ever saw," muttered one man.

"Heard of it, but never saw it," another said.

Jason Vance lay the gun on the table and sat back, awaiting the inevitable, cursing to himself that he had been involved in trouble on his very first night in town.

It only took the sheriff a few moments to arrive, and Jason Vance groaned inwardly when he saw Sheriff Winslow. He knew the type well. A middle-aged man who had grown up fighting the Mexicans and the Indians and the Yankees with equal fervor, he was an official who would insist on upholding the letter of the law and had the tenacity to make it stick. Winslow's gray hair and slight paunch did not fool Vance for a moment. He knew he was in for it.

"What happened here?" the sheriff asked in general after surveying the scene.

"I saw the whole thing, Sheriff," offered the portly bartender. "Rogers, there, insisted on playin' poker with the stranger. We all know he cain't play worth a damn, 'specially when he's drinkin', which he usually is. He's losin' heavy and the stranger keeps tryin' to quit, but Rogers just gets ugly, demandin' a chance to get his money back. Then he starts yellin' how the stranger is cheatin' him. You know how he gets. Threatens to draw on the stranger who ain't carryin' no gun. The stranger tries to tell him he ain't packin', but Rogers starts to pull out his gun where he's got it hid in his belt, under his coat. Then we hear a shot an' Rogers is hit. Stranger shot him with a sleeve gun."

"This it?" asked the sheriff, picking up the derringer. Vance nodded. The sheriff examined the gun with great interest and then looked over at Rogers who sat, still clutching his arm. "Somebody go fetch the Doc. You all right, Rogers?" The man sat with a dazed expression. He nodded vaguely. "Sleeve gun, huh?" The sheriff seemed fascinated. "Professional gambler's trick. You a gambler?"

"Yes, sir, I am," Vance replied, no hint of emotion in his voice.

"Don't see your kind around here much. Watcha doin' in Rainbow?" the sheriff asked with deceptive mildness. Vance could see that those eyes did not miss a thing.

"Actually, Sheriff, I came here looking for a little peace and quiet." He smiled at his own irony. "I had hoped to settle down around here and do a little ranching, if I could find a suitable place."

The sheriff obviously did not believe this story, but did not comment. The doctor arrived and began to examine Rogers's wound.

"I reckon I better take you in," said the sheriff with a sigh of resignation, as if he knew his duty but regretted having to fulfill it, at least in this instance.

"Look Winslow"—it was the bartender—"the gambler weren't doin' nothin' wrong. Fact is, he done everything he could to avoid a fight. Rogers just wouldn't let up. Forced him to shoot. At that he just winged him."

"How d'we know he didn't try to kill him and just missed?" asked the sheriff with dogged logic.

Jason Vance stood up solemnly. Shuffling through the cards still spread on the table, he pulled out the three of hearts. "Sheriff, if you will permit me a small demonstration?" he asked.

"Go ahead, mister," said the sheriff, frankly curious.

Vance walked over to the window and stuck the edge of the card into the crack where the window frame met the wall. Walking back to the sheriff, he took his derringer and, turning quickly, fired the remaining shot through the middle of the three hearts on the card. Gasps and murmurs from spectators filled the room. "You see, Sheriff," said Vance, returning the gun to the lawman, "if I had wished to kill Mr. Rogers, I could just as easily have shot *him* through the heart. I tried to avoid trouble, but when I could not, I tried only to disable my opponent." He turned to the doctor. "I trust he is not seriously injured."

The medical man looked up, gave a disgusted snort, and said, "No bones broke. He'll be hurtin' some, but he'll be fine."

"Mighty impressive shootin'," the sheriff decided reluctantly. "Mighty impressive talkin', too. Anybody see anything different here?" he asked of the crowd. When no one responded, he turned back to Vance. "Guess I won't need to arrest you, but we'll take it kindly if you'll just leave town on the stage tomorra." It was a mildly worded request, but Vance knew he dared not ignore it.

"Sheriff, the gentleman said he wanted to settle in Rainbow, and now you're gonna run him out because Rogers is stupid?" It was a female voice and all eyes, including Jason Vance's, turned to Rita Jordan who had just made her first appearance of the evening. Vance had to agree with Ol' Zeke. She sure wasn't hard to look at. She was tall for a woman, about five and a half feet, Vance judged. Ignoring the fashion of the day which called for curls and crimping around the face, she wore her jet black hair pulled severely back from her face in a simple chignon, a style that served to accentuate her large green eyes with their unnaturally thick, black eyelashes. Those eyes were now holding Sheriff Winslow in thrall, much to that gentleman's discomfort, and her full, red lips were quirked into a knowing smile.

She was not really beautiful, Vance thought. Her lips were too full, too sensuous, her nose a bit too long and straight, her chin too pointed, but the creamy white skin that covered it all and curved so enticingly down her long neck and disappeared into the daringly low-cut bodice of her green silk gown made a man willing to overlook her imperfections. What that green silk covered was very enticing, too. Needing no corset to lift her high, pointed breasts or to cinch a naturally slender waist, she allowed her natural charms freedom under the thin material, a freedom that made a man's imagination run wild and his breath come hard and fast.

"He a friend of yourn, Miss Rita?" asked the sheriff uncertainly.

Rita's emerald eyes shifted over to Vance, taking him in from head to foot in one quick glance; then she looked back to the sheriff. "I'll vouch for him."

"I don't know," said the sheriff, visibly reluctant to shirk his duty. "Man like that, just naturally causes trouble. Like tonight. He might not start it, but it happens 'cause he's here."

"What if I said he works for me and I need him here?" Rita asked, stepping closer to the sheriff, who was obviously becoming unnerved by her nearness.

The sheriff swallowed loudly. "Well, if you'll take the responsibility, I guess he can stay, but first sign of trouble, out he goes," he added with determination.

"Of course, Sheriff. Won't you stay and have a drink?" she offered, with a slow, suggestive smile.

"Not while I'm on duty, thank you anyway," said the lawman, anxiously backing away from Rita. When he reached the door, he turned back to Vance. "One sign of trouble, and you're out. Don't forget." Vance did not miss the warning glint in his eye.

"I won't," replied Vance. Completely baffled, he turned back to Rita who was disappearing behind a door on the back wall of the saloon.

"Drinks for everybody, courtesy of Miss Rita," called the bartender, as the doctor and some others escorted Rogers out.

Vance sat back down at his table and began to pick up the cards, as he tried to figure out what had happened and

91

more importantly, why. He had come into the saloon earlier, more to get a feel of the place and meet the important people there than anything else. It was a little fancier than he had expected, with wooden floors instead of the usual straw-covered dirt, and with a genuine mahogany bar. A third-rate painting of a voluptuous nude hung behind the bar, a luxury seldom seen in such a hick town. Several tables with miss-matched chairs were scattered about the room, completing the sparse but adequate furnishings.

He had made conversation with the bartender and bought a bottle, which he planned to share with anyone who seemed so inclined, since he never drank himself. He saw no sign of Rita Jordan but did notice the door behind the bar. It had a fancy screened design on it, and from the way the bartender kept glancing at it, Vance had decided that Rita Jordan must be behind it, able to see without being seen. He had passed a few pleasant hours, giving drinks to some of the locals, learning more about the town and the area, and then Rogers had come in, already drunk. He had joined Vance's group and recognizing that Vance was a gambler, demanded a game. Vance had been reluctant, not wanting to win from the townspeople his first day there, but rather unable to lose very much, either. He had looked to the bartender, hoping for some disapproval, but after checking with whoever was behind the door, he had nodded to Vance, so they had played. At first, several others had joined in, but they soon dropped out, seeing how surly Rogers was becoming. Vance tried to let him win, even passing him good cards, but he was either too drunk or too stupid to play well, and Vance consistently out-bluffed him without making the slightest effort to do so. Finally, in a rage, Rogers had gone for his gun.

Vance shook his head. Why had Rita stood up for him, a total stranger? Had she been serious about the job? He sat alone until closing time asking these questions of himself. When everyone else was gone, he rose to remove the card he had shot from the window frame when a female voice stopped him.

"Leave it there," she ordered. He turned to see her standing in the doorway, a disturbing presence in the empty room. "What's your name, mister?"

"Vance. Jason Vance. And you are Mrs. Jordan?" he asked.

She laughed at this, a deep, throaty laugh. She eyed him again, not quickly this time. "You want a job?"

"I'm willing to consider any offers you may make, Mrs. Jordan," he replied, his voice carefully expressionless.

This also amused her. Her lush mouth quirked into a suggestive smile. "I need a man," she purred. He raised his eyebrows and her smile widened. "To help Will here," she added with amusement, indicating the bartender. "The trail drives'll be startin' soon and a lotta new cowboys'll be comin' through town. Sometimes things get wild, and Will ain't as young as he used to be. You can gamble whenever you find some suckers. I'll pay you fifty a month, and you keep all your winnings."

It was a generous offer. Most places demanded a percentage of winnings and didn't pay wages. Of course, in such a small town, the winnings would necessarily be small. He could not bleed them dry. Not if he wanted to stay around for a while, and he might need to do that.

"You're very generous. I accept your offer with gratitude, Mrs. Jordan." He bowed gallantly. This pleased her.

"You got a room?" she asked, toying idly with the low neckline of her dress.

"Yes, I'm staying at the hotel," he replied, his eyes naturally drawn to the swell of her bosom but managing to remain expressionless.

"Tomorrow, you move your stuff over here. I got a room upstairs for you." Her green eyes glowed mysteriously, her lashes fluttering down to cover them. "Right next to mine." It was Jason Vance's turn to smile.

Stella Wilson stood at her bedroom window, staring out into the darkness.

"You can't keep him here, Stella," said George, who was sitting on the bed, watching her.

"What are you talking about, George Wilson?" she snapped, but without rancor.

"You know perfectly well what I'm talking about, my dear," he explained patiently. "You can't keep Dusty from leaving if he wants to."

Stella looked at him in feigned amazement. "What makes you think he wants to leave here?"

"The same thing that makes you think it," he informed her with satisfaction. "Look, Stella, the man's not getting any younger. He wants a home, a place of his own. There's nothing here for him," George argued.

"There're a lot of people here who love him," Stella argued back.

"If you love him, then you have to let him go. He may seem like one of the family, but he's still just a hired hand. No amount of love can change that fact, and it's eating away at him. I've seen it; you've seen it. Dusty

Rhoades wasn't born to work for another man. He's done well here because he felt he owed Ben something, but he can't pay him back forever. Stella, be realistic," George pleaded.

Stella sighed. "I just want him to be happy."

"And you think the only way the people you love can be happy is under your watchful eye," he accused.

"That's not true, George, and you know it. Why, it was me encouraged my own sisters to get married to the men they loved, even though it meant they'd have to leave here," she pointed out.

George smiled in the darkness. "You're right, of course, but that was only because you were sure they'd be happy if they did. Tell me, my dear, are you afraid that if Dusty leaves, he'll never be happy, or are you afraid he'll be happy and you won't know it?"

"Why are you always tryin' to figure me out, anyways?" snapped Stella. "I'll tell you one thing. Dusty Rhoades'll never be happy outside Texas."

"Then maybe he'll find some land to homestead out in the Panhandle. People say there's good land out there. God knows he'll never be able to afford land around here." Stella didn't answer. After some thought, George said, "That's it, isn't it? You have it all planned out that some day Dusty will get back the old Rhoades place. You're dreaming, Stella. It'll never happen. You have to face reality."

Stella sighed again. "It has to happen. I've prayed for it enough times. God couldn't be that unfair."

"Stella, I think . . ."

"You think too much," she interrupted. "You ought to trust your feelings, George." She looked out the window and said in a faraway voice, "I have a feeling that

Dusty isn't going anywhere, now or ever."

"Does this feeling have anything to do with that new schoolteacher?" asked George suspiciously.

"Whatever makes you think that?" Stella asked with false innocence.

"Seems that I recall your saying something about matching Dusty up with her unless she turned out to be absolutely hopeless," said George.

"I never said no such thing," she denied indignantly.

"Not in so many words, but your intentions were crystal clear, at least to me. Even down to instructing me to stay in town this afternoon so they'd have the ride out here alone to get acquainted. Well, I'm afraid your little scheme backfired." With great amusement he told her about what had happened with Dusty and Priscilla at the stage. "Didn't you note the tension, not to say hostility, between them?"

"Yes, I did!" said Stella with great excitement. "This is better than I could have hoped for!"

Puzzled, George asked, "You think it's good that they don't get along?"

"It's very good. You just wait. You'll see." She rubbed her hands with glee.

George scowled at his wife. "Whatever made you think they'd get along in the first place? Before you'd even met her, I mean, and don't bother to deny that you planned this match before she even left Philadelphia."

Stella gave her husband a pitying look. "Men!" She sniffed. "I don't know how you could have missed it. You read all her letters to Daddy, too, didn't you?"

"Yes, but . . ."

"But you only read the words, I guess. That's a man for you. I read between the lines. Anybody could see she had a sense of humor and was pretty clever into the bargain. Just the kind of girl Dusty usually steers clear of. Ever wonder why?" Stella did not bother to wait for an answer. "Of course you didn't. Men never think about things like that. Prob'ly Dusty never thought about it either. It's because he likes that kind of girl best, and he's scared to death of gettin' caught!" she concluded triumphantly.

George shook his head. "Stella, I think . . ."

"Don't start doin' that! You'll ruin everything!" Stella cried in mock horror. "Just think for a minute, though, what might happen if there was a girl, just the perfect girl for him, and she was in a place, right under his nose, where he couldn't ignore her or stay away from her. Just think what might happen."

George heaved a gusty sigh. "Stella, I think . . ."

"Oh, no," Stella laughed. "Forget I said to do that! I told you, you think too much. You gotta go by your feelings."

George chuckled. "All right, you win. I'll strike a bargain with you. If you'll come to bed, I'll stop thinking and start feeling."

Stella laughed softly. "You got a deal, mister."

The next day, Stella waited for her chance with Dusty. After the noon meal, for which Priscilla did not appear, she watched for Dusty to go into the barn as he often did to check on his mare. She followed him there and found him currying the horse.

"She sure is pretty," Stella remarked after Dusty had acknowledged her presence. "Gentle, too. I swear, you've done a job on that horse. Why, I'll bet Matthew

97

could ride that mare."

Dusty looked at her skeptically. "Matthew *has* ridden this mare and you know it. What're you after, Stella?"

"Me? Nothin'!" she said in amazement. "It's just that Daddy, well, he suggested that . . ." she trailed off uncertainly.

"That what?" he asked suspiciously.

"Well, Priscilla—you remember, the schoolteacher?"

"I remember," said Dusty dryly.

"She can ride."

"Oh, I'll bet she can!" he replied sarcastically.

"That's my opinion, too," said Stella confidentially. "But you know Daddy. She said she can ride and Daddy thinks she should have a horse to use. And with her bein' a city girl and all, why, we can't have her ride one of them wild mustang ponies. She'd get kilt!"

"Why you tellin' me all this?" he asked, the suspicion back in his voice.

"Well, you done such a good job gentlin' that mare, we thought maybe you could gentle a horse for her, too," Stella said hopefully.

Dusty snorted in disgust. "Stella, I got more important things to do than pamperin' a tenderfoot."

"I know that," said Stella defensively, "but you know Daddy, once he gets an idea in his head." She thought a moment. "'Course there's always your mare . . ." she suggested tentatively.

"Oh, no, she ain't gettin' my horse!"

Stella nodded agreement. "She prob'ly won't want to ride *your* horse anyway. It was a bad idea."

"Whadda ya mean, she wouldn't want to?" he asked, a scowl marking his forehead.

"Well, she's prob'ly used to riding fancy, eastern

horses. You know, thoroughbreds and the like."

"I'll match this horse against any thoroughbred anywhere," he declared belligerently.

"The horse could use the exercise. You don't get much chance to ride her," Stella suggested.

"I never said I'd let her," he insisted.

"'Course, I can understand you not wantin' her to make unfavorable comparisons to your horse. Why you'd even be ashamed . . ."

"Tell her she can ride the mare!" Dusty said in disgust.

"Why, Dusty, that's mighty generous of you. You're a real gentleman," said Stella with admiration. She turned to go and then turned back as an afterthought. "I'm goin' down there right now and take her some dinner. Why don't you saddle up and bring her down so Priscilla can get a look at her? That'd be a right friendly gesture. Yes, sir, a real gentleman."

She walked out into the sunlight, smiling as she heard Dusty call after her, "Stella, someday you're gonna go too far!"

A few minutes later, Stella arrived at the schoolhouse with a plate of food covered by a napkin. "Anybody home?" she called.

Priscilla appeared at the back door, dressed in a simple, black cotton skirt and white shirtwaist, wearing an apron, with a scarf tied around her head. "Hello! I've just been unpacking," she called gaily. Priscilla had intended to lie awake for a while the night before and analyze her feelings for Dusty Rhoades and hopefully to determine why she had permitted him to kiss her. Even more important, she had wanted to determine why she had kissed him back, a fact she had been reluctant to admit, even to herself, but which was quite true, nevertheless.

Her body, however, had not been nearly as concerned with the problem as her mind and had promptly fallen asleep as soon as it was stretched out on the bed. Morning had given an air of unreality to all the events of the previous day, and Priscilla had decided that the kiss had probably not been as important as she had previously thought. In fact, she felt quite certain that she could forget it, and its giver, with equal ease once she set her mind to it, a task she meant to undertake as soon as she was unpacked.

"Since you didn't make it for dinner, thought I'd bring you a little something," Stella was saying.

"That's so thoughtful of you. Come on in." They went inside and sat down at the table. Priscilla uncovered the plate of food and flashed Stella a grateful smile. "I opened a can of peaches for breakfast, but I think this was what I really needed," she said as she began to devour the beefsteak and flaky biscuits Stella had brought. "Truthfully, I just woke up a little while ago. I'm afraid I slept half the day. It's so quiet here and I guess I was really tired."

Stella was looking around. Priscilla had filled the bookshelf and set around some pictures and a few knickknacks. "Shore startin' to look homey here."

"I already feel like it's home. You've certainly helped by making me feel so comfortable."

They chatted for a few minutes until they heard a horse approaching. "Who could that be?" asked Priscilla as she heard the gate swing open.

"It's Dusty," said Stella without looking, and she smiled as Priscilla jumped up, tore the scarf from her head, and pulled off her apron as she dashed to the mirror. Dipping the corner of her apron in the water pitcher, she wiped imaginary smudges from her face and hurriedly straightened her hair.

"Hello, the house," Dusty called.

"Come on in," Stella called back and by the time he appeared in the doorway, Priscilla was standing demurely in the center of the room, completely composed.

"Well, hello, Mr. Rhoades," she said coolly. "How nice of you to stop by." She had not expected to see him again so soon, at least not until she had succeeded in putting him out of her mind, but she was pleased to note that she could greet him without betraying any embarrassing emotion. Betraying, of course, being the key word, since she was certainly feeling such emotions. How could his mere presence disturb her so? she wondered, putting a casual hand over the place where butterflies were struggling in her stomach. Why, he was hardly even looking at her.

Dusty risked one brief glance at Priscilla, just long enough to determine that she did not seem the least bit upset by what had happened. Maybe she was used to having men grab her and kiss her. It was no wonder, the way she flirted so shamelessly. Not that she'd flirted with him, of course. No, he didn't have that excuse. Didn't really have any excuse except that she was so damn . . . He forced himself to touch the brim of his hat and nod politely in her direction before turning an expectant look at Stella.

Stella appeared not to notice. "Well, Priscilla," she said looking around, "while we have possession of a big, strong man, is there any rearranging you'd like done in the furnishings?"

From the way Dusty was glaring, Priscilla guessed that this was not why he had come and that Stella knew it perfectly well, but since she did have a job to be done, she decided to risk it.

"Yes, I surely would love to have my trunk moved over here by the wardrobe. The wardrobe will have to be moved over a little, though," she suggested with more confidence than Dusty's look inspired.

Dusty stared at Stella in stony silence for a moment and then wordlessly went about the task outlined for him. When he was finished, he went back to the doorway, put his hands on his hips, and again looked at Stella as if expecting her to say something. She could hardly suppress a smile as she asked, "Is there something you wanted to tell Miss Bedford?"

Priscilla saw his eyes narrow and his jaw muscles twitch as if he were quite angry. Then reluctantly, he turned his icy blue eyes to her and said, "Stella says you can ride."

What was all this about? she wondered, glancing at Stella who was looking out the window, completely unconcerned. Left on her own, she decided to play along with the role Stella had obviously assigned her. She looked back at Dusty and answered, "Yes, I can."

"Well, I got a horse—a mare—you can ride when you want to. She's real gentle. Won't give you no trouble."

Remembering how certain George and Ben had been last night that Dusty would never allow her to use his horse, Priscilla wondered how Stella had managed to accomplish this miracle. Had Dusty developed some tender feelings for her overnight, after their kiss? Had he volunteered the mare? No, judging from his expression, Stella had coerced him in some way, but Priscilla was appreciative enough of her efforts not to refuse the offer. "Thank you. That's very kind."

"She's outside if you want to take a look at her," he told her grudgingly and stomped out the door. Priscilla turned a puzzled face to Stella who ignored her and followed Dusty outside. Left with no choice, Priscilla joined them and when she saw the mare, she forgot everything else.

"Oh, she's wonderful!" Priscilla exclaimed, examining the mare very carefully, stroking her. The mare, she noted irrelevantly, was the same chestnut brown as her own hair, with a white star on her forehead and white stockings on her front feet.

"Dusty raised her from a foal," offered Stella.

Priscilla had ridden since childhood and recognized the clean lines that marked the quality of the animal. The fact that Dusty was responsible for her lifted him considerably in her estimation. A man who could raise a horse like this couldn't be all bad. "What's her name?" she asked.

Dusty was just able to suppress a smile as the irony of the situation occurred to him, and he said with studied nonchalance, "Well, like I said, she's real gentle, won't give anybody any trouble, knows how to act right. So I call her 'Lady.'" He looked up just in time to catch Priscilla's wince.

"It suits her," Priscilla said, also with creditable nonchalance, although she was inwardly smarting. Obviously, she did not meet his qualifications for being a lady. Not that she cared. And if he ever tried to treat her as if she weren't . . . again . . . well, she'd show him. "May I ride her?" she asked. "Now?"

Dusty was reluctant. He still wasn't quite used to the idea. "She ain't broke for no sidesaddle," he protested.

Priscilla gave him a disgusted look. "Neither am I,"

she said, and without waiting for a helping hand, nimbly straddled the horse. Thanks to Dusty's long legs, the stirrups were within easy reach of the ground, but she found that once astride, she could not reach them. Having ridden bareback as a child, she found this no deterrent. After adjusting her skirts as modestly as she could, she gripped tightly with her knees and kicked the horse into motion. "I won't be gone long," she called over her shoulder as they trotted away. Dusty had left the schoolyard gate open and once over the hill and out of sight, Priscilla kicked the mare again.

Dusty and Stella, watching from the schoolyard, stood dumbfounded as a cloud of dust proved she had broken into a run.

"Damn fool, she'll break her neck!" predicted Dusty.

"Don't count on it," said Stella.

Dusty ignored her and sat down on the step to roll a smoke. "Hope she don't get lost. I got work to do."

Stella watched as he kept pausing in the task of building a cigarette to scan the horizon with anxious eyes. When he had finally managed to get it rolled and lighted, Stella said, "Well, I got things to do. Tell Priscilla I'll see her later."

As she trudged off, Dusty rose swiftly to his feet and opened his mouth to lodge a protest. Fortunately, he caught himself in time, though, and closed his mouth with a snap. What was he going to do, beg Stella not to leave him alone with her? He wasn't afraid to be alone with her. Or at least, not much. Of course, if he had his druthers, he'd druther not. She might say something about last night. Or he might. He had no intention of it, but then he'd had no intention of kissing her either, and that hadn't stopped him. Somehow things just happened around Priscilla Bedford, like a man just wasn't in control any more. With an exasperated sigh, he plumped down on the stoop again and took a deep drag of his cigarette.

He had finished that one, rolled another, and almost finished it before his apprehensive vigilance was rewarded with the sight of Priscilla returning. Rising swiftly, he took one final drag, flicked the butt to the ground, and attacked it savagely with his boot heel. Where in the hell had she been, anyway? She could've gotten lost or fallen off and been hurt. Lady had obviously enjoyed her run. She was stepping high, fairly dancing, as she trotted into the yard. Even more irritating was the sight of Priscilla's face and the realization that the brilliant smile she was wearing had nothing to do with his presence.

He'd never seen her look lovelier, her eyes shining, her cheeks flushed, her hair coming loose, blowing every which way. Comes from riding without a hat. Wasn't safe to ride without a hat. Person could get sunstroke. Well, maybe not in March, but it was a bad habit to develop. She *could* get sunburned, though. Maybe that red on her cheeks was sunburn; maybe she'd even get freckles, he thought maliciously. A highfalutin lady like her would probably faint if she got a freckle. It would serve her right.

Priscilla had seldom enjoyed a ride more. Used to city life where she had been confined to promenades in the park, she found the freedom of the Steele ranch intoxicating. She was even willing to forgive Dusty Rhoades his boorishness in return for the great service he had done her in lending her Lady. "She's marvelous," Priscilla reported when she got within earshot of Dusty.

105

So happy was she that she failed to notice he did not share her good humor. The mare had a soft mouth, and it took only a slight pull on the reins to halt her a few feet from where Dusty stood. Priscilla reached down and gave Lady's neck an affectionate pat. "She may be gentle, but such spirit!" she announced to no one in particular, and leaning closer to the horse's ear, she crooned, "Yes, a lady *should* have spirit."

Ignoring her provocative remark, he strode up to her, hands on hips, and demanded tersely, "Where have you been?"

Priscilla stared at him in astonishment. He was actually angry. "I don't think I left the state," she replied with disarming sweetness.

Fighting down an urge to do her bodily harm, he barked, "You could've gotten lost."

"I stayed on the road," Priscilla informed him loftily. "I'm not a fool." The sooner this conversation ended, the better, she decided. She had best get off the horse and send him on his way before . . . well, before anything untoward happened. Or anything at all. But, as she considered the problem of dismounting, she suddenly realized her dilemma. Getting up was one thing, but getting down, without the aid of a stirrup, wearing a skirt and with Dusty Rhoades watching, presented an insurmountable obstacle. Before she had a chance to think any further on the subject, however, two large hands reached up, clasped her rather rudely around the waist, and plucked her from the saddle.

A second later her feet were planted on the ground, so suddenly that she staggered, clutching his forearms for support, as the rough hands at her waist steadied her. She brought her wide-eyed glance up to his face, marveling at his apparent rage. The muscles under her clutching fingers were bunched with fury, and those sky-blue eyes were sending out storm warnings.

"Not a fool?" he raged, fighting an irrational desire to shake her. "You could've fallen off, broken your neck!"

"I've never fallen off a horse in my life," she lied, matching his angry tone. "Would it matter to you if I did?"

An indignant denial rose to his lips but got no further as he suddenly realized that it *would* matter—it would matter a great deal. And that was part of the reason he was so angry. He had gotten mad that she had endangered herself and then gotten madder because he had cared. Of all the damn-fool situations, he mused as his grip on her waist lightened into a caress. She felt so soft today, he thought, as he fingered her uncorseted figure and looked down into those great, dark eyes, marveling at the way the fire was burning out in them and they were growing even larger, the closer he got to them.

Priscilla had watched his face in amazement as the wrath had evaporated right before her very eyes, to be replaced by a curious play of emotions she could not read. She felt her own anger die as the muscles under her hands relaxed and his clutching fingers began to embrace. A strange new light was shining out of those blue eyes, a light whose danger she recognized. Well, if he tried to kiss her again, she thought, as his face came toward hers, she would . . . let him, she realized in the last instant before his lips touched hers.

His mouth closed over hers, gently at first, but before she had time to savor the sweetness, his arms closed around her, crushing her to him, the heat of his desire melting her resistance, molding her softness against the lean length of him. An answering heat rose in her own body, turning her blood to a molten fire that scorched through her, burning away all thought, all inhibition. Her hands were on his back, clinging, searching out the warmth of him, the strength of him, drawing him ever nearer.

One of his hands still held her tightly against him while the other found the mass of her hair. As his long fingers tangled into her fallen locks, she barely noticed the sharp stabs of stray hairpins. Instead, she was only aware of the sensation of his tongue as it traced the contour of her bottom lip. The thrill she felt made her gasp, inviting his further invasion. Mindlessly, she reveled in this strange intimacy, an intimacy no one had ever dared before, as his rough tongue explored the tender skin inside her lip, flicked over the surface of her teeth, and then plunged into the warm depths of her mouth. The shock of his assault sent waves of response singing along her nerve ends, out and out until her fingers and toes curled in reaction and she arched against him, instinctively inviting his caress. He did not fail her. The hand buried in her hair slipped out and around, skimming the heated skin of her throat, following that satin trail down the V of her blouse until the well-worn button holes surrendered to his insistence, freeing her sweet treasure for his exploration. Brushing aside the silken barrier of her chemise, he captured that treasure in a worshipful embrace that stopped her breath. A moment later she released that breath in a shuddering sigh as his thumb found one pebble-hard peak and began a sensuous torment that weakened her knees, forcing her hips to lock with his, demanding a closeness, a unity that she did not understand but could only crave with the force of a primal need.

How could mere flesh and bone cause such pure pleasure, she wondered dazedly, or feel it either? If only she could make him touch more of her . . . The thought jolted her, and her consciousness, which had been soaring heedlessly, came thumping rudely back to reality. What was she doing, behaving like a wanton, and with a man who had already made it clear he thought she was no lady! Jerking her face away, she began to struggle against him.

For a moment Dusty did not comprehend her movements. Robbed of her mouth, his lips tried to settle on the satin of her neck until the violence of her struggle broke through to his besotted brain. Just as he released her, she managed to land a glancing blow on his shoulder with her ineffectually tiny fist.

Staggering backward a few steps, Priscilla regained her balance and clutching frantically at the edges of her blouse, drew herself up to her full height. "Take your hands off me," she demanded breathlessly and totally unnecessarily, since his hands were no longer anywhere near her.

Dusty stared at her dumbly, one of those hands moving absently to rub the spot where she had struck him. What on earth had happened? He had been certain that she was responding, kissing him back for all she was worth, and then . . . He watched fascinated as she took a deep breath, pulling the light cotton of her shirtwaist taut across her erect nipples. No, he hadn't been mistaken. She *had* responded. Then why had she pulled away?

Priscilla took a calming breath and raised her free hand to restore some order to her hairstyle, a futile gesture since her neat chignon now hung in a hopeless tangle down her back. "Thank you for allowing me to ride your mare, Mr. Rhoades," she said with as much breathless dignity as she could muster. She would never let him know how he had shaken her. "Good day to you, sir," she added, turning on her heel and heading for the safety of the schoolhouse.

Dusty watched her haughty march with reluctant admiration. She sure was put together, he thought. Like a thoroughbred. If only she wasn't so damn . . . Muttering another curse on all the female sex, he jerked his hat brim low over his eyes, wincing slightly as the schoolhouse door slammed shut, and mounting Lady, rode slowly back to the ranch.

It took Priscilla quite a while to calm down as she alternated between sitting and standing and pacing and then sitting again. The nerve of the man, she thought, mentally replaying the events of his visit. Maybe he considered that kiss as payment for doing her a favor. Well, if he expected any more payments, he was going to have a long wait. Was he always so highhanded, so forceful in his dealings with women? If so, she wondered that he was allowed to run around loose, and if not, then why had he forced himself on *her*, not once but twice? Flushing with shame, she realized that once might have been an accident but that twice would never have happened without her cooperation. She should at least have slapped his face last night, thereby saving herself the humiliation of her response to him today. Well, it would not happen again, she resolved, no matter what the circumstances. If he so much as made a move in her direction, she would freeze him out so fast, he'd think he'd been caught in a blizzard. Having decided that, she returned to her unpacking, the chore that Stella's visit had interrupted.

Later in the afternoon, when she had finished arranging her room and the classroom to suit herself, Priscilla changed into a respectable dress of blue flowered calico and walked up the hill to the ranch. She found Stella enjoying an untroubled hour in the parlor while her two youngest children napped. Stella smiled when she saw Priscilla in the doorway. "Enjoy your ride?" she asked as Priscilla came in and sat down in a chair opposite her.

Priscilla fought down the wave of irritation she felt rising inside her and answered calmly, "Yes, it was very nice."

Stella studied her thoughtfully for a moment. "Did Dusty give you any trouble?"

Priscilla could not control the blush that stained her cheeks. "Not about the horse . . . I mean . . . no," she replied lamely, trying unsuccessfully to avoid Stella's prying eyes. Finally, exasperated, she blurted, "Is he always so disagreeable?"

Stella considered the question for a moment. "Matter of fact," she decided, "Dusty Rhoades is one of the most *a*-greeable men I know."

Priscilla almost gasped in her surprise. She found this impossible to believe and said so.

"It's true," Stella affirmed. "Why, I'll bet there's not a girl in five counties wouldn't lay down and die for a chance with him."

Priscilla shook her head in disbelief. He must only use his brute force on her. "Well, his charm escapes me," she said with a little less than total honesty.

"That's 'cause he ain't used it on you," Stella asserted.

"What do you mean?" Priscilla asked suspiciously.

Stella thought a moment. "You may've noticed that Dusty's different from the other cowboys."

"I certainly have!" she said with spirit and more truth than Stella could have guessed.

Stella smiled. "No, what I mean is, most cowboys're mighty bashful around women. Comes from not seein' any for months on end, I reckon. Anyways, Dusty never did have that problem. I guess growin' up around here with all us girls, he just had to learn to get around us to survive. So he learned to get around us. I ain't hardly ever knowed him to meet a woman and not shine up to her. Young, old, pretty, ugly, it don't matter. He charms 'em all. Sometimes I think he does it just to keep in practice." She paused so Priscilla could soak this all in. She could see Priscilla was intrigued by the whole idea, so she continued. "Yes, I've never known Dusty to fight shy of a pretty girl before, but maybe in your case, he's got a reason."

Priscilla turned guiltily away from Stella's probing glance. He had not exactly been fighting shy of her, although he *had* been far from charming.

Misinterpreting Priscilla's guilty look, Stella remarked, "I'll bet he gave you back as good as he got, though."

"Better," Priscilla affirmed, trying to remember only his barbed comments and not his heated kisses. "He doesn't show any sign of letting up either. Did you catch that 'Lady' remark?" she asked indignantly.

Stella laughed appreciatively. "With both hands! But don't you let him get you riled," she warned, much too late. "Tell you what. You just be as sweet as pie to him, no matter what, and before you know it, he'll be eatin' outta your hand."

Priscilla shook her head. Those tactics had no place at all in her plans. "No, thanks. I'd probably lose a finger!"

Stella laughed again. "Well, don't forget, he's lendin' you his horse. As a rule, cowboys don't let nobody ride their horses and this one's his special pet. He paid you a big compliment."

"Oh, Stella, I know you made him do it," Priscilla protested, remembering Dusty's surly attitude.

Stella grew serious. "Honey, nobody, not even me, can make Dusty Rhoades do anything he don't want to, and don't you forget it."

Chapter Four

That evening, Jason Vance started his new job at the Yellow Rose. He had spent the day exploring the nearby countryside after having closed the deal on the horse Zeke had gotten him. The saloon was crowded, word having spread about the previous night's shooting, and everyone wanted to see the now-famous three of hearts and the man who had shot it.

Vance got a bottle and some glasses and generously treated his admirers to drinks. He held court all evening at a corner table, occasionally glancing up to Rita's door, but she failed to appear. As he approached the bar to get a new bottle for his companions, Will leaned his girth against the mahogany and commented, "Noticed you ain't a drinkin' man."

"In my business, you need a clear head and a steady hand," Vance replied.

"Miss Rita noticed it right off," Will said, using his rag to wipe at an invisible spot on the shiny wood. "She was mighty impressed. She likes a man who don't drink."

"That can't be very good for her business," remarked Vance wryly, returning to the table.

Much later, when the crowd had left, Vance helped Will close up, and then Will said, "I put your bags in your room. It's upstairs, the second door on the right," he explained, pointing to the screened door Vance had noticed before and which led to the second floor stairs.

The stairs were dark and narrow, but the upstairs hall was lighted by a lamp hanging on the wall. Only two doors led off the hall so Rita's door was not difficult to find. When Will left, as Vance could hear him doing even now, Rita and Vance would be completely alone, a fact that made Vance feel a little uncomfortable. Rita Jordan was a very attractive woman, but Jason Vance traveled alone. He was particularly uninterested in forming any close relationships at the moment because of his special purpose in being in Rainbow. After a brief hesitation and a great deal of apprehension, he tapped lightly on her door. "Come in," she called, and he knew she had been listening for him. Taking a moment to straighten his coat, he gingerly opened her door and stepped into her room. What he saw there stunned him, so that it was a full minute before he remembered to breathe, but fortunately, Jason Vance was used to concealing his emotions and his face betrayed nothing.

Rita Jordan was sitting in a chair opposite the door wearing a green silk wrapper—which was barely wrapped. She had allowed the skirt to fall open, revealing her long, shapely legs, which were crossed to the thigh. The bodice was negligently closed to expose a large expanse of cleavage. The small portion of her breasts that was covered was clearly outlined by the sheer material.

"Good evening, Vance," she purred provocatively. "I wanted to explain your duties to you."

He forced himself to keep his eyes on her face, although even that was not safe. Her green eyes were almost hypnotic in their effect on him, and there was an air of vulnerability about her, in spite of the obvious seductiveness, that might almost have passed for innocence. Perhaps it *had* passed for innocence once.

"You're probably wondering why I wanted you," she continued. Vance did not smile at her little play on words. He was a naturally suspicious man and this whole setup was too . . . well, too set up. Almost like a test, and it was a test he'd have to pass if he wanted to stay in Rainbow. "Will's a good man," she was saying. "Been with me a long time, and he looks real mean, and that's usually enough. But, past couple years, Will's been sufferin' from the rheumatism. It cripples him up some, and I'm just afraid that if things got rough, he'd be outta the game." She leaned forward a bit and Vance caught his breath. He had a glimpse of one dark nipple before forcing his glance back to her face. "Now I can see you're a man who don't look fer trouble but who knows what to do with it when he meets it. Your job'll be to sit around and make yourself conspicuous-like. Help Will out when he needs it and play your cards." She sat back again and waited for his response.

"Is that all?" he asked blandly.

She nodded, a small smile curling her luscious lips.

"I'm very grateful to you, Mrs. Jordan." He bowed slightly. "Good night, ma'am." He turned to go.

"Vance," she called and he turned back. Her green

117

eyes glinted with curiosity. "Do you like women?"

"I like women very much," he replied without expression.

Her brows rose. "Do you like me?" she asked. That air about her became stronger, making her seem even more vulnerable, almost as if she wanted him to think he had the power to hurt her. She was very good, he thought.

He pretended to consider the question and looked her over very carefully, as if he hadn't really paid much attention before. He studied her for a long time, too long, until she stiffened with annoyance. "Yes, Mrs. Jordan," he concluded at last, "I like you very much."

"And you were still going to leave?" she asked accusingly.

He smiled, a slow upward straining of his lips that never quite reached his eyes. "You called me here to tell me my duties," he explained. "You said I was to help Will. I assumed that if I had any other duties, you would tell me about them."

She threw her head back and laughed heartily at this. "You're right, Vance," she said when she had recovered. "If I want you for anything else, I'll let you know."

"Your servant, ma'am," he said, bowing himself out of the door and closing it softly behind him. He paused for a long moment, closing his eyes with relief. He had been right. It had been a test, and he had passed it with flying colors. For a moment he let himself wonder what might have happened if he had made a move on her. Undoubtedly, she would have stopped him. She was not a woman to suffer unwanted attentions. But how would she have done it? He shrugged off the question and turned down the hall.

The door to his own room stood ajar, and as he stepped

118

in and looked around, he found himself quite pleased with the accommodations. His room contained a brass bed with a passable mattress, a washstand, and a wardrobe. A somewhat battered armchair completed the furnishings. He noticed that his window, like Rita's, overlooked the street and was graced with lace curtains. After unpacking his meager belongings, he removed his clothing, carefully hanging his suit and shirt in the wardrobe, and slipped on a fine linen nightshirt. When he moved to his bed, he carried with him his belt. As he first sat and then lay on the bed, he turned the belt over, and reaching into a slit he had cut there himself, he pulled out a yellowed paper. Opening it carefully, he studied it for a long time. It was a map, a map he now knew by heart, but somehow, looking at it helped it to seem more real. The writing was in Spanish, but he had in the past few months managed to translate it all so that he now knew what it said.

"Not yet, but soon," he said aloud. Refolding the map, he returned it to its hiding place and shoved the belt up under his pillow. Leaning back on the pillow, he put his hands behind his head and recalled the strange sequence of events that had put the map into his hands and brought him to the town of Rainbow.

Jason Vance's luck had run out. He'd eaten the last of his food the day before, his horse was played out, and he was lost. Then he saw the buzzards. They were the first living things he had seen since he had become lost in the vast wasteland of the Texas Panhandle. They circled slowly, waiting. Now, a buzzard could mean a dead anything, but it might mean a dead man. If it were a dead white man, he might have had supplies with him, even some food, if he hadn't starved to death, and if not, he probably came from somewhere, and Vance could backtrack him to find out where. At any rate, he had nothing better to do, so he rode to where the buzzards were circling. The first thing he saw was the dead horse. It was already stiffening and swelling in the hot sun, but it had a saddle, which meant it was a white man's horse. Then he saw the man. He was lying in the shade of a rock and at first Vance thought he, too, was dead, since he did not move. Vance could see the tracks in the dust where the man had dragged himself from the dead animal. When he was closer, he climbed down and walked over to the rock.

"Howdy, stranger," said a rasping voice. "Set a spell."

The man was alive but just barely. He was an old man, although how old it was difficult to guess. His weather-worn face bore a thousand wrinkles, stained here and there by blood and bruises.

Jason Vance squatted on his heels beside the old man. "Your horse drag you?" he asked. He could see at a glance that one of the old man's legs was broken, and from the way he lay twisted, he must also be injured internally.

"Yep," answered the old man, matter-of-factly. "Managed to git my gun out and shoot 'im, but not soon enough. Got skeered by a rattler, I reckon."

"Not much I can do for you. I could try to set that leg, though," Vance offered, genuinely sorry for the old man's plight, but still anxious about his own.

"No! Don't touch me, son," he ordered. "I been layin' here since yestidy. I ain't got long, boy, an' I knows it, so don't go makin' it worse by tryin' to make it better."

120

"I haven't any food myself, or I'd offer to fix you something to eat. I do have coffee."

"I got a pack horse somewheres around here. She ketched up with us late last night. I keep hearin' her back over in there." He pointed vaguely. "Maybe you kin ketch her. She's loaded with grub."

Vance felt a vague sense of triumph as he rode a short way and succeeded in capturing the pack horse. He had made the right decision in following the buzzards. After bringing back the pack horse, he built a fire, made some coffee, and fried up some bacon.

"I ain't hungry," said the old man when Vance offered him some, "but I sure could use some coffee." Vance served it to him. "There's somethin' you kin do fer me, friend, and I'll pay ya dearly fer it."

"Pay me?" Vance was amused. "Why, old man, I can take everything you have right now."

"Not everythin'," he said with a sly smile, although his eyes were glazed with pain. "Look in my left saddlebag offin' that dead hoss. You'll find it."

Vance did as he was told and he found, among several worthless items, an ancient, yellowed map. It was drawn in great detail, noting many landmarks. The legends were written in Spanish but Vance could understand a little of it, especially the word "oro."

"Is it a gold mine?" he asked when he had returned to the old man.

"Better," said the old man, and for a moment he convulsed with pain. "It's buried treasure. Spanish gold. It was a payroll fer the Spanish soldiers up in Natchidotches. They used to carry it up the old Spanish Trail, through San Antone and across."

"You mean to tell me they buried one somewhere?"

121

Vance asked skeptically.

"This time they did. Got skeered by Injuns or sumpin' an' buried it. Never did get back fer it. Near as I kin figure, there was at least $50,000 in gold."

"Well, old timer, now I've got the map, what's to stop me from leaving you here?" Vance asked with a touch of amusement.

The old man coughed a bit and when he was done, he gave Vance a pitying smile. "You got you a good map there. Covers about five square miles. Enny idee where them five miles might be?" Vance looked at the map. There were no towns or any other directions to give an exact location.

"You've got me," said Vance with grudging admiration. "What is it you want me to do?"

"I been layin' here all this time, thinkin' how terrible it'll be when I'm daid, havin' the buzzards pick out my eyes and my innards, 'til I'm a pile a bones. It surely would be a comfort to know I'm gonna be buried proper."

Jason Vance was not an evil man. At least he prided himself in being civilized, and he had planned to dispose of the old man in some way, but digging a grave out of the parched ground in the hot sun was not exactly what he had had in mind.

"You've got a deal, old man. Now tell me where it is," he said.

"First," the old man grinned, "you dig the hole." Vance hesitated for a moment, trying to think of another option.

"Fifty thousand in gold," the old man taunted. "Jist think, the next hole you dig'll be filled with gold."

Reluctantly, Vance got up and, taking the pick and shovel from the old man's gear, he began to dig. It was hot work. The ground was hard and dry. He glanced over at the old man now and again. Once he saw him drawing in the sand. When he'd dug a hole about three feet deep, he decided to stop for a rest. Walking back over toward the rock, he called, "Hey, old man, you want a marker on this grave?"

Silence was his only answer. The old man was dead. Vance started to swear when he noticed the crude map drawn in the dirt in front of him. Squatting down, he saw a dot labeled "San Antone" and another labeled "Astin" with lines coming out from each, intersecting at a point southeast of them. The old man had even given approximate mileage. "Thanks, old man," he said aloud. Jason Vance's luck had changed.

After he buried the old man, he loaded up only the necessities from the old man's pack and struck out on the dead man's back trail, figuring, correctly, that his last camp would have been at a water hole. There he rested a day, giving his horse a chance to recover, and with the two horses, the dead man's provisions, and an idea where civilization lay, he made it to Tascosa inside of a week.

By then, the map had begun to haunt him, almost as if the old man's ghost had lingered on it, urging him on. He began some discreet inquiries as he moved slowly eastward, toward central Texas. The closer he got to San Antonio, the more he learned about dozens of stories of buried Spanish treasure. It was a subject men loved to discuss, and they all knew of someone who owned or at least had seen a map. There was something about the subject of gold that made men eloquent and raised their enthusiasm to a fever pitch. Jason Vance was not immune to such influences. By the time he reached San Antonio, he was obsessed with his treasure, or the idea of

123

it, and it was there he learned that a town had sprung up near the place on the dirt map where the two lines crossed, the town of Rainbow.

"What do I do now?" Priscilla asked, using a flour-covered hand to push a stray lock of hair out of her eyes and leaving a white streak across her forehead.

Aunt Sally's weather-beaten face settled into a scowl. "First, you wipe the flour off your face." He could hardly believe she was really here, in his kitchen. When she had asked him to give her cooking lessons, he had consented without believing for a minute that she was serious. He had thought she had only been trying to get one up on Dusty, and he had been only too glad to help her. Then, this morning, she had appeared at his door for her first lesson, ignoring warnings from all the Steele girls about bearding the lion in his den, and even more amazing, he had been glad to see her. Oh, he hadn't liked her at first. When she'd showed up at the ranch that night wearing that fancy dress, he had marked her down as one of those silly eastern women, nice to look at but a head stuffed with sawdust. Then she had started flirting with the boys, and his disgust had grown until she'd gotten to Ed. Ugly Ed they called him now and probably always would, and he loved it! That was when Aunt Sally had realized that she wasn't really flirting, only trying to make the boys feel good. And when he'd noticed Dusty's reaction, he'd realized she was also trying to irritate him. That was fine, too. Dusty Rhoades needed to be taken down a notch or two. Wouldn't hurt him a bit.

Priscilla's laughter broke his reverie. Holding out her white hands for his inspection, she said, "I can't very well wipe my face with these, can I? Will you do it for me, please?" Aunt Sally harrumphed self-consciously and then picked up a towel and awkwardly wiped off the smudge. "Thank you," Priscilla giggled, amused at his clumsiness. "Now what do I do with these biscuits?"

Clearing his throat again, Aunt Sally handed her the rolling pin. "You roll out the dough. Then you cut out the biscuits."

"It's so easy!" she exclaimed, accepting the rolling pin. "How thin shall I roll it?"

"Just start rolling. I'll tell you when you got it right." He watched with approval as she began her task. She sure was a pretty little thing, even in a plain shirt and skirt. Would serve Dusty right if he did fall for her. A lady like her would never give him the time of day.

Finally, Priscilla had placed the last of her three-dozen biscuits on the baking sheet. "Thirty-six biscuits for seven men?" she asked incredulously. "Will they eat all of them?"

"They will if they're good," Aunt Sally replied dryly, placing the large tin sheet into the oven. It was amazing, he thought, watching how Priscilla's eyes sparkled. She was like a little kid, so excited over a mess of biscuits. "How come you never learned to cook?" he demanded.

His rudeness did not bother Priscilla. Somehow she felt he had a right to pry into her private affairs, as if he really were her Aunt Sally, or at least her Uncle somebody or another. "Too much of a tomboy, I guess," Priscilla shrugged. "My mother died when I was very young and our housekeeper was even more formidable than you," she explained with a twinkle. "I never would have dared ask her to show me anything in 'her' kitchen. She would have probably refused on the grounds that I

125

would break something, and she would have been-right. I was a very clumsy child." Aunt Sally's skeptical look told her he did not believe that for a minute, but she disregarded it. "Now you have to tell me how you came to be called 'Aunt Sally.'"

"Don't rightly remember," he hedged, but she was having none of it and told him so. "Well, cooks is usually called some female name or another, sort of like a joke," he explained noncommittally.

"But why did you get 'Aunt Sally'? There must be a story." When he did not respond, she asked, "What's your real name?"

"Tom," he snapped with what she guessed was feigned irritation. "Some real clever fella pointed out one time that they couldn't very well call me 'Uncle Tom.' That started a war once, near as I can recollect. So he said it'd have to be 'Aunt Sally.' The name just stuck." Before she could comment, he added, "You'd better scoot now. I hear the boys comin' in." She, too, could hear them riding into the yard.

"I want to stay and find out what they think of my biscuits," she protested.

"You can't stay here," he insisted.

"Why not?" she challenged.

"'Cause no tellin' what you'll hear. You won't want the boys to know you're here, not if you want honest opinions, and the boys talk mighty rough when there's no womenfolk around."

Priscilla stared at him a moment and then burst out laughing. "Do you think I've never heard a man swear?" she asked. "I was raised in a house full of men—my father and his friends. I've heard every swear word there is. I won't be shocked."

126

Aunt Sally was dubious. "You ain't never heard a cowboy swear. It's, well, it's like an art to him."

"I'm not leaving," Priscilla insisted. "If you want me out of here, you'll have to carry me out," she added smugly, fully aware that Aunt Sally would die before doing such an outlandish thing.

Before he could renew his arguments, they heard someone enter the front door of the cookhouse. "Aunt Sally!" It was Dusty Rhoades.

"Quick, get out of sight," Aunt Sally whispered urgently. "Get in the pantry," he told her, giving her a gentle shove in the proper direction. "In here," he called to Dusty when she had closed the door behind herself.

A moment later, Dusty pushed open the swinging door between the kitchen and dining room of the cookhouse. He held up a rather soiled and bloody flour sack. "Got some pods here for you. Save 'em up 'til the day of the dance. The boys figure they'll need 'em then." With a short bark of laughter at Aunt Sally's disapproving grunt, he dropped the sack on the work table and left. Snatching up the sack, Aunt Sally looked around frantically for a place to hide it, as Priscilla poked her head out of the closet. Seeing that the coast was clear, she left her hiding place.

"What are pods?" she asked curiously, eying the dirty sack with disfavor.

"Nothin' at all," Aunt Sally told her, trying to hold the sack behind his back.

"Don't be silly," she chided, amused at his efforts to protect her from something he obviously considered unfit for her delicate sensibilities. "It's obviously something. Tell me!" she implored.

"Nothin' a lady needs to know about," he told her,

127

depositing the sack in a corner behind a chair.

Priscilla stared at him in exasperation for a moment before she thought of the perfect solution. "Then I'll just have to ask Dusty," she said threateningly and started for the door.

"Oh, no, you don't!" Aunt Sally bellowed, blocking her way with remarkable swiftness. He tried to intimidate her, but he was no match for the determined glint in those brown eyes. Priscilla waited patiently, a small smile curving her mouth. At last he gave in. "All right," he began, his embarrassment acute, "pods are . . . the part of a he-calf that they . . . cut off to . . . make him a steer."

Priscilla looked blank for a moment at this obscure explanation, but then the light dawned. "Oh, like when they geld a horse," she interpreted.

"That's right," he agreed with relief, turning to begin dishing up the men's noon meal.

Priscilla considered this for a moment. "But why did he bring them here?" she asked, trying to remember exactly what Dusty had said.

"No reason. Just his idea of a joke, I reckon," Aunt Sally supposed but without much conviction.

At last Priscilla reached a conclusion, as illogical as it seemed. "Does he want you to cook them?" she asked suspiciously.

"'Course not," Aunt Sally replied, but she could see he was lying.

"Do they *eat* them? How awful! Why on earth would they do that?" Priscilla waited in vain for Aunt Sally's reply. At last she said with an exaggerated sigh, "I guess I'll have to ask Dusty."

Aunt Sally turned from his work, ready to stop her

once more from carrying out that threat, but swift action was not necessary. She was waiting patiently for his explanation.

Recognizing his defeat, he cleared his throat noisily and stammered, "They . . . they think it . . . makes them . . . more . . . manly." Seeing she still did not understand, he went on, "Like if a fella's gettin' married . . . he eats 'em before he . . . goes on his . . . honeymoon." Aunt Sally's voice trailed off as he saw comprehension dawn on her face.

Priscilla could not suppress the gurgle of laughter that rose in her throat. "Does it work?" she could not resist asking.

Aunt Sally gave a snort. "How should I know?" he asked in disgust. "I never had no truck with women except for a few times I . . ." He stopped dead, suddenly remembering to whom he was speaking.

Was he actually blushing? she wondered. It was hard to tell, his face was so sunburned. "Except for a few times you visited bawdy houses?" Priscilla asked wickedly.

"Miss Priscilla!" he gasped, visibly shaken.

"Oh, did I shock you?" she asked in mock dismay. "Did you think I wouldn't know what a bawdy house was?"

"You *shouldn't* know, that's for sure," he declared.

"All good women know about those places," she explained, gleefully ignoring his outraged sensibilities. "It's important to know what the competition is," she added artlessly.

Aunt Sally stared at her sweet face a moment before he asked in a last-ditch effort to divert her attention, "Do I smell your biscuits burnin'?"

With a squeal of dismay, she ran to the oven and

managed to extract the sheet of biscuits—which were not burned at all but a luscious golden brown—only scorching two fingers in the process.

Aunt Sally sent her scurrying back to the pantry as he rang the dinner bell, and she listened intently from her hiding place to the sounds of the men trudging into the adjoining room, the scrape of chairs, and the clank of eating utensils. For a long time she heard nothing but the faint sounds of men eating. She would learn later that the men wasted no energy on conversation when it was time to eat. Finally, she heard the indistinguishable murmur of a man's voice followed by a burst of ribald laughter. Someone must have told a joke, she surmised. Then she heard another murmur and more laughter. Twice more the process was repeated, and then someone—she was almost certain it was Dusty Rhoades—called Aunt Sally. Opening the pantry door a crack, she was able to hear him—it *was* Dusty—ask, "Aunt Sally, you reckon you could remember how you made these biscuits?"

"'Course I can. I make 'em every day," Aunt Sally replied irritably.

"No, I mean *exactly* how you made this particular batch," Dusty insisted.

Priscilla opened the door a little farther and stuck her head out, not wanting to miss a single word. "I reckon," Aunt Sally was saying. "Why? You like 'em?"

"Well, the boys an' me was figurin'," Dusty said, ignoring the question, "if you could make up some more like these, an' if we could find anythin' sharp enough to cut 'em up with, why, they'd make fine bullets. Save us a heap of ammunition."

The men's loud laughter covered Aunt Sally's scathing reply to Dusty's outrageous suggestion, but it made her feel a little better to know he had not meekly swallowed such an insult, even if it was not personal to him. A few seconds later, a very angry Aunt Sally stomped into the kitchen, stopping short when he saw Priscilla standing dejectedly in the pantry doorway. "You hear?" he asked unnecessarily. She nodded and shrugged fatalistically. "Don't pay no attention to them critters," he ordered her, going over to where she stood and awkwardly placing a leathery hand on her shoulder. "Them no-accounts wouldn't know . . ."

They both looked up as the door swung open. Dusty Rhoades entered, carrying one of the infamous biscuits, and the grin on his face told Priscilla he had come to needle Aunt Sally some more. "Another thing, if you could . . ." he began, but stopped when he saw Priscilla and Aunt Sally across the room. His absolute astonishment was clearly visible on his face, and for a moment he just stood there, mouth gaping. Then he saw Aunt Sally's hand on Priscilla's shoulder and an unreasoning rage washed over him. How dare that old man put his hands on her? he wondered illogically, ignoring the fact that he had several times put his own hands on her quite improperly. "What's she doin' here?" he asked venomously.

Priscilla had watched wide-eyed as Dusty's astonishment had faded, and those bluer-than-blue eyes had narrowed down, flashing fire. She was just about to answer his impudent question by asking what business it was of his, when Aunt Sally spoke, his hand tightening reassuringly on her shoulder for a moment before dropping back to his side. "For your information," he snapped, "*if* it's any of your business, which I doubt, Miss Priscilla helped me make dinner today, and it was

131

her that made the biscuits." His look of triumph showed Priscilla that he thought he had succeeded in embarrassing Dusty, but she doubted this. His answering grin proved she was correct.

"Well, now, Miss Bedford," he said, all anger now vanished from those sapphire eyes to be replaced by pure deviltry, "I think you may be on to something. I always heard that diamonds was the hardest thing on earth, but these biscuits . . ."

"Ain't you got no manners, a-tall?" Aunt Sally blustered, horrified that Dusty dared to insult a lady right to her face.

"No, he does not," Priscilla stated coolly. Patting Aunt Sally's arm, she reassured him, "Don't worry, he can't hurt my feelings." She gave the cook her warmest smile. "Thank you for the lesson. Maybe next time I'll do more justice to your very fine instruction. I'd better be going. I'm sure Mrs. Wilson is wondering where I am." With a last, frosty glance at Dusty and another friendly smile to Aunt Sally, she slipped gracefully out the back door.

Dusty was completely disconcerted. No manners! Look who was talking! He knew how it must seem to Aunt Sally, but the cook had no idea how she had provoked him in the past. And then, when she'd smiled at Aunt Sally. She'd never smiled at *him* like that. He felt a pang that was mighty akin to jealousy, but he ignored it, trying instead to follow what Aunt Sally was ranting about.

". . . a fine girl like that. You got no call to act like a no-account. I met Yankees act better'n you. You apologize to that girl or you're never eatin' in my kitchen again!" Aunt Sally decreed, crossing his scrawny arms over his narrow chest.

Dusty wasn't afraid of Aunt Sally's threats. He'd heard too many of them, but he had the sense to realize that the cook would be only too happy to tell the rest of the boys about his villainous behavior, and knowing their opinion of the schoolteacher, he also knew that the men would side with her, and his authority would be seriously undermined. He was between a rock and a hard place. "I'll go talk to her," he mumbled grudgingly, reluctantly following her out the door.

She was already halfway across the ranchyard, and he had to call her name twice before she stopped and turned stiffly to wait for him. A little daunted by the chilly reception she gave him when he finally caught up to her, he stood awkwardly for a minute, shifting from one foot to the other and trying to think of a way to pacify her without really apologizing. Those brown eyes were glittering like glass and it gave him an uneasy feeling. Finally, he managed a sheepish grin and said, "Those *were* about the toughest biscuits I ever ate."

Priscilla bit down on her lip to keep from smiling. Honestly, he was the most infuriating man. How could he possibly look so appealing while saying something that should make her angry? And she was still angry at him for his earlier behavior, the memory of which still made her feel hot with shame. At least, that was what she blamed for the very uncomfortable warmth she felt in his presence. "I'll try to do better next time," she said as blandly as she could and turned to leave, eager to get away before she betrayed her softer feelings.

He couldn't let her go yet. "Wait," he said, frantically grabbing her arm.

She turned back slowly, casting an imperious look at his restraining hand. If he thought he could manhandle

133

her right here in the ranchyard, in full view of any number of people . . .

Swiftly withdrawing his hand, he cursed himself silently. It seemed like he was always grabbing her, whether he intended to or not. It was a dangerous habit. This whole thing was getting out of hand. "I didn't know you made the biscuits," he began, stopping when he remembered that even when he had known, he had been obnoxious.

"Really, Mr. Rhoades," she said contemptuously, "I can't understand how a man like you became foreman. I mean, if you treat everyone with such insolence . . ."

"But I don't . . ." he tried to explain.

"But you do," she pointed out. "The other night when you introduced me to the men, you either interrupted them or would not let them speak at all."

"No, I didn't," he denied, not remembering such cavalier behavior, only recalling how he had tried to keep her from flirting with the men.

"You most certainly did," she insisted. "You never even let Happy say a word, you cut Curly off in mid-sentence, and Tucking Comb, why, he was never able to explain how he got his name."

"It's not a very interesting story," he said lamely, feeling more and more like a fool every minute.

Priscilla crossed her arms over her breasts, her mouth pressed into a disgusted line. Was he going to apologize or not? she wondered. She had been certain that that was why he had followed her, but if that had been his reason, he was certainly not rushing right into it.

She was waiting for something, he was sure of that, but what? Could she want to hear the story? It seemed a little far-fetched, but then she never had made any sense to

134

him. "There's this place along the trail, Doan's Store, where the drovers stop on their way to Kansas," he explained, not noticing Priscilla's blank look. "Doan had some girls there. Nice girls," he added hastily, in case she misunderstood. "They were his nieces, I think. Anyway, Tucking Comb, he offered to buy one of them a treat at the store, candy or something, but when he took her in, she looked at all the stuff and said, 'If it's all the same to you, I'd rather have one of those tucking combs.' We've all called him that ever since."

It had taken Priscilla a while to figure out what on earth he was talking about, and when the truth had finally dawned on her, she could only continue to listen with amazement and growing amusement. He was, without doubt, the strangest man she had ever met. Was he trying to make her forget that he had offended her?

When he had finished the story, he waited for some response but none was forthcoming. After an awkward pause, he said, "I told you it wasn't a very interesting story." He made a helpless gesture with his hands. "Look, Miss Bedford, I never meant to . . ." To what? Make her mad? That was exactly what he'd intended.

Noticing his predicament, Priscilla came to his assistance. "You never meant to get in trouble with Aunt Sally? Is that what you were going to say?" she asked maliciously.

No, it hadn't been, but he had to acknowledge that it was the truth, and that it was a little silly, too, and that he felt awfully foolish standing here where anybody might see him, trying to make up to a woman without saying he was sorry because he wasn't the least bit sorry. As the absurdity of the situation dawned on him, he could no longer suppress a grin. "Aunt Sally's pretty horrifyin' when he's on the warpath," he conceded.

Priscilla gasped in outrage. He actually had the nerve to admit that his only reason for following her had been to pacify the cook. Of all the ridiculous . . . yes, it was ridiculous. So ridiculous that she, too, could not suppress a smile as her sense of humor overcame her injured pride. The boyish innocence of his grin was hard to resist. It struck a chord deep inside her, weakening her resolve, and she forgave him in spite of herself. "I'm afraid the thought of you trembling in your boots at the prospect of Aunt Sally's wrath is more than I can bear. You may tell him that I have forgiven you," she informed him magnanimously. "But"—she raised a warning finger to interrupt his attempt to reply—"it won't be true! I have not forgiven you, nor will I forget," she added perversely. And, she added mentally, I will repay you at the very first opportunity. With that, she walked away, leaving him frowning at her very shapely back.

Not forget! That sounded like a threat! It was almost funny, her threatening him. She was no match for Dusty Rhoades, mean as she was. 'Course, he couldn't get too mean, himself, not to a woman, and he had a hunch it would take a bit of doing to out-mean Priscilla Bedford. No, he'd have to think of another way. Her being female sort of limited his options, but he'd think of something. Meanwhile, he'd steer clear of her. That was probably the best thing to do anyway. And for sure keep his hands off her. If he could. With a weary sigh, he returned to the cookhouse to tell Aunt Sally her lie.

Chapter Five

By the time Saturday night rolled around, Priscilla felt as if she had long been a part of the Steele household. Ben Steele treated her as if she were another of his daughters. Stella involved her in the preparations for the party. The younger girls took her in hand and taught her the rudiments of square-dancing. George promised faithfully to claim her for the first few dances until she felt more sure of herself. Dusty ignored her.

Preparations for the party proved more elaborate than Priscilla would have imagined. As Stella explained, they could not dance in squares, or many squares at least, in the confines of the parlor, and so a larger space was required. Since the March weather might not hold and they might need a fire, the barn was unsuitable, also. That left the bunkhouse as the only building large enough, and so all the men cheerfully moved their bunks and belongings into the barn. When Priscilla pointed out that in the event of foul weather, the men would be sleeping in the unheated barn, in her opinion a much graver situation than dancing in a cold building, Stella reassured her by telling her the men slept outside half the time anyway and would consider it a luxury just having a roof over their heads. Besides, Stella argued, she could not pass up the opportunity to give the bunkhouse a thorough cleaning, something that had not occurred in recent memory. It took two days and the labor of all the females on the place to accomplish this feat, but by the appointed day, even Stella was satisfied with the results.

Priscilla had been debating with herself for several days about what dress she should wear to the party and had at last decided to risk wearing her very best ball gown. It was far from being the height of fashion since it was, in fact, last year's gown, but she had been in mourning for her father and had not had anything new made up in months. Not that anyone in Rainbow would know, of course, and the dress had the advantage of having a slightly fuller skirt than the more current styles, something that would prove helpful when square-dancing, she was certain. On the other hand, it was rather fancy for a small party in a small town and Priscilla did not want to give a bad impression by being overdressed. Unable to decide, she finally sought Stella's opinion.

"You mean that red dress?" Stella asked delighted, remembering it vaguely from watching Priscilla unpack.

"Yes," Priscilla admitted reluctantly. The dress was not actually red, but rather a delicate shade of rose, more a deep pink than a true red. "Red" sounded so, well, sinful.

"Wear it!" Stella decreed. "It's just the thing, something that'll set 'em on their ears."

"I'm not certain I want to do that, exactly," Priscilla protested.

"Yes, you do. No sense hidin' your light under a bushel. Won't do no good anyhow. Just make 'em want to peek under the bushel." Stella's broad wink brought an involuntary gurgle of laughter from Priscilla, and thus her decision was made for her.

On Saturday afternoon Priscilla joined the Steele girls for a frenzy of bathing and curling and primping and pressing. Even the youngest of the Steele sisters wanted to appear to advantage, and Priscilla helped them all get their ribbons in place and their curls turned just so. Finally, she and Ruth retired to Ruth's room—having her own room was her privilege since she was the oldest girl still at home—and completed their own toilettes. Priscilla helped Ruth slip into the simple pale blue frock that matched her eyes and accented her slender figure. Then Ruth helped Priscilla squeeze into her corset and assisted her in lowering the yards of heavy satin over Priscilla's head and in doing up the myriad of tiny buttons that ran down Priscilla's back. Heaving a sigh of exaggerated relief when she had finished the tedious task, Ruth stood back and playfully ordered, "Now turn around and let me see how it looks."

Priscilla turned obediently, but her anticipatory smile faded when she saw Ruth's enormous eyes and gaping mouth. Certain she had made a terrible mistake in her choice of attire, she asked, "What's wrong, Ruthie?"

"Oh, Priscilla, you're *beautiful*!" Ruth groaned with such patent envy that Priscilla almost laughed with relief.

"You're beautiful, too, Ruthie," Priscilla said with

perfect sincerity. Ruth shook her head determinedly, but Priscilla overrode her objection. "Yes, you are!" she insisted.

"Not like you!" Ruth said with perfect honesty.

"Not yet," Priscilla conceded, "but you will be. You already have a lovely figure and it will fill out even more in the next few years, and your face is very pretty and your skin is perfect and . . . well, as Stella would say, you'd better watch out because you'll be beating the men off with a stick. In fact," she added, giving Ruth a careful scrutiny, "maybe you'd better carry a stick with you tonight."

Ruth flushed with pleasure. "Do you really think so?" she asked uncertainly, looking down at her simple gown.

"You'll see for yourself. Just wait!" Priscilla assured her as they found their shoes and put the finishing touches on their coiffures.

When they were finished, they joined the rest of the family who were waiting impatiently for them in the parlor. Ruth's entrance caused a murmur of approval from those assembled, a murmur that ceased abruptly when Priscilla entered the room. Every eye examined her from head to foot and back again, and every tongue was momentarily stilled by the sight.

The dress that Priscilla thought of as rose appeared almost wine-colored as it shimmered in the lamplight. The bodice of the dress was constructed of a series of drapes and folds that molded ingeniously over Priscilla's curves, serving both to enhance the roundness of her breasts and to accent the slenderness of her waist. The drapes were echoed on a larger scale in the skirt which fell in a bell-shaped series of flounces to the floor, an elaborately simple style that had taken all the cunning of a very clever dressmaker to create. But as impressive as it was, everyone in the room found himself staring at where it wasn't, namely at Priscilla's chest. The stately bodice did not begin at all until quite low on Priscilla's torso, leaving bare a remarkably smooth pair of shoulders, a rather large expanse of pure white bosom, and just the barest hint of cleavage.

Priscilla watched their stunned expressions in dismay. "Oh, dear, is it . . . too much?" she asked in despair.

George leaned over to his wife and whispered, for her ears alone, "No, I'd say she's got just the right amount," earning himself a very sharp elbow in the ribs as Stella rose to reassure her friend.

"Didn't I tell you it'd knock them on their ears?" she asked triumphantly.

More sure than ever that this was not the reaction she wanted to create, Priscilla tried to protest, but Stella would have none of it, and at Stella's urging, the rest of the family joined her in insisting that Priscilla's dress was perfect. Outgunned, outmaneuvered, and outflanked, Priscilla found herself on her way to the bunkhouse where the musicians were warming up and the guests were beginning to arrive.

"Priscilla said I'll need a stick to beat off the boys tonight," Ruth volunteered proudly, trying to divert the attention that Priscilla was finding so embarrassing on the walk across the yard.

The younger girls were impressed, but George took the opportunity to whisper to Stella, "If Ruthie needs a stick, I hope Priscilla's got a gun on her somewhere."

Stella gave him a warning glance and another poke in the ribs just as they arrived at their destination. The large, empty room was now lined with chairs and benches of every description, gleaned from every corner of the ranch. At one end, on an improvised raised platform, sat the "band," two fiddlers and a harmonica player. At the other end of the room, Stella had set up a refreshment table holding an assortment of cakes, pies, and pastries, and a bowl of punch. "Unspiked punch," Stella had informed her with a sniff. Stella did not approve of spirits but had to allow her father to provide a keg of whiskey for the men, although she insisted on keeping it out of sight in the yard, beside the bunkhouse, where it would not offend the ladies.

The Steele's cowboys were mingling with the few early arrivals when the family arrived. Priscilla's entrance would have caused a stir no matter what she had been wearing, Stella insisted in a fierce whisper as Priscilla balked in the doorway after two of the men had choked on their punch. A firm hand on her back, which she discovered belonged to a grinning George, propelled her into the room and up to the nearest cluster of guests to be introduced.

Her initial unease quickly vanished as she read the admiration on the faces of the men and the envy on the faces of the women. The envy she handled easily with her naturally gracious manner and a few well-chosen compliments. The admiration she simply ignored, treating each man she met with equal, and restrained, warmth. Names and faces soon began to run together in her mind as the crowd swelled to over a hundred people—just a small group, George insisted—and equally soon she lost track of how many men she had promised to dance with. George reassured her, telling her that *they* would no doubt remember, and when it came to the Belle of the Ball, it was first come, first served on every dance anyway.

Dusty had been glad that his back had been toward the door when she had come in. His first clue that something was wrong had been when Tucking Comb had strangled on his punch. Pounding the hapless cowboy on the back, Dusty had turned to see what had caused such a reaction. He had almost groaned aloud at the sight of her. Good God, she looked like a dance-hall whore. What had possessed Stella to let her show up in a dress like that? Half-naked, that's what she was. If she didn't catch her death of cold, it'd be a miracle. And what would happen when a fella danced close to her, like in a waltz? He'd be able to see clear down to her navel! Dusty found himself strangely ambivalent about that possibility: totally averse to anyone else having that opportunity but strangely eager for it himself. Well, he'd just make sure that *he* was the first one to waltz with her. That way, if there were a view . . . he'd mention it to Stella. Let her take care of it. He'd do Priscilla that much of a good turn. Feeling very virtuous, he had watched her progress around the room through narrowed eyes, feeling a growing irritation at the way she smiled and laughed with each new acquaintance. A born flirt, that's what she was. It was a good thing she'd never tried that stuff on him. A damn good thing.

Priscilla could not help but be aware of Dusty's scrutiny or of his potent disapproval. The knowledge that she had displeased him gave her a new confidence as she joined George for the first dance. As good as his word, George claimed her for the first two dances, although he had to face down a dozen anxious cowboys to do it. By then she was feeling secure enough to follow the steps without his guidance, and George begged off, saying he feared for his life if he monopolized her any longer and steering her to the refreshment table.

While George was pouring her a glass of punch, Priscilla noticed Dusty with two cowboys she did not know standing on the other side of the table, their backs to her. She could not pass up the opportunity to examine his attire as he had earlier examined hers. Hatless, he had oiled his hair, managing to tame it into a semblance of order, which she knew instinctively would not last long. It made him look like a little boy whose mother had slicked him up for church in the hope that the effect would last at least until he reached the church door. He was wearing a yellow checked shirt that someone had lovingly starched and pressed—someone female, she supposed, who had been charmed into performing the favor—and a brand new yellow silk scarf hung around his neck. His long legs were encased in equally new nankeen trousers, from which that female person had also pressed the "store-bought" crease. The trousers were tucked into a pair of glossy, star-topped boots decorated with the large single star in honor of the Lone Star State. She had to concede that although he would have been laughed out of any party she had ever attended back east, he was, in this place, something of a dandy and was dressed fit to kill, a fate she soon thought might well be too good for him.

One of the cowboys that Priscilla did not know was saying to Dusty, "I ain't seen you dancin' with the schoolteacher yet."

George started to say something to them to warn them she was there, but Priscilla silenced him with a gesture.

The other cowboy said, "She sure is a pretty little thing."

"Oh, she's tolerable, I reckon," Dusty allowed, annoyed that he had noticed.

At this, George was determined to break in, but again Priscilla restrained him.

Dusty continued, "But I suppose I'll do her a favor and ask her to dance." He craned his neck, looking over the crowd. "Now where'n hell'd she git to, anyway?"

"I'm right here, Mr. Rhoades," Priscilla informed him gleefully. All three men started as if they had been struck and turned sheepishly around. Priscilla smiled coquettishly and batted her eyes. "But you needn't do me any favors," she continued sweetly. "I have more than enough partners, so you don't need to trouble yourself." Still smiling, she took George's arm and strolled away.

As she danced through the next few sets, Priscilla tried to enjoy the feeling of satisfaction that embarrassing Dusty Rhoades had given her, but another, deeper feeling prevented her. That feeling, as much as she hated to admit it even to herself, was relief. Relief that she would not have to dance with Dusty Rhoades, not have to be held in his arms, and that, she knew deep down, was the real reason that she had refused to let George warn him of her presence. She had been hoping he would let something slip, hoping she would catch him, and then do exactly what she had done. Oh, she could have handled the situation differently. She could simply have made her presence known and waited very smugly for a public apology, or she could have agreed very demurely to dance with him, thanking him for the great favor he was bestowing upon her. Either tactic would have been a master stroke and would have humiliated him in front of his friends, who in turn would have repeated the story to everyone at the party. But those solutions had one drawback: she would have had to dance with Dusty Rhoades. For three days she had been dreading the

moment when he would take her in his arms. The mere
thought of those strong arms going around her, those big,
rough hands touching her, was unsettling, and the
memory of what had happened the last two times she had
been held by those arms was positively unnerving. Not
that he would try anything like that on a crowded dance
floor, of course. She knew that, but she also knew that
allowing his touch was inviting disaster. Why, just the
touch of his hand the other day in the ranch yard when
he had been trying not to apologize to her about the
biscuits . . . Well, she had nothing to worry about
tonight. She had successfully driven him away, and she
would be safe the entire night. *Safe?* What an odd choice
of words, she thought vaguely as she tried to execute the
dance caller's command to "alemand left." But safe she
would be, and the knowledge brought a new gaiety to her
laugh, and she truly began to enjoy herself. She could not
help but notice that Dusty danced practically every
dance, but he always managed to be in a different square,
and, she also noticed, to be with a different girl each time.

At one point, a short time later, Priscilla stood talking
for a moment with Ruth, who also had not lacked for
partners, when Dusty approached with Curly in tow.
Priscilla bristled a moment, thinking he meant to speak
to her, but he managed to irritate her even more by
totally ignoring her. "Why, Ruthie," he was saying, the
admiration plain in his demeanor, "I do believe you went
and growed up when I wasn't lookin'!"

Ruth blushed rosily, unable to conceal her delight.
"Oh, Dusty," she protested shyly.

"Curly noticed, too, didn't you, Curly?" Dusty asked
rhetorically, since he did not even bother to pause to
allow his companion to answer, but instead leaned

conspiratorially close to Ruth and confided, "Reason I know he did is 'cause the sight of a beautiful woman always knocks him speechless, and he can't say a word right now." For some reason Priscilla could not fathom, Curly did not seem to mind being talked about in such a derogatory manner and just stood there, grinning. Dusty continued, "But the fact is, he'd be mighty pleased to dance with you even though he ain't able to say so right now."

Ruth seemed a little surprised but covered it well, replying with becoming modesty, "That would be fine," and took his offered arm. Priscilla observed Dusty in amazement as he watched the happy couple take their places on the dance floor, brushing his hands against each other as if he were congratulating himself on a job well done. Before she could think to turn away, he caught her staring.

"Miss Bedford?" he said in feigned surprise. "Not without a partner? I maybe could find you somebody if you're desperate."

Unable to think of a suitable reply, Priscilla had to content herself with giving him a scathing look and gliding away to the arms of her next partner as the musicians struck up a waltz.

Dusty frowned as he watched her whirl away in the arms of another man in what should have been his dance. It had been a mistake to speak to her, he knew, but he had been unable to resist needling her a little, even if there hadn't been anyone around to hear him. And he still didn't like that dress. It just wasn't decent.

From the corner of her eye, Priscilla caught his displeasure and supposed that he was disappointed because she had not stood there and crossed verbal swords with him. Perhaps that was the best way to conquer him, she thought. If so, she would never be able to succeed at it, since her fertile brain had already thought up the blistering reply that she should have given to his suggestion that she might need a partner. It would keep, though, until next time, and she was certain there would be a next time.

Several dances later, the musicians took a much-needed break and paid a well-earned visit to Ben Steele's whiskey barrel. Priscilla took the opportunity to seek out Stella and gladly sat down beside her for a rest.

"You havin' a good time?" Stella asked solicitously.

"Yes, a marvelous time," Priscilla answered quite honestly.

"I see you ain't short on partners."

"Oh, no, all the gentlemen have been most attentive," Priscilla agreed.

Stella looked at her thoughtfully. "Has Dusty asked you for a dance?"

"No," Priscilla replied blandly.

"That boy! Where's his manners? An' you, the guest of honor. I'll skin him alive!" she threatened.

Priscilla smiled politely. The musicians were taking their seats and preparing to play again.

"Oh, here he comes now," Stella observed with satisfaction. "He'll ask you now for shore."

Priscilla managed to look unconcerned as she mentally rehearsed her brilliant refusal. Dusty approached them, and bowing with almost comic formality said, "Mrs. Wilson, may I have the honor of this dance?"

A little startled, Stella looked over at Priscilla who seemed to be very interested in something happening across the room. Uncertainly, Stella rose and walked out to dance with Dusty. After they had waltzed a few steps, she demanded, "Why ain't you asked Priscilla to dance yet?"

Assuming a wounded expression, he explained, "She heard me say I was gonna ask her, and she said not to bother, she had plenty of partners without me."

Stella studied that face she knew so well. "There must've been more to it than that!" she accused.

"You ask her. That's the truth!" he insisted. Somehow he managed to look both wounded and innocent.

Stella wasn't fooled. Dusty had been up to his tricks, no doubt about it. But exactly what had he done to have Priscilla refuse to dance with him? It must have been a doozy, she decided with a worried frown. Nothing that couldn't be smoothed over, she was certain, but enough to ruin things for tonight, and she had had such plans for tonight. Priscilla in that dress, and Dusty all decked out, and dancing, and moonlight . . . what had gone wrong? This whole situation had gotten out of hand, but Stella Wilson was just the person to get it back in hand again, just as soon as she figured out just where things had gotten off the track.

The next time the musicians took a break, Priscilla was surrounded by admirers anxious to earn her attention, but she still managed to notice that Dusty was standing in a far corner, talking very earnestly with a buxom blond girl she thought was the storekeeper's daughter. The girl was listening to him with such wide-eyed adoration that Priscilla felt like laughing until she saw them walking outside, arm-in-arm. She covered the pang she felt with forced gaiety, charming the group of cowboys who had gathered around her.

The night wore on, and Priscilla, being unused to such

exertion, begged her latest partner for a rest, so she sat out one dance while he went to get her some refreshment. While she was sitting, watching the dancers, Dusty wandered over, apparently without noticing her, and sat down right beside her, ignoring several other empty chairs. For a moment he sat there, stretching out his long legs, picking an invisible thread from his pant leg, watching the dancers. Then suddenly, he noticed Priscilla.

"Miss Bedford! Not dancin'! Shore you're not without a partner!" he said, feigning surprise.

"Of course not," she said sweetly. "I'm just resting. My partner went to get me some punch."

"Mighty glad to hear it," he said reassuringly, then added seriously, "I got me a big problem." Priscilla had no intention of encouraging him, so she sat silently, staring at the dancers, but he continued without any encouragement. "Yes, a mighty big problem. You see, I've danced one dance with every woman here, an' now I have to decide who to dance with twice." Now they both knew that he hadn't danced with Priscilla, but she would have died before mentioning it. "You have to be real careful with womenfolk. You pay 'em too much attention and they start gettin' funny ideas." Priscilla stiffened in outrage. Could he possibly mean *her*? Well, if he thought she had any "funny ideas" about him, he was sadly mistaken, but before she could reply to his outrageous statement, he slapped his knee in discovery and said with great excitement, "Well, I'll be. There's one lady here I ain't danced with yet!"

Priscilla was ready for him now. Just let him ask. She had a reply that would send him reeling. She smiled in malicious anticipation but, to her surprise, he leaped to

150

his feet and muttered, "Excuse me, ma'am." Before she could open her mouth, he was across the room addressing a little old lady. Wasn't she the storekeeper's grandmother? That blond girl's great-grandmother? Why, she was eighty if she was a day. Dusty had to shout in her ear several times to make himself understood, and when he succeeded she fairly dragged him out onto the floor and proved to be such a lively partner that soon all the other dancers had stopped to watch and shout encouragement. Seeing Dusty the center of attention after so successfully insulting her was more than Priscilla could bear. Casting about for a means of revenge, she spotted the cowboy who earlier in the evening had told Dusty he thought she was pretty. She sidled up to him. He looked to be about her age, a rather homely boy with a front tooth missing. She smiled her sweetest smile and said, "I don't think we've been introduced."

He turned beet red and stammered, "N . . . No, ma'am."

"I'm Priscilla Bedford," she offered.

"I know," he said, his embarrassment almost painful to behold. "I mean, everybody knows who you are."

"And who are you?" she asked with interest.

She would have thought it impossible, but he turned even redder. "I'm Gus Stanford. I ride for the Circle R. That's Ol' Man Rogers's outfit."

When the hilarity with Dusty and Grandma Smith was over, the musicians struck up a waltz, and Priscilla induced Gus to dance with her.

While they danced, or rather while Priscilla danced and Gus walked around with her, trying not to step on her feet, she flattered him. "You were very gallant to defend me to Mr. Rhoades."

The compliment obviously turned his head, but his loyalty to his friend won out. "Don't be too hard on Dusty, ma'am," he urged. "He didn't mean no insult. He was just showin' off."

She lavished on him her most approving look and said, "Now I *know* you are gallant, Gus, standing up for a man who is your friend in spite of the fact that he is the rudest, most obnoxious creature I have met in the state of Texas." For a moment she was afraid Gus's eyes would pop out of his head, but gathering her courage, she proceeded to further vilify Dusty Rhoades until she was certain Gus could not fail to repeat her denunciations to every cowboy in the place. As soon as the dance was over, she released him to do just that. With a triumphant sigh, she turned to her next partner.

Gus was conscientious in his mission, and the group of men gathered around the whiskey barrel outside were laughing uproariously when George and Dusty approached. They fell silent as George took a cup and proceeded to fill it.

"You ain't gonna take a drink, are ya George?" someone asked with mock seriousness.

"You know me better than that, boys," chuckled George, and they all laughed as he took a mouthful of the liquor, swished it in his mouth, and spat it out, emptying the cup on the ground.

"That ought to do it," commented George.

"Stella'll be hoppin' mad when she smells that stuff on you," warned Curly.

"I'm counting on it," smiled George.

"Never could understand why you do that, George," someone else said.

"That's because you know nothing about women, my

boy," said George. "Stella will get angry, I will beg forgiveness, and she will forgive me. Now, a forgiving woman is a loving woman. Need I say more?" The bawdy laughter that followed said he need not, and with a sly wink, he left the group as Dusty took his turn at the whiskey barrel.

With great delight, one of the more intoxicated cowboys related Gus's conversation with Priscilla to Dusty, and while he was chafing under it and the added comments his friends were making, a large and singularly ugly cowpoke named Jake spoke up and predicted, "Why, I'll bet that girl'll never give you the time a day agin'!"

Through his anger and humiliation, Dusty's cunning mind was already seeking revenge, and he jumped on Jake's statement like a duck on a June bug. With a strange gleam in his eye, he clapped Jake on the shoulder and said, "Friend, did you say the word 'bet'?"

Priscilla was sitting down taking a rest between dances when Dusty entered the room. She tried to stifle a yawn. It would soon be morning and as much fun as she had had, she was looking forward to removing her shoes and crawling into her bed at the schoolhouse. The thought had put a small smile on her lips and a far-away look in her eyes, and she did not notice when Dusty approached her. He startled her when he spoke.

"Excuse me, ma'am," he said in such a respectful tone that Priscilla gave him a moment of careful scrutiny. "There's a cowboy outside who's been just achin' to dance with you all night, but he's just so bashful, it's a sin. An' he asked me, well"—he looked around in apparent embarrassment, such an uncharacteristic gesture that Priscilla was intrigued, and continued—"since I know ya, he wanted me to introduce ya to him, sorta break the ice." Seeing the doubtful puzzlement on her face, he hurried on. "The party's almost over and he's skeered he'll never get another chance." She was still trying to decide if he were telling the truth. "We could just sorta walk outside, kinda casual-like," he suggested.

Priscilla's better judgment told her not to go, but it was such a good story! Try as she would, she could not think of a single man present with whom she had not danced at least once—except Dusty, of course—but if he were really shy, she might not have seen him. Yes, if Dusty were telling the truth, it was very flattering, and if he were lying, what could he possibly have up his sleeve? Her curiosity got the better of her. She would play along, she decided, vain enough to think that he could not get the better of her if she were aware that he was planning some trick.

"All right," she agreed with just the proper degree of kind condescension and rose gracefully from her chair. Dusty offered his arm, but she ignored it, walking regally ahead of him out the door. Pausing outside the bunkhouse, she turned to await Dusty's further instructions. He indicated she should proceed in the direction of the cookhouse. As she walked into the shadows, away from the lighted area around the bunkhouse, she thought vaguely that this fellow must be shy indeed to be hiding away over here. The whiskey barrel and the men congregated around it were off in the other direction entirely, and Priscilla could not see a single soul in this part of the yard. A tiny shiver went down her spine, and she blamed it on the night chill which had felt so good when she had first stepped out of the overheated bunkhouse, and not on her sudden awareness of Dusty Rhoades. He was so close behind her that she could hear him breathing, so close that if she stopped and turned, he would . . . She caught herself remembering another time that had happened, the first time he had kissed her, and the heat that suffused her body could not be blamed on any other cause. Was that why he had brought her to this deserted spot? The suspicion angered her, especially when she could plainly see that there was no anxious cowboy waiting for her arrival. When she had almost reached the cookhouse door, she stopped, stepping carefully out of his way and looked around expectantly. "Where's your friend?" she asked, letting him hear her skepticism.

Again Dusty looked around as if embarrassed and shuffled his feet awkwardly. "I reckon it's me, ma'am," he said.

Priscilla stared at him in wonder. Did he really think this clodhopper act would fool her, make her forget all the nasty things he had said to her all evening? With a disgusted sniff she wheeled away from him, heading back toward the dance, but he stepped quickly in her way and cried, "Wait!" in such a panicked voice that she stopped dead. What had caused the desperation in his plea? What could be so important to him that he had created this elaborate scheme to get her out here and made him willing to beg her to stay? It must not have been what she had first thought, she realized with an odd sense of disappointment. He had just passed up a perfect opportunity to take her in his arms. She had seen his hands come up when he had stepped in front of her, but he had pulled them down again, as if resolved to avoid physical contact. Then why else would he have brought her here? Could it be . . . could he possibly be *sorry*? Deciding at least to hear him out, she crossed her arms and raised her eyebrows in silent challenge.

"I wasn't lyin'," he began hesitantly at first. "I really do wanna dance with you. I don't know why I acted like such a fool. Maybe it was Ben's whiskey talkin'." He paused to study the dangerous glitter in her eyes. He'd have to do better than that if he wanted to persuade her, he decided. And keep his hands off of her. It was hard, with her so close and all. Keep talking. If only the words didn't stick in his throat.

"No, I can't blame the liquor. Anyways, not for the first time, 'cause I hadn't had any then. That time I was just showin' off for my friends. I didn't want them to think . . ." No use going into that, he thought, quickly changing the subject. "Then when you burned me, I got so mad, well, I just wasn't responsible anymore." She was still listening, so he lowered his voice and said in a very injured tone, "A man don't like to be laughed at."

"A woman doesn't either!" she replied tartly.

"Nobody would've laughed at you," he said truthfully, and she knew that he was right. His ill-chosen words were only insulting because she had overheard them. No one else would have taken them seriously. Sensing her slight capitulation, he continued. "I really did want to dance with you. Shoot, every man there wanted to. Why should I be any different?" he added defensively, not wanting her to guess more than he was willing to say out loud. "Then I got to thinkin', the party's almost over, and I missed my chance by actin' low down, and what could it hurt if I said I knew it and asked you to overlook it, and maybe you'd feel sorry for me and dance with me after all, just once, and if not, I'd be no worse off." He made an appealing gesture with his hand. "So how about it? Will you?" He could see she was thinking it over.

It was a heady experience, she had to admit, having Dusty Rhoades plead for her company. The obvious compliment was certainly gratifying and if he had not actually apologized, he at least had admitted his fault. And he wasn't trying to bully her. Or manhandle her. And she had to admit that while all of his insults had been private, except the first one which she had already dismissed, she had retaliated publicly, knowing how he would be embarrassed in front of his friends. She had more than paid him back for his slights. If only he were sincerely sorry, if only it weren't so dark, if only she could see his eyes. He *sounded* repentant, but if she could see his eyes, she would know for certain.

Suddenly, Ben Steele's voice boomed out from inside the bunkhouse. "This here's the last dance, folks, so gents, grab your favorite gals!"

"Well?" he asked in appeal.

What harm could it do? she wondered, for some reason forgetting all the reasons she had had earlier for not wanting to dance with him. He seemed so harmless. It *was* the last dance, and he had taken so much trouble to convince her, and she did want him to be sorry. "All right," she said with the air of one granting a great favor, and she was shocked to see how pleased, no, how delighted he was. He actually threw back his head and laughed! What could have made him so happy? Of course! He wanted everyone to see that the Rhoades' charm had prevailed once again, and that she was just one more in a long line of helpless victims. Except that she was not yet helpless. "On one condition," she added, and that sobered him instantly.

"What's that?" he asked warily.

"That we dance"—she looked around, satisfying

herself that they were indeed fairly isolated—"right here."

"Here? Why?" he asked incredulously.

"I know exactly what you're up to, Mr. Rhoades," she informed him, "and I will not be displayed like a trophy, just so you can soothe your wounded pride." She lifted her chin determinedly.

Dusty opened his mouth to lodge a protest, but at that very moment the music started. Swiftly he considered. If he dragged her back to the party, she would be furious and he'd never get a dance with her. On the other hand, if they danced here, no one would see them but at least they would be dancing. With a resigned shrug and a wry grin, he offered her his arms.

The sight of those arms caused Priscilla's stomach to lurch dangerously. What was wrong with her? she asked herself irritably. He was just a man. She had danced with scores of men this very night. This one was no different. Or was he? Of course he was, she told herself sternly. He had kissed her as no other man had kissed her and that made him different, but different was not dangerous. Not when she detested him. He would take no further liberties with her, not if she had anything to say about it. He would simply dance with her, accepting the favor she so graciously granted him. She had nothing to fear from him. Fear. Now where had that alarming thought come from? she wondered, ruthlessly squelching the surge of panic that tried to rise as she stepped bravely into his arms.

Taking a deep breath, she placed one hand lightly on his shoulder and slipped the other very gingerly into his. He took it with equal caution and placed his other hand very carefully on her back. She realized at once that he was a much better dancer than any of the other men she had danced with that night, as she followed his strong lead to the lilting strains of the waltz. He seemed so much larger than usual, looming over her in the darkness. But as they moved, the light fell on his face and she saw that he was smiling. It was such a winning smile, so boyishly innocent, and she loved the way his lips curled back from his teeth and the way his eyes crinkled up on the corners. Unable to resist, she smiled back at him.

Dusty was handling her gently, as if he were afraid she might break, but of course that wasn't the real reason. He knew good and well she wasn't the least bit fragile. No, it was more like handling nitroglycerin—the least little jolt and it might blow up on you. The thought made him grin. When he twirled her around again to face the light, he saw that she was grinning back. She had the prettiest little mouth. And the sweetest, he remembered against his will. Involuntarily, he tightened his grip on her ever so slightly. This would never do, he chided himself. If he didn't think about something else quick, he'd soon be doing something he'd regret.

Priscilla felt his hand squeeze hers, but before she could react to the tingle this sent up her arm and down her spine, his arm tightened around her waist, and she felt herself swung almost off her feet as he began to spin her around and around, faster and faster, turning and turning, an invisible force pulling her away, but his arm holding her to him like a steel band. He was laughing now, a deep, rich sound that struck a chord within her and caused the laughter to bubble up and out of her own throat. At last, breathless and dizzy and laughing, and clinging, they stumbled to a halt. For a moment, Priscilla rested her head against his chest, clutching his shoulders for support while the world whirled on without her. His hands tightened on her waist as she swayed drunkenly, and he pulled her to him protectively. The intimate contact as her softness was crushed against his hardness made Priscilla breathe in sharply, and that served only to flood her senses with the smell of him, the smell of whiskey and tobacco and the musky scent of sweat that made her only too aware of how close they were, how her fingers gripped the solid muscles of his shoulders, how his heart was pounding against her breasts. Or was that her own heart? Startled, she looked up to find the laughter had faded from his face also.

Dusty stared down at her in wonder. God, she was beautiful. Why had he never noticed it before? Or had he? It was hard to remember, hard to think at all right now, the way her body curved into softness under his hands, the way her hair smelled like flowers, the way her eyes looked so dark and deep, a man could drown . . . She stiffened slightly under his scrutiny, and instinctively he knew she was afraid he was going to kiss her. Wanting to, but sensing her reluctance and afraid she would pull away, he began to move his feet once again in time with the music that still floated over from the bunkhouse. She followed his shuffling lead, their movements no more than the barest excuse for remaining in each other's arms. Priscilla's hands relaxed their grip, and as she moved them to rest more comfortably on his broad shoulders, his own hands shifted to her back, drawing her nearer until her breasts, now strangely sensitive, brushed against his shirt front. She saw, because her gaze had locked with his, a strange blue fire burning in his eyes. Breathing took a conscious effort, a phenomenon she could no longer blame on the strenuous dancing, and she could not help but notice that the rise and fall of his own chest was rather labored also. They were even closer now. She could feel his thighs moving against hers through the layers of their clothing. She felt an odd tingle up the back of her legs that settled in her loins. As if sensing her response, or perhaps reacting to one of his own, Dusty slipped his hands down her back, into the curve of her waist and cupped them over her hips, drawing her body into intimate contact with his, a contact that made her gasp but not resist. How long they stayed like that, locked together, bodies swaying in an intimation of a waltz, savoring each other's desire, Priscilla never knew, but it seemed like forever as she watched that blue fire blaze more brightly, and saw the small struggle as he tried to hold himself back and heard the soft groan deep in his chest as he failed.

No gentleness this time, his lips met hers hungrily, demanding a response that she was powerless to deny. Her arms slipped around his neck as his embrace lifted her feet from the ground. Clinging to him, her fingers buried in the thick softness of his red-gold hair, her mouth locked greedily to his, she was only vaguely aware that they were moving, that he was moving her, until she felt the rough wooden boards of the cookhouse wall against her back. In total darkness now, in the shadow of the building, she could not see him as he pulled away from her for a moment, but she could feel his hot breath on her face and hear him groan again, more agonizingly this time, as he pressed his body against hers, pinning her against the wooden wall, flattening her breasts against the equally unyielding wall of his chest. Her heart was pounding now, sending streams of wildfire through what had once been her body but what now seemed to be no more than a blazing mass of need. A small, pleading sound escaped her lips as his mouth moved in a fiery path down her throat and his hands slid up her ribcage to catch and hold the fullness of her breasts.

This was what he had been longing for all evening, ever since he had first seen her—the chance to touch and taste her creamy skin, to explore and discover the delights of her softness. He moaned again as the warmth of her skin seemed to burn his lips like a fine liqueur, heating his mouth with intoxicating sweetness. She cried out faintly when his tongue found the tiny crevice between her breasts, savoring the lush smoothness that made the satin of her dress seem rough in contrast. Through that satin he could feel her breasts swelling, the nipples hardening to pebble-roundness under his palms.

Priscilla arched against him, offering herself with an abandon that might have shocked her had she been able to think, but she was now ruled solely by a primitive need, a need to get closer and then closer still to the heat of his body and the unspeakable pleasures offered by his hands and his mouth. His lips had zealously searched out every inch of exposed skin, as if he would devour her with his desire, but she reveled in it, in her own desire to be consumed. Her breasts swelled in his grasp, straining against the heat of his hands as if they would burst free, and that was what she wanted, she realized, as those hands slid up, fingers grazing her sensitive skin, seeking the hidden delights beneath the neckline of her gown. In another moment those delights spilled free as he eased the rose-colored satin down and down. The night air chilled her heated skin, only barely visible in the deep shadows, and then she was warm again, no, hot, as his eager hands captured her fullness and his searching mouth began to explore, finding first one stiffened peak and then the other, laving each adoringly and then moving to the other and then back again, as if afraid one might suffer from too much neglect. Someone was moaning softly, she noticed hazily, as she began to rock her hips against his in response to his gentle urging.

She was actually purring, he thought vaguely, sliding his hand down from the soft cushion of her breast to curve around her hip, guiding her into the secret rhythm while his mouth continued to savor the musky flavor of her skin. Groping, he tried to find her curves beneath the heavy satin skirt, and failing that, with a grunt of exasperation and a quick lunge, he managed to delve under the skirt and the petticoats and up again to caress her thigh, her hip, her belly, and then lower, to the place that burned for him as he burned for her. Her vibrant flesh quivered under the thin layer of silk that barred him, and he wanted her in that moment with a desire that was actually painful, wanted her and needed her and so much more. But not here, some still-sane voice inside his head demanded, not here.

Priscilla surrendered drunkenly to this new invasion, parting her legs slightly to allow his questing fingers the freedom they demanded, the freedom to coax this newly discovered part of her to life. The fire that had smoldered there since the first time he had kissed her now blazed forth and Priscilla hoped it would consume her. No one could feel like this and survive. If only she could touch him the way he was touching her, she thought as her hands caressed him almost frantically. She longed to be free of all these constraints, all these things making it so hard for him to . . . Free! That was it. She wanted to be free, in his arms—set free in some nameless way.

In one great burst of will, Dusty raised his head and found her lips for a long, mind-numbing kiss, and then he managed to lift his mouth from hers, just a fraction of an inch so that he could still feel the tiny gasps as her breath came and went but he could still speak. His own breath was ragged when he asked in a hoarse whisper, "Can we . . . go . . . somewhere?"

Priscilla could not think. Go somewhere? There was no other place she wanted to be, no place except here, with him, in his arms, feeling his hands, his lips . . . and then she realized what he meant. A place more private, where they would be more alone, where they would be free . . . Yes, oh yes! her mind screamed and the word trembled on her lips for one heart-stopping moment, but before she could utter it, a Rebel yell split the night.

He pulled away so suddenly that she would have fallen if she had not had the solid wall against her back. "Fix your dress," he ordered in an urgent whisper, as she watched the shadow of his hands reach down to smooth her skirt and then up to smooth his hair, the hair she had so eagerly caressed just moments ago. Mechanically, not really comprehending, she adjusted the neckline of her gown, only gradually beginning to realize that they were no longer alone in the yard. More yells and catcalls and shouts of approval broke through the passionate haze that had surrounded her. As her breathing and her heartbeat slowed to normal, and her consciousness turned outward, she became aware of the crowd of men moving toward them, yelling and cheering, and intent on congratulating Dusty no matter how reluctant he was to receive those congratulations, and he was very reluctant indeed.

Priscilla looked to him for some explanation of their

sudden popularity, and although it was too dark to see his face, she could tell by the way he stood, the stiff way he tried to draw the crowd's attention away from her, that something was very wrong, and that she was somehow involved in that wrong. Could they have seen—did they know what had happened and what had almost happened between them? It seemed impossible, and yet the thought made her stomach churn with apprehension. Frantically, she fluffed her skirt and fingered the folds of her bodice and searched the twists of her hair to determine if anything were out of place. It was so dark, perhaps no one would notice, she thought distractedly, watching the milling crowd.

The yells and shouts began to take on meaning in her numbed brain. What were they saying? "You won!" "You did it!" "Never thought she'd do it!"

Do what? she wondered frantically. What were they talking about? Overcoming her panic, she fixed a frozen little smile on her face and asked, just loudly enough to be heard, "What's going on here?"

"He won the bet!" someone yelled. She thought that it was Curly, but it did not matter.

"What bet was that?" she asked in dread of the answer.

"We bet him he couldn't get you to dance with him and . . ."

Priscilla never heard the rest of Curly's explanation. Horrified, she replayed the whole scene in her mind: Dusty's mythical "friend," his ingratiating apology, his elation when she had agreed to dance. Every word had been a lie. He had no personal interest in her. He was only trying to save face with his friends. He had used her, and how willing she had been! No, not willing, but eager.

Humiliation stained her cheeks as she remembered what else she had been eager for. Grateful for the darkness that hid her shame, she could not keep from shrieking, "This was a bet?"

Instantly, the men fell silent. They looked at her, quite unable to read her expression in the darkness but certainly recognizing the fury in her voice. They had not expected her to be angry and they shuffled awkwardly, each waiting for another to speak, to somehow smooth things over.

Priscilla felt the rage rise in her, an ugly, overpowering force. "A bet?" she shrieked again, her voice quivering with an intensity that made the men literally draw back. Pulling herself up to her full height, she treated them to the most scathing look she could muster, only hoping that they could see it. "Every one of you, you are all a bunch of lowdown, dirty, sneaking . . ." Words failed her for a moment, but then it came to her, "Polecats!" They seemed to shrink under her wrath.

Then she turned to Dusty and he could feel the anger emanating from her small body like a palpable force. When she thought of what he had done, how he had humiliated her, how she had almost let him . . . She felt the rage inside her grow, overwhelming her female body's ability to contain it, and for the first time in her life she wished to be a man so that she could thrash Dusty Rhoades as he deserved to be thrashed. She had no words to express her contempt for him so she performed the only act of violence open to her. She threw back her arm and slapped his face with a force that whipped his head half around. Then turning swiftly before anyone could see her tears, she ran off into the night.

166

For a long time nobody moved, then slowly Dusty's hand came up to touch his burning cheek, and he remembered how she had been before. How she had been when all that anger had been passion, when she had molded herself against him, answering him kiss for kiss, fairly purring in her pleasure at his touch. She would have gone with him, too. He was sure of it. In another moment she would have agreed, and by now she would have been lying in his arms. . . . His eyes narrowed as he examined the men so sheepishly watching the direction where Priscilla had vanished into the night, and the words that had failed her came readily to his lips. He began to curse the men who stood around him, questioning not only their good judgment but also their ancestry and their moral turpitude. It took only a few invectives to rouse them from their stupor and all two dozen of them began to defend themselves in no uncertain terms, raising such a din that Priscilla might have heard it at the schoolhouse if she had not been so busy raising a din herself.

It was daylight by the time Stella had exacted testimony from all the witnesses and determined what had really happened. In her court she served as prosecutor, judge, and jury. George made a feeble attempt at the defense, but it was soon apparent that there was none, so he settled for the role of impartial observer.

"We didn't mean no harm," wailed Gus. "We never thought she'd get so mad!"

"She called us polecats," complained Jake.

"Well, you are," snapped Stella, "an' a lot worse'n that! You've gone an' done it this time. She'll prob'ly leave on the next stage."

"Leave? 'Cause've what we did?" asked Curly apprehensively.

"Certainly," Stella affirmed. "You boys insulted her, humiliated her. I wouldn't blame her a bit."

"We meant it as a compliment," protested Gus.

"Well, I reckon you can plead insanity then, and nobody'd question it," said Stella. "Now, your only hope is if you go down there and apologize and do it mighty humble." She looked around but nobody would meet her eyes, and nobody moved. It would take a little something to get them moving, she realized. "An' it might be a good idea to ride into town first an' you each get her a present."

"A present?" someone asked.

"Yeah, you know, a box of candy or some doodad that girls like, an' while you're gone, I'll go down to see if I can't get her in a forgivin' mood."

"It's Sunday!" Curly said. "Ol' man Perkins'll never open up on Sunday."

"You tell him I said to. Tell him we might lose our schoolteacher. He sets store by that school. He'll open up," she assured them.

Slowly, they filed out to find their horses until only Dusty remained sitting in a stony silence, his red cheek giving mute testimony to his guilt.

"An' you, boy," Stella said threateningly, "you'd better come back with somethin' made of solid gold, an' you'd better dee-liver it on your knees."

Glaring at her coldly, he got up and walked out without saying a word.

Stella sighed and turned to George. "I reckon she's at the schoolhouse. Walk down there with me, honey."

George left her at the door, and she could hear the muffled sobs coming from inside. She knocked softly and called, "Priscilla? Honey, it's me. Can I come in?"

There was no answer, so she went on in. Priscilla sat on the bed, trying to wipe her eyes. "Do you know what they did to me?" she quavered. Stella nodded. "They bet on me, as if I were a horse or something." The sobbing started again and Stella went to her and held her for a while, cooing words of comfort.

"It seems a lot worse than it was," Stella said. "You're wore out, an' everything seems worse then. Tomorrow you'll laugh about it," she suggested, but she could see that that was little comfort to Priscilla. "They told me their side of it. Why don't you tell me yours?" Stella urged.

After making liberal use of Stella's handkerchief, Priscilla began at the beginning with Dusty's first insult and continued until she got to the place where he had finally asked her to dance outside the cookhouse. "So I agreed to dance with him right there," she sniffed, trying not to blush at the memory of what she had no intention of telling Stella. "When the dance was over, all the men came rushing out and told me about the bet. I've never been so humiliated in my entire life," she cried.

Stella noticed her heightened color but attributed it to Priscilla's natural embarrassment in such a situation. "Now, now, don't take on so. Fact is, they never meant no such a thing. They thought you'd be flattered!" Stella declared.

"Flattered!" Priscilla was incredulous.

"I know it don't make no sense, but they're men an' they don't have to make no sense. To look at it from their side, to them the most important thing about coming to the party was to get a dance with you. When you froze out Dusty, that was the worst punishment a man could get. Now, I ain't excusin' the way he acted all night 'cause, Lord knows, there ain't no excuse for it, but in spite of that, he still couldn't stand the insult you give him, so he tried to get back some on it. The others, they should never have told, but they wanted you to know how how much store they set by you. They also figured you'd get a little put out with Dusty, but they never dreamed you'd get mad at them, too." Stella chuckled. "I guess when you called 'em polecats, they just about layed down an' died. You never saw men so insulted."

For the better part of an hour, Stella cheered and consoled, until finally they could hear the thundering of hooves in the distance.

"They must've lathered them horses gettin' to town an' back so fast. Now, honey, you just step right out there. Hold your head up. You got nothin' to be embarrassed about. Make 'em crawl, though," Stella cautioned. Priscilla almost smiled at that, but she could not quite make it.

The two women stepped out onto the stoop as the riders, about two dozen of them, approached and then dismounted.

Aunt Sally stepped forward, removing his hat and glaring at the rest until they had done so, too. "First off, Miss Priscilla," he said respectfully, "I didn't know nothin' about this until Mrs. Wilson got the story from these"—he looked around contemptuously—"these coyotes. If I did, I'd've stopped it right off. Anyway, they're all too ashamed to speak right up to you, so they ast me to step in." He cleared his throat importantly, and continued. "These no good cowpunchers are almighty sorry for the dirty trick they played on you and are beggin' yer forgiveness."

"We didn't mean no insult, ma'am," offered Curly.

"Shoot no," added another Priscilla didn't recognize. "There weren't another girl at the party we'd pay five cents to dance with, an' I'll guess over $300 changed hands over you!" The others nodded agreement, and Priscilla's mouth fell open. She looked at Stella who affirmed it.

"I told you so," Stella whispered.

Nobody moved for a minute and then Aunt Sally spoke with disgust. "Give her the presents, you fools!" One by one, they all rather shamefacedly approached to leave their wrapped offerings at her feet.

Finally, Priscilla found her voice. "What's all this?" she asked, gesturing to the growing pile.

"Them's presents to show how sincere they all are," explained Aunt Sally.

"That's not necessary!" insisted Priscilla. "I can see now that you meant no harm. I was too easily offended." She meant it, too. They were not to blame. Dusty Rhoades held that honor.

"We ain't takin' no chances, Miss," said Curly. "We shore don't want you to leave here."

"Leave?" she asked in genuine amazement. "You think I'd leave because of this?" The thought *had* crossed her mind but only briefly. She could not let them think her so poor spirited. Nor could she let Dusty Rhoades know how thoroughly he had demeaned her. "Oh, no," she assured them, "I plan to stay here a good long time." She managed a small smile.

Murmurs of relief went through the crowd as the last of the gift-givers deposited his offering. Suddenly, Stella was looking around very intently. "Where's Dusty?" she demanded. Priscilla had not realized he was supposed to be with them.

At first no one answered, and then Curly spoke. "He didn't come back with us."

"He'd better be headed for Mexico then," snapped Stella. Someone snickered.

"He said to tell you he had some business in San Antone. He'll be back tomorrow night," explained Curly as the riders mounted up.

Aunt Sally considered, "Guess he figured there weren't no present big enough in Rainbow to make up for what he done."

No, thought Priscilla, nor anywhere else.

Chapter Six

As promised, Dusty returned the following evening, but Priscilla was too busy to think of him. School had started, and she found herself overwhelmed with lessons and recitations and pranks, including a garter snake in her desk. She made the discovery that most of her finishing-school education would be wasted in her new job, which required little more than an ability to read, write, and cipher, and to pass those skills along. Her class ranged in age from fifteen-year-old Katie Steele and a few of her friends down to six-year-old Joe Wilson and contained at least one child of every age in between. Fortunately for Priscilla, their abilities did not vary as much as their ages because none of them, not even the older ones, had had more than a few terms of school. With the school term lasting only three months every year, and some years being skipped altogether for lack of a teacher, the students had acquired little more than basic knowledge, so Priscilla grouped her sixteen pupils according to size and spent her energies on improving such skills as they possessed, resolutely putting aside her visions of introducing them to the wonders to be found in Ben Steele's library. She never laid eyes on Dusty who, she was told by a very informative Ben Steele, Jr., had returned empty-handed from his trip.

In fact, it was no accident that she had not seen him. Dusty skulked around the ranch, checking his back trail and carefully scouting before appearing in the open, lest he meet Priscilla by chance. Stella caught him the first afternoon after his return.

"What are you up to?" she demanded, cornering him outside the cookhouse.

"Nothin'," he insisted with forced innocence.

"You been down to apologize to that girl yet?" she asked, her piercing blue stare attempting to pin him down.

"Not yet," he admitted, shifting uneasily under her scrutiny.

"What are you waitin' for, Christmas?" Stella's fists rested on her ample hips as she stared down at him menacingly.

"I'll do it when the time is right," he assured her.

Stella snorted in a very unladylike manner. "When'll that be?"

"Soon, real soon," he promised, edging away from her and fairly running to the refuge of the bunkhouse.

The second day after his return, just as everyone was coming in for supper, a freight wagon pulled into the yard, causing quite a flurry of excitement. Everyone gathered around to see what it could be bringing, and George stepped forward to ask the driver what his business was.

"I got a dee-livery fer the schoolhouse," the driver explained.

"For the school?" Priscilla asked. "Whatever could it be?"

"Says here," said the driver, studying a soiled, wrinkled bill, "that it's a desk, fer the schoolhouse."

Priscilla was delighted. She flashed a smile at Ben Steele. "Why, Mr. Steele, what a wonderful surprise! The school certainly does need a new desk."

Ben Steele was puzzled. "It ain't from me. If the school board had any money at all, we'd raise your salary, Miss Priscilla."

While everyone stood puzzling over the mystery, Stella's eyes were scanning the crowd around the wagon. One face was conspicuously absent. "Well, now," she said before anyone came to the conclusion she had just reached, "let's show the gentleman where the school is so he can unload. He'll be wantin' his supper."

Children scrambled into the wagon, the hands mounted their still-saddled horses, and the others walked off, all shouting directions and instructions. Stella held Priscilla back as the others left.

"Who could have sent it?" Priscilla asked, genuinely puzzled.

"Well, it must've come from San Antone," Stella remarked casually, studying Priscilla's face. "Do we know anyone's been to San Antone lately?"

It took only a moment for Priscilla to realize the truth, and she could not stop the scarlet wave that stained her cheeks. That man! If he thought he could buy her forgiveness with a desk . . . well, she'd never forgive him. Never. She was too ashamed of her own behavior to forgive his and the knowledge left her too angry to speak for a few moments. Finally, she blustered, "I . . . I'll send it back. I won't keep it!"

"Why not?" asked Stella mildly.

Priscilla fumbled for a reason that sounded reasonable. "It . . . it's not proper. I could never accept a gift like that from a man who's . . . well, practically a stranger."

"It ain't fer you, it's fer the school," explained Stella more reasonably. "Besides, no one'll know who sent it."

"Everyone will know! If you figured it out, so will everyone else," Priscilla pointed out with ruthless logic.

"What folks think is their own business, but it's fer shore he'll never admit to it, so officially, no one'll know," Stella argued. "No one says you have to keep it. When you get married, you can just leave it fer the next teacher . . . unless you marry Dusty, of course," she added with a twinkle.

"The chances of that are very remote," fumed Priscilla, as she fought another blush. Stella could see she was wavering and started her walking toward the school.

Priscilla was considering. She did *deserve* some sort of peace offering, even if she had no intention of making peace. "If it weren't just such an *enormous* thing . . ." she murmured.

"He had to do something with all that money," Stella offered. To Priscilla's questioning look, she replied, "He won over a hundred dollars."

"A hundred dollars!" Priscilla repeated and she walked a little faster toward the school.

There, eager hands had unloaded the crate and pried it open. When Priscilla arrived, the desk was sitting on the grass before the schoolhouse, surrounded by a very quiet

176

circle of children and cowhands. The circle opened to admit Stella and Priscilla, who gasped audibly when she saw the desk. It sat resplendent, catching the gleam of the late afternoon sun in its polished mahogany finish. Adorned front and back with elaborate carving and scrollwork, it had rendered those humans around it awestruck.

Priscilla could hardly believe her eyes. "It's beautiful," she breathed.

Stella was the first to recover. "Well, Priscilla, show the boys where you want it put." That seemed to break the spell, and suddenly men were falling over each other in their haste to carry the unique object inside. In a matter of minutes it was placed, and Stella herded everyone out, reminding them that their supper was waiting and inviting the freighter to join them. She also had a suspicion that once Priscilla was left alone, she would be receiving a very special visitor.

Priscilla found a rag and began to polish the travel dust off her new acquisition. It was hard to believe that the man who had been so cruel to her could have chosen such a piece. Maybe he had some good qualities after all, although, she admitted to herself, good taste hardly indicated good character. No, she would not allow herself to be bribed into thinking well of Dusty Rhoades. As attractive and charming as he undoubtedly was, she would not fall under his spell. She knew him now for the deceiver that he was, a man who would take advantage of a situation he had created for monetary gain. Her cheeks burned at the recollection of what else he had almost gained, but that only served to stiffen her resolve. She would not be taken in again.

It was quiet now. Everyone had gone back to the ranch

for supper. Everyone except Dusty Rhoades. She was as certain of that as she was of her own name, somehow sensing his presence long before she heard his booted step on the schoolhouse porch, as if every pore in her body had opened to perceive an invisible aura that preceded him. Not bothering to look up when she finally did hear him, she continued polishing, barely managing to appear composed, while inwardly she was so aware of his nearness that it was frightening. Apparently, her body remembered the pleasure he had given it in spite of the fact that her mind found his conduct despicable. When at last he stood beside the desk—so near she could almost feel the heat emanating from his body—she braced herself for the impact of those sky blue eyes and glanced up, her outward poise unruffled.

Oh, she was a cool one, all right, he decided. It was hard to believe she was the same woman he had held in his arms a few short days ago, the same woman he had almost . . . well, no use thinking about that now. He had a job to do. A nasty job. "Nice desk," he began, matching her coolness.

"Yes," she agreed mildly. "It's a real work of art. I can't imagine who sent it," she added in a tone that told him she knew exactly who had sent it.

He never batted an eye. Two could play this game, he decided. "It's a puzzle all right," he agreed and bent to examine the carving on one drawer. "Whoever sent it must think a lot of you," he surmised, drawing back again.

An involuntary response to his implied compliment warmed her, but she fought down those warmer feelings with a ruthless determination. "Either that or he has a very guilty conscience," she said archly.

He considered that a moment, turning his hat in his hands, examining the hatband. He did feel guilty—a little bit, anyway. The bet had seemed like a good idea at the time, but now it seemed awful foolish. Wonder why it was that almost every time he had dealings with Miss Bedford, he ended up feeling foolish. All he wanted to do was get the upper hand, take her down a notch or two, but every time he tried, he was the one who got knocked down. Oh, she'd been embarrassed at the dance, all right, but the upshot of that had been that everyone else had come bowing and scraping and begging her forgiveness, and now it was his turn. Made a man wish he'd never set eyes on her, but it was too late for that, now, especially now that he'd set more than his eyes on her. He forced that memory back into the oblivion to which he had assigned it. It would do him no good now.

With a kind of mindless fascination Priscilla watched his large hands turning his hat. It was a brand new hat, she noticed irrelevantly, still pure white, and the hatband that he was paying such close attention to . . . Good Lord! It looked like a snake skin! Almost hypnotized, she watched those long brown fingers caress the hat brim, the same way they had caressed her . . .

"I wasn't lyin' the other night," he murmured, startling her out of her reverie.

Pulling her thoughts back from where they had so shamelessly wandered, Priscilla replied, "To which night are you referring, Mr. Rhoades?" She would not make it easy for him, she resolved.

Dusty bristled. She was the only person in the world who called him "Mr. Rhoades." He was "Dusty" to everyone who knew him, and "Rhoades" to the occasional stranger, but "Mister" to no one. She probably knew how much it irritated him, probably did it on purpose, but he swallowed his irritation, determined not to let her rile him. "The other night at the dance," he replied calmly, "when I told you how much I wanted to dance with you, and all that. It was all true. I'd been cussin' myself all night for seven kinds of a fool." That much was true, at least.

"And cussing me, too?" Priscilla asked perceptively.

Dusty almost winced. That was also true, but no use admitting it. "Oh, no, ma'am, you was justified in the way you treated me. And the things you said about me, I reckon they're all true, too." He almost choked on that. Had she really called him a "boorish ruffian"? She must have. Gus couldn't have made up something like that. He was too dumb. "It's just my pride was hurt, an' I guess I had a few drinks, an' when Jake offered to bet me"—a small deviation from the truth—"it just seemed like a good excuse to try to get you to dance, which is what I wanted to do anyway."

"And profit from it at the same time," Priscilla added venomously.

Dusty almost groaned. "Oh, no, ma'am," he assured her, still studying his hatband. It *was* a snakeskin, and he'd paid a pretty penny for it in San Antonio. He kept his gaze fixed resolutely on it, not daring to meet her eyes. If he did, she might be able to guess how much of his apology was sincere and that would never do. "It was mostly my pride, an' I figured, you bein' a real lady an' all, you couldn't help but forgive me if my apology was humble and heartfelt enough." At last he felt safe in meeting her eyes and he looked up, staring directly into those dark brown pools. "I never meant no harm to you, ma'am." That much was absolutely true, and he let her see it.

She did see it, but his earlier remark about her being a "real lady" brought back memories of what else had happened that night. She could forgive him for the dance and the bet, but she could not forgive him for her response to him. The recollection brought her to her feet. She found it entirely too difficult to be angry when he was so close and so conciliating. No, she would not forgive him just yet, she decided, trying to take a step backward but finding her chair was in the way. He had other things to apologize for, although how she would remind him was a problem. Could she accuse a man of taking liberties when she had been perfectly willing at the time? "Your . . . your conduct was . . . ungentlemanly," she reminded him falteringly.

She need not have spoken at all. He could clearly read her thoughts in those expressive brown eyes, and he knew all too well what she was thinking, what she was fearing. "The bet was only that I could get you to dance. That's all," he assured her. "The rest . . . what happened . . . just happened," he lamely excused himself. It was bad enough that she thought him a "boorish ruffian." He didn't want her to think him a complete cad, a man who would wager a woman's honor.

In spite of the fact that she had convinced herself he would not have done such a thing, she felt the surge of relief that followed his assurance. It brought a brittle laugh to her lips and she asked recklessly, "You mean you didn't profit from that, too? Why did you even bother?"

She realized, too late, what a provocative question it had been as she saw his eyes kindle and flame into the blue fire she had found so dangerous in the past.

181

Helplessly, she watched his strong fingers crush the brim of his hat and then fling it onto the top of the desk.

"You know why," he whispered hoarsely as those fingers closed around her waist, drawing her toward him.

Totally against her will, her face tipped up to meet his kiss, and the awareness she had known before flared into the wild desire she always felt in his arms. His kiss was seeking, and she did not disappoint him, parting her lips at his gentle insistence, meeting his tentative thrust, drawing a groan from him as her tongue tangled with his in a sweet duel. His hands were everywhere, exploring her back, her shoulders, the curve of her hip, and finally cupping the softness of her buttocks to draw her into intimate contact with the hard evidence of his desire.

As always, her mind ceased to function as she surrendered to the realm of sensation, glorying in his hands, his lips, the male hardness of his body. Answering her unspoken request, he palmed her thrusting breasts, feeling the pebbled suggestion of her arousal even through the material of her dress. The heat from his hands swept through her like wildfire, melting her very bones, rekindling the blaze that he had started before, that all-consuming fire that burned within her loins and demanded to be fed.

It hadn't been a dream, he realized with wonder as he fumbled with the buttons on her dress. She *had* responded to him that night, just like this. He'd been afraid that the whiskey and the darkness had exaggerated his recollections, but no, she had been just like this, wild and passionate and eager and . . . just like he'd always imagined it would be when he met *the* woman, that special one. The buttons freed at last, he pushed past the silk and lace, seeking and finding the

cushioned softness of her breast, teasing and torment-
ing until he heard, no, felt that strange, ecstatic sound
she made for him. Only for him.

Once again Priscilla heard that soft moaning and was
mildly surprised to know it came from her own body. But
only mildly surprised. She was incapable of any emotion
stronger than the need to feel his hands on her, all over
her, and she threw back her head as his mouth left hers,
offering him the white column of her throat, to which he
paid eloquent tribute before continuing on to scale the
peaks of her breasts with ravening greed. Back and forth,
first to one and then the other he went, tasting, suckling,
until both tips sparkled rosily and Priscilla was gasping
with pleasure. His hands had locked onto her bottom,
cradling her against his hips, urging her into the pulsing
tempo that would give them the assuagement they both
were seeking.

Still holding her against him with one hand, his mouth
still feasting on her velvety flesh, he disposed of a few
more buttons, and finding the spot where her chemise
disappeared into her waistband, he followed it down,
down beneath the silken covering that had hindered him
before, until he had the warm, moist core of her, and then
he knew. She was the one; she was ready for him, for only
him. He had known it. He had always known it would be
like this.

Priscilla cried out in alarm at his intimate intrusion.
As much as she had wanted it, craved it, his touch was a
violation that shocked her back to consciousness. Only
then did she hear and understand the words he was
muttering against her quivering skin.

"I knew it," he said, unaware that he had spoken
aloud. "I knew it."

What did he know? she wondered and then went rigid as the truth dawned on her. Of course! He had known that he could convince her, charm her, and then make love to her, if he just put himself to the task. She had been so easy, too, a willing partner in her own conquest.

Feeling her sudden stiffness, he raised his face to read her expression, ready to coax her past her understandable reluctance, but she broke free of him, wrenching his hands away from where they had trespassed. Desperately, she pulled her dress together, backing away from him while clumsily working a few of the buttons back into their holes. He stared stupidly at her furious face and heaving breasts, unable to fathom her sudden change of mood.

"You knew it, did you?" she gritted, trying to still the trembling of her hands and the pounding of her heart, her face scarlet with shame and indignation.

"What?" he asked blankly, trying to make sense of her sudden withdrawal, wanting nothing more than to have her back in his arms.

"You *knew* that I would fall victim to the famous Rhoades Charm! That's it, isn't it? Just like at the dance, you come down here and wheedle and cajole and worm your way into my affections—" She could have bitten her tongue. "Affections" was the last word she should have uttered, but she went doggedly on. "But this time it isn't going to work, *Mr.* Rhoades." She gloried in the way he flinched every time he heard that "Mister" and this time she reveled in it. "Oh, your apology was very well done. Your 'heartfelt' was excellent, although your 'humble' could stand some improvement." She stopped for a moment as she saw something that looked suspiciously like pain flicker across his face, and for just that moment she was willing to forgive him, yes, follow her heart and forgive him completely and be grateful for the opportunity. But then she saw his expression harden into the more familiar animosity, and she hardened her heart accordingly. "I am amazed at your ability to apologize while at the same time managing to appear completely innocent of wrongdoing. It is a remarkable characteristic," she added.

Dusty stretched his lips into a mirthless grin. "I'm a remarkable fella, *Miss* Bedford," he informed her. But not remarkable enough to figure you out, he added mentally. Where on earth had she gotten that business about the famous Rhoades Charm? And as far as his being humble was concerned, he was getting quite a bit of practice at that every time he ran into Miss Bedford, but he'd never let her know it. "Then you won't accept my apology?" he asked harshly, with a meaningful glance at the desk.

"Oh, I'll accept your *apology*," she said with her own significant look at the desk. "It would cause too much ill will and . . . gossip," she admitted reluctantly, "if I did not. But," she told him, "rest assured. I know you now for what you are, and you will not get around me so easily in the future. In fact, you won't get around me at all!"

Dusty's lips thinned in the effort to contain the words he wished he was not too much of a gentleman to say. What on earth did she know him to be now, if he'd been a "boorish ruffian" before? What did a man have to do, anyway? Get down on his knees? He'd already spent almost all his winnings on the desk, just to make it up to her, and then he'd apologized, pretty humbly, too, no matter what she said. Any other woman would have . . . Well, who needs her, anyway? He'd thought for a minute

185

there that she was something special, but he'd been wrong. It wasn't the first time he'd made a mistake about a woman, but no harm was done. There were still plenty of women out there who appreciated him. He'd just go find one. The hell with Priscilla Bedford. Retrieving his hat from the desk top, he smashed it down on his head. "It's been a pleasure, Miss Bedford," he said sarcastically, and turning on his heel, he stomped out.

Watching him go, Priscilla tried to enjoy her moment of triumph but found it rather hollow. Win or lose, it was not fun to argue with Dusty Rhoades. And, she had to admit to herself, that very strong physical attraction that had caught them both several times before was still in operation, no matter how at odds they happened to be. It was unnerving and a little frightening to recall how she melted at his touch. The only solution seemed to be staying away from him completely, something she guessed he would assist her in now that she had wounded his pride. The thought should have consoled her, but instead she felt strangely bereft.

On the fourth day of school, a new student appeared. At least he said he was a student. He stood half a head taller than Priscilla and was rather broad shouldered, although he was otherwise skinny and gangly. He was smiling and very polite, but something about him made Priscilla suspicious. And a little leery.

"My name's Judd Slaughter, ma'am. I shore could use some larnin'," he said, clutching a poor excuse for a hat tightly in both hands.

"How old are you, Judd?" she asked.

"Sixteen, ma'am, but I ain't had much schoolin'."

"Well, Judd, I won't turn you away if you really want to learn. Find a seat in the back, please."

The morning passed uneventfully, except for a strange undercurrent in the classroom, something more felt than seen or heard, a sort of general restlessness among the children. At one point, Katie Steele whispered to her, "Watch out for Judd. He's a bad one."

Twice Priscilla caught him staring at her, almost leering, and he hadn't bothered to look embarrassed when she caught him either. When lunchtime came, the children scrambled outside into the warm spring air. Priscilla watched them from the window, in case Judd tried to bully anyone, but he did not. In fact, the younger boys gathered around him, almost in admiration, and he was talking to them about something that had their complete attention. Priscilla couldn't hear them, but she watched for a while and then went to eat her own lunch.

"She ain't skeered of nothin'," young Ben Steele said. "I put a snake in her desk an' she didn't even scream, just picked it up and threw it out the window."

"I kin skeer her," said Judd knowingly. "You just wait. I'll skeer her 'til she starts bawlin' and screamin' and carryin' on. You'll see. Right when we go inside, first thing, I'll do it. Then there won't be no more school fer the rest of the day."

The younger boys continued to argue but Judd was unmoved. At last Priscilla rang the bell and they all filed in, all except for Ben junior who slipped away over the hill to the ranch house.

All the children took their seats, a bit quietly Priscilla noticed, except for Judd who walked right up to her desk and leaned over it, grinning at her.

"Please take your seat, Judd," she said, a little taken

aback by his boldness.

"You know, Miss Bedford," he said in a low voice that only she could hear, "you're quite a woman. Why, I'll bet, you bein' a teacher an' all, there's all kinda things you could teach a man. Maybe there's even some things I could teach you. Why don't you send all these younguns home so you an' me kin have us some fun."

The shock went over Priscilla in a wave, but except for the two spots of color that appeared in her cheeks, she managed to maintain her poise. "Judd, I think you'd better leave," she gritted in a low voice.

Judd's homely face creased into a scowl. "Maybe you think I'm just a kid. You're wrong, though. I've done it, done it lots a times. You won't be sorry." He grinned confidently as he rubbed the telltale bulge in his pants. "You'll see . . ."

"Judd," Priscilla's voice held a warning that went unheeded.

"You want it. All women want it. Don't pretend you don't. Get rid of these kids and I'll show you," he whispered urgently. He went on, but she was not listening. She had remembered something—something that had been in the old desk when she arrived, and without knowing why, she had transferred it to the new one. She eased open the drawer. There it was under her hand. He was still talking, whispering, saying ugly things, things she did not understand or would not let herself understand. She was not frightened, only angry, furious that this monstrosity could invade her school and presume to insult her, terrorize her. Her hand closed around the riding quirt in the top desk drawer and without wasting a motion, she brought it up and slashed it across his face. His look of pained astonishment was almost funny, but it quickly changed to rage. She hit him twice before he grabbed her hand and tried to wrest the quirt from her. She jumped to her feet, sidestepping the desk to clear the space between them.

Ben junior reached the ranch yard just as the hands were saddling up fresh mounts for the afternoon's work. Dusty was the first one he saw. He was out of breath from running, but he managed to gasp out his message: "Judd Slaughter's gonna hurt Miss Bedford!"

In an instant, Dusty was in his saddle, racing for the schoolhouse.

Judd Slaughter was strong, stronger at least than Priscilla, and he had caught both of her hands now. She realized it was useless to struggle, so she began to kick him in the shins, again and again, first one and then the other, over and over, until he released her hands and turned to escape. She laid the quirt across his back several times as she chased him down the aisle, her fury making her oblivious to the other children's shrieks of terror. He fell down the front stairs but was instantly on his feet again and running, limping a little she noticed irrelevantly as she stopped at the doorway. She stood on the step watching his escape, absently slapping the quirt against her skirt and allowing her anger to drain slowly away.

"Afternoon, Miss Bedford," Dusty called. He had pulled up about a hundred feet from the school to witness Judd's exit and now was walking his horse closer to the school. She sure is pretty when she's mad, he thought, for once enjoying the sight since it was not he toward whom her anger was directed. He had taken no time to consider his motives when he had made the decision to ride down here, but seeing her again made him painfully aware of what those motives were. Of course he had feelings for her. You couldn't kiss a woman the way he'd kissed her and not have some feelings for her. It was only logical, and if he didn't really want any more to do with her himself, he surely didn't want to see her hurt, certainly not by Judd Slaughter, although he now realized that Priscilla Bedford was more than a match for the likes of Judd.

Priscilla was mildly startled to hear Dusty's voice, and it was the surprise, she told herself sternly, that caused her pulse to quicken. What was he doing here anyway? she wondered. Her anger had abated somewhat, now that Judd had so unceremoniously removed himself, and as she took a calming breath, she allowed herself the pleasure of watching Dusty Rhoades ride closer. It was the first opportunity she had had to observe him on horseback, and she marveled at the easy way he sat his horse, as if he had been born to the saddle, his long, muscular legs gripping the horse with a powerful ease. He was grinning that boyish grin he had, and she felt something inside her melt. It simply wasn't fair that he could look so appealing today and make her forget what had happened just the day before. She took a last calming breath and managed to ask with creditable coolness, "Did you come for some lessons, Mr. Rhoades?"

A look of mock alarm crossed his features as he stopped his horse by the schoolhouse porch. "Oh, no, ma'am," he assured her with a meaningful look at the quirt. "I ain't too sure I like your way of givin' lessons." He glanced over his shoulder in the direction in which Judd had disappeared. "I just heard a rumor that there was trouble down here and that you might need some help. Guess I shouldn't be listening to no rumors," he

190

added, leaning forward and crossing both hands on the pommel of his saddle.

Priscilla slapped the quirt against her leg one last time, annoyed at her desire to step closer to his horse and rest her hand on that well-muscled thigh and smile up into those twinkling sapphire eyes. "That's right, you shouldn't," she told him, a little more sharply than was necessary. "I'm perfectly capable of handling unruly students myself. If I ever need your help, I'll let you know."

Her curtness did not seem to bother him at all. In fact, he relished it. It gave him an opportunity to indulge himself in looking at her without being tempted to take her in his arms. At least, as long as he stayed on his horse, he was safe. "And just how would you let me know, ma'am?" he goaded, reluctant to let the conversation drop, because then he would have to leave.

He was teasing her, she knew, and she was irritated because she was enjoying it. "Wellll . . ." she considered, casting about for an answer, and then she noticed the bell-rope which was still swaying slightly from when Judd had brushed by it. "If I'm ever *really* in trouble, I'll ring the bell, loud and long. Then you'll know to come running." The thought of Dusty running to her rescue brought a small smile to her lips, and then she realized that that was exactly what he had been doing just now. Why would he have done a thing like that? He didn't really care about her. No, she was just a challenge to him, a threat to his masculine superiority. That was it. He had come to help her today so that he could prove that superiority. Well, if that were true, she'd certainly shown him! She smiled a bit more. "Then you'll be able to perform a genuine rescue. I'm sorry you wasted your time today."

If he was the least bit frustrated, he did not show it. Instead he contorted his fine features into a parody of solemnity and informed her, "It weren't no waste of time, ma'am. Why, watchin' you in action is an education in itself. It purely is."

She shook her head at his teasing, fighting off the feeling of warmth spreading over her. Maybe he did care, just a little. After all, if *he* were in danger, wouldn't she set all their differences aside to help him? The fact that he had been willing to do that was certainly comforting, and even a little touching, too. She guessed he must have some good qualities after all. But she wouldn't let that change her opinion of him. He was still the most infuriating man she had ever met. "Good afternoon, Mr. Rhoades," she scolded mildly and returned to the chaos of her classroom to settle the children down after the spectacle they had just witnessed.

Dusty sat there for a while longer before finally turning his horse and walking it back to the ranchyard. That Priscilla Bedford sure was something, he decided, not like any woman he had ever known. He still couldn't decide if that were good or bad.

Chapter Seven

Shortly after all the students had left, Priscilla was startled to hear a horse ride up and a strange masculine voice holler, "Hey, schoolteacher! Git out here!"

Her earlier experience should have made her cautious, but she was more curious than alarmed. She went to the doorway to find a large, middle-aged man sitting his horse in the schoolyard. His jaw dropped when he saw Priscilla.

"Are you the schoolteacher, ma'am?" he stammered.

"Yes, I am," she replied coolly.

Instantly, he jumped down from his horse and snatched off his hat, obviously embarrassed. "Excuse me, ma'am, you see"—he seemed momentarily at a loss for words—"I'm Ed Slaughter. My boy come home all cut up an' said the schoolteacher beat him fer nothin'. I figured . . . I mean, we thought you had to be a *man*."

Priscilla could not suppress a smile. "As you can see, I am not a man. Your son was quite unruly, so I was forced to punish him."

"He ain't my son, ma'am. Leastways, not my real son. His real pa was hanged, years ago. He weren't never no good. I married his ma an' give the boy my name, but he's still his father's son, I reckon. Runs with a bad crowd. I hope he didn't do you no harm."

"Whatever he did, he was rewarded for, I assure you, Mr. Slaughter," Priscilla replied, mulling over this new information about Judd Slaughter.

"I'll do my best to keep him away from the school, ma'am. I'm sure sorry he bothered you," Slaughter apologized.

Priscilla sighed as Slaughter rode away. It was nice not to have to worry about Judd's coming back. At least, she hoped she would not have to worry.

On Friday after school Stella had arranged for Priscilla to go to visit Hazel Rogers for a few days so she could have her clothes altered. Priscilla had met Hazel and her husband, John, at the party. Hazel seemed like a very pleasant woman, although her husband was a rather remote, almost unsocial man who carried one arm in a sling. Priscilla had wondered at that but thought it best not to inquire.

According to previously made arrangements, a wagon from the Steele ranch would take her out to the Rogers' place and someone from the Rogers' place would take her home. To Priscilla's great surprise, when the Steele wagon arrived Dusty was driving it. She had not given any thought to this possibility. After all, Dusty was the foreman and far above such menial tasks as taxiing ladies all over the countryside, and he could not possibly find the job pleasant. Since the day the desk had been delivered, except for the time he had ridden to her rescue, he had studiously avoided her all week, and she had returned the favor. Since they could not meet without arguing—or doing something far worse, she admitted reluctantly—it was better if they did not meet at all. She had been certain of that, but if she had been so certain, why had her stomach done a somersault when she had first seen him driving up in the wagon? Apprehension, she decided. Pure and simple. Nothing more.

Dusty pulled the wagon up beside the school, tied the reins to the brake handle, and lifted his hat to Miss Bedford before climbing down from his seat. Yep, she was a cool one, all right. He had been a fool to come on this trip. He should have asked one of the other boys to do it. Any one of them would have been glad to. That, he had to admit, was the main reason he hadn't asked them. They were all half in love with her already. Given any encouragement . . . well, he'd see to it they got no encouragement. That was his responsibility as foreman. He'd just forget any personal problems he had with Miss Bedford. He could be polite to her for a few hours. He could be polite to *anyone* for a few hours. It would be good practice for him, too; good practice in ignoring her. If they were going to both be living on the ranch, he'd have to learn to do that, and it wasn't like he didn't have plenty of experience. He'd been ignoring women for years, ever since one almost got her hooks in him. Not that he'd ignored them completely, of course. He was always willing to take whatever was offered, as long as there were no strings attached, but when a girl started hearing wedding bells, he was gone. It was a practice that had served him well, and the fact that he was still a free man attested to that. He just wished she didn't look quite so cute in that perky little bonnet with that red bow tied under her chin. Thank God she was wearing that duster again, the same one she'd had on when he'd first seen her. Of course, now he knew what it was hiding, but it would be a big help not to have to look at it all afternoon. If only he could forget what she looked like and keep in mind some of the nasty things she'd said to him, he'd be all right. "You got a bag or somethin'?" he asked as impersonally as he could.

For a moment she allowed herself to study his carefully expressionless features. If he were still angry with her, he was concealing it well. Personally, she was no longer actually angry, but like the old saying went, "once stung, twice shy," and she was wary of him even in his present innocuous mood. They would, she conceded, have to learn to get along sooner or later, since they would both be living on the ranch and could not avoid each other completely, but why would he subject himself to her company like this when it wasn't necessary? Well, it would be good practice for her, good practice in ignoring him, or tolerating him, whichever proved most expedient. "Yes, I have a suitcase inside," she informed him and waited on the porch while he went in and got it. He loaded it into the back of the wagon while she locked the door, and then he wordlessly handed her onto the wagon seat.

Neither spoke for a while, and Priscilla smiled as their silence reminded her of the first time they had met. Her attempts to start a conversation then had been disastrous, but she felt a little more capable of keeping things on an even keel now. "Nice weather we're having lately," she said blandly, making it as much a question as a statement.

Dusty shot her a puzzled look, but then he caught the

twinkle in her eye and also remembered their first encounter. He also knew what she was trying to do—make things easier between them—and that was something he was willing to work toward, too. "It's warm for March, and that's a fact," he agreed cheerfully. "Hope that don't mean a real hot summer."

She smiled triumphantly. At least he was willing to cooperate with her. "Everything here is so different from back home. What do you call those blue flowers?" she asked, pointing toward the hillside covered with a flower that seemed to have bloomed overnight.

"Those are bluebonnets," he explained, thus beginning a conversation about the strange plants and flowers that grew in the Southwest. Priscilla had a hundred questions and Dusty patiently answered every one.

Priscilla could not help a small sense of smugness. Dusty Rhoades was no different from any other man. She could handle him if she just put her mind to it, she acknowledged, congratulating herself on the fact that they had been riding for nearly an hour and were neither arguing nor embracing. All she had to do was set the tone for their relationship, a certain cool aloofness, and he would have no choice but to maintain it. It gave her a rather heady feeling, something akin to what a lion tamer must feel, she guessed, knowing that he could control a wild beast. The thought of Dusty Rhoades as a wild beast under her control was even more than heady, she realized as a small thrill went through her. That he could be wild, she knew from experience, and that he could make her feel that way, also, she knew to her sorrow. But he would not do it again, she vowed with a renewed smugness. A small smile of resolution curved her lips.

Dusty glanced over. Maybe she was out of questions. He hoped so. She was acting so sweet and feminine that he was starting to like her, and that was the last thing he wanted to do. She had a way of looking at a man when he talked, like she was hanging on every word. Made him feel important. Too important, especially when he knew what she really thought of him. He glanced over again. She'd taken off that bonnet, let it hang down her back with the red ribbon still in a bow at her throat. He ought to tell her not to be out in the sun without a hat, but then, he kind of liked the way her skin had turned a little brown. It made her look healthier, not so pale, like when she'd first got there. No sign of freckles either. And he liked the way her lips curled up when she smiled.

"You gettin' hungry?" he asked abruptly.

Priscilla blinked in surprise. "I . . . I suppose so, but we're not even near the Rogers' ranch yet, are we?"

"No, but . . ." Dusty shifted uneasily in his seat, and felt his neck getting red. "Stella packed us a picnic," he told her reluctantly. He had been mortified when Stella had presented it to him, especially when he had seen that matchmaking gleam in her eye and that knowing smirk on her mouth, but he hadn't known how to refuse it without embarrassing himself further. He couldn't exactly explain how things were between him and Priscilla, especially because he wasn't sure himself.

Priscilla felt the heat rising in her cheeks. She should have known Stella was behind this whole thing. It had the mark of her meddling all over it. She had known Dusty would not have escorted her of his own free will, and judging from the uncomfortable way he was squirming, he'd had no part in planning the picnic, either. Just wait until she got her hands on Stella Steele Wilson. "How nice," she managed to say quite convincingly, although she, too, was mortified by Stella's matchmaking. "Is there a place we can stop?" she asked, looking uncertainly at the rather barren landscape.

"Up ahead there's a real nice spot," he said, careful not to look at her, not wanting to know if she, too, suspected Stella's motives. In a few minutes they came upon a small copse of trees growing around a seep of water. It sat well off the road and the foliage created a private little glen for them to eat in.

Priscilla knew a small pang as she wondered how many other picnics he had had on this spot, and with whom. Squelching such concerns as unimportant, she considered practicalities. "What will we sit on?" she asked, thinking with dismay of grass stains on her skirt.

Relieved that she did not seem upset by the prospect of Stella's picnic, he replied, "I got a tarp in the wagon. Keep it there all the time," he added, in case she suspected he'd had any part in this.

After parking the wagon in a shady spot, Dusty helped Priscilla down and then handed her a bulging flour sack that he retrieved from under the seat. Then he reached into the back of the wagon and came up with a tarp in one hand and a stoneware jug in the other. Seeing Priscilla's rather startled expression, he hastily explained. "Cider," he said, indicating the jug, and she nodded with relief.

In a few minutes, after some awkwardness—for some reason he was all thumbs—he had the tarp spread out in a sunny spot, and he sat down, Indian style, and began to delve into the picnic sack.

Priscilla had removed her duster, feeling suddenly warm in this sheltered, sunny spot, and she sat down across from him, primly folding her legs beneath her. She stared with some amazement at the amount of food Dusty had removed from the sack, but after watching him eat, she was amused instead. In short order he devoured three beef sandwiches and most of an apple pie—he did save one piece for her. When he was finished, she was still nibbling her sandwich in a very ladylike manner. He poured some cider into a tin cup for her and then, to her delight, hoisted the jug over his shoulder and took a long drink. He was, she decided, the best looking man she had ever seen, without doubt, and she could not resist an admiring glance or two as he unfolded his long legs and stretched out, half-reclining, with a groan of satisfaction. She loved the way his jeans molded those long legs and those trim hips and the way his muscles moved under the cotton of his shirt. He was, she realized with some surprise, dressed up. That shirt was the same yellow checked one he had worn to the dance, as was the yellow silk neck scarf. Those jeans that fit so well were almost new and disappeared into those shiny star-topped boots she had admired before. The new white hat, which he had carefully placed on a far corner of the tarp, was looking slightly less new but still quite presentable, even if it did have a snakeskin hat band. Yes, he made quite a picture lying there, and she quickly averted her eyes, trying to remember how impossible he could be. The effort brought a smile to her lips as she considered her absurd reactions to him and tried to study the surrounding trees.

She looked so pretty when she smiled. Right now she looked almost content. Remembering her earlier interest and seeing the way she was examining the scenery, he remarked, "You really like it here, don't you?"

Priscilla looked at him in surprise and her heart skidded to a momentary halt when her eyes encountered the cerulean depth of his. He looked almost concerned, as if he really cared for her happiness. Something heavy seemed to settle into the pit of her stomach and it sent a strange warmth spreading throughout her body. Unwilling to reveal how oddly impressed she was by his apparent concern, she replied with a gush of enthusiasm, "Like it? I love it! Do you realize it might be snowing in Philadelphia right now?"

She actually seemed sincere, however unlikely he thought it that she should prefer an isolated Texas ranch to the wonders of the big city. "Just wait 'til July," he cautioned dampeningly. "You'll be wishin' you was back in Philadelphia."

Priscilla laughed. "You wouldn't say that if you'd ever been to Philadelphia," she informed him.

Dusty winced. She had the prettiest laugh. It sounded like little bells. And her words had stung. Did she think he was a country hick who'd never been twenty miles from the spot where he'd been born? "I been to Philadelphia," he replied rather curtly.

Priscilla stared in surprise, as much at his defensive tone as at the statement itself. "You have? When?" she asked with genuine curiosity.

"In seventy-six," he snapped, picking up a twig and tossing it forcefully away.

For a moment she did not make the connection, and then her own memories came flooding back. "The Exposition! You went to the Centennial Exposition!" she cried, almost clapping her hands in triumph.

She was actually impressed, he realized with a small sense of pride. "Yeah," he admitted with becoming modesty. "Ben wanted someone to go with, so since Ben junior was too young, he took me."

"My father took me almost every day," Priscilla recalled with an exaggerated enthusiasm. She did not take the time to analyze why she felt so excited at the fact that they had a shared experience to discuss. She only knew that she had sensed a small withdrawal on his part for just a moment and she wanted to recapture the mysterious warmth she had felt when he had looked at her just minutes ago. "It was so exciting! Just think, we might have passed each other in the crowd one day."

Her enthusiasm was contagious and Dusty grinned. She was cute as a button when she got excited, he decided. "I don't think so. I doubt you spent much time at the livestock exhibitions," he teased.

Priscilla was inordinately pleased to see that adorable grin. "Oh, but I did," she informed him with delight. "My father was very interested in the different breeds of cattle and horses. I suppose we spent most of our time there."

Dusty scowled. That didn't make much sense. Why would her father, a city man, be interested in cattle? "Was your father a farmer or somethin'?"

"No, he was a printer," she replied. Then noticing his puzzled expression, she explained, "He was very interested in the West, though, and ranching and things like that. He read a lot on the subject. I guess that's why I first became interested in it, too." She was not, however, interested in discussing her personal life. She was interested in talking to Dusty Rhoades and getting him to smile at her and maybe even make him laugh, so she turned the subject back. "I'm sure I must have seen you. I looked at every western man there." Could she once have seen him and forgotten? At this moment it seemed unlikely, she decided, studying the way his eyes crinkled at the corners as he recalled pleasant memories.

"Me an' Ben weren't dressed western, so you prob'ly didn't notice us. Ben outfitted us both in suits, like we was bankers or somethin', so we wouldn't look strange," he explained with a degree of pride, basking in her undivided attention. What was it about those eyes that made a man feel so important?

Apparently, he had forgotten that virtually every western man had gotten himself a stylish eastern suit to wear. "It didn't matter what you were wearing. Western men just naturally stood out from the rest. Maybe it was the sunburned faces or the loud voices. I don't know, but I do know that after a few days, even I could pick a big Texas cattleman out of the crowd. Then I'd send my father over to talk to him."

Had she really hung around the stockyard? It seemed unlikely. He would have noticed. He would definitely have noticed, and his grin said so. "Well, for shore I never saw you, and I know I looked at every pretty girl in Philadelphia," he said.

Priscilla blinked. Had he actually said he considered her pretty? Well, what did she think? A man didn't kiss a girl he wasn't attracted to. That knowledge quickened her pulse and set a warm glow over the afternoon. "You wouldn't have noticed me," she assured him. "I was only fifteen then, and a very gawky, tomboyish fifteen at that." And skinny, too, all knees and elbows, hardly the type of girl that would attract Dusty Rhoades's attention. She recalled how upset she had been on that magical day when she had seemed to change overnight from child to woman. She had thought that all her fun was over until she had discovered that men were interested in talking to her now, answering her questions, and if they didn't always stay on the subject she wanted to discuss, she simply used her barbed tongue to prod them back again. Right now, however, she had no urge to change the subject, as much as she had always detested such word games between men and women. This time she wanted to encourage him, perhaps win another compliment or even . . .

Dusty was doing some fast figuring in his head. She really was as young as she looked. Not that a few years should make that much difference, but somehow it did. It made him feel oddly protective, although why he should, he had no idea. She was looking at him, waiting for him to say something. What had she just said? Something about being a tomboy and ugly. Involuntarily his eyes skimmed over her, taking in the way her breasts rounded out that thin cotton shirt she had on, how tiny her waist was even without a corset, and the way her hips curved out below. "You've changed a lot," he said, his voice suddenly husky with the desire she always aroused in him.

Something inside Priscilla responded to that strange tone in his voice, and she felt her senses quicken with a new awareness. It was dangerous to feel like that, she knew, but she was powerless to stop. "Hadn't we better be going?" she asked faintly in an attempt to divert those too-blue eyes from their apparent effort to hypnotize her.

Dusty stared at her for a long moment. She looked almost . . . what? Frightened, that was it. Was she frightened of him? Good God, she didn't need to be scared of him. He *loved* her! Didn't she know that? No, of course she didn't know that. He hadn't known it himself until just this moment and the knowledge jolted him to the core. What had he been thinking of, to fall in love with a woman who hated him, who ended up half hysterical every time he put his hands on her; a woman, he reluctantly admitted, that he had no right to touch at all. Humbled by that admission, he readily agreed. "Guess we'd better go," he said, scrambling to his knees and snatching up the empty flour sack. He began to gather up the remains of their picnic and stuff them into the bag, and after a moment Priscilla began to help. Once their hands accidentally touched, and they both jerked away as if the contact had burned them, their eyes meeting for one awful moment and then darting nervously away. When everything had been safely gathered, Dusty closed the sack, set it aside, rose to his feet, and offered Priscilla his hand.

Priscilla hesitated only a moment. After all, it was silly to be so skittish, but when she placed her hand in his she realized that it had not been silly at all. The warmth from his hand spread swiftly through her body as he used his strength to pull her to her feet, and the blazing blue of his eyes entranced her so that she did not realize that her legs weren't working properly until they refused to hold her weight and she almost fell.

At her startled cry, his arms instinctively went around her, catching her sagging body and lowering it gently to the ground again. Half-embarrassed at her clumsiness and half-disconcerted by his closeness, Priscilla could barely think and made some inane, confused explanation of how her legs must have fallen asleep.

Dusty didn't hear her. He was too intent on watching her face and savoring the way her body cradled against him. Vaguely aware that she was no longer talking, he tried to say something back, something that made sense, something that might explain why he continued to hold her, but all he could manage was, "Oh, Pris . . ." as he

205

gently cupped her lovely head in his hands.

Priscilla gazed at him in wonder. It was true, she realized with stunned amazement. The thing she had denied so long was really true: she loved him! In spite of his rudeness, his crudeness, his . . . in spite of everything, she loved him! She might have even told him so at that very moment had her mouth not been busy with something else entirely.

The wonder on her face turned her eyes into two large, brown, liquid pools, and Dusty found himself longing to drown in their depths as he slowly lowered his lips to hers. Their kiss was infinitely sweet and full of the longing they both felt.

Priscilla's hands gripped the front of his shirt as she sought to hold him close, but after a few moments, he drew back, ending the kiss, his brilliant eyes searching her face for some sign, some clue. Impatient with such hesitation, she used her grip to pull him back to her, wanting only to feel him against her once more, and this time she slid her arms around his back so that he could not escape. In response, his own hands moved down to her shoulders and then enfolded her gently. She felt his strength, the tightly leashed power trembling through him, but she had no desire for such restraint. Provocatively, she tightened her arms around him, pulling him down to her as she fell backward onto the tarp. He followed helplessly, crushing her breasts against the unyielding wall of his chest. Parting her lips, she flicked her tongue against the firmness of his mouth. Exulting in his groan of defeat as he lost the battle to his passion, she opened to his sweet invasion, tangling her tongue with his, and pliantly yielding her body to his urgent hands. The familiar warmth had become a fire, smoldering somewhere deep within her loins, sending its heat throughout her body wherever his hands happened to touch, and they were touching everywhere. Her back, her shoulders, her buttocks, her hips—his hands inflamed every part of her, and when at last he caressed her breast, finding the sensitive peak with his thumb, the fire engulfed her completely, destroying her strength and her will and all her senses, save one. This was what she had wanted, his whole length pressed against hers, his body half covering her, his weight a delicious burden, his hands moving freely. When the cool air touched her heated skin, she felt a slight surprise that he had opened her shirtwaist so easily. In another moment, he had disposed of the ribbons of her chemise and pushed back the delicate silk to reveal the alabaster globes of her breasts, which stiffened delightfully as the cool air kissed them.

"Oh, darlin'," he breathed, glorying once again in the sight of her. "You're so beautiful."

Beautiful? Was she? She did not know. She only knew that she wanted to be, for him. For an electric moment his hand explored, finding one pink crest to torment with its sandpaper roughness, and when she thought she would cry out from the sheer pleasure of it, his warm mouth found the other crest, and she did cry out, arching against him, her hands forcing his head more tightly against her softness.

His leg had tried to entrap hers, to still her ecstatic thrashing, but had succeeded only in becoming entangled, his thigh moving instinctively between her legs, stroking rhythmically against the heat of her desire. Unthinkingly, she stroked back, urgent with a need she felt but did not understand. She moaned a protest when his hand moved from her breast but sighed with satisfaction as she felt it touch her hip and then slide down to her thigh and, oh yes, back up under her skirt now, searching out those secret places that ached for him.

Dusty was barely able to think, but still he somehow knew that she would stop him soon, the way she always did, and driven by that knowledge, he continued to explore the depths of her passion, finding at last the center of her, so hot, even through the silk, that he groaned. Fumbling frantically, before she could think to stop him, he found the waistband tie of her pantalettes and stripped the garment from her.

Far from wanting to stop him, Priscilla helped, lifting her hips and kicking her feet free of restraint, the whole of her now free, open to his touch, and touch he did, his fingers leaving trails of fire along her quivering thighs, seeking out her warm, moist core. She had never dreamed a man could give such pleasure and his name trembled on her lips in grateful tribute when his mouth swallowed hers in a long, drugging kiss that left her only vaguely aware that he was doing something, something down below, something new, and then he lowered himself onto her, his body covering hers completely. Her eager hands clasped him to her, finding to her delight that his waistband was loose and she could reach under his shirt, that beautiful yellow shirt, and actually touch him. His skin was hot and soft, soft yet hard, like satin over steel, and she reveled in her discovery as her busy hands explored his back, only half aware that something hot and hard was probing, prodding, insisting. It took a moment for her to realize what was happening, and she knew a tinge of panic when she did.

"No, stop," she gasped against his mouth, but it was too late. He had broken the barrier of her innocence and her cry of pain became a sigh of pleasure as he slowly filled her. She knew instinctively that this was it, what she had been longing for since the day they had met, the perfect completion of the love that had been growing between them since then. But he was pulling away! Frantically, she grasped his flanks and drew him back. As he returned, he brought with him tingling sensations that went singing along her nerve endings, and soon she was caught in the timeless rhythm that became increasingly more urgent as it lifted them higher and higher. Just when Priscilla thought she could bear no more and live, the spasms shook her, sending a thousand colored lights to explode inside her brain, blotting out all else. She was only barely aware when Dusty groaned and shuddered out his own release, and for what seemed a long time, she lay in a golden haze, trembling with the aftershocks and savoring his glorious weight upon her sated body.

Slowly the fog of passion lifted from Dusty's brain, and into its place crept a chilling horror at what he had just done. How could he have let it happen? Hadn't he just realized that he was no good for her? And why had she . . . ? But she hadn't, not really. For a while there he had thought that he was not the first. She had seemed so eager, so . . . but no, she was innocent. Hadn't she tried to stop him? She had simply waited too long. Only a truly innocent woman would have let things go so far without realizing the dangers. Now he had two choices. The most obvious one, of course, was to marry her. When dealing with a decent woman, the rules were simple: if you bed her, you wed her. Priscilla would probably agree, too, even though she did not love him, could never love him, but although he would like nothing better than to have her, just like this, for the rest of his life, he couldn't force her to accept him. The thought of living with her, loving her, and knowing she only tolerated him because she had been foolish one time in her life—had given in to that strange physical thing that was between them—made him cringe. When he saw the rest of the picture, her locked away in that tiny cabin, Ben Steele's foreman's cabin, as the wife of a hired hand, her tolerance turning to outright hatred as the years robbed her of youth and hope, he felt physically ill. His only other choice was to pretend that this had meant nothing to him and walk away. He had tumbled other girls and walked away. Never anyone like Priscilla Bedford, of course, but then they hadn't been bad girls, either. Not really. He had experience at it, anyway. He should be able to pull it off, if that was what he had to do.

Priscilla had never been in love before. She felt exhilarated and contented and a thousand other things, all at once. And to think, this was only the beginning. They had their whole lives to enjoy it, to explore it, to test it to its limits. Love was a wondrous thing, even when the words had yet to be spoken. She would be the first to say them, she decided, trying to imagine how his face would look, all softened with love and tenderness for her. Would he be all choked up or delirious with joy? He was moving now, lifting his weight from her. She would tell him as soon as she saw his face, those blue eyes glowing with shared pleasures. But when he pulled back and she saw those eyes, distant and troubled in a face so stiff it might have been carved from granite, the tender words froze on her lips.

In a moment he had levered himself off of her and was

on his feet, adjusting his clothes. He almost stepped on her pantalettes which were lying on the grass where he had discarded them. He scooped them up and tossed them in her direction, not allowing himself to look at her. "Better get dressed," he said, his voice strained. "Somebody might come by." And he walked over to the wagon, keeping his back to her.

Hurt and bewildered, Priscilla stared after him. She wanted him to hold her, to tell her how beautiful she was, how much he adored her, and he had simply walked away. But then she recalled his words and realized that she was lying half-naked, outside, in broad daylight where anyone might come by and see her, see them if they continued making love in such an inappropriate spot. No wonder he was acting so strangely. He must be awfully embarrassed to have lost control like that. She might even be embarrassed herself if she didn't feel so wonderful. Swiftly she dressed, hoping that she looked reasonably decent and made quick work of repinning her hair. Fortunately, her hair *never* looked really neat so that a little dishevelment was hardly noticeable. Besides, she had the bonnet that she had left on the wagon seat. Between that and her faithful duster, she could look at least presentable. When she got to Hazel's, she could change her clothes immediately, claiming travel dirt or something. If only she didn't have to go to Hazel's now! She would so much rather go with Dusty someplace, anyplace, but that would hardly do. When they failed to arrive at the Rogers', a search party would be sent after them, and how embarrassing that would be. At least they had a little time together, the rest of the trip to Hazel's. It wasn't much but it would have to do, for now. "I'm ready," she called to where he still stood, his back to her.

Dusty cringed at the sound of her voice. She sounded so normal, as if nothing had happened. No hysterics or vapors or recriminations from *her*. Yes, she was a real lady, first class all the way through. Oh, he'd known it all along, ever since that first minute when she'd gotten off the stage. She might be teaching school now, but any fool could see she was used to better things. And those clothes! Yes, she'd known a better life before and would again, he was sure, but that life held no room for Dusty Rhoades. Where would a lowly cowboy fit into a life like that? She should marry somebody with money and education, something to offer her. What did he have to offer her? A two-room cabin on Ben Steele's ranch and a life of drudgery. If he had any sense at all, he'd walk out of her life right now. It would be the kindest thing he could do. Unfortunately, he didn't seem to *have* any sense at all. Turning, he strode purposefully back, wordlessly folded up the tarp, and then picked up the jug.

Following his lead, Priscilla picked up the flour sack and stood a little uncertainly, not knowing exactly what to say or do next. It was so *awkward*!

Dusty gave her an inquiring glance and, seeing the odd look on her face, surrendered to despair. She must feel ten times worse than I do, he thought bleakly. After all, she was a virgin, for God's sake, and to do it with a man she didn't even really like . . . No wonder she looked so strange. Maybe he should apologize or something, he thought wildly, and he might have if he had had any idea at all of what to say. Instead he just said, "Let's go," in a voice so subdued as to be barely recognizable.

Priscilla nodded her head and followed him obediently to the wagon. Wasn't he going to say anything or do anything? Wasn't he even going to kiss her?

212

When the things had been loaded into the wagon, he handed her up onto the seat as impersonally—no, more impersonally—than he had when they had first met. What was wrong? Did he not trust himself or did he not care? Priscilla felt the prickle of tears behind her eyes, but she blinked them back resolutely. No tears. Not now, she vowed.

Wearily, Dusty climbed to his own seat and took up the reins, but instead of starting, he sat for a long moment, carefully lacing the leather straps through his fingers. Finally, his concern overriding his better judgment, he asked, "Are you all right?"

Priscilla almost did weep at that, so tenderly spoken were his words, but she managed to retain her composure and answer with only a slight constraint. "Yes, I'm fine, thank you," she lied. She was actually a little sore, as she had noticed when she sat down on the hard wooden seat, but it was nothing he needed to be concerned about. She didn't dare look at him for fear of weeping or doing some other foolish female thing, so she picked up her bonnet and very busily put it on.

He was glad that she was fine. He would never be fine again, he feared as he clucked the team into motion. A lump of pure misery settled into his stomach when he tried once more to decide what to do. If he married her, he would never have her love, and if he didn't marry her, he'd never have her at all. It was a perfect case of "damned if he did and damned if he didn't." In the uneasy silence that followed, the miles fell behind them quickly and soon he began to notice the painfully familiar landmarks. That was all he needed, he decided—to come out here on top of everything else.

"You're very quiet," Priscilla pointed out somewhat

timidly when she could stand the silence no longer. They had things to talk about, plans to make, or at least she hoped they did. She could understand how he must feel about what had happened, but after all, if she didn't mind, why should he?

He fought down the irritation he felt. She had a right to talk to him if she wanted to, and he owed it to her to talk back. It was common courtesy, but he had a feeling she wanted to talk about things he didn't. "It's just . . . I ain't too fond of comin' out here," he hedged. It was part of the truth, at least.

Priscilla looked around. If anything, the countryside was more beautiful than before. She could see nothing to make him unhappy. "But why?" she asked.

He took so long to answer that she recalled the westerner's aversion to personal questions and began to wonder if her new status still did not give her the right to ask them, when he finally said, "Because this place used to belong to my family."

So that was it! Stella had told her the story but had neglected to make the connection for her. That made it doubly strange that Dusty would choose to drive her out here. "Stella told me what happened," she said with sympathy. "Coming here must bring back a lot of unhappy memories."

"It ain't that," he explained with impatience, a little offended that she thought him so sensitive. "Fact is, it brings back mostly good memories. It's just that, well, it pains me to see the way ol' man Rogers has let the place go down."

"How do you mean?" she asked with genuine interest. "Is he a bad rancher?"

"Not so much bad as just plain don't care. You see"—

he gestured to the land around them and, warming to his subject continued—"now, a tenderfoot like you might not notice, but this is perfect cattle country, lots of good graze, plenty of water. Fact is, all a man'd have to do is sit back and wait for his cows to drop calves, and he'd be rich, but Rogers ain't rich. He's dirt poor."

Priscilla had automatically bristled at the "tenderfoot" remark, but she let it pass, sensing that it had just slipped out. "Why is that?" she asked encouragingly, truly intrigued.

"Runs a rawhide outfit," he said obscurely. And then, seeing her confusion, he interpreted, "That means it's run so loose, it's like it's held together with a piece of rawhide. His hands steal from him, he don't have no idea how many head he's got, his stuff's scattered all over, he don't ever have a proper roundup. Don't seem like he even cares about makin' money, and a man with a wife and four kids should be thinkin' about that most of all."

Priscilla nodded her agreement but did not reply. His remark, and the trace of bitterness she had heard beneath it, had triggered a series of thoughts that led to a very surprising conclusion. Could Dusty possibly be concerned because he had no money, no way other than his job with the Steeles to support her? That was so silly when she . . . but how could she tell him that? Very tactfully, she decided, but before she could discover a way to do it, they rounded a hill, and the sight of the Rogers' ranch buildings blotted everything else from her mind. Suddenly she understood everything: why Dusty hated to come here, why Rogers did not make money, why Hazel took in sewing. The shabbiness of the place was evident even at this distance, although the natural setting was breathtaking. A crystal-clear stream flowed by the property, lined with all manner of trees—walnut, pecan, hackberry, elm, wild plum—and dipping into the sparkling water were the weeping willows. The ranch buildings were built around a gently sloping hill that sat back from the water, and there on top . . . was nothing. That "nothing" assaulted her eye, as a sour note assaults the ear. It disturbed her, puzzled her.

"It's all wrong," she said aloud, without meaning to.

"What is?" he inquired, all that had passed between them suddenly forgotten.

"Why, the house"—she gestured—"should sit on that hill. That's the perfect spot, overlooking the water, commanding attention—not down below, where it is. It's all wrong," she decreed.

Dusty looked at her strangely for a minute. "Funny you should notice that. When my folks lived here, that's where my Pa built the house."

"Where is it now?" she asked, experiencing an odd sense of loss.

"It burned a few years back," Dusty informed her quietly. "Rogers was too lazy to clear off the spot so he just put up a house down below."

"I see what you mean by a rawhide outfit now," she murmured.

He accepted her remark and nodded in agreement, feeling unaccountably close to her suddenly. "The place was never run down like this when I was a kid," he confided. "Pa kept it in perfect running order; never a bent fence post or a rotten board anywhere. Now look at it," he added in disgust.

Priscilla felt a surge of sympathy but resisted the urge to express it. Somehow she knew he wanted none. Instead she simply said, "It's a pity," and in the companionable silence that followed, they reached the Rogers' ranch.

Hazel Rogers awaited them at the door, her two youngest children clinging shyly to her skirts. Childbearing had expanded Stella Wilson's figure, but it had made Hazel Rogers gaunt. Her plain face had been worn down to hollows and angles, and her simple but well-made dress could not conceal her protruding bones. Still, she was as neat as a pin, with every strand of her prematurely graying hair tucked lightly into a bun, and her faded brown eyes still holding a certain undaunted liveliness. She greeted them both warmly.

"Good to see you, Miz Rogers," Dusty exclaimed with a dazzling smile. "That a new dress? It looks mighty nice on you," he added with unabashed enthusiasm.

Priscilla stared in astonishment at Hazel actually blushing like a schoolgirl as she laughed and chided Dusty for being a shameless flatterer. He'd never smiled at Priscilla like that! And he'd certainly never complimented her, at least not directly like that, either. Annoyed that she felt, not jealous exactly, but certainly neglected, she accepted his offered assistance out of the wagon with a cool reserve that caused Hazel, a careful observer, to raise her eyebrows in speculation. Priscilla greeted Hazel with the proper degree of friendliness and thanked her prettily for allowing her to come.

"Think nothing of it," Hazel assured her. "I'm glad for the company. I don't get many female visitors. Dusty," she added, turning to him, "you'll stay to supper, won't you?"

"Thank you, no, ma'am," he said with a self-conscious glance at Priscilla. "We had a . . . that is, Stella packed us a picnic and we . . . ah . . . we stopped on the way and . . ." His voice trailed off uncertainly, his acute embarrassment at what had also happened robbing him of his usual poise.

His stammering explanation brought a crimson flush to Priscilla's face despite her efforts to appear unconcerned. She tried to convince herself that Hazel could have no idea what had happened at that picnic, but Hazel's raised eyebrows told that she had a pretty good idea, nevertheless.

To escape Hazel's knowing look, Dusty made haste to retrieve Priscilla's suitcase from the wagon and set it inside the door of the ranch house. After saying goodbye to Mrs. Rogers, he turned to Priscilla. "Guess I'll see you on Sunday, Miss Bedford," he said a little too formally, tipping his hat.

He looked a little apprehensive about it, too, Priscilla decided as she favored him with an equally formal smile. "Yes, you will," she informed him, her eyes dancing mischievously, telling him that she was far from finished with him. "Thank you so much for bringing me out here today," she added sweetly.

Dusty bit his tongue. He had almost said, "My pleasure, ma'am." That would have done it, all right. Instead he muttered, "You're welcome," and quickly made his escape, leaving Hazel staring after him, wondering.

"That Dusty's such a nice boy," she remarked, watching closely for Priscilla's reaction.

Priscilla was careful not to have one. "Is he?" she asked innocently and preceded Hazel into the house.

To her surprise, Priscilla found the inside of the Rogers' home as neat and cheerful as the outside was slovenly and depressing. Evidence of Hazel's talents with

218

a needle were everywhere, and it seemed that Hazel had created her own cozy little world, rising above the circumstances of her life in every way that she could.

Hazel explained that her husband, John, had business in town and that they would have the house all to themselves. After a pleasant supper, during which Priscilla renewed her acquaintance with Hazel's two older children who were in school and got to know the two younger ones, Hazel put the children to bed. She and Priscilla then unpacked Priscilla's suitcase and the two of them sat up most of the night, talking and sewing.

Hazel Rogers had grown up on a small tenant farm in Virginia, but after the war, her parents had decided to move west. Somehow they had ended up in Kansas, her father working on the railroad while her mother tried to keep body and soul together by taking in washing. Hazel helped by doing sewing. Her luck changed when the cattle came to Abilene, where they were living, for with the cattle came men and to serve the men came the prostitutes. For a long time, Hazel did not quite understand what those girls did for a living but whatever it was, they needed fancy clothes to do it in, and Hazel was the best dressmaker in Abilene. Soon she was the pet of all the madames, making dresses costing hundreds of dollars. Of course, the madames demanded kickbacks on the orders they sent her, but even still, Hazel did very well indeed.

Her success came too late to help her family, however. Both her parents died in quick succession, and not long afterward Abilene died, too. The prostitutes, the cowboys, and all who profited from them were driven out by the decent people of the town, and these undesirables created new cattle towns further west, leaving Hazel without her main clientele. Decent women would not use her any more, and, although the chippies begged her to move on with them to Ellsworth, she could not bear to go, orphaned as she was. It struck her too much like camp following. So she married a man who promised her a ranch, a home of her own, a life of ease and luxury. Hazel had never been pretty, had always been shy, and now she was alone. John Rogers was the first man who had ever paid any polite attention to her, and she was easily wooed. She had often wondered why he had bothered with her. Perhaps it was the fact that she had her own business, and he thought she would have some money saved. He had been right about that, and he had used the money to buy the ranch. He had already had it picked out. A speculator had bought it from a widow and was holding it until he got the right price.

They had set up housekeeping with enthusiasm, John promising her that within a matter of months they would be rich beyond their wildest dreams. Even to Hazel's unschooled mind that seemed a bit premature. She knew enough about cattle to know it was a year-to-year business requiring hard work and patience—some years being good, others not so good—but John was so certain, almost as if he expected to find a gold mine on the place. Of course, he did not, and the years went by, almost nine of them now, and she had four children and a husband who drank too much sometimes and never tended to his business, a business that would have made him a wealthy man. Hazel knew he was bitter, although she did not know why, and John was not a man to share his secrets with anyone, least of all his wife. Now he carried his arm in a sling from having been shot in the saloon. He had taken to gambling, too, something he was even worse at than ranching, and he had almost gotten himself killed because of it. Hazel Rogers shook her head when she thought of it, but she did not think of it often. She had her children to think of and her home. As long as there was food on the table and clothes on their backs, she would make the best of things. That was her way.

Not having seen the latest styles in quite a while, Hazel was impressed by Priscilla's clothing. They laughed long over Priscilla's inability to climb into a wagon or even walk correctly in two of the dresses, but Hazel decided she could at least make them usable again. Hazel was as different from Stella Wilson as night from day, but Priscilla took to her as she had taken to Stella, respecting the inner strength and quiet dignity she possessed, and the weekend passed all too quickly for them both.

Hazel and Priscilla had skipped church on Sunday morning so that Hazel could finish Priscilla's clothes. Hazel had teased her mercilessly about how the men had spent Saturday night gambling over who would have the honor of driving her home to the Steele ranch, but Priscilla had retorted that by now she was used to having men gamble over her favors. It was practically becoming a regional pastime.

Early on Sunday afternoon, they heard a wagon pull into the ranch yard. Priscilla had paid little attention until Hazel, glancing out the window, had exclaimed, "It's Dusty!"

The sound of his name, announcing his presence so unexpectedly, caused her heart a small lurch which she tried to ignore as she hurried to the window to see for herself. "What's he doing here?" she asked of no one in particular when she had verified that it was indeed he. "He knew someone from here was supposed to take me home." Or did he? She had not told him, assuming that Stella would have, and he had said that he would see her on Sunday, but she had thought . . . surely, someone at the Steele ranch should have seen him hitching up the wagon and stopped him.

Someone had tried to. Stella and George had been sitting on the porch when Dusty had driven the wagon out of the barn. George had called for him to stop and warned him that he was making an unnecessary trip, but Dusty had stubbornly insisted that he was not. "I told her I'd pick her up on Sunday," he had said, stretching the truth a bit, and when George would have argued, Stella had stopped him. "Maybe there's been a change in plans," she had said to George, warning him with her eyes not to interfere, and they had both watched him drive away, his back stiff, his face set mulishly.

Dusty had cussed himself the entire way out to the Rogers' place. He had known perfectly well that he was not to return for Priscilla, but something had compelled him to, anyway. Maybe it was the way he had dreamed about her the last two nights, or maybe it was the way he couldn't quite forget how she felt pressed against him, or maybe it was because the thought of her being alone with another man for that long ride filled him with unreasoning rage. Not that he thought anything would happen to her. Nobody would dare lay a finger on her. Nobody but him, he admitted reluctantly, but that was different. Yes, it was different, somehow, although he wasn't quite sure how. And there was always the possibility, however unlikely, that she might not mind another man kissing her—might even like it, might even encourage it. It was when he got to that part of his imaginings that the unreasoning rage took over, and he decided that he would go after her himself.

Hazel stepped out to greet him. "You're in a heap of trouble, Dusty," she told him smilingly.

"How's that, ma'am?" he asked, smiling guilelessly back, as he hopped down from his seat.

"One of my boys was supposed to take Priscilla back. I'm afraid you just might have a fight on your hands if you try to cheat him out of his chance," she warned.

Dusty looked sincerely puzzled as he lifted his hat to scratch his head and threw an inquiring look at Priscilla who had followed Hazel outside. "Didn't I say I'd be back to pick you up?" he asked innocently.

Priscilla was not fooled by his innocent act. She had seen it too often now, and she knew that she should be very flattered that he had come for her. Not bothering to conceal her smug little smile of triumph, she shook her head.

Dusty achieved a look of comic exasperation. "Well, I'll be. I could've sworn I was supposed to come back," he lied shamelessly and shrugged. "Guess I'd better go make peace talk with the boys. Wouldn't want to get shot in the back some dark night," he added with a mischievous wink at Hazel as he turned and made his way to the bunkhouse.

Priscilla sighed as she watched him walk across the yard with that curiously rolling cowboy gait that came partly from spending most of his life astride a horse and partly from trying to keep his balance on his two-inch boot heels. "That man," she murmured unconsciously while reluctantly admiring the breadth of his shoulders and the leanness of his hips.

Hazel's quick eyes and ears had immediately caught Priscilla's unconscious reaction to Dusty, and her equally quick mind had put that reaction together with Dusty's unscheduled appearance here today. Like Stella and most married women, she was an incurable matchmaker, and she was certain that she could smell a budding romance. "You all packed up?" she asked Priscilla as she turned back into the house.

"Almost," Priscilla responded absently, her attention still fixed on Dusty's retreating figure. He had reached the bunkhouse, in front of which were clustered the Rogers' cowhands, and from their stance, they were not at all pleased to see Dusty. She watched, fascinated, as he thumbed back his hat, grinned engagingly, and began to address the assembled men. There was a bit of arguing, but Dusty's grin never wavered, and although she could not hear a word that was being spoken, she knew exactly what was happening: Dusty was charming those *men* into forgiving him for his usurpation. Gradually, she saw each of them grudgingly relent until only one—probably the one who actually was to drive her home, she guessed— continued to rant belligerently. At last, Dusty took the offended man aside and put his arm around the stiff shoulders. Dusty spoke long—and persuasively, it appeared—for the man's stiffness gradually left him and soon he and Dusty were shaking hands, as if sealing a bargain. What had he done now? Priscilla wondered in increasing exasperation. Finally, she turned on her heel and went inside to finish getting her things together.

A few minutes later, Dusty appeared at the ranchhouse door and announced that he had come to terms with Hazel's men and was no longer in mortal danger. "I'm glad to hear that," Hazel laughed. "I know you'll want to get started right away, so you can take your time getting back. No use rushing on such a pretty day," she added slyly.

Priscilla knew that in not inviting Dusty to stay to supper with them, Hazel was breaking one of the cardinal rules of western hospitality which decreed that all visitors, invited or not, must be fed and even housed if necessary. She also knew that they had no reason to start back immediately. After supper would be plenty of time, but she saw the matchmaking gleam in Hazel's eye and knew any protest would be useless. Besides, she didn't really want to make one. A long, leisurely drive back suited her perfectly, and if they stopped along the way, well, so much the better, she thought with a silent giggle.

After saying goodbye to Hazel and thanking her profusely for her help, Priscilla allowed Dusty to help her into the wagon, reminding him that now he would never have to lift her as he had before. As the wagon clattered out of the yard and away from the ranch, Priscilla turned around once to wave a last farewell to Hazel and her children and then turned back, folding her hands primly in her lap and settling in with a sigh. She had plenty of things to say to him, but she decided to let him make the first move, or rather, she decided to see if he would make the first move.

Dusty risked a glance at Priscilla. It was warmer today and she wasn't wearing that duster, just a sort of jacket that matched her skirt. He couldn't help but notice by the way she moved under the jacket that she wasn't wearing a corset, either. Made a man's imagination run wild, it did. He wondered if she was mad because he had come after her. No reason she should be, unless she wanted someone else . . . He fought down the rage that tried to bubble up inside him. No use being a damn fool. She couldn't possibly prefer the company of that dried up old prune, he decided, considering the cowboy who'd been supposed to take Priscilla home. Or could she? He shifted uncomfortably at the thought. She certainly hadn't done anything today to show she preferred his company to *anyone's*. In fact, she was just sitting there like a stone. Maybe she *was* mad at him. She had every right to be, he conceded, but she wasn't acting mad exactly. She usually talked a lot when she got mad. Well, there was one way to find out. He made a tentative effort to break her reserve. "You have a nice visit?" he asked with mild interest.

Priscilla looked up. It wasn't much of an opener, but she decided it was good enough. "Very nice, thank you. Hazel is quite a seamstress. You should see what she's done with the inside of that house," she began, carefully working the conversation around to where she wanted it to be, namely a place where she could casually mention her ability to purchase a ranch. "You were right about the rest of the ranch, though. It's a real rawhide outfit." Dusty raised his eyebrows at that but made no comment, so Priscilla kept on talking. "Is it really as easy as you said to be a successful rancher?" she asked naïvely.

Dusty grinned, a little startled by her curiosity and amused that a woman like her would be interested in a subject like ranching. "There's more to it than that, of course," he allowed, and, darting a quick look in her direction, decided to give in to temptation. It was a lot safer than doing what he really wanted to do. "But with a few good hands, even *you* could make money ranchin'," he added slyly.

Priscilla stiffened under his disparaging remark, forgetting her intentions for a moment. Did he think that she would stand for his insults now that they were . . . well, he had another thing coming. "Do you have a low opinion of all women, or is it just me, Mr. Rhoades?" she inquired indignantly.

So, we're back to "Mr. Rhoades" again, are we? he thought, vastly pleased that he had gotten a rise out of her. He loved to see the sparkle in her eyes when she was good and mad. "I ain't got a low opinion of you, Miss Bedford," he complained, feigning offense.

"You assume I know nothing about ranching. Well, I'll have you know that I know quite a bit about it," she informed him.

Those reddish eyebrows lifted again, disappearing under that unruly shock of hair that hung down on his forehead. "You do, huh?" he asked with a little too much amazement. "You done a lot of ranchin' in Philadelphia?"

"Of course not!" she responded, unaware that she was playing right into his hands. "But I've read books on the subject."

"Books!" He almost whooped and pretended to be vastly impressed. "For example?"

"Well, for one, *The Beef Bonanza or How To Get Rich on the Plains* by James Brisbin," she said importantly.

Dusty gave a disgusted snort. "I'll tell you how to get rich: write a book tellin' a lot of tenderfeet how to get rich. That'll do it. You can't learn everything from books, teacher," he chided.

His sarcasm had Priscilla really angry now, and his condescending attitude was insufferable. She had been certain that he would be impressed when she mentioned Brisbin's book. Simply everyone back east had read it and thought it was wonderful. "It certainly wouldn't hurt you to read a book now and then," she said acidly.

So that's what she thought of him, was it? That he was an ignorant, illiterate cowboy. The knowledge wounded far more than his pride. "You think I never read a book?" he asked, even more acidly.

Priscilla gasped in astonishment. She had only meant to . . . well, she *had* meant to insult him, but she had obviously done much more than that. He actually looked hurt. It had been a very tactless remark, but she had had no idea he would be so sensitive on the subject. "I didn't say that . . ." she faltered.

In exasperation, he was pulling the team to a halt, hardly aware of what he was doing, only conscious of a need to give her his undivided attention. "Or maybe you think I can't read, is that it?" he demanded, turning to her, truly angry now.

"Of course not!" she cried in frustration. "Why are you trying to force me to insult you?" she begged.

"I don't notice you needed no forcin'. You just sorta jumped in voluntary," he pointed out bitterly.

Priscilla stared with apprehension at those eyes, narrowed down until only a spark of blue fire shown from each, and that handsome face, twisted now into a mask of rage. "Why did we stop?" she asked quite meekly.

Dusty felt a small sense of satisfaction as he read the anxiety on her face. "So I could have both hands free to strangle you, Miss Bedford," he gritted rashly.

Priscilla gasped again, her hand automatically flying to her throat. Not that she was really afraid, at least, not exactly. It was just that he looked so wild and she suddenly realized that she had been terribly wrong to think she could control him.

Dusty groaned aloud when he saw the very real fear his

228

impulsive remark produced. He wasn't really going to hurt her. It was just that she got him so crazy. "If only you weren't so damn . . ." he began and stopped when he realized that he had reached for her. Balling his fists, he groaned again and hastily jumped from the wagon, pausing only a second to tie the reins before he strode away, out of sight behind a boulder.

Priscilla sat for a while staring after him, trying to figure out what had gone wrong. Why was nothing ever simple where Dusty Rhoades was concerned? She had planned everything so carefully. She guessed her mistake had been in not telling Dusty what he was supposed to say and do. She smiled a little at that and at the knowledge that no one would ever control Dusty Rhoades. Not that she would want to—not really. It was just that a little cooperation would be so helpful! Why didn't he come back? she wondered, anxiously watching the rock behind which he had disappeared. After another long moment of consideration, she decided to go after him. It wouldn't hurt anything to be a little placating. He'd had a chance to cool off now, and if she could just get him to listen to reason, she would explain and . . . well, no use making more plans, she thought, climbing down from the wagon. First she had to find him.

That was not hard to do. He was standing on the other side of the rock, his back to her, and he was, of all things, throwing pebbles that he had apparently collected. Not tossing them gently but throwing them violently, as far as he could out into the empty field. It didn't look as if he had calmed down appreciably. "Mr. Rhoades," she called hesitantly. It sounded so stupid, even to her ears, but she had never yet called him by his first name and her tongue rebelled against framing it, especially when she really wanted to call him something far more endearing. But one did not call a man who had threatened one with murder "Darling."

Dusty wheeled around instantly at the sound of her voice. She *was* trying to provoke him to murder, he thought wildly, calling him "Mr. Rhoades," but his wrath cooled when he saw her standing there looking so timid, so uncertain. Why couldn't they get along? Why couldn't things be right between them?

He knew the answers all too well, unfortunately, and those answers only posed more problems. He sighed. "Why is it everytime I talk to you I end up yellin'?" he demanded, sending all his remaining pebbles flying in one bunch.

Priscilla had been wondering the same thing. Perhaps it was because he didn't want to talk about the important things. Perversely, she goaded him into doing just that. "That's not exactly how you 'end up'. Usually, you 'end up' by forcing yourself on me!" she accused, clenching her fists and planting them firmly on her hips.

Dusty gaped at her. "Forcing?" he demanded incredulously.

Priscilla lifted her chin in defiance. It wasn't strictly true, but true enough. "Yes," she insisted haughtily. "Forcing!"

Of all the lying little . . . She really believed it, too, he thought savagely, unconsciously noticing the enticing way her breasts rose against her shirt when she struck that arrogant pose. He had half a mind to . . . "Force! I'll show you force!" he promised, long legs closing the distance between them in two strides.

His arms closed around her in a grip that drove her breath from her lungs, and his mouth crushed down on hers in a punishing kiss that mashed her lips against her teeth until she would have cried out in pain had she been able to breathe. As suddenly as he had taken her, so suddenly did he release her, and she staggered backward, gulping in air, raising the back of her hand to her throbbing mouth.

Dusty stared at her, horrified at the naked terror in her eyes. He had not meant to hurt her. He had never meant to hurt her. Hadn't he decided to give her up so that he wouldn't hurt her again? Or had he? He couldn't remember just now. Not that it mattered. After this she'd hate him for sure.

Priscilla stared back at him, trembling from head to toe from his attack, yet strangely sensitive to the remorse she saw so clearly reflected in his eyes. One large brown hand reached slowly out to touch her cheek. She could not keep from flinching as a long finger grazed her face, but neither could she fail to notice the pain that flickered in those so-blue eyes when she did.

"Oh, Pris," he whispered sadly, "I never meant . . ." The hand that she had pressed to her mouth reached out to touch his lips, stopping his words, and he tenderly kissed her fingertips.

She had been wrong! She *could* control him! She knew it instinctively, with the inborn intuition that was hers as a woman. It was so easy, so natural. Why had she not discovered it before? With confidence in her new power, she moved her fingers from his lips, across his cheek, around his ear, and buried them in that thick, red-gold hair, using her other hand to remove that gorgeous white hat and send it sailing. If he cared, he did not let it show. Instead he stood as if mesmerized by some special secret he was reading in the depths of her chocolate eyes.

Priscilla tipped her face, offering him the lips that still tingled from his assault. Powerless to resist, he accepted her offer, lowering his mouth to hers with a care that bordered on reverence, but Priscilla was having none of that. Wrapping her arms around his neck, molding her lush curves against him, she broke his restraint, and the next moment they were on the ground, neither knowing or caring who had pulled whom down, heedless of the rocks and the dirt, each aware only of the other and of the overwhelming urgency that inflamed them.

There was no time for gentle caresses, and no need. In a frenzy of fumbling they came together, and he took her in one swift stroke that made her gasp and cling to him as one in danger of drowning. "Yes, oh, yes," she breathed as he began to move within her, beating out that sacred rhythm that climaxed oh, so wonderfully. She met each throbbing stroke with an ardency that had him calling her name over and over as he tried to bury himself, his whole self, in her dark, sweet depths, reaching and striving again and again, until nothing existed for either of them but that frantic quest. Priscilla's breath came in heaving sobs as she labored, desperately, for that ultimate unity—her hands, her legs, her mouth urging him on, helping him, demanding that he carry her with him, and then they were there. The explosion shook Priscilla from her chin to her toes, the vibrations pulsing through her in giant waves so that she cried out, almost in fear as they overwhelmed her again and again. From a great distance she heard Dusty cry out, too, and wondered hazily why it sounded almost like a protest.

It had been a protest. In that one moment when he had felt a satisfaction, a completeness he had never known before, he had railed at the injustice of it all. Now, when it was all over, he rolled away from her and lay staring unseeing at the sky, beside her but not touching, gulping air into his throbbing lungs and cursing heaven or fate or whoever was responsible for his misery. He'd had no right, no right at all, to take her once, much less twice. Oh, she had been willing enough, but who could blame her? That first time had been so good and she was innocent, and she probably thought that . . . oh, hell! She might not know how things like this turned out, but he did. He'd seen it often enough. A couple who couldn't keep their hands off each other, couldn't get enough, and then, by the time their first kid was born, they couldn't stand the sight of each other. Just because he and Priscilla were good together—or great, he admitted reluctantly—didn't change who and what they were or the fact that once the novelty of the sex wore off, they'd probably murder each other. Made a man want to put a gun to his head. He had been right. He should have walked away after the first time. He would not make the same mistake again.

Priscilla wondered if she would ever feel normal again. Had she felt this glow the first time? She could not remember. Not that it mattered. Nothing mattered now, except that they were together, and that they would stay together. Always. With a contented sigh she turned her head to study his profile. His breathing, like hers, was almost normal now. He looked so serious, almost grim in fact, and she smiled at the thought that he might be embarrassed again, might even feel a little guilty for taking advantage of her. That was actually funny when she considered how she had forced him to kiss her. If there was any guilt, it was hers. Maybe she would tease him about it, she thought, reaching over to touch his face, but his words stopped her hand in mid-air.

"This shouldn't have happened," he said, his voice flat. Hastily, he adjusted his clothes and rose to his feet. "Try to make yourself look halfway decent so we can get out of here," he added gruffly, not looking at her, and he strode away, making a small detour to retrieve his hat before moving out of sight around the rock.

Priscilla stared stupidly at his retreating back, hurt and humiliation washing over her in a sickening wave. Then, suddenly aware of her near-nudity, she quickly, with trembling hands, made herself decent again as he had said. Decent! Now there was a laugh, she thought as she noticed with dismay how he had torn her pantalettes in his hurry to remove them. She'd never be decent again. She'd let a man use her. No matter that she had given herself in love, no matter that she had been convinced that he must feel the same way. He did not. Irrelevantly, she remembered a Bible story she had once read about one of King David's sons who had loved his half-sister so much that he had raped her, but afterward—and she remembered this with startling clarity—he had hated, and the hate with which he hated her was greater than the love with which he loved her. That Dusty now despised her was evident. That she despised herself was even more true. She had behaved like . . . like a bitch in heat, rutting on the ground like an animal. The raw pain that knifed through her brought tears to her eyes, but she blinked them back furiously. She would not cry. He would not see her cry. Hastily, she brushed the dust off of her clothes and made what repairs she could to her disheveled hair, hoping that she did not look as ravaged as she felt. To her great satisfaction, her hands barely shook as she put in her hairpins. Taking a deep breath and wrapping the ragged shreds of her pride around her for protection, she started toward the wagon where Dusty now stood, still unable to face her.

At the sound of her returning footsteps, he stiffened, waiting for her approach. Painfully aware that she was standing just a few steps away, as stiff and erect—and as brave—as a soldier, and that he must now say words that would humiliate her, he turned to face her. It was worse than he had expected. Her face was set and expressionless, but her eyes! He would never forget the anguish that he saw there. Drawing on his deepest reserves of courage, not daring to meet her eyes again, he chose a spot some inches above her head to look at and repeated his cruel decision. "That shouldn't have happened."

"It didn't happen," Priscilla replied, her voice as brittle as broken glass. She was gratified to see the shock register on his face as he was forced to meet her eyes, eyes which she hoped betrayed nothing.

She was right. Dusty stared into eyes suddenly gone blank, two brown mirrors which told him nothing. "What did you say?" he asked in bewilderment.

"As far as I am concerned this never happened," she explained. "It was a mistake, I'm sure you'll agree, and one that is better forgotten. By both of us," Priscilla added with remarkable coolness, considering that inwardly she was quaking.

"Sure, whatever you say," he muttered, wondering how she, a mere woman, could be so calm when he felt that he should double over, so great was the pain he felt. Yes, she *was* first class. Hadn't he always known it?

"Fine," she said, and, scorning his offered hand, climbed up onto the wagon seat. Staring fixedly ahead, she nevertheless knew when he took his own seat and untied the reins, but the wagon did not move as she had expected. Instead he simply sat there a moment, just as he had before, apparently engrossed in lacing the reins through his fingers.

At last, and completely against his will, since to show concern deviated from his chosen plan, he asked gruffly once again, "Are you all right?"

"I'm fine," she gritted, furious that this small scrap of consideration touched her. Clenching her hands together until the knuckles turned white proved distraction enough to keep the tears from coming to her eyes. Would he never stop asking that question? Would she never stop lying? Would she ever, truly, be fine again?

Dusty nodded a silent reply and clucked the horses into motion. A heavy weight settled in somewhere close to his heart. She truly hated him now. She would never forgive him for his cruelty. Indeed, he could only forgive himself by remembering what he had saved her from. With some bitterness he considered his fate. Twice in his life he had loved. The first woman had been beneath his touch and that love had died as quickly as it had been born. This time—and he could not help but appreciate the irony—*he* was beneath *her* touch, but he knew his love would not die so easily, if it ever died at all.

Priscilla felt very fragile, as if she might fly into a million pieces if the wagon so much as jolted the wrong way, but somehow she managed to maintain her composure during the seemingly endless ride back to the schoolhouse. Mercifully, he took her straight there, so she did not have to face anyone. If Stella had even looked at her . . .

When at long last he halted the wagon in the schoolyard, she jumped down before he even had time to set the brake. Fumbling for her key, she quickly unlocked the door and shut herself safely inside her own room. To her horror, she heard him get down from the wagon and come all the way to the porch, but then she heard the thump as he set her suitcase on the stoop. After a long moment, during which her heart pounded with apprehension, he left, and soon she heard the wagon clattering away.

Sagging with relief, she staggered to her bed, at last succumbing to the tears she had held in check for so long. She had been a fool, an absolute, love-sick fool, and she had no idea how she would hold her head up or look him in the eye again. Would he gloat over his conquest? Would he brag of it? Somehow she doubted it, clinging to the memory of how he had inquired about her welfare, but then one could never tell what a man might do. If a man could so humiliate a woman whose only crime was loving him, he might do anything. Suddenly, she felt dirty, soiled, unclean, and with a haste bordering on frenzy, she drew water and heated it, and when it was as hot as she could stand, she poured it in the tub. Stripping off her clothes and leaving them in a heap to be washed separately, she immersed herself in the steaming water and ruthlessly scrubbed away every trace of Dusty Rhoades. If only, she thought as the salt tears splashed into the bath water, she could wash him out of her heart so easily.

Chapter Eight

Priscilla slept soundly that night and if she had been plagued by dreams, she could not remember them. Surprisingly, when she looked at herself in the mirror the next morning, she seemed unchanged. Except, she amended after a more careful examination, for a trace of hurt deep in her brown eyes, a hurt that she knew would remain there as long as she lived. Seduced and abandoned. The words had always seemed so comically melodramatic to her, as silly as the woman who would let herself be victimized. Now, of course, she knew how painfully serious that situation could be, how devastated a woman could feel when she had trusted and been betrayed, but she also knew the anger of that betrayal, and that anger was her salvation. She would never let anyone—least of all Dusty Rhoades—know how he had hurt her.

Once again she considered going home, running away to Philadelphia, but as before, she decided to stay. Her decision to leave the east had been a wise one and was no less wise because she had made a mistake. She had responsibilities here and she would fulfill them. When she met Dusty Rhoades, as she knew she must eventually and often, she would treat him like the cold stranger he had become, and if he chose to brag about his achievement, she could handle that, too. It would be his word against hers, and she felt at least adequate to treating any rumors with disdain. That settled in her mind, she prepared to meet her students for the first day of her second week of school. To her great relief, the children seemed to notice no difference in her and behaved just as they always had. Soon Priscilla's own self-consciousness faded, and the day passed without incident.

That evening when Priscilla appeared for supper, she found the Steele family in an uproar. George had brought the mail from town and included was a letter from the second Steele daughter, Abigail. Stella staunchly refused to open it until everyone was finished eating and the others were in near rebellion when Priscilla arrived. During dinner they explained to her the very romantic story of how sister Abigail had been carried off to northern Texas by a shockingly handsome rancher named Ed Deal.

"You see," Stella explained after all the younger girls had tried to tell the story but failed to make it comprehensible with their giggling and blushing, "Dusty went up the trail that year to Dodge." Priscilla felt her face grow slightly warm at the mention of his name but no one else seemed to notice her momentary discomfort, and she steeled herself against betraying any emotion. "I guess he was about twenty-one at the time. Daddy made him the trail boss and everything. Anyway, when he gets to Dodge, he meets up with this fella, Ed Deal. Now Ed had just brought in his own herd—he has a small ranch up near Henrietta. Ed's filthy rich, havin' just sold his herd, and he an' Dusty commence to paint the town. Now Dusty, he's thinkin' about how everybody in Rainbow's been teasin' him about Abigail and expectin' him to hitch up with her, so he starts droppin' a few choice remarks to Ed about her. Ed starts to get interested, so Dusty suggests they travel back to Texas together. By the time they get to Henrietta, Ed's so desperate to meet Abigail, he gets Dusty to take him home with him for a visit."

"Now the way Dusty tells it," interrupted George, with a gleam in his eye, "is that when he got to Henrietta and saw how ugly the girls were there, he was sure Ed would even be impressed by the Steele girls!" At this point the Steele girls all told George what they thought of his interruption and then Stella returned to the subject at hand.

"Well, Dusty comes ridin' in one day with Ed. Poor Ed, his tongue was almost hangin' out. I reckon he was in love with Abigail 'fore he even set eyes on her. She's a right pretty girl, too, and that didn't hurt none. Well, to make a long story short, a month later she went back to Henrietta with him. That was four years and two babies ago."

"I'm curious, Stella," Priscilla asked, surprising herself at her ability to speak of him. "Didn't anyone ever tease Dusty about *you?*"

"Not much, honey. You see, I was just eighteen when I married George. That was the summer Dusty went up the trail the first time and while he was gone, I met an' married George."

"When he came home," George added, "everyone teased us both about my having stolen Dusty's girl while he was gone. I think that was the first time he realized that people expected him to marry one of the Steele girls. So when Abigail reached eighteen he hit the trail again."

"Didn't you tell me he found a husband for your other sister, too?" asked Priscilla perversely. She could not seem to stop, like someone probing a sore tooth to see if it still hurt.

"That's right," said Ruth, eager to tell something. "Tim Kelly. He has a ranch over west of San Antonio. Daddy had sold him some stock and sent Dusty to close the deal, and Dusty brought Tim back for a visit."

"I suppose there are no pretty girls over west of San Antonio, either," guessed Priscilla, her natural sense of humor overriding her momentary lapse into self-pity.

"Of course not!" boomed Ben Steele. "We keep all the pretty ones right here. Somebody wants one, they have to come an' get her!" General laughter ended the story-telling, and, caught up in the gaiety, Priscilla found her spirits lifting.

After dinner, the family gathered in the parlor for the reading of Abigail's letter. Fortunately, Priscilla had heard Stella send Ben junior to fetch Dusty in to join them, so she was prepared when he came in looking remarkably the same as he always had, just as if he had never been so unspeakably cruel to her. She did notice, however, that when he nodded her a greeting, he did not quite meet her eyes. Perhaps, she thought with a small measure of satisfaction, he was experiencing some pangs of his own.

When everyone was seated and finally quiet, Stella opened the letter and read importantly all the ranch

242

news, the children's progress reports, and news of an expected addition to the Deal family in late summer. Near the end of the letter was a special note.

"To Dusty a message from his good friend, Mr. Ikard." Everyone laughed at this except Priscilla who did not understand the joke. "He says to tell you that a while back, two ranchers named Lee and Reynolds walked seven carloads of Herefords from the railroad to the LE ranch west of Tascosa. Now at least someone else believes in those things besides Mr. Ikard and Dusty." Everyone enjoyed the private joke immensely, and even Dusty was chuckling.

"I don't understand. What are Herefords?" asked Priscilla, oddly irritated at being left out.

Ben Steele hastened to explain. "They're a breed of cattle, my dear. A fine breed, lots of beef. Dusty and I saw them at the World's Fair in Philadelphia a while back. We met Ikard there. He and Dusty really took to those cows. Ikard finally brought some in, but they'll never catch on here."

"Why not?" Priscilla asked, genuinely curious.

"Too short legged," Ben said. "Not a lotta water in Texas an' a cow's gotta be able to walk miles and miles sometimes. Those Herefords'd never make it."

Dusty jumped in, anxious to defend his preference. "You gotta admit, Ben, they shore are pretty critters, though, with them curly white faces." He looked to Priscilla, and she saw with amazement that he was strangely intent on justifying his opinion to her. "I been workin' with longhorns all my life an' I ain't never seen one didn't have blood in its eye. But them Herefords, they're so gentle, they'll walk right up and lick your hand. One look at them big brown eyes an' you know you ain't gonna have no trouble." In the long moment of silence that followed, Priscilla found herself unable to look away from the blue intensity of his eyes. He seemed to be sending her a silent message, and inexplicably, she wanted desperately to understand it.

Stella broke the spell. "Dusty always was a sucker for big brown eyes," she said.

Priscilla, her face flaming, quickly turned the only pair of brown eyes in the room down to where Matthew was playing at her feet, so that she would not have to look at anyone. She did not see Dusty's expression, but she could imagine his embarrassment at the laughter from Stella's remark. She heard him mumble something and glanced up to see him leaving the room.

"Guess some folks can't take a joke," said Stella, looking knowingly at Priscilla. Priscilla could not quite meet that gaze, choosing instead to give Matthew her renewed attention, so she missed Stella's speculative frown.

Priscilla was wishing that she had had the courage to watch Dusty's reaction. Maybe she would ask Ruth about it later, she decided. Not that she really cared, of course. It was just that she needed to know in order to know how to react to him in the future. Yes, that was it, although why she should care was beyond her. It shouldn't take much advance planning to outfinesse a man like that. He was nothing but an ignorant cowboy, even if he had been to Philadelphia once. He might know a lot about cows and horses, but she had it all over him in every other area. How she could ever have thought she cared for him— how she could ever have thought he deserved her attention—was beyond her. When she thought of it like that, it seemed ridiculous that he had even managed to touch her emotions, he was so far beneath her touch. Hadn't Ben Steele warned her about getting involved with a cowboy? Yes, and he had told her not to waste herself. Well, she'd never waste herself again. That resolution made her suddenly restless, and she soon got up and left the group in the parlor still discussing Abigail's letter.

Priscilla wandered through the large ranchhouse until she came to Ben's office, and on impulse she went in and began to examine his library. Soon she was lost in a rediscovery of certain books that had once been her favorites. The more "old favorites" she discovered, the greater grew her sense of smug superiority, and Stella found her much later, actually humming as she thumbed through one dusty old tone.

"There you are!" Stella said. "I been wonderin' where you got off to."

"Stella, someone has been very careless with your father's books," Priscilla informed her with asperity. "Just look at how worn this one is, and they all seem to have dirty fingerprints and smudges on every page," she complained.

Stella glanced at the offending objects and smiled. "You sound just like Aunt Ellen," she mused. "I can hear her now: 'Dusty, you wash your hands before you start messin' with those books!'"

Priscilla felt something heavy drop into the pit of her stomach. "These are Dusty's fingerprints? In all these books?" she asked, her skepticism evident.

Stella shrugged almost apologetically. "I reckon. That one there"—she pointed at a work by Emerson—"he packed up the trail with him the last time. That's how it got so poorly." She shrugged again, looking around.

"He's prob'ly read every book here. He takes 'em when he goes places. That's how he gets 'em dirty. Don't always wash his hands; sticks 'em in saddle bags and bed rolls. He's always . . . What's the matter, Priscilla?"

Priscilla was stunned. She felt her new-found superiority draining away. "It's . . . it's hard to believe, that's all," she said faintly. No wonder he had been so insulted when she had suggested he read a book. Why, he had probably read more than she, or at least as many. With all these books behind him, he was as educated as any college man she knew. "The way he talks, you'd never guess," she added, defensively.

"Pshaw!" Stella exclaimed. "He can talk as good as you. I've heard him and George go at it, arguin' over some idea or another. In front of the boys, though, he talks like them. Doesn't want 'em to think he's puttin' on." Stella considered a moment. "Speakin' of puttin' on, he does just the opposite with you."

"What do you mean?" Priscilla asked, strangely reluctant to hear the answer.

"I mean he talks ignorant on purpose when you're around, more so than usual," Stella said.

Now that made absolutely no sense at all. "Why would he do that?" Priscilla demanded.

Stella started to answer and then stopped and looked archly at Priscilla. "That's somethin' you'll have to figure out yourself, honey," she replied and left Priscilla standing open-mouthed with a very dirty book in her hands.

Priscilla did try to figure it out, irritated that she wanted to and even more irritated that she could not. It made no sense at all. If Stella were right, and Priscilla had no reason to think she would make up a story like that, then Dusty had taken pains to appear ignorant and perhaps even rude and crude in her presence. Why he would do such a thing was baffling. Ever since she had become a woman, men had been taking great pains to impress her—bragging, boasting, preening, showing off, doing whatever they felt necessary to win her admiration—but Dusty Rhoades, for reasons incomprehensible, had done just the opposite, as if seeking her disapproval. Why? Perhaps he was simply not interested in her, Priscilla tried to suggest to herself but immediately dismissed such a notion. If he had not been interested, then he would not have done anything at all, needing only to ignore her to be successfully ignored in return. No, he had been interested, all right, Priscilla recalled bitterly as she remembered how he had kissed her, time after time, how he had tried to seduce her at the dance, and how he had, at last, made love to her. It was almost as if, unable to fight his own attraction for her, he had tried to repulse any attraction she might have for him. The supreme irony of it was that in spite of his efforts, she had actually fallen in love with him.

Priscilla considered this new idea carefully. Had she really fallen in love with him despite his faults or had it been because of them? How infuriating to think that was true! So many intelligent, attractive men had courted her back home. They had all been polite and well bred and had never offended her in any way. While they had been so predictable—and so boring—Dusty Rhoades had been tantalizingly aloof. Was that his secret, that he had been immune to her charms? Well, not quite immune, she had to admit, which brought her back to her original problem of why he had been so disagreeable, if he did indeed find her attractive.

Sighing with exasperation, Priscilla shook herself out of her reverie and, choosing some books which were obviously some dirty-handed someone's favorites, she made her way slowly through the growing twilight back to her room at the school. She tried to read, but her eyes kept wandering to the smudges on the edges of each page and then her mind would wander, too. At last she closed the book, blew out the lamp, and lay down in the darkness, wondering about herself. What was it that she really wanted out of life, the true reason she had come west? Reluctantly, she asked herself if it could have been the memory of those cattlemen at the Exposition that had brought her. She had made excuses, saying she wanted adventure, but when she remembered those men with their booming voices, their brown faces, their broad shoulders, their . . . aliveness, she wondered if she had not really come west hoping to find a man, a *real* man. It seemed incredible that she could have been drawn by such a primitive urge, and yet, when she had met a man—and Dusty Rhoades was every inch that—she had given in to that urge willingly, gladly. When she thought about it—his conduct to her aside—he really wasn't all that bad, either. He was attractive, certainly, and knew it, too, but did not seem conceited about it. He was, if Stella told the truth, intelligent and even educated in a rough sort of way. He had the trust of his employer, the admiration and respect of his community, and the friendship of his peers. Men followed his leadership and women doted on him. He was, in short, a man any woman would want, and indeed, it seemed that many women had and did want him. Priscilla was one of them, she admitted sadly, angry that she still felt that way in view of the way he had treated her but honest enough to admit it was true. As hard as she tried, she could not forget how he had been that first afternoon, how gentle, how sweet, how ardent. She had been so certain that he loved her then, just as she loved him, but why had he changed? Priscilla knew there was an explanation, the same one that would explain his uncharacteristic behavior to her all along, if only she could discover it, and when she did . . . Priscilla smiled in the darkness as she remembered Stella's remark about how Dusty could not resist big brown eyes. If that were true, she decided as those big brown eyes glinted dangerously, then Dusty Rhoades would be hers, but before that, for a little while at least, he would suffer, just a bit. Yes, a little revenge was in order and would make him so much more grateful when she finally accepted him. With growing certainty, she began to plan that small revenge, forgetting that she still had not solved the basic mystery of Dusty Rhoades. She planned many things long into the night, long after she should have been asleep, and that was what saved her.

Priscilla had only dozed for a few moments when she heard the sounds of a horse approaching the schoolhouse. For a wild instant she imagined it might be Dusty. Her thoughts had been about him for so long that she thought she might have conjured him. But no, she knew it could not be he. Who would be out so late? She sat up and looked out the window. A full moon lighted the night but she could distinguish only a shadowy figure on a horse. Then a voice called in the darkness.

"Teacher, I come fer ya!" It was Judd Slaughter! She felt a cold chill as she watched him climb unsteadily from his horse and mount the steps to the door. His slurred speech and faltering gate proved he had been drinking. Oddly, Priscilla felt no fear until he began to rattle the doorknob. The door was locked, of course, but suddenly Priscilla realized how flimsy was the barrier that protected her, and this time she had no roomful of children to inhibit Judd's baser instincts, and she was certain they were quite base. A shiver slithered down her spine as she heard him throw his weight against the door. She must get away. Already the doorframe was splintering against his onslaught. She could run through the front of the school and up to the ranch, but could she outrun him, barefoot, in the dark? The bell! Of course, she remembered frantically, she had told Dusty she would ring the bell if she were in trouble. She scrambled off the bed just as the door gave way with a resounding crash, and Judd staggered into the room. Taking advantage of his momentary disorientation, she tried to dart around him to reach the classroom door, but the room was too small. Without any effort, his bony hand snaked out, catching her by the shoulder. Wrenching and twisting out of his grasp, she felt his fingers lose their grip on her solid flesh, only to clutch desperately at the thin cotton of her nightdress. His other arm was around her now, crushing her to him, pinning her protesting arms between their bodies.

He was laughing now, an evil sound, and she gagged at the putrid odor of his breath in her face. Fighting back the gorge that rose in her throat, she thrashed wildly, kicking frantically but ineffectually with her bare feet and pushing madly with her imprisoned arms.

"A real wildcat, ain't ya? That's what I like. I'll tame ya down, all right. Where'd I put that quirt?" Still clutching her nightdress in one hand, he released her long enough to reach for the quirt he had dropped in the struggle. With one last burst of strength, Priscilla jerked away from him. The delicate fabric gave way under his ruthless grip as he tried to pull her back, exposing one full, milk-white breast to his lecherous gaze. It seemed to glow in the moonlight. "God Almighty," he swore thickly as he lunged toward her retreating figure. She dodged but was unable to elude those long arms which closed around her. Off balance, they both fell, his weight carrying her backward to the floor. She fought him in a frenzy of terror as his hands moved insolently over her body, feeling, clutching through the thinness of her gown. Oblivious to her blows, he muttered unintelligibly, and her writhing only seemed to arouse him more.

Priscilla threw her right arm over her head in a desperate effort to strike a telling blow, when her fist struck something solid. The wood pile! Almost instinctively her hand groped over the small stack of wood she kept handy for feeding into the stove and closed convulsively around a piece of the wood. She brought it down with all the strength she possessed, but the angle was poor, and she managed only a glancing blow against his ear. Howling a startled exclamation, he reared back just enough to give her purchase and using the stove wood for leverage, she pried herself free, scrambling to her feet. Roaring his outrage, Judd lunged, wrapping his arms around her calves. With the last ounce of her strength, she raised the club above her head with both hands and brought it down on the back of Judd's skull with all the might she possessed. He grunted when the blow fell and then went limp, his face smashing ignominiously to the floor between her feet.

A strangled sob escaped Priscilla's lips at what she had done, and the stove wood slipped from her suddenly nerveless fingers. Judd groaned and the muffled noise filled Priscilla with renewed panic. She turned, groping madly in the dark until she found the classroom door. Flinging it open, she ran tripping and stumbling in her mindless haste to where she knew the bell rope hung.

Dusty had lain awake for hours, his thoughts divided about equally between cattle and women, or rather a woman. He was remembering an old dream, a vision of the ranch he would one day own. It was something he tried not to think about too often lest he find his present situation unbearable, but Abigail's letter had brought it all back to him. He'd been planning for it, saving for it all his adult life, knowing that his destiny must be more than just living out his days as someone else's foreman. The ranch would be in West Texas, or maybe Montana or Wyoming or Colorado or . . . He'd never felt compelled to make a final decision, trusting that when the time came, he'd make a good choice. He'd start small and build, maybe get some backing from back east or even Europe. Lots of folks were doing that. He'd breed Herefords, too, maybe mix them with Longhorns to get the best of both breeds. Then he'd build a house, a stone house, with lots of rooms, a house fit for a queen, and *then* he'd marry. His wife would be beautiful and smart and, oh, hell, he thought bitterly, she'd be, if he had any power to make her so, just like Priscilla Bedford, or he'd never even be able to look at her. Why, oh why, he asked himself for the thousandth time, had he met her *now*? If only he'd met her five years from now, when he would have been a successful rancher, the kind of man she deserved.

Time and again he forced his thoughts back to plans for his ranch, and each time he ended up back at the same question, the question for which there was no answer. He was wrestling with it once again when he heard the school bell clanging in the distance. It took a moment for him to recognize the sound and another moment for the significance to register. Of course! Priscilla was in trouble! In an instant he was on his feet, pulling on his jeans, stomping into his boots, his hat somehow automatically on his head. Reaching for his rifle, he impulsively changed his mind and grabbed the gunbelt he seldom wore, strapping it hastily around his hips. The Colt .45 slipped easily from the holster, and as he checked the loads, the other men in the bunkhouse began to stir, the insistent bell finally disturbing their sleep.

"What's goin' on?" asked Curly groggily.

"Trouble at the school," Dusty called over his shoulder as he left the building. Snatching a halter from the outside wall, he ran to the barn and caught up Lady. Jumping on her bare back, he raced toward the still-ringing bell.

Priscilla clutched frantically at the rope, pulling and pulling with every fiber of her being, ringing and ringing and ringing and still no one came. Where could they all be? It had been hours and hours. Her arms ached with the effort and still no one came. Were they all dead? Had Judd murdered them all in their sleep so no one could help her, save her from him? Half-hysterical, she never heard the clatter of horses' hooves in the yard, the booted feet on the stairs, or even the pounding on the door.

"Priscilla! Open up! It's Dusty!"

His shout penetrated her single-minded concentration, and with a cry of relief she threw herself at the door, fumbling in the darkness for the latch. Then he was there, strong, solid, safe, his largeness filling the emptiness, and she threw her arms around him,

253

clutching at his strength, drawing it into her. His arms closed around her in a spasm of comfort and at last she felt safe, safe enough to cry out her terror, and so she did, sobbing into his chest as his hands patted and stroked and tamed the wildness of her hair.

"Easy now, honey, it's all right. Don't cry, sweet girl, I'm here now," he murmured, feeling almost weak with relief to find her all in one piece. His soothing, caressing tone calmed her and she forced back the sobs that wrenched her, fighting for control. Sensing her struggle, he urged her on. "Are you hurt? Are you all right? What happened?" he demanded, forcing her to think, to respond.

She shook her head against his damp shirt front. "I . . . I'm all right," she managed in a choked whisper.

Desperate now to know what had reduced her to such a state, he placed his hands gently but firmly on her shoulders and pushed her slightly away. "Then what . . ." he began but broke off as his eyes took in her appearance and his expression changed from concern to shock. She followed his gaze downward to where it rested on her bare breast jutting boldly out from between the two ragged edges of cloth. With an expression of dismay, she hastily, clumsily pushed the torn material back in place to cover herself.

"Good God, what happened?" he demanded.

"Judd Slaughter . . . drunk . . . broke in . . ." she stammered, renewed horror washing over her.

A scalding rage boiled up inside him and his fingers tightened convulsively on her shoulders, his fury hurting her more than Judd's brutality had. "Did he . . ."—his suddenly hoarse voice seemed to grope for words—"did he . . . *hurt* you? Did he *do* anything?"

Wincing from the pain of his grip, it took Priscilla a moment to realize that he wanted to know if she had been raped. "No, no," she assured him. "I fought him off. He . . ."

"That son of a bitch! I'll kill him! I'll bust his head wide open. I'll . . ." He stopped his ranting as he felt Priscilla go limp in his arms. The expression on her face was awful. "What is it?"

"I . . . I think I already killed him," she whispered.

He blinked in a moment of surprise and wondered that he felt oddly disappointed. "Where is he?" he asked in a voice demanding obedience. Still clutching the tear in her nightdress, she gestured with her free hand toward her room.

So suddenly did he release her that she staggered, grabbing the wall for support. She leaned against it, watching him move swiftly into the darkness. She flinched as he drew his gun, and then her knees gave way and she sank to the floor.

Dusty entered her room cautiously, his eyes searching the darkness for potential danger, and then he heard the soft moaning and picked out Judd's crumpled form lying on the floor. Warily, he approached the boy, and seeing he posed no threat, Dusty reached down and roughly checked him for weapons. Finding none, he gave the boy a vicious kick to turn him over on his back. Judd groaned.

For one horrible moment a red haze covered Dusty's eyes as he allowed his rage full rein, and when the haze lifted he saw his gun pointed at Slaughter's head, the hammer drawn back and his finger tight on the trigger. One small squeeze and the boy's bloody brains would scatter across the floor, and this . . . this thing, this piece of filth that had dared to touch Priscilla would no longer

255

exist. So vivid was this image that his finger actually tightened, but at the last instant some still-sane impulse stopped him. No, he could not do it. He could not foul the room where she slept, where she ate, where she lived. Nor could he, he discovered, foul his own hands with Slaughter's blood. How would she look at him if she knew that he had killed a man who lay defenseless? Knowing her as he did, he feared that she would judge him more harshly for such an act than she would judge Slaughter for his attack. She would never desire the ultimate revenge. Appalled at the way she had unmanned him without even being present, he took out his frustration by giving Judd another kick. "You bastard, I oughta blow your brains out!" he hissed.

Judd stared up, uncomprehending. "She busted my head," he muttered. "I never even . . . what'd she hit me with?" The liquor and the blows had dulled him so that he did not even recognize Dusty as a potential threat.

With a sigh of exasperation, Dusty jammed his gun back into its holster, struck a match, and lighted the lamp on the table. It was plain to see what had happened. The door jamb was splintered; one hinge hung loose. A piece of firewood lay on the floor; bits of bark and splinters clung to Judd's hair.

Dusty grabbed a fistful of Judd's shirt and lifted him half off the floor. "What'd you do to her?" Dusty demanded malevolently.

Finally startled out of his fog, Judd's homely face contorted in fear. "Nothin'! I swear to God! I just wanted to scare her, get her back for the beatin' she give me, but soon's I got through the door, she hit me with something." He groaned again, holding his head.

Dusty could hear riders approaching. By now the rest

of the boys would have caught up their horses and would be coming to see what the ruckus was about. He ruthlessly slammed Judd to the floor and started back to where Priscilla still huddled by the front door, but when he saw her, he realized she was only wearing her torn nightdress. Not wanting the boys to see her like that, he went back to her bed and pulled off the cover. Walking to her, he put it carefully around her shoulders and lifted her gently to her feet.

"Are you all right?" he asked.

Priscilla felt an hysterical urge to laugh. It seemed he was always asking her that question and she was always lying when she answered it. "I'm fine," she lied once again, but this time at least he did not believe her, and her voice sounded strange and distant to her own ears as well.

His hands still gripped her upper arms, and he squeezed her tenderly, comfortingly. She was, he realized, in shock, but he had no time to deal with that now. The boys were riding into the schoolyard. With a reassuring pat on her shoulder, he reluctantly left her and stepped out on the porch to meet them.

"You boys think I'd need help?" he asked with a slight swagger.

"Naw," said someone, "we figured you could handle it. We just come along to watch."

"What happened?" asked Curly, who showed the concern they all felt.

"Judd Slaughter got drunk, broke in on Miss Bedford," Dusty replied tersely. Angry murmurs rose from the group. "He never got a chance to do nothin', though. Near as I can figure it, Miss Bedford clubbed him a coupla times with a piece of firewood soon's he come in the door," he lied. Obviously, Judd had laid hands on her but no one else needed to know that. "He's layin' out there around back." Two men got down to retrieve him.

"I say we string him up," Aunt Sally suggested venomously, and the others voiced their snarling approval.

Dusty hesitated. That was what he wanted to do, too, but . . . He stepped inside to where Priscilla was still standing, staring wide-eyed, her face starkly white in the moonlight.

"They want to string him up," he told her gently.

"What does that mean?" she asked. He could tell by the tremble in her voice that the shock was starting to wear off.

"Hang him," he said baldly.

She swayed as the realization hit her, and he caught her just in time. That was why he had hesitated to agree with Aunt Sally. He knew now that she would never be able to cope with it. He leaned her back against the wall and stepped outside again. The boys were bringing Judd around, and he was swearing by everything holy and a lot that wasn't that he had never touched her and never meant to. They dropped him on the ground in front of the school and waited for Dusty's verdict.

"Look, boys, Miss Bedford's pretty shook up, an' her bein' eastern an' all, well, if we hung him, we might just have to bury her, too." He considered a moment. "He never really did her no harm. Shoot, he prob'ly couldn't have done her much damage even if he'd had the chance." The sexual innuendo went over Priscilla's head, but the men caught it, and they grinned. "Whaddya say we take him out and teach him a little lesson and then run him outta the country?"

This suggestion met with general approval and the men

258

loaded Judd onto his horse while Dusty instructed them where to take him, saying he'd be along as soon as Priscilla was taken care of.

"Stop by the house an' tell 'em what happened," he added. "Tell 'em to send one of the girls down to take care of Miss Bedford and to bring along a horse for her."

When they were gone, he went to Priscilla and guided her gently back to her room, seating her on the bed. She was shivering now, probably from the shock since it was not cold. He took another blanket and spread it over her lap. She stared with unseeing eyes. He wanted to hold her, to comfort her, to take away the terror and soothe that frightened look from her eyes, but he realized with a stab of pain that he had forfeited any right to do that when he had rejected her. With brutal honesty, he had to admit that in Priscilla's eyes, he must be no better than Judd Slaughter. True, he had used seduction instead of force, but his aim—to use her beautiful body for his pleasure—had been the same as Judd's and, like Judd would have, he had discarded her afterward. Yes, he had deliberately cut himself off from her, and knowing how she must feel about him, he stepped away, jamming his hands into his pockets.

Priscilla felt so strange, as if she were inside her body and yet not inside of it at all, but outside, looking on. For a while she had been numb, but that numbness was wearing off now, and she found that although the stark terror had passed, she still felt afraid, although she found Dusty's presence somehow comforting. She looked down at her hands. There were splinters in them. She stared a moment. "I never actually harmed anyone before," she said aloud without realizing it. Her voice was soft and almost childlike.

"You didn't hurt him much." It came out more gruffly than he had intended, but he was still upset.

"But to hit someone in anger, an act of violence . . ."

"You weren't angry, you were scared. You was just defendin' yourself. Don't take on about it," Dusty ordered. He was angry now, at Judd, at himself for not shooting Judd when he had had the chance, for letting her weakness prevent him from doing the right thing.

"They were going to kill him," she said incredulously, still trying to come to grips with a situation that every moment seemed more unreal.

"Yes, an' they should have," he told her bitterly, regretting that decision, also.

She looked at him, her eyes searching, wanting to understand, but certain that he was wrong. "But why couldn't you have just arrested him, put him in jail?" she asked.

He was getting impatient. "If you put him in jail, then you gotta have a trial. You wanna stand up in court and tell everybody what happened here tonight?" he asked brutally.

She looked away, shame scorching her face. Of course not. That would almost be worse than actually going through it, she thought. But hanging?

"Look, Miss Bedford, I don't know how they treat womenfolk back where you come from, but here we treat 'em pretty special, an' any man who raises his hand to a woman had better be ready to get his neck stretched." He was past discretion now. "I don't know what he planned to do here tonight or what you think he planned, but I know one thing. When he was done with you, he would've had to kill you." Priscilla gasped in horror. "That's right. So you'd never be able to tell who done it.

260

See, a man who harms a woman ain't safe anywhere in the West. Hell, folks in Wyoming'd hang him if they heard he hurt a woman in Texas. He knows that, or he should. So don't go cryin' cause you hurt him a little. You prob'ly saved your own life and for shore, you saved his."

Priscilla considered this. It was brutal justice, but it was justice, she decided, and then she heard his words echo back to her: "Here we treat 'em pretty special." Had Dusty's treatment of her been "special"? she wondered. In a way, as brutal as Judd had been, he had been less cruel than Dusty. Judd had not touched her heart. Physical bruises healed, but what about bruised hearts? Slowly, she raised her eyes, the question glowing in them, and found him watching her. He had no trouble reading the accusation there, and the agony it brought twisted his face. Priscilla watched in detached fascination for a moment until the clatter of horses in the yard broke the spell.

It was Ruth, riding one horse and leading another to take Priscilla back to the house. Obviously, she had simply thrown a dress over her nightdress, and when Dusty stepped outside, she helped Priscilla do the same, tactfully ignoring the jagged tear in Priscilla's gown. When they got to the house, Stella was waiting and led Priscilla gently inside while Ruth and Dusty took the horses back to the corral.

"You got there mighty quick," Ruth commented, eying him sharply. Dusty said nothing. "Guess that's 'cause you didn't take time to saddle up. Or put your shirt on." He suddenly realized he was in his undershirt. The front of it was still damp where Priscilla's tears had wet it. He touched it, remembering how she had clung to him

261

and for a moment he wondered if maybe . . .

"George'll go with you," Ruth interrupted his thoughts. "He wants to make sure everything's done proper or something."

"It'll be proper," Dusty said grimly, and he walked off to saddle a horse.

Stella took Priscilla into her and George's bedroom, closing off the questions and curious stares of the rest of the family, knowing Priscilla would not yet be ready to face them. She sat Priscilla on the bed and knelt in front of her. "Honey," she asked softly, taking Priscilla's icy hands in hers. "Did he hurt you? Are you hurt anywhere?"

Looking into Stella's sweet face, Priscilla suddenly realized the full horror of what had happened and what might have happened. "Oh, Stella, he put his hands on me, all over . . ." Her voice broke, the tears coming once again, great sobs racking her body as Stella cradled her and rocked her like a baby.

After a while the storm subsided, and Stella, hating herself for having to, asked, "Darlin', tell me now, did he rape you?"

A shudder of revulsion shook her. Rape. That word had been horrible enough when it represented only something dark and unknown. Now that she knew what intimacies existed between a man and a woman, the thought of enduring such things from someone like Judd Slaughter horrified her. "No, no, he would have, I guess, but I got away," she replied in a strangled voice.

"Thank God for that," Stella whispered. "You feel like a bath?" she asked in a more normal voice.

A bath? Priscilla asked herself, wondering if she had heard correctly and then remembered how she had felt

262

the other day, wanting to cleanse herself of all trace of one man, and realized that now she truly did feel filthy and defiled. "Yes, oh yes," she told Stella fervently, amazed once again at the way Stella always seemed to know just what she needed.

In a very short time Stella had drawn the bath and undressed Priscilla as if she were helpless. Ignoring Priscilla's feeble protests, Stella bathed her, too, with the loving hands of a mother soothing an ill-used child. When Priscilla was clean and dry and swaddled in one of Stella's own nightdresses, Stella tucked her into her and George's bed and held her until she was fast asleep. Only then did she murmur a prayer of thanksgiving and close her own eyes.

It was dawn when the men returned. Stella and her Mexican woman, Maria, had prepared a hearty breakfast for them, since Aunt Sally had gone along to administer justice. The men smiled grimly as they rode up, silently telling Stella everything had gone well. She did not ask what had happened. She trusted her men to do what was right.

As they dismounted, Dusty inquired, for all of them, "How's she doin'?"

"She's just fine," Stella replied. "She cried some, but not as much as you'd think. That girl has sand. Maybe we'll make a Texan out of her, yet."

Ben told all the men to sleep until dinner, which they were glad to do. Priscilla woke up late in the morning and when she had dressed and eaten, she sat down in the parlor with Stella.

"Might help if you talked about what happened," Stella suggested. "Thing like that might not seem so bad, talking it over with a friend in the light of day."

Priscilla agreed gratefully. Already it seemed like a bad dream, and she was eager to exorcise the demons that had plagued her all night.

"And then I found the bell rope," she finished. "I had mentioned to Dusty just a few days before that I'd ring the bell if I had trouble. It was a joke then. It seemed so long while I was ringing it, like hours and hours, before he finally came."

"Couldn't have been five minutes from the time I first heard it 'til it stopped. I reckon that's when Dusty showed up."

"Yes, and I never was so glad to see anyone in my entire . . . Oh, no!" Priscilla's hand went to her mouth and her face turned scarlet, remembering how she had thrown herself into his arms. It was hardly the way to behave with a man who had scorned her just a day earlier.

"What is it, honey?" Stella asked, alarmed.

Priscilla's blush deepened. How could she explain her embarrassment? "Oh, I . . . when he got there, I threw my arms around him and held on to him like, like, I don't know what! What must he think?" she asked, deciding the truth was explanation enough.

"He prob'ly thought you was glad to see him, which I expect you were," Stella assured her.

"How can I ever face him?" she murmured thoughtfully. It had been difficult enough before.

"Honey, what you do when you're upset don't count for much. I doubt he'll ever mention it," Stella said.

Perhaps not, Priscilla thought, but he would think about it, and that was almost as bad. What conclusion would he reach when he asked himself why she had clung to him? Would he realize that she loved him or would he, as Stella had suggested, simply decide that she had been overwrought? Perhaps she could influence his conclusion by the manner in which she treated him now, but then, which conclusion did she wish him to reach? Pride and common sense decreed that she conceal her love from him. No good could come of exposing herself until she understood him better, but then she need not be completely aloof, either. No, a lukewarm approach would be best. She would treat him as a friend, express her gratitude for his help, but not let him see the depths of her feelings. Her feelings, she had to admit, did run deep when she remembered how kind he had been that night, how gentle with her, how protective. Even when he had rebuked her, it had only been when she had tried to take some of the blame on herself, and unless she was very much mistaken, he had experienced some measure of guilt about his own treatment of her, too. Yes, a mildly friendly, polite acknowledgement of her gratitude would keep him guessing and salvage her pride at the same time. With that in mind, she watched for her opportunity.

It came a little later, when the men had arisen and eaten their dinner. They were saddling up, preparing for what work they had the energy for, and Dusty, being the first one mounted, took the opportunity to lope over to the house and inquire after Priscilla's welfare, a subject that he had discovered concerned him very deeply. To his surprise, Priscilla herself stepped out onto the porch to greet him. She looked, he thought with amazement, strangely untouched and pure, as if she had already risen above the ugliness of the night before and perhaps even forgotten what had passed between them, as well.

"You're lookin' some better this mornin'," he said, a little uncertain of whether he should make any reference to what had happened.

"I feel fine, thank you." And she looked it, too, although he could not know that the color in her cheeks was from vigorous pinching and not from health. "I wanted to thank you for coming to my rescue last night." That had been easy enough, she thought, clasping her hands tightly together. She didn't want to fidget in front of him, make him think she was nervous. She felt perfectly capable of controlling the conversation as long as he did not ask any pointed questions about her behavior. She would almost rather face Judd Slaughter again than try to explain herself. She took a deep breath and awaited his reply.

Dusty could not help but admire her courage. It could not be easy for her to talk about it. He shrugged. "It sure wasn't much of a rescue. In fact, Miss Bedford, I'd appreciate it if you'd do something for me," he said, leaning forward in his saddle.

"What's that?" Priscilla asked warily.

"Well, ma'am, twice now, I come rushin' down to the schoolhouse when I thought you needed help, an' both times you already took care of the situation yourself. I'd be much obliged if, next time, you'd send for me a little sooner. I'm sorry to say it, ma'am, but you got a way of makin' a man feel plumb useless!" He twisted his face into a comic mask of despair and was rewarded with a small smile.

Priscilla would not have believed that he had the ability to make her smile over what had happened, and yet he had. Not accidentally, either, she realized with small surprise. He had deliberately set out to cheer her. The knowledge warmed her. "You may rest assured, Mr. Rhoades, that I will endeavor to do just that," she told him. "I had no idea that I had hurt your masculine pride.

Please forgive me."

Dusty tipped his hat and bowed slightly, pleased to see her behaving more normally. Her tongue was not quite as sharp as usual, but her spirit was unbroken, he noticed with relief. He had just started to turn his horse to go, when he recalled something, a question that had been nagging at the back of his mind all night. He should, he knew, simply ride away and forget it, but something compelled him to rein his horse back again.

Priscilla had just released the breath she had been holding in a sigh of relief as she watched him turn to leave but caught her breath again as she saw him turn back as if he had just thought of something.

"Excuse me, ma'am," he began, trying to keep his voice light, "but I been wonderin' if, let's say, Aunt Sally or one of the other boys had been the first one down to the school last night, would you have hugged them the way you hugged me?"

Priscilla refused to blush. The fury that rose up in her lifted her chin, and her hands twisted together until the knuckles turned white. Just a moment ago she had been convinced that her instincts about him had been correct, that he really wasn't so bad after all, but now she knew she had been wrong. He *was* rude and cruel, trying to embarrass her and get her to admit she cared for him in spite of the horrible way he had used her. "Of course I would have," she replied with a haughty toss of her head. "And if it had been anyone else *but* you, I would have kissed him, too!" she added indignantly. With that, she turned on her heel and slammed back into the house, leaving Dusty sitting dumbfounded.

Well, what did he expect, he asked himself, a declaration of undying love? He already knew how she felt about him, and he'd given her no reason to change her mind. Yet, for that one moment last night, he had felt so close to her. He had been so sure that she . . . Well, he had been wrong, he told himself sternly. No use making a fool of himself over it. It didn't change anything anyway. They were still the same people they had been on Sunday when he had decided they would never suit. With a savage jerk on the reins, he turned his horse away from the porch and joined the other men.

Stella had both hands over her mouth when Priscilla returned, trying not to laugh out loud, but her shoulders were shaking. Priscilla was too angry to notice and began pacing furiously around the room.

When Stella recovered herself, she said, "Reckon that'll make him tuck in his tail and run."

"Of all the rude, conceited," Priscilla stammered. "How could he be so . . . so . . . ?" Words failed her.

"Maybe he just wanted to know did you like him better'n the other boys," Stella suggested.

Priscilla doubted this. "Then why didn't he just ask me instead of trying to embarrass me?" she demanded, knowing the answer already. He had wanted to trick her into revealing herself. She was certain of it.

Stella was thoughtful. "Honey, there ain't a man alive brave enough to ask a question like that, 'specially if the answer is important to him."

"How could it possibly be important to him?" she snapped, certain that the only reason it could be important was to feed his enormous conceit.

"Maybe 'cause he's so crazy in love with you," Stella suggested mildly.

Priscilla stopped in mid-stride, almost stumbling, and fell into a chair. She sat there for a moment, trying to make sense out of what Stella had said. "That's impossible," she finally decided.

"Is it?" asked Stella, unconcernedly picking up her sewing. "Think about it. He let you ride his horse, the one he's savin' special to breed, the one he never let no other grown-up person ride, just the children a time or two. An' did you notice he was the one took you out to the Rogers' place?"

Priscilla remembered how strange she had thought that, considering how strained their relationship was. "I thought you had ordered him to," she offered.

"Ordered?" Stella sniffed. "Nobody ever ordered Dusty Rhoades to do anything in his life. I asked him to get one of the boys to take you out, an' it ain't like every one of them boys wouldn't give a month's pay to be alone with you for five minutes. He just couldn't stand the thought of it, so he took you his own self. And what about him comin' back to pick you up?" Stella added. "We all tried to stop him, tell him he wasn't supposed to, but he wouldn't listen, insisted on goin' anyway."

Priscilla stared at her stupidly, recalling how Dusty had pretended to think he was supposed to return for her. Had he simply wanted another opportunity to seduce her? Had he planned it all along, right from the beginning? she wondered, a hot flush pouring over her. No, that couldn't have been it, she realized. The picnic had been Stella's idea, and he had been just as embarrassed as she had about it, and they had been leaving—at his suggestion—when she had fallen and then they had . . . And when he had come back for her, he had acted so strangely, almost deliberately taking offense at something she had said, leaving her sitting in the wagon so he wouldn't be tempted to murder her, or so

269

he had said. Had he really been afraid of doing something else? She had been the one to follow, to continue to provoke him, and in the final analysis, she had demanded that he kiss her. She had been so certain then that he loved her, but afterward he had turned so cold. She had not been able to figure it out, but perhaps Stella had a clue. "If he really . . . I mean, if what you said were true, why is he always so, well, the way he always is with me?" she asked.

"I been ponderin' on that myself," Stella said. "Ever since you come here, Dusty Rhoades's been walkin' around here like he's got an itch an' don't know where to scratch. Near as I can figure, there's a fly in the ointment somewheres."

Priscilla leaned forward eagerly. "What do you mean?"

Stella smiled a little at Priscilla's obvious concern. "Well, I'm positive he loves you, but there's somethin' holding him back, somethin' stuck in his craw, else he would've been on your doorstep with his hat in his hand long before this."

Priscilla had reached the same conclusion, of course. "What do you think it is?" She didn't realize that she was betraying herself to Stella.

Stella paused a moment to study Priscilla. "The way I figure it, it's one of two things. Either he don't think he's good enough for you—"

"I doubt that," Priscilla exclaimed, unable to imagine such a thing.

"Or else he thinks that *you* think he ain't good enough."

That was it, of course! She had been so horrid to him, insulting him. How deeply she had cut him with her remark about reading a book. She forgot all the things he had said and done to earn her barbs. Guilt flooded over her. Then she saw Stella's knowing look and realized what Stella was thinking. Instantly she recovered herself. Coolly, she said, "Stella, this is all so . . . so preposterous. I can't believe a word of it."

"You could test him, see if it's true," Stella offered.

"How?" Priscilla's eagerness betrayed her again, but this time she did not care.

"Let me ask you this, first. You interested in *en*couraging him or *dis*couraging him?"

Priscilla smiled mysteriously. "Let's just say I'm *interested*, shall we?"

Stella laughed. "All right, honey, you wanna know fer shore how a man feels about you, try to make him jealous."

What a perfect idea! Why had she not thought of it herself. "With whom?" she asked delightedly.

"That's a question, all right," Stella agreed, "but it could be anybody. If he's as far gone as I think, he'd be loco if you smiled at Aunt Sally. Keep your eyes open for an opportunity."

Priscilla vowed she would.

Chapter Nine

Priscilla insisted on holding school the next day, as usual. She wanted things to get back to normal. The door to her room had been mysteriously repaired and strengthened, and a bar had been added. Stella sent Dusty to town on an errand. By now, she knew, the story of Judd Slaughter's attack would be all over and she wanted to be sure the story was told in such a way that Priscilla's virtue would not be in question. That was Dusty's errand, and he handled it well. Eating his noon meal at the hotel dining room, he told the story to a group of interested businessmen. While buying a few supplies at the store, he told it to some wide-eyed ladies and a few loafers. Smoking on the sidewalk, he held forth for some out-of-work cowhands and a few drifters.

On his way to the Post Office, he encountered a man who called him by name. Dusty thought he looked familiar but could not place him. Dusty recognized the type though. He had seen that type in every cattle town from here to Dodge.

"You're the foreman at the Steele place, aren't you?" the stranger asked.

"That's right," Dusty replied cautiously.

"I heard what happened out there. I hope Miss Bedford was not injured." The stranger seemed genuinely concerned.

"No, he never even got near her," said Dusty suspiciously. "You a friend of hers?"

The man smiled an embarrassed smile. "An acquaintance, you might say. She and I arrived here on the same stage. Jason Vance is my name." He put out his hand and Dusty shook it. It was surprisingly soft.

Of course, he remembered Vance now. He had seen him at the stage. But the name was familiar, too. Then he remembered that Jason Vance was the gambler who worked at the Yellow Rose. They studied each other carefully for a moment. Both men knew that Jason Vance had no right to be inquiring about a decent woman. It was practically an insult for him to even know her. Men like Vance had been horsewhipped for less. Dusty stiffened a little.

Vance hastened to explain. "I hope you won't mention that I asked about her. It's just that"—Vance gestured helplessly—"a man in my line of work rarely meets a lady like Miss Bedford. I'm afraid my admiration for her colored my good judgment. I meant no slander to her."

Dusty saw he was sincere and could not really blame the man. Priscilla did have a way of exciting admiration, as Dusty knew to his sorrow. He had been discreet, too, approaching when Dusty was alone. "Don't worry, Vance. I won't say nothin'," he assured the gambler.

"Say, can I buy you a drink?" Vance offered, and he

was shocked by the strange look that passed over the cowboy's face. It was not exactly fear. Alarm? Not that either—more like a sudden wariness, like an animal sensing danger.

Dusty studied Vance's face and decided that the gambler did not know. But then why should he? There had been gossip about Vance's living in the saloon with Rita, but even if it were true, that did not mean that she would have told him anything. And there were probably a lot of other cowboys who never went to the saloon, although he could not name one just then. He hesitated before replying. It was a grave insult to refuse a man's offer of a drink, and Dusty knew the story of how Vance had shot Rogers. Dusty wasn't wearing his gunbelt, in deference to the sheriff who frowned on such things within the city limits, and Vance didn't appear to be wearing a gun either, although that could be a false impression. Of course, those details wouldn't prevent a showdown if Vance took offense. They would merely delay it, and Dusty wasn't a man to flee from trouble, if he couldn't avoid it. Having nothing personal against Vance, however, he felt inclined to avoid it this time, and when he considered the source of his dilemma, he decided he was damned if he'd have a shoot out because of that woman.

Remembering something he'd read once about discretion being the better part of valor, he flashed Vance a conciliatory grin. "That's mighty friendly of you, Vance," he said cheerfully. "Hope you won't take this personal, 'cause I got nothin' against you, but let's just say it's a mite early in the day for me. Another time, maybe."

Vance lifted his eyebrows in surprise. Far from being

offended, he was amused, having interpreted Dusty's strange reaction as embarrassment and believing that he had guessed the problem. Vance had met many men who could not hold their liquor but few with the courage to stay out of saloons, and he had to admire Rhoades for that. "Of course, I understand," Vance assured him, remembering how magnanimous Rhoades had been in telling him about Miss Bedford. "I'm not a drinking man, myself."

When they parted, Dusty stood and watched Vance walk across the wide street toward the saloon, and he thought he caught a flicker of movement at an upstairs window. He could almost picture those hate-filled green eyes boring into him, and a chill passed over him. Calling himself a fool, he shrugged off the feeling and went on about his business, while upstairs, over the saloon, a shadowy figure moved to another window to better observe his disappearing figure.

"Vance!" Rita called sharply when she heard his footsteps in the hall. Vance came to her door.

"Yes?"

"What were you talking to *him* about?" she demanded.

"Him, who?" asked Vance, knowing very well whom she meant, but trying to put some things together in his head.

"Don't play your gambler's games with me. You know who—Rhoades. What were you talking to him about?" Her eyes were flashing now, glittering like green glass. With anger? No, it was hatred.

"There was some trouble over at the Steele place yesterday. A boy attacked the schoolteacher. I was inquiring after Miss Bedford's welfare," he explained blandly.

276

"Miss Bedford's welfare," Rita mocked. "Well, aren't you the gallant one? What happened?"

Vance told her the story as he had heard it on the street, and then what Rhoades had told him. Rita had heard the story of the events of the dance and the arrival of the desk. She had begun to suspect Dusty's interest in Priscilla, and now he had been the first to rush to her rescue. It gave her joy, but there was pain in it, too. Here, at last, was a way to get to him, but the thought that he might love another woman . . . She turned her face away from Vance who was watching her curiously, trying to determine her emotions.

"Did he say anything else?" she asked with forced indifference.

Vance considered, realizing it was important. He had offered Rhoades a drink as a conciliatory gesture and in doing so had struck a nerve. What would it strike with Rita? "I offered to buy him a drink."

Rita's head turned sharply around. "What did he say?" she asked eagerly.

"He said it was too early in the day for him."

She laughed a long time. It was an evil laugh, a satisfied laugh. Then she turned to Vance. "He's a coward. Oh, he looks strong, so tall and handsome, but he's afraid. He's afraid all right. Afraid of a woman." She laughed again, a laugh that sent chills down Jason Vance's spine.

He tried to make sense of it. Rita Jordan hated Dusty Rhoades. For some reason, he would not come into her saloon. For a cowboy to deny himself use of the only saloon for miles around was unthinkable, and to risk insulting a known gunman by refusing to drink with him was foolishness, but Rhoades had done both, so he must have good reason. Watching her now, he was consumed with curiosity about what could make a woman hate like this. He had no answers, but he was sure of one thing: Rita Jordan would be a bad enemy to have.

Rita saw the puzzled expression on his face. He would be curious now, prying. He was smart, too. He would figure things out. Of course, he could never know the whole story but he could figure out enough of it to be dangerous. Jason Vance was a man, and men liked Dusty Rhoades. Vance might take up for him, even feel it was his duty to warn Rhoades. That would never do. She would give Jason Vance something else to think about. Something that would put him on her side permanently. Yes, that was it. It was time for it, anyway.

That night when Jason Vance rolled over on his side to go to sleep, he was grinning. Now he knew why old Sam Jordan had died with a smile on his face. Vance had known many women, women for whom sex had been a profession, but never had he known a woman like Rita Jordan. He considered himself a man for whom life held few surprises, but she had surprised him and amazed him. Now, he thought, he would not mind if the business that had brought him to Rainbow took a long time to complete. Rita Jordan had a way of making time pass pleasantly.

Thinking back, he wondered if he should feel somehow offended or insulted by Rita's attention. That evening, after Will and Vance had closed the saloon, Will had informed him that Rita wanted to see him in her room. Her wanting to see him was not unusual since she spoke to him almost every night after closing about something or other, but she usually did it in the saloon with Will present. Tonight she had retired earlier than usual, a fact Vance had noticed but dismissed as unimportant. Now she wanted him to come to her room. Remembering what had occurred the first and only other time he had been in there, Vance took a moment to brace himself before knocking on her door. He was glad that he had.

"Come in," Rita's husky voice had called.

Vance opened the door and entered the room cautiously, allowing himself a full minute before trusting himself to close the door, so astounded was he by what he saw. Rita sat in her bed, propped up on several pillows, wearing a green ribbon in her hair and, quite obviously, nothing else. She was smiling in that way she had that made her look vulnerable and was absently curling a lock of her long, raven hair around one finger. The hair cascaded down her pearl-white shoulders, just touching the sheet that she had pulled up barely far enough to cover her breasts. Not that the sheet concealed very much. It was so sheer that he could actually see the dark triangle between her legs, legs that were long and slender and slightly parted under the cover, as if in invitation.

Most men would have found the situation self-explanatory and would not have hesitated for a moment taking what Rita so obviously offered, but Vance was not like most men. He stood patiently, his carefully schooled expression void of emotion, waiting for a sign from her.

Suddenly, Rita laughed her smoky laugh. "Well, don't stand there like you don't know what you're supposed to do," she ordered.

At last, Vance allowed himself a small smile. It was not a smile of satisfaction. That would come later, if he were indeed satisfied. Nor was it a smirk or a leer. It was simple amusement at the way she had so arrogantly changed their relationship, without even so much as hinting at her intentions until this very moment.

Vance walked slowly over to a straight-backed chair which sat near the bed and removed his coat, hanging it carefully on the chair back. "Am I correct," he asked, as he removed his shirt and laid it likewise on the chair, "in hoping that this will now become one of my regular duties?"

Rita considered, twirling her hair thoughtfully as she watched him remove his shoes, socks, and pants. "I reckon that depends on how well you do the job, Vance," she replied with a guileless smile.

Clad only in his drawers, Vance made his way to her bed, watching her all the time, cautiously, as the prey watches the predator. He reached over and took hold of the sheet where it lay across her breasts and drew it back slowly, deliberately, studiously examining each inch of flesh as he uncovered it. Rita lay completely still under his observation, her lazy smile changing to a questioning look.

"You're a very beautiful woman, Mrs. Jordan," Vance concluded coolly, the only evidence of his own arousal a vein that beat rhythmically in his temple.

Rita smiled again, a slow, feline grin, as she moved toward him. Her fingers deftly disposed of the buttons at his waist and she slipped her silken hands inside to peel the cotton drawers down over his hips. A sharp intake of breath was his only response to her touch, and he stood stoically as she observed his swollen manhood.

"And you, Mr. Vance," she concluded, "are a very beautiful man."

Vance groaned as she lowered her face and began to caress the object of her admiration, but he suffered her tribute, as pleasant as it was, for only a few moments before pushing her away. She was, he realized, a woman

280

who knew many ways to pleasure a man, but as tempting as it was to discover them, he felt an overwhelming need to control, to dominate, and yes, to subdue her.

His hands cupping the satin of her shoulders, he bore her backward onto the bed. Looming over her for a long moment, he watched her expression change from mild surprise to curiosity to excitement, unaware that her excitement only mirrored what she saw in his own eyes.

Rita stared up at Vance's expressionless face, intrigued that even now he managed to control it. Only his eyes, smoky with desire, gave away his arousal, and for the first time in many years she felt a small stirring in her own body, a tightening in her loins that spread a warmth over her whole body. It was odd, she thought, that a woman could live without a man for years and never miss it, and yet . . .

Of their own accord, her hands came up, fingers trailing lightly across the smooth wall of his chest, teasing his hardening nipples for a moment before moving up, over his shoulders and around his neck. She tugged gently, but he held himself stiff, aloof, making no move or gesture. Irritated, Rita shifted restlessly, seductively. He would not refuse her, could not. No man could, she reasoned. The tightness between her legs became an ache, a moist emptiness. Her breath came quickly now as the longing washed over her. Her arms tightened urgently around his neck, her fingers twining into his thick, dark hair. "Vance," she breathed his name, imploring him for they both knew what.

Still he did not move, allowing himself one last look at her, a small smile of triumph tugging at his lips, and then he lowered himself, almost reluctantly, onto her willing body. Her eager mouth found his, but he gave her no satisfaction. Pausing only briefly at her parted lips, he moved on, brushing feather-light kisses over her face, her eyelids, her ears, and then the hollow below her ear, and down the sensitive cord of her neck to the now-throbbing pulse at the base of her throat. His hands had found the soft fullness of her breasts and now his lips sought out their hardened tips, sucking, tasting, nipping, until she cried out with pleasure, arching herself toward him. His hand splayed across her abdomen and then tangled in the silken hair below. Lower still he found her wet and ready, too ready to long withstand his searching fingers.

"Vance!" Her cry was halfway between entreaty and command, and at last Vance moved to answer her. He entered her carefully, savoring his possession, and when he moved, it was with deliberate slowness. He stroked her leisurely, almost indolently, in defiance of her restless hands that urged him on.

Rita hated him then. She had not intended, or even expected, to feel anything. Her purpose had been to gain control over Vance in the most basic way she knew. Never did she dream that he might have the same objective. Whether he had or not was irrelevant now, she realized, as she felt the ecstasy building, building, growing larger and larger with each plunge. She clung to him now with legs and arms and hands and lips—touching, feeling, tasting every part of him she could reach—and still he held her back, until, in desperation, she cried out his name again, begging for her release. Like a benevolent despot, he granted her supplication. Slipping his hand between their bodies, he found the nub of her desire and fondled it as he increased his pace.

Rita met him stroke for stroke, faster and faster, her

breath coming now in tiny moans. She wanted only for it to go on and on and only for it to end. Not another minute. She could not stand another second. She would scream, and scream she did as the world exploded, and her body shuddered again and again with the shock waves.

Vance smothered her outcry with his mouth and lay still for a long time until the last of her spasms had died away. He had intended to withdraw, regain control, and take her again, but her limp body came suddenly to life as he began to move away. She was much stronger than he would have imagined and she wrapped her legs around him. He could still have broken loose, but now her hands were on his buttocks, doing things that made him forget his intentions. She was moving too, squeezing and undulating. In his last rational moment, he realized she was punishing him for making her lose control, but he no longer cared as he plunged into the abyss of sensation. Rita clung to him when he cried out as the shudders of release shook his entire body, a small smile curling her lips. When at last he was still, a dead weight on her slender body, and she felt him go limp within her, she allowed herself a small chuckle. "Looks like you're human, after all, Vance," she announced with satisfaction.

Vance levered himself up onto his elbows and looked at her thoughtfully. "I still haven't decided about you, Mrs. Jordan," he said as he slid down her damp body until his mouth could fasten on one of her still-erect nipples. His caress was none too gentle as he used teeth and tongue to bring her breasts to stiff peaks. Once again she was arching to him, in spite of her voiced protests.

"No, Vance, stop it," she was saying without much

283

force, but Vance knew she meant it. Ignoring her, he began to work his way downward, biting, nipping, licking, until he reached her most vulnerable spot. "Damn you, Vance," she moaned, making a feeble effort to push him away, but he had slipped his hands beneath her hips, and between his fingers in back and his mouth in front, Rita was lost. Again and again he brought her to the brink, and again and again, he let her slip back. Each time she cursed him and begged him and cursed him again, until at last he was able to enter her once more. This time, as if it were a contest of wills, they both held back, each testing the other's control to its limits, and this time it was Rita who slipped her hands in between them, forcing Vance over the edge with delicate fingers and at last allowing herself to follow.

It was a while before their breathing returned to normal and a while after that before Vance had the energy to roll off of Rita's body. Without a word or a backward glance, he turned onto his side and allowed himself a small smile, a smile of satisfaction.

"Vance?"

He did not answer, feigning sleep, but she was not fooled.

"I know you're awake." She forced him to roll over on his back so she could see his face. "You know, I think I'm starting to like you, Vance." Still he did not answer. This was not a subject he wished to discuss. "Don't you want to know why?" she asked, suddenly seductive again.

"Nothing could interest me less, Mrs. Jordan," he replied with utter boredom.

This amused her, as he had known it would. "Good. Then I'll tell you." Her face grew serious. "I like you, 'cause I can't figure you."

"That shouldn't be too difficult. I am a simple man, nothing more than you see." He was trying to end the conversation, but he knew it was a useless effort.

"Liar," she said, not with malice. "You shoot Rogers an' never bat an eye, and then you give money to his wife to pay the doctor." He was surprised that she knew that, but he should not have been. She had a way of knowing everything that happened in town, although she rarely left the saloon. "I seen you givin' money to those kids that hang around in the street. An' the way you let them suckers win at cards. It's a disgrace, Vance. You could've bled this town dry in a week and gone on with a pretty nice stake."

"But, Mrs. Jordan, why should I want to do that? I've told you, I plan to settle in Rainbow, maybe even take up ranching," he replied.

Rita swore at him, but she was not angry. "That's the story you give, so's you can have an excuse to go ridin' all over the country. But I know you're lookin' fer somethin'. Must be somethin' worth lookin' for, too, or else you'd never waste your time here, in a hick town like this," she mused.

Anxious to turn the subject, Vance replied, "And why do you waste *your* time here, my dear?" She started at the question, and he could see the green eyes turning cold. "Surely, a woman with your, ah, talents, could make a fortune in, say, San Francisco or New Orleans. Even San Antonio would be better than this place." He had angered her now, and he was relieved. She would ask him no more questions tonight.

But Rita Jordan was not fooled. "It appears we've both got secrets, Vance. Don't worry, I won't ask no more tonight, but I'll find you out." Before he could reply, she added, "Now get out. I don't want you in my bed all night."

Back in his own room, Vance lay awake for a long time in the dark. What kept Rita Jordan in this town? It was a question he had asked himself many times, but until today he had had no answers. It could not be love, since Rita had no other lovers. In fact, Will had mentioned that Vance was the only other man besides himself who had ever been upstairs in the saloon. There was so obviously nothing between Will and Rita that even the gossips had given up on that. If it was not love, only one other emotion could motivate a woman like Rita Jordan. He had seen hate in her eyes when she spoke of Dusty Rhoades. Could that be it? But what could the cowboy have done to make her hate him so? Could he have scorned her? The idea was inconceivable that a cowboy would have refused her. Why, most men would have killed for her. There had to be more to it than that. Suppose, just suppose, she had wanted more. Suppose she had wanted to marry Rhoades, and he had refused. Not that there weren't many men who would have married her. A lot of prostitutes had married and become respectable. Come to think of it, Rita herself had married. As a wealthy widow, she could have made a new life somewhere back east, if she had wanted to. Instead, she was here. Was Rhoades one of those men with principles, too good for a girl who had worked the line? Vance considered. He knew little of Rhoades except what he had observed and heard. Obviously, he was well liked, a young man with ambition and a future—and a choice. He was not wealthy, but he would be welcomed into the home of any respectable family in the state. He could choose among any of the daughters of Texas for a wife if he wished. Vance pictured a certain woman's face in his mind. If he had a choice between Rita and a woman like . . . like *her*, well, there would be no choice.

As he slept, Jason Vance dreamed he held a woman in his arms. Her body was Rita Jordan's body, but when he saw her face, it was the face of Priscilla Bedford.

The next Sunday Priscilla joined the Steeles, as usual, for dinner after church. The preacher, Reverend Allen, had also been invited and had proven a very interesting companion, keeping them all entertained with stories of his adventures while preaching in various Texas towns. He made a party out of an otherwise dull afternoon.

Priscilla had especially enjoyed sitting under Reverend Allen's preaching because he was such a pleasant looking young man with red hair and bright blue eyes. After sitting with him for an afternoon, she could see he also had a way with the ladies, as her grandmother used to say, and a plan began to form in her fertile brain.

The shadows were growing longer in the yard when Priscilla made her excuses to return to her room. Reverend Allen had been so particularly attentive to her, she felt certain he would be willing to accompany her on her walk to the school. She had seen Dusty loitering out in the yard and hoped for a chance to test Stella's theory using Reverend Allen as bait. She did not even need to ask the preacher to accompany her, for as soon as she rose to leave, Reverend Allen begged to be allowed to walk her back. Delighted, she consented.

As they crossed the back yard, she could see Dusty was leaning against a post on the bunkhouse porch, watching them.

"Reverend Allen, the way is quite rough between here and the school. Would you mind if I took your arm?" Priscilla asked demurely.

"I should be delighted, Miss Bedford," he said almost too eagerly and offered his arm with a flourish that should have stood Dusty on his ear.

They walked off slowly over the hill and across the flat toward the school, Reverend Allen discussing the sad state of culture and the arts in Texas—he was from New York, himself—until finally, he came to the point. "And so you see, Miss Bedford, why I feel so fortunate in having met a young lady with your background. You have so much to share in this wilderness."

"I would hardly call Rainbow a wilderness, Reverend Allen," she scolded lightly. "In many ways it is very civilized."

"Yes, and with your help, it will become even more so, but I fear your true talents are wasted in the schoolroom," he told her.

"Why, what do you mean?" Priscilla was becoming suspicious that Reverend Allen had more than culture on his mind.

"Well, a lady like yourself needs a special position in the community from which to exert her influence," he declared.

"What sort of position?" Priscilla was very much afraid she already knew.

"Well, for example, as the wife of an influential man," Reverend Allen suggested.

Priscilla laughed lightly, hoping to divert what she was now sure was coming. "No influential man has asked me to become his wife, Reverend Allen."

Reverend Allen stopped. They were now almost to the

school. He turned to face her and looked into her eyes with such earnestness that she almost laughed out loud. Instead, she smiled tolerantly and endured what was now inevitable. It was not the first time.

"Miss Priscilla, I know it is difficult for you to imagine myself as an influential man, but I know I need not remind you of the power of the church in civilization. As the towns around here grow into cities, the churches will grow also, and so will the role of the ministers. I see the church as a moving force in the state of Texas, and I can think of no other woman I would rather have at my side when that happens than yourself."

It was such an obviously prepared speech that Priscilla had to fight off an impulse to applaud. Instead, she very kindly smiled at young Mr. Allen and said as gently as he could, "You are undoubtedly right about the future of the church, since you would know far more about that than I, and it flatters me very much that you think me worthy to assist you in such a great undertaking. However, I must, with great regret, refuse your generous offer."

The preacher did not intend to be refused, but before he could charge into another argument in his favor, Priscilla continued, "Since you did not speak of love to me, I must conclude that I will not break your heart when I tell you that I am in love with another man and therefore could never be so unfair to you as to accept your proposal." The words came to her lips with surprising ease and far less pain than Priscilla would have imagined. It seemed that Stella's theory had made the situation bearable, somehow.

"Another man! I had no idea. Are you engaged?" he stammered.

"No, not yet. And no one knows, not even the man in question. But I hope soon to be able to tell you his name and to require your professional services," she said blithely with a silent prayer that it was not just wishful thinking.

Poor Reverend Allen was looking rather downcast and Priscilla could not leave him that way, especially when she had it in her power to raise him up again. "If you will soon—and I certainly hope you will—be considering other young ladies, may I suggest someone to you?" Priscilla asked gently.

Reverend Allen perked right up at this prospect. "Yes, please do," he urged.

"Ruth Steele."

"Ruth Steele! Why, she's just a child," he judged, frowning slightly.

"She's seventeen, a woman by western standards, and she has the added advantage of already being in love with you." She could not help smiling at his embarrassment. His face turned scarlet. Why did redheads always blush so?

"Why, wh . . . wh . . . wh . . . what makes you say that?" he stammered.

"Well, I first became suspicious when I noticed how intently she listens to your sermons. Surely, *you* have noticed that, too," she asked with a mischievous smile.

"Oh, yes, but I thought, I mean, I assumed, I mean . . ."

"Reverend Allen, you are an excellent speaker, but no one is *that* good. And then she began to study in her Bible the passages from which you preached. And finally, the proof positive, she began to quote from your sermons, *word for word*!" Priscilla announced triumphantly.

Reverend Allen thought this over, considering the evidence carefully. "Just today she asked me a very thoughtful question about the Trinity . . ." he murmured.

"You see. How many other seventeen-year-old girls have ever asked you a question about anything?"

Reverend Allen wanted to be convinced. "But she's so young," he tried once more.

"The Bible says, 'Train up a child in the way he should go.' Ruth would be clay in your hands. You could mold her, teach her everything you know of the finer things in life." She could see that his eyes were looking into the future, seeing Ruthie as the great lady he could help her become. She struck her final blow. "Mrs. Steele, I'm told, came from a fine old Virginia family. With her breeding and Ben Steele's blood in her veins, Ruthie has the potential to become anything at all." That did it. She had made him a happy man.

"Miss Bedford, how can I ever thank you," he gushed, pumping her hand. "You've opened my eyes to what was God's will all along. The Lord will bless you for this."

"I certainly hope so," Priscilla murmured, but he was gone, hightailing it back to the ranch house. Priscilla stood for a moment looking after him, shaking her head. "Well, Ruthie will make a man out of him if anyone can," she thought and walked around to the rear entrance to the school. She suddenly noticed a strange noise coming from the hill on the north side of the building. Walking around to investigate, she was startled to see a horse—one of Dusty's horses—and then Dusty himself, repairing what she knew must be an imaginary hole in the wire fence. Could he have been so jealous that he had followed them here to see what would happen?

Could he have overheard what they'd said? There was only one way to find out, and Priscilla stalked up the hill.

"Is there a problem with the fence, Mr. Rhoades?" she asked as seriously as she could manage.

Dusty did not meet her eye. "Nothin' serious, ma'am, just a little weakness I noticed yesterday and forgot to come back and get. Thought I'd better get it now, 'fore some enterprisin' cow finds it." Another prepared speech? Priscilla thought so. "What'd *he* want?" Dusty jerked his head to the departing figure in black.

Automatically, Priscilla turned to look at the fleeing Mr. Allen as the realization struck her. He really *had* followed her and was jealous enough to inquire into her personal business. A stab of joy made her forget exactly what question Dusty had asked, so she stammered around. "Oh, well, I mean . . ."

"Did he insult you?" Dusty's eyes were blue fire and the shock brought back her self-control. "'Cause if he did, preacher or no preacher, I'll . . ."

"Oh, no!" she interrupted, laughing, as much amused at his hypocrisy as at the thought of Reverend Allen's insulting her. Dusty could insult her, but no one else was permitted. "At least I don't think many women consider a proposal of marriage an insult," she commented and was thrilled to see how much that upset him.

"A proposal of marriage?" he asked quietly, a twisting agony beginning in his stomach. Priscilla looked longingly at the figure disappearing over the hill, nodded, and sighed. "Oh," he said and began very violently repairing the fence. "He's a lucky man," he said tightly.

"Yes, he is," Priscilla responded gaily, enjoying his implied compliment. "I turned him down."

"You turned him down!" He had said it too loudly, let his relief show. He had tipped his hand, and he knew it, but it was too late now.

Priscilla pretended not to notice. "Yes, I could never do that to any man."

"Do what?" He had forgotten the fence now.

"Marry a man I didn't love." While he was absorbing that, for good measure she mumbled, as if to herself, "If I had wanted to do that, I could have stayed in Philadelphia." His head jerked back as if she'd struck him. "Don't act so surprised. Do you think no one's ever proposed to me before?" she asked indignantly. *Just because you didn't,* she added mentally.

"Uh, I mean, well, seems like every other teacher we ever had here came to get married." He gestured apologetically, acutely embarrassed at the subject under discussion.

"I cannot speak for the other ladies," she said haughtily, "but *I* came here to teach school. If I'd wanted to get married, I could have taken one of the offers I received back home or . . ."—she paused for effect—"I could have married the man who asked me on the train from St. Louis"—she could see he was paling now—"or the man at the hotel in San Antonio. It's just as Mr. Steele said . . ."

"*Ben?*" he interrupted, his face mottling. "*He* asked you, too?" It was almost more than he could stand.

"Mr. Steele? Oh, no!" she laughed. "He simply gave me some good advice on the subject of marriage."

"Oh, yeah? He's an expert, all right," Dusty gritted, starting on the fence again.

"I don't know if he's an expert or not, but he told me

not to throw myself away on a thirty-a-month cowboy and to marry only for love, and I know that's good advice."

"You know it, huh? I guess schoolteachers know just about everything." He had been right about her not wanting a man like him, but the knowledge gave him little comfort.

"Well, I know a lot of things. For instance," she said, delighted with her new discoveries and turning to go back down the hill, "I know there was no hole in that fence."

By the time he thought of a reply, she was gone.

Dusty had a hard time falling asleep that night. He had cussed himself for seven kinds of a fool and then done it over again, but that had not helped. He had really done it, this time, letting Priscilla see how jealous he'd been of Reverend Allen. She'd put him in his place, too, with all that talk about "thirty-a-month cowboys" and reminding him how she'd never marry a man she didn't love. He knew she didn't love him. She didn't have to rub it in. He was no "thirty-a-month cowboy," anyway. He earned a lot more than that. He even had money saved, and Ben let him run his own brand, so he had cattle, too. But for a woman like that, he knew he'd need a lot more than a few cows to impress her. So far, she didn't seem impressed at all. Dusty was used to girls who swooned over him, like that Sally at the dance. He'd only asked her to go for a walk in the moonlight because he'd seen Priscilla watching them, and then he'd practically had to hold her at arm's length to keep her from kissing him. All the girls acted like that, all except Priscilla. Oh, she'd responded all right, but she hadn't wanted to, not really, and she regretted it now, as much as he did. The difference was that while he was trying to pretend that nothing had happened, she was going to make him pay, punish him for it, and he'd given her the perfect tool.

If only he'd met her later, he thought for the thousandth time, after he had his ranch. He was almost ready for it, too. With the money he had saved and the sale of the cattle he would send north this year with Ben's herd, he would have a good stake, more than most men started with, but first he had to find land. There was plenty of it out there, and he was sure he would know the right place when he saw it, but where would a woman fit into all this? He smiled grimly when he tried to picture packing Priscilla Bedford into a wagon and heading out for God-only-knew-where, riding for months on end until he found what he wanted, then putting her out to set up housekeeping in a soddy or a dug-out or a lean-to until he could build a house. Even then it would take years to put the ranch on a paying basis. It never occurred to him that a woman might be willing to do those very things for the man she truly loved, and even if it had, he would never have asked her to. His pride rebelled at the mere suggestion. He had seen his mother struggle and do without for too many years. No wife of his would have to suffer, and even if he might have considered it for a lesser woman, he would never ask it of Priscilla Bedford. Besides, she would laugh in his face!

No, he could think of no way to fit Priscilla into his life, even if she were willing, which he was sure she was not. The best course of action now was to spare himself as much misery as possible and that meant getting as far away from Miss Bedford as fast as he could. The time was perfect. They would be starting the roundup soon. Dusty and Ben usually hired a trail boss or used one of their own men on the years Dusty did not go up the trail. Dusty would simply tell Ben he wanted to boss the drive himself this time. He could say he wanted the extra money and wanted to oversee the sale of his own stock. No one could question that. Then just before they left, he would tell Ben he was not coming back and say his last goodbyes. Once in Dodge, he could make contacts and inquiries, get a lead on good ranch land, maybe even buy a small herd of young stuff, and drive it with him. If he were ever going, now was the time. The roundup would keep him on the range until time to leave, and he could probably avoid Priscilla completely. No use torturing himself, and he knew that every time he saw her would make it that much harder to leave. Too many encounters and he might never go at all. It was settled, then. A few, careful weeks and he would be gone. Forever.

Jason Vance cut a striking figure astride his black horse. He became a familiar sight, too, riding off in various directions at least several times a week. To people who were curious, he explained he was interested in ranching, a story no one really believed. But no one ventured to call him a liar, at least not to his face. He was, of course, looking for the landmarks described on his map, a job he had not realized would be so difficult to one unfamiliar with the country. Any native could probably have glanced at the map and pinpointed its location immediately, but Vance had no intention of showing the map to anyone. Thus, he was forced to do a lot of exploring. It was rather pleasant and it gave him something to do, away from Rita's watchful eye. He knew she rarely missed anything that happened in or around town and his rides gave him a curious sense of freedom. He had a sense of urgency, too. While it was true that he had wanted the gold before he got to Rainbow, his trip here on the stage had awakened in him a desire he did not know he was still capable of feeling. Now he wanted the gold for something more than simply what it could buy. He wanted it for what it would enable him to do. On the stage he had met Priscilla Bedford. A lady. As he had explained to Dusty Rhoades, he seldom met a lady. She had recalled to him memories of a way of life he had left so long ago. Scenes of his childhood and young manhood had drifted before him in a haze of courtesy and refinement, qualities he still prided himself in, despite his rugged years in the West.

Jason Vance was the son of an old Virginia family. Or rather, one of the sons. He had three older brothers, all of whom had fought in the War and all of whom had lost. When the unpleasantness ended, the Vance family, like most of the South, found themselves beaten down but not quite destroyed. They managed to maintain a sort of genteel poverty and hold on to most of their land. As the years passed, they recovered somewhat, although they would never again know true wealth. When the time came, Vance's father sent him to college, not because it was economically feasible, but because all his sons went to college.

Young Jason enjoyed the social life of college but chafed under the restrictions his meager allowance imposed on him, so he supplemented his income by gambling. He showed a definite talent for winning and soon many old Southern families were contributing to his enjoyment of the good life. Unfortunately, among his associates was a young man whose financial situation was much like his own. Young Sneed, however, was not very skilled at cards. He lost heavily, and then lost some more, far more than his family could ever afford to pay. Rather than confess to Vance or disgrace his family, he shot himself, thereby doing both. The scandal that followed somehow managed to implicate Vance in the boy's death and Vance suddenly found he was no longer received in the homes of old friends. He could have stayed and perhaps ridden out the storm, but it seemed too good an opportunity to pass up, so he used his "ruin" as an excuse to escape to the West. He spent several years learning his trade on Mississippi river boats, then had drifted west to work the cattle towns and mining camps, winning and losing several fortunes in the process.

His chosen profession had successfully closed the door to any possible reconciliation with his family and his old way of life. As a gambler he was worse than a nobody, lower than white trash, no matter how much money he might win. He had thought himself content however, until the moment he had entered that stagecoach. She was just a young woman reading a book of poetry, but then they had spoken. He had asked what she was reading, and they had discussed poetry for a while, then literature in general, then places they had been. She brought back to him memories of women with honeyed voices who laughed softly and blushed if gentlemen admired their beauty.

Priscilla Bedford had stepped out of his life as suddenly as she had stepped in, and yet she remained, a shadowy presence on the periphery of his existence, her name mentioned casually by cowboys recounting a humorous story and then a not-very-humorous one.

Vance's concern for her had prompted him to overstep the bounds of propriety by inquiring after her, something he, as a southern gentleman, would never ordinarily have done. Yet, his feelings for Priscilla Bedford were not ordinary. He knew what he usually felt about women—either attraction, romance, or lust—but his feelings for Priscilla were none of these. A nameless longing surrounded his memory of her, a longing graced by magnolia trees and cool drinks on shaded porches. Why, if he were a rich man . . . He was not sure just when his brain had made the connection, but sometime soon after he arrived in Rainbow he had realized that the ancient Spanish gold could buy his freedom and return him to his family with untainted wealth as an adventurous boy who had made good in the West. The prodigal returned. Never again to sit in a smoke-filled saloon with unwashed ruffians, any one of whom might kill him at any moment on the slightest provocation. To pass his life in genteel idleness, perhaps even marry a woman like . . . And so he rode the hills, eyes searching the horizon for a familiar lay of land, a bent tree, a large stone, and, finding nothing, he rode on.

Chapter Ten

Priscilla's spirits soared for days after discovering that Dusty was jealous of Reverend Allen in spite of the fact that she saw very little of Dusty. She was beginning to suspect that he was deliberately avoiding her, and that made her even happier until Stella brought her back down to earth with the news that Dusty was going up the trail with the cattle drive and would probably be gone three months or more. That did not sound to Priscilla like the action of a man in love, and for once even Stella was stumped for a theory. Stella did point out, however, that after a trail drive, a man was mighty anxious for female company and might be anxious enough to forget a lot of silly notions he might have had in his head. Priscilla could only hope that was true, and the more she thought of it, the more convinced she became that perhaps it was all for the best. The cattle drive and the separation would give them what they both needed: a fresh start.

The weeks of the roundup passed quickly, and Priscilla

fell more deeply in love with Texas as the April breezes blew. She saw the men only briefly since they camped out most nights wherever they happened to be working stock. Priscilla took the opportunity of Dusty's absence to ride Lady daily. She had ridden the mare before, but not often since she had not wanted to seem to be taking advantage. Now Dusty had no time for the horse and he could not use her to work the cattle since a mare was too disruptive to a *remuda*, so Priscilla rode her and groomed her with the love and enthusiasm she would gladly have spent on the horse's master, if he had allowed it. Another motive was to prove to him that she would take good care of the mare while he was gone so he would not begrudge her the use of the horse. If Dusty knew of or appreciated her care of Lady, she never knew, since she had not seen him to speak to since the roundup had begun. In fact, she had become convinced that he was avoiding her and had to content herself with the thought that he must indeed be afraid of her.

From dinner table conversation, Priscilla knew that the roundup was almost complete and Ben Steele expected to send about 2500 of his own cattle and another 250 of Dusty's up the trail to Dodge City. Priscilla had been surprised to learn that Dusty actually owned cattle, too, and that even Curly had started a small herd of his own, taking stock from Ben in lieu of part of his pay. Emotions were running high around the Steele home—excitement over the adventure of the drive, concern for the safety of the men who would be involved, and interest in the price of beef—but Priscilla was completely unprepared for the mood she found the family in when she appeared for Sunday morning breakfast.

The dining room, usually boisterously loud with the clatter of dishes and the voices of children, was strangely silent. A deathlike pall hung over the group assembled there. Stella and George would not meet her eyes, Ruth sat stonily, her eyes red from crying, and the younger girls wept openly. Young Ben sat staring at his plate, obviously wanting to join the girls in weeping but feeling the burden of his manhood upon him. Ben Steele sat looking as if catastrophe had struck, and even the younger children were oddly subdued.

No one spoke, so Priscilla was obliged to ask, fearfully, "What has happened?" although she did not really want to know.

For a long time no one spoke, the adults exchanging glances as if mutely trying to decide who should break the news. At last Stella spoke up. "Last night Dusty rode in to tell Daddy they're almost ready to start." Stella paused.

"That can't be all," Priscilla insisted.

Suddenly, Ruth made a small, strangled sound and rushed from the table. No one seemed to notice. Stella continued, "Dusty also told Daddy that after he gets the herd sold, he's quittin', goin' on from there to find a place where he can take up ranchin' on his own. He's never comin' back here."

Stella spoke the words as kindly as she could, but each one was like a knife driven into Priscilla's vitals. Never coming back! She would never see him again. Never. The word numbed her brain, and she sank into the chair, thankful that the pain was too great for tears, and that she would not make a fool of herself in front of everyone. She sat woodenly in front of her empty plate, making no pretense at eating, until the others were ready to leave the table, and then she found that she had to face an ordeal that would test her self-control to its limits. Ben had asked Dusty to stay at the ranch all day, to go with them to church and have Sunday dinner with them as a last farewell. Judging from the mood of the family, it would not be a joyous occasion.

Dusty, who had taken refuge somewhere during breakfast, brought the wagon around for the women. He was as grim faced as everyone else and if he did not look directly at Priscilla, he did not look directly at anyone else, either, obviously feeling the pain of separation from those who had loved him like a son and a brother. If he felt any other pain, Priscilla could not tell and chose not to study him for signs of it. Instead, she contrived to sit in the back of the wagon, as far from Dusty as possible, for the long drive to church. She heard not one word of the sermon that morning, but when Reverend Allen prayed long and loud for the lost lambs who had wandered far from the fold, there were no dry eyes in the Steele's pew.

Dinner was even worse, with the three men forcing themselves to be pleasant while the women sat in brooding silence.

Finally, even George could stand it no longer. "Dammit, women, you should be glad for the boy! He's worked hard for this chance. He has a right to expect some enthusiasm from us. We're the only family he has."

"Don't blame them, George," said Dusty solemnly. He had failed to realize that in leaving Priscilla, he would also be leaving the Steeles, and only today had he realized the full implications of his act. "I know how they feel. I feel just as bad leavin' them. Like you said, you all are my family. But it ain't like I'm dyin'! Shoot, soon's I get things goin' good, I'll come back for a visit so's you can

304

see how prosperous I am. Better yet, get ol' Ben to pack you all up and bring you to see me."

Dusty's forced cheerfulness soothed no one, and once again Ruth left the table abruptly. This time Priscilla followed, offering to comfort her but finally, in the privacy of the girl's room, indulging herself in a few tears, also. While they were gone, the dinner party broke up to mope in various parts of the house. The men retired to Ben's office where they did not have to endure the women's sad faces. Priscilla wandered outside, alone, too depressed to sit with Stella and Ruth. When she reached the barn, she realized with a pang that Dusty would be taking Lady with him. During the past weeks she had come to love that horse. Impulsively, she slipped into the barn and went to Lady's stall. The mare came eagerly to her and whinnied expectantly. Priscilla stroked her nose and caressed her neck, speaking to her softly. She was so engrossed that she did not notice Dusty had come in until he spoke.

"Reckon she'll miss you." He had had no intention of speaking to her at all, had intended to slip out of the barn again when he had seen her there, but somehow, he could not force himself. After all, after today, he'd never have another chance to see her again.

"I'll miss her, too." Priscilla could not bear to look at him, so she continued to pat Lady. Then she had an inspiration. "Would you consider selling her? I could pay you what she's worth. I have some money my father left me."

It was too dark in the shadowed barn to read his expression. "I could never sell Lady," he protested. "I might . . ." He caught himself. He had almost offered to give her the horse. It was an impulse born of his feelings

305

for her and the pain he was enduring, but what would she think? That he was paying her off. She would be insulted. Besides, he was selfish enough to want to keep Lady as a reminder of Priscilla, the only one he would ever have. "No," he said, half to himself. "I could never sell Lady."

To turn and walk away seemed so final that Priscilla could not force herself to do it. Impulsively, she asked, "May I ride her once more?"

"Shore," Dusty replied quickly, unreasonably glad to be able to please her in something. "Mind if I tag along?" he heard himself say as he slapped a saddle on Lady's back. It came as no surprise that he wanted to, but to actually say it . . .

Priscilla did mind, but she reasoned that this would be her last encounter with him and her last chance to solve the mystery that was Dusty Rhoades, if that were possible.

They rode in silence for a while, each feeling the enormity of loss, each wondering how deeply affected the other was. At last Priscilla gathered her courage and managed to decide on an inoffensive way to begin what she felt might be the most important conversation of her life.

"I can certainly understand how you feel, leaving the only home you've ever known," she began. "It helps if you have something that you are working toward, though. I know that was what helped me." She stopped to study his face, but he was staring rigidly ahead, almost as if he had not heard her. "Of course, I did not have so many people loving me and wanting me to stay," she continued, hoping he would at least wonder if she fell into that category.

"What about all them beaus you had back east?" he

asked with such sudden, unexplained anger that Priscilla jumped. "They must've wanted you to stay."

Priscilla blinked. Was that bitterness she heard underneath the anger? Emboldened by the thought, she replied, "What about you? From what I hear, you'll be leaving a string of broken hearts all across Texas." Seeing she had shocked him gave her the courage to ask the question that had been haunting her all day. "Come now, isn't there some pretty girl you'd like to pack up on your saddle and carry off to Kansas with you?" She had tried to sound playful, but there was a definite edge in her voice.

Dusty felt that edge. She just couldn't let him go without sticking him one last time, could she? Now she wanted him to admit how difficult it was to leave her so she could have the last laugh. He cast her a considering look. Their horses were walking slowly, side by side, and he checked his mount, waiting until she had stopped, too, and as they sat not an arm's length from each other, he said very quietly, "Even if there were, Miss Bedford, I wouldn't do it."

Priscilla searched his face. She was close, so close, if only she could keep him talking. "Why not?" she asked with such intense curiosity that he was compelled to answer.

"A cattle drive's no fit place for a woman," he explained, a little uncertain exactly why he wanted her to understand. "After that's over, I gotta head out into some pretty wild country, without even knowin' where I'm goin' and nothin' there when I get there."

Was that all? Could that be his only reason? "The right girl would wait for you," she insisted. Could he tell that she was that girl—could he read it in her eyes?

His confusion was obvious. What was she getting at? Did she want him to ask her to wait so she could turn him down, or worse yet, so she could agree and then jilt him when he had gone? He would not give her the chance. "You're talkin' three, maybe even five years of waitin', Miss Bedford," he informed her with just a hint of sarcasm. "No girl would wait that long. No man would ask her to." With that he turned his pony's head and wheeled around, heading back toward the ranch. "Time we was gettin' back," he said brusquely and kicked his horse into a trot.

Priscilla stared after him for a moment before urging Lady to follow him. She had to face the truth and it was not a pleasant prospect. Regardless of how Dusty felt about her, and she still believed he cared for her in some way, he had no intention of including her in his life. How did a woman fight such logic? How did she convince him that his arguments were foolish? And were they? To him, she had to admit, they were not, and she felt unequal to the task of showing him otherwise.

When they came to the fork in the road, Priscilla took the turn to the schoolhouse, and after a moment's hesitation, Dusty followed her. When they reached the schoolyard, she dismounted before he could help her. She did not trust herself in his hands. She stood with her back to him, taking one long, last look at Lady. The horse seemed to sense her mood and nuzzled her affectionately. Priscilla's eyes blurred and she buried her face in Lady's neck until she could fight back the tears. He would not see her cry. With an iron will she composed herself, and, squaring her shoulders, she turned to face him, forcing her lips into a smile.

"Well, I guess this is goodbye," she said as lightly as

she could, extending her hand to him. It seemed a prosaic ending for their tumultuous relationship, but she could think of nothing else to do.

He took her small, soft hand in his large calloused one. Never had he seen her more lovely, her hair windblown, her cheeks flushed, her eyes bright with unshed tears. He knew she had been trying not to cry. Were those tears for him or the horse? Not that it mattered. This would be the last time he would ever see her. The last time. Ahead of him stretched hundreds, maybe thousands of miles—dangerous, difficult, lonely. Lonely campfires with other lonely men. How long before he would even see another woman, let alone a woman like this? When would he stand with one, alone like this, holding her hand, the sun streaming down on her hair, making it shine like a halo, her eyes glistening? He cursed the fate that had brought her here, and he cursed himself for falling in love with a woman he could never have. The injustice of it infuriated him, quickly, without warning, and he wanted revenge, or at least a token of it. Well, why not? he asked himself, and before an answer came, while he still held her right hand, he slipped his left arm around her waist. Pulling her to him, he kissed her soundly on the mouth.

Before she could resist or assist, he released her and for a moment she stood too stunned to move. How dare he! Of all the rotten . . . ! Cold fury canceled every other emotion she had felt before and she threw back her left hand to slap his insolent face. He still held her right one in a convulsive grip. Then she froze. He was not insolent. He was braced, expecting her blow, desiring it to cancel out his shameless act.

He flinched as her hand came swiftly up, but instead of striking him, she wrapped her arm around his neck and

309

pulling him toward her with the hand she still held, she kissed him with all the fire and passion of a woman who wanted to be remembered with regret. Although his mind was completely stunned, his body took only a moment to respond and the next instant he held her in a bone-crushing embrace. How could he have forgotten what she felt like, how she tasted, how she smelled, how she molded her softness to him so eagerly, how intoxicating her essence could be?

Priscilla surrendered to his arms, her body also remembering past delights, and lost herself in the world of sensation. She had been right! He did care for her! His coldness had been all an act, a lie to somehow protect her from what she no longer remembered or cared to remember. She only knew, with some primal instinct, that this was the way to subdue him, to conquer him, to overcome his silly notions, and she returned his kiss with a fervor that inflamed them both.

Dusty's hands explored her body, rediscovering half-forgotten wonders, marveling at the way she seemed to melt beneath his touch, but even as he did so, he heard some soft warning voice, deep in his brain, repeating an alarm. What had he to fear? he wondered vaguely as he found the sweet mounds of her breasts thrusting eagerly into his palms.

Priscilla curved into his fevered touch, savoring the two-fold ecstasy that came from his body and from her knowledge that when he took her this time he would never leave her again. She would force him to confess his love, use her woman's body to seduce from him the truth, and then he would be hers, completely.

"Oh, Pris, I . . ." he murmured drunkenly against her mouth, almost allowing the betraying words to escape but stopping himself just in time.

"What, my darling, what?" she whispered back, her breath sweet honey against his lips.

"I . . ." he began, but forgot the rest as she drew herself from his embrace and began backing away from him. Fascinated, he stared at her slowly retreating figure, trying to figure out why she was moving away when he knew from her eyes that she wanted to be close. Before his mind could decide, his body had begun instinctively to follow, one sure step and then another, and then she was turning, throwing one sassy look over one beckoning shoulder and running toward the schoolhouse. He was right behind her, his long legs easily overtaking her, long arms reaching out for her, but she twisted free, her tinkling laugh taunting him to try again, but before he could, she threw open the schoolhouse door and fled inside. He might have stopped had not her tantalizing laughter rung out again to bring him stumbling into her room.

He paused a moment, his breath rasping in the room's stillness, seeking her in the sudden dimness, and then he found her, standing on the other side of the room's partition, her back to the bed's iron footrest, hands clinging to the metal as if for support, her breasts rising and falling rapidly in the aftermath of her flight. He watched that rise and fall as one hypnotized, hardly aware that he was moving toward her, closer, ever closer, until her hands reached out and touched him. That touch released a torrent of emotions in him that seemed to drown them both as he crushed her to him in a kiss that had no end.

Priscilla yielded to him in blissful abandon. This was the man she had waited for, the moment she had waited

311

for all of her life, and she gloried in it, gloried in the feel of him, the touch of him, his lips, his hands as he worked feverishly to get to her, to find her beneath all those layers and layers of cotton and silk. She was searching for him, too, pulling and tugging and wrestling with buttons as they tumbled together in a struggling heap upon the bed. Dusty rolled away a moment in a frantic attempt to pull off his boots, but Priscilla drew him back with a tiny cry of protest at such niceties. She wanted him and she would have him now, all of him, she told him with her body and her hands and her urgent kisses.

Unable to deny her, he responded with renewed fervor, devouring the ripe swell of her breasts with his ravenous mouth while his busy hands sought out the secret source of the fire that now raged out of control.

Priscilla moaned in ecstasy as his calloused hands grated over her softness, spreading her gently like the petals of a precious flower, and then in answer to her imploring cry, he filled her, forcing that flower to bloom with such intensity that for a moment Priscilla thought she might not survive such exquisite pleasure.

Dusty, too, doubted his ability to survive as he endured the dual rapture of losing himself in her sweet depths and knowing she was as lost as he. From somewhere, a vague sense of foreboding prodded him, but before he could remember where it came from, it was gone again, lost in the avalanche of sensation that always came with intimate knowledge of Priscilla Bedford.

Priscilla marveled at the splendor of him as she ran her hands over his burning skin and felt the power beneath it. She met each vibrant thrust greedily, joyous in the knowledge that each plunge brought them closer to the unity that she yearned for, the oneness that would win

312

from him the confession that she craved. In anticipation she wrapped her slender legs around him, her still-stocking-clad feet rasping against the denim of the jeans she had given him no time to remove, her restless hands finding the sleekness of his lean flanks, compelling him to join with her, to blend with her, to merge with her. Hungrily, she tasted the salty sheen of his exertions as her mouth explored the brawny expanse of his shoulder while his hands mercilessly tormented the sensitive tips of her breasts, sending tingles down, down into the very core of her, to throb there, throb and pulse and build, larger and larger until she could hold it no longer, bear it no longer, and she let it explode, sending its pulsing waves out and out, convulsing her with blissful fulfillment.

As always, her release triggered his, and he followed her into the oblivion of delight, gasping out his satisfaction, clinging to her until the tremors died away and rationality returned. It returned with harsh clarity, and even as his lips still lingered in the curve of her shoulder, his sated body stiffened and he pulled away, groaning softly. What had become of all his good intentions, all his carefully laid plans? Everything had gone so well, so perfectly! If only he had not kissed her. He should have known better, should have known that once they started . . . No use looking back now, though. It was far too late for that. But not too late, if only he could get away from her. No, that would not be enough, not this time, he knew instinctively. She would expect some sort of commitment and walking away would not be enough. She would not give up so easily, not after giving herself the way she had. No, if he were to get away, to save her from a life he knew was all wrong for her, no matter what she might think, he would have to hurt her, wound her pride with an insult she could never forgive. It was, he decided grimly, the only way.

Priscilla followed him as he rolled away, curling herself against his side, sighing contentedly and staring with fascination at the cloud of red-gold hair that blanketed his chest and which she had been too busy to notice before. He was magnificent, she thought, studying the symmetry of his body, the way his firm flesh molded over the massive bones, and she loved him so, she thought her heart would burst from it. That love shone from her eyes, if only he would turn his head to see it, but he did not.

Instead, he pulled his lips back from his teeth in a parody of a grin. "I'll shore miss you, darlin'," he said carelessly, amazing himself with his acting ability. "You really got a way of makin' a man feel like a man," he commended her, wrestling with his pants and then swinging his still-booted feet to the floor, ignoring her startled gasp. "Don't know where I'll find your match. 'Course, I reckon it'll be fun lookin'," he remarked, scooping up his shirt and rising to his feet.

Priscilla felt as if she had received a stunning blow. Her whole body was paralyzed by the impact of the words she was hearing but was unable to believe. It was impossible! He could not be saying these things, could not mean them, not after the way he had just made love to her. The man she loved could never do such a thing, and yet he was doing it.

Shrugging into his shirt, he turned to face her, looking down with an insolent smirk to where she still lay in a satisfied coil. His affront revitalized her frozen body and in a desperate lunge, she snatched up the edge of the coverlet to conceal her nakedness from his insulting gaze. Shame scorched her face as the pain of betrayal twisted her heart.

"Maybe I will pack you on my saddle, just like you said, an' take you with me. A piece like you could keep a bedroll mighty warm . . ." The crack of flesh against flesh halted his speech, a fact for which he could only be grateful as he raised his hand to the cheek she had just slapped. Slowly, he turned his eyes back to where she now crouched like a wild thing, clutching the blanket around her, her eyes blazing with hate and something else.

"You bastard!" she hissed, trembling with rage and shame. "Get out of here! Get out of here!" she shrieked, terrified that he would not leave before she broke down.

Pausing only a moment, savoring that one last look, he swung away, his eyes making one last sweep of the floor to be certain he had left nothing behind, and, discovering his hat where it had fallen beside the door, he retrieved it and made his way hastily from the room. Outside, he took a minute to button his shirt and otherwise make himself presentable while at the same time remembering how she had looked in that last instant, the picture of her face just before he had fled vivid in his mind. She had looked, he realized with stunning certainty, as if she had been *hurt*. Oh, she had been angry and humiliated, that he had intended, but she had also felt pain. He had seen too much suffering in his life to be mistaken, and the knowledge devastated him. How could he have hurt her so much unless she really loved him? It was inconceivable that she should, and yet he had seen the irrefutable evidence on her face. Inconceivable, and humbling, too, when he realized another awful fact: if

315

she had ever loved him before, she could not love him now, not after the things he had just said to her. That had been his plan, and he admitted reluctantly that he had succeeded all too well in his efforts. She would never so much as speak to him again now, and he could not blame her. Sighing in his victorious defeat, he lifted one hand toward the school in silent salute. "Goodbye, Priscilla," he whispered. "You win the last hand, my love." Catching up Lady's reins, he mounted his own horse and rode slowly away, leading the mare.

Priscilla never heard him leave. As she sobbed into her pillow and cursed the man she loved—still loved in spite of his treachery—with every swear word she knew, she could not help but recall his face, the way it had looked in that last moment. Those sapphire eyes had blazed with a fire that still scorched her, and when the storm of her anger had abated and she could think more rationally, she remembered that look and identified it. With a surge of wonder that brought her head up and stopped her tears instantly, she realized that the look she had found so searing had been raw pain. He had destroyed her with his cruelty, but he had felt the pain himself. It made no sense, yet it was true. She had seen the irrefutable proof, the twisting agony in his eyes. Why? Oh, why? she asked herself over and over, and how could he have done such a thing, said such awful things to her, if he loved her? It was completely unlike the Dusty Rhoades she knew, she decided, and seizing that thought, she worried it like a dog worries a bone, long into the night until at long last she had solved the mystery of Dusty Rhoades.

Dusty rode back to camp that night, promising the Steeles he would check in with them before leaving to say a last goodbye. It seemed easier to postpone it until the time when he would be in a hurry. He did not look forward to it.

The next morning, after an almost sleepless night in which he replayed that final scene with Priscilla over and over in his mind, he drove his men with unnecessary ruthlessness, as if getting the branding and roundup finished were a matter of life and death. He himself did the work of two men, pushing himself to his physical limits so he would not have the time or energy for contemplation. At their nooning, all the cowboys were commenting on the sudden change in their usually relaxed foreman.

"Hasn't the boss got a wiggle on himself today," commented one to Curly.

"Yep. If he'd made this ol' world, he'd have made it in half a day an' gone fishin' in the afternoon—if his horses had held out," Curly responded. Dusty heard the joke but did not join in the general laughter. His friends sobered immediately. Dusty was usually the first to laugh at himself. Something was wrong with him, very wrong. They exchanged glances and mutely decided to give him a wide berth.

When work resumed, Dusty chose a horse to match his mood, a mustang he had named Cyclone. All of the cowponies were wild to some extent, and most would buck a time or two everytime they were ridden, just for meanness. Cyclone, however, had a peculiar trait. Dusty explained it by explaining how the horse was named: "That horse is just like a cyclone. Most times, you don't need to worry about it, but when it starts acomin', you just can't never tell where or what it's gonna hit." Cyclone would go for days or even weeks as gentle as a lamb and then, without warning and with slight provocation or no provocation, would begin to buck. A bucking horse was no great challenge to a cowboy, especially one like Dusty Rhoades, but then Cyclone would take off running and nothing would stop him until he decided to quit. Dusty did not mind that either and, in fact, was hoping Cyclone would give him a good run this afternoon.

The horse took the saddle calmly, even though Dusty was intentionally rough, trying to inspire him. He took the rider calmly, too, as if waiting for an opportune moment. When Dusty spurred him, that was the moment. Cyclone leaped and came down stiff legged, then lowered his head and bucked in earnest several times. Both horse and rider knew this was part of the game and Dusty kept his seat firmly. Then he spurred the horse again, and Cyclone took off as if his tail were afire. The pounding, driving ride with the wind searing his face was heaven to a man in Dusty's frame of mind, but his paradise suddenly faded as he saw that Cyclone was heading straight for a cut bank, twenty feet down to the creek bottom. With iron hands, he tried to slow or turn the horse, but nothing would swerve Cyclone once he had decided on a course. Desperately, the edge of the bank only a few feet ahead, Dusty kicked his feet clear of the stirrups, threw a leg over the horse's head, and jumped as Cyclone disappeared over the edge of the bank.

Priscilla was having a hard time concentrating on the children's lessons. Her mind kept wandering back to yesterday and reanalyzing everything that had happened in view of what she had decided about Dusty. He was, she knew, a very complex person, proud and stubborn, and when she charged him, as Stella had, with the fault of thinking himself not good enough for her, she was able to

318

explain every unexplainable bit of his behavior, even down to his cruelty of yesterday. Had he not just told her, in no uncertain terms, that he had nothing to offer a wife, and having nothing to offer would deny himself? Then when she had sought to trap him—how he had sensed that she would never know—he had lashed out at her, driving her away in a manner he knew would free her from him once and for all. It was all so simple, she wondered that she had never figured it out before, but at the same time, she realized the futility of understanding. Knowing what kept him from her would not bring him to her, and in a few days he would be gone from her life forever. Short of riding out to the roundup camp and crawling into Dusty's bedroll, Priscilla could think of no way to even see him before he left, much less speak to him of such private matters.

Her frustration was unendurable and the schoolroom suddenly seemed stifling. Leaving the children to their memorization, she walked to the open door and breathed deeply of the April air. As she gazed off across the green grass, she saw a strange sight. Watching for a moment, listening intently, she began to hear an even stranger sound. At first she doubted her senses, but then she was certain, and she hurried down the stairs. Scrambling up the hill beside the school, she stood at the barbed wire fence that protected the schoolyard from wandering cattle and stared with wondering eyes at the spectacle approaching.

It was the chuck wagon, not an unusual sight in itself, although it should not have been returning to the ranch at this hour. Aunt Sally was driving and singing at the top of his unmelodious voice a song whose words seemed strangely appropriate to Priscilla's state of mind:

> *When you are single*
> *And living at your ease*
> *You can roam this world over*
> *And do as you please;*
> *You can roam this world over*
> *And go where you will*
> *And shyly kiss a pretty girl*
> *And be your own still—*

Stranger yet was the din coming from the back of the wagon. It was a man's voice, shouting, and from what Priscilla could make out above Aunt Sally's singing, he was cursing abominably. Priscilla waved, trying to get Aunt Sally's attention as he continued to sing:

> *But when you are married*
> *And living with your wife,*
> *You've lost all the joys*
> *And comforts of life.*
> *Your wife she will scold you,*
> *Your children will cry,*
> *And that will make papa*
> *Look withered and dry.*
>
> *Come close to the bar, boys,*
> *We'll drink all around.*
> *We'll drink to the pure,*
> *If any be found;*
> *We'll drink to the . . .*

"Whoa!" Aunt Sally had seen her waving and pulled up the wagon within calling distance. "Howdy, ma'am!" he shouted and instantly the cursing from the interior of the wagon ceased.

"Is anything wrong?" Priscilla called.

"Not really, ma'am," he assured her blandly. "Dusty got hisself hurt an' I'm just takin' him back to the ranch."

"Hurt? Is it serious?" Priscilla tried to sound only mildly concerned, although she was gripped in an icy fear.

"He's stove up some, hurt his hi . . . uh . . . his le . . . uh . . . his side," Aunt Sally struggled to present the facts without offending a lady's sensibilities. "Don't look like he broke nothin' though."

Priscilla breathed a sigh of relief. "What happened?"

Aunt Sally considered a moment and then his face cracked into one of his rare smiles. "Seems like he fell off his horse, ma'am." Aunt Sally ignored the muttered imprecation behind him and continued to smile at Priscilla, one of the few women he had any use for. He had never quite forgiven Dusty for the way he had treated her at the dance and Aunt Sally felt justified in adding insult to injury.

"Oh, my," was all Priscilla could think of to say. She pretended she had not heard Dusty's muttered curse. "Tell Mrs. Wilson I'll be up as soon as school is out in case she needs any help."

"Shore will, ma'am," said Aunt Sally, tipping his hat in an uncharacteristic gesture and driving off.

At the ranch, George helped Aunt Sally get Dusty out of the wagon and into the bedroom of the cabin. They almost had him to the bed when Stella protested.

"He ain't messin' up my sheets with them dirty clothes. Help me strip him down."

With the men's help, she removed his vest and shirt,

leggings, and boots. When she started to pull off his jeans, he groaned, as much from embarrassment as from pain.

"Stella, you don't leave a man no dignity at all!" he complained.

Stella smiled but continued. When they got him onto the bed, Stella covered him and, walking to the foot of the bed, she commanded, "Unbutton your drawers and I'll pull them off."

"What?" he shouted.

"Do it, or I will," she ordered.

Certain she would, he did as she said. After she had pulled his underwear out from under the covers, she stepped around to the side of the bed.

"Now, throw back them covers and let me see it," she said, indicating his left hip, the spot where he had landed when he had jumped from Cyclone's back.

"No," he protested.

"I understand you're bashful, but listen here. We ain't even sent for the doc yet. It'll be hours, if he's in town, before he gets here, days if we have to go lookin' for him. Meantime, I'm the one's gotta look after you an' I can't do nothin' less I know what's wrong. Now throw back them covers."

Dusty looked appealingly to George, who nodded. "Do as she says," he advised.

Gingerly, Dusty moved the quilt to expose his hip. Raising his head, he saw it himself for the first time and groaned. Stella gave a slight gasp, George shook his head, and Aunt Sally whistled.

Dusty had meant to land on his feet when he jumped from the horse, but somehow he got the angle wrong and landed instead on his hip. Miraculously, nothing was

322

broken as the cowboys had determined before moving him, but he had a glorious bruise, the pain of which was excruciating.

"You've done it this time, boy," Stella observed. "Can you move your leg?"

With great difficulty he proved he could.

"I reckon you'll live, but we better fetch the doc up here just to make sure everythin's all right," Stella decided.

"I'll go," George offered. "Aunt Sally has to get back to the men. They'll be wanting their supper."

"I reckon Mr. Steele'll want Curly to take over," said Aunt Sally.

"I'm sure he will, but check with him before you leave. He'll want to know what happened to Dusty," said George.

Stella had a thought. "Get this boy some whiskey, George. He looks like he needs a drink."

"Whiskey! Where would I get whiskey, my dear? You know you don't allow it in the house," George said innocently.

"Don't get smart with me. I know you got a bottle hid around here somewheres. But just give him a little. No use gettin' him drunk."

After the men left, Stella started gathering Dusty's discarded clothes. "I'll get some hot water and we'll put some hot rags on it. That should help some," she said. "Guess this is one trail drive you'll miss."

"What?" Dusty repeated. He seemed genuinely shocked. He had not had time to consider the implications of his injury.

"You ain't goin' nowhere with that hip, especially not on the back of a horse. I'll bet the doc keeps you in bed two weeks or more."

Dusty groaned again. As Stella turned to go, she heard a metallic clink. Looking down, she saw a small gold coin had fallen to the floor. Picking it up, she smiled. "Here's your gold piece," she said, placing it on the bedside table. "I'll put it here since you ain't got no pockets." She ignored the unkind things Dusty had to say to her as she left the room.

Priscilla was genuinely worried when she reached the ranch, but Stella's matter-of-fact explanation of Dusty's condition calmed her fears. The doctor arrived soon after, and his diagnosis was the same as Stella's. Ruth and Priscilla had to retreat to the house during his examination because the doctor's probing inspired Dusty to new extremes of profanity that could be heard clearly in the yard. The doctor also prescribed periodic manipulation of the leg to keep the joint from stiffening, a procedure he showed Stella how to do. Dusty's protests could be heard even inside the ranch house.

Priscilla and Ruth helped Maria get the family's supper, and Stella began to prepare a tray for Dusty.

"Well, I ain't takin' him his supper," Stella announced. "I heard enough cussin' for one day. I declare, I been hearin' cowboys cuss all my life, but Dusty Rhoades taught me some new ones today. I never seen a man so broke up about bein' hurt. He was bad enough 'til he found out he'd miss the trail drive. Then he went plumb crazy. You'd think something terrible was gonna happen to him if he stays here one more day."

Priscilla considered this. Was he afraid of facing her again? Of course he was, and rightly so, she decided.

"Ruth," Stella said, "you take this tray to Dusty."

Ruth's eyes grew large and moist. "Not me!" she

declared with as much determination as meek Ruth ever mustered.

Stella's eyes narrowed. "He wasn't cussin' at you, too, was he?"

"No," Ruth said. "Even worse."

"Worse?" Stella stared in shocked surprise.

"Yes," Ruth replied miserably. "When I was in there before, I was just trying to be cheerful and nice, and he accused me"—tears were rolling down her face now—"he accused me of bein' *glad* he was hurt so he couldn't leave." She looked at Priscilla's and Stella's amazed faces. "The terrible part is he was right!"

Maybe it was the scare they had had, followed by the great relief that made them giddy. At any rate, when Stella and Priscilla heard the reason for Ruth's misery, they dissolved in gales of laughter.

"Quiet! He'll hear you," cautioned Ruth, and that made them laugh even harder, clinging to each other until the tears began to fall. Finally, too weak to continue, they dried their eyes and with great difficulty composed themselves.

Holding her side, Stella said, "You should have seen his face when I told him to take off his drawers!"

"Stella, you didn't!" Priscilla gasped, and when Stella nodded, they dissolved again.

A solemn Maria broke their hilarity by her appearance. Catching her breath, Stella eyed Maria and said, "Well, Maria, you can take Mr. Dusty's dinner to him now."

Maria replied in very rapid Spanish. The words were unintelligible to Priscilla, but she grasped their meaning just the same. Stella pretended to be shocked. "Maria! What would your priest say if he heard you talk like that?"

Maria sniffed. "He no take Señor Dusty his dinner either."

Priscilla started to laugh again until she saw Stella's blue eyes fixed on her expectantly.

"Oh, no," she protested.

"The boy's gotta eat," insisted Stella. "He won't cuss and carry on in front of you." Ruth begged her, Stella pleaded, but it was her own realization that this was just the opportunity she had been waiting for that caused her to consent.

As she started out the door, tray in hand, Stella added casually, "You'll have to feed him, 'cause he can't sit up. It hurts him too much."

"Stella, you didn't tell me that!" Priscilla started back in, but Stella closed the door, so she was trapped.

The closer she got to the cabin, the more apprehensive she became, until she remembered that he would be just as nervous about seeing her as she was about seeing him. In fact, he had been in the wrong so he should be more nervous. And what if she were not upset at all about what had happened? That would really throw him, she decided and marched the rest of the way to the cabin with determined steps.

As she opened the cabin door, a contortionist's trick with the laden tray, she was startled by a bellow from within: "Stella, where's my supper!"

Priscilla tiptoed through the front room and peeked into the bedroom. Dusty was lying in the bed, and she was shocked by the sight of his bare chest covered with all that red-gold hair. She had never seen another man's naked chest before and was still not used to Dusty's, and she almost dropped the tray. With a little shiver she remembered Stella's remark about removing his drawers,

326

and she had to assume he was completely naked under the covers. Well, now, what would her friends in Philadelphia think about that? She had him just where she wanted him, naked and helpless, and she intended to make the most of it. Drawing a deep breath, she went in.

Just as she crossed the threshhold, Dusty again shouted, "Stella!"

Priscilla smiled, and trying not to look too cheerful so as not to be accused of Ruth's crime, she sang out, "Here's your supper."

For a minute he was too stunned to move and then in a frenzy of embarrassment, he snatched the covers up to his chin, eying her with suspicion.

"We're all so glad you weren't seriously injured," Priscilla said sweetly.

Dusty could not believe she was really here. "Where's Stella?" he demanded.

"Oh, she . . . what's that expression? Oh, yes, she had too many irons in the fire and so she asked me to take care of you." Priscilla set the tray down and pulled a chair up beside the bed and sat down. She shook out the napkin and placed it on the blanket over his chest, picked up the plate and spoon, scooped up some food, and offered it to him.

"Now, eat your supper like a good boy," she cajoled.

"What in the hell are you doin'?" he snarled, uncertain whether he was more embarrassed at being caught in such a predicament or terrified at her cheerful attitude.

"My goodness," she chided. "Stella said you wouldn't swear at me. I'm feeding you. Stella also said it would be too painful for you to sit up and feed yourself."

"She did, huh? Well, nobody's feedin' me like I was a

baby," he said.

"Suit yourself. Can I help you?" she offered.

"No!" he snapped and tried to push himself up to a sitting position. The effort cost him. His face turned white and beads of perspiration popped out on his forehead until finally he fell back in surrender.

His pain brought tears to Priscilla's eyes. So that he would not see, she quickly jumped up and began to moisten a towel in the water pitcher, blinking back her tears. Then she wiped his face off, and when his breathing returned to normal and the color came back to his cheeks, she again offered him food, and he ate grudgingly and silently.

As she was feeding him, she noticed the gold coin lying on the bedside table. Curious, she picked it up. It looked like a coin except that it was square and worn smooth by much handling. "What's this?" she asked.

He chewed and swallowed before answering and the irony in his voice was unmistakable. "It's my lucky gold piece."

Priscilla barely managed to stifle a smile. When he had finished eating, she asked, "Would you like anything else?"

"No, you can go now." It was as much an appeal as a statement, but Priscilla was not quite finished.

"It must be a big disappointment to you not to be able to make this trip." She sounded very sincere, but he refused to look at her or reply. "Yes, it must really be a disappointment, especially after you kissed all the girls goodbye."

His head jerked around toward her and he stared a moment, his jaw muscles quivering. He had known she would call him. Well, here it was. He would face it like a man. Deliberately, he said, "I only kissed *one* girl goodbye, and I'm mighty sorry I did." It was as close as he could come to an apology without betraying himself.

Priscilla feigned surprise. "Why, Mr. Rhoades, it isn't very gallant for a gentleman to say he is sorry he kissed a lady."

What did she want, anyway? "I ain't sorry I kissed her," he tried again, his voice strained. "I'm just sorry I did it that way."

"And what way was that?" she asked innocently.

How could he answer a question like that? "A way she didn't like," he hedged.

Priscilla considered a moment. "Are you certain she didn't like it?" She had liked the kiss and the loving. It was the rest of it that had upset her—his lies. "I mean, did you ask her permission? Did she refuse to kiss you? And when you did, did she slap your face or kiss you back? You see, a lady will often slap a man's face when she would prefer to kiss him back, but she will never kiss him back if she prefers to slap his face." Since she had done both, she reasoned, that should give him something to think about. Snatching the napkin from his chest, she rose to leave.

Dusty's mind was reeling. He knew she was trying to tell him something but her meaning was lost in the barrage of words, and he could not understand what she was telling him. Maybe it was George's whiskey. Now she would leave, and he would never know what she meant. Reaching for her hand, he begged, "Wait!"

What other words he might have spoken were lost forever in a howl of pain, however, for as he reached over to grab her, he inadvertently rolled onto his injured hip. His yell filled the room with people. Obviously, Stella had been vigilant, expecting Dusty to give Priscilla trouble. Priscilla explained briefly that he had apparently moved wrong and then as Stella and the others tried to settle him down, Priscilla slipped out. She would give him time to think over what she had said and draw his own conclusions. Meanwhile, she could be as maddeningly aloof as he.

Chapter Eleven

Jason Vance could hardly believe his eyes. He passed his hand over them for a moment to make sure he was not hallucinating. No, there it was, exactly as the map had shown. The hills all in place, the river flowing in an S shape around them, the landscape he had pictured so vividly in his mind for so many months. What he had not pictured were the ranch buildings sitting on the hills. He had held off exploring this part of the country because he knew whose ranch lay in this vicinity. Most probably this was it, and his gold—for he now thought of it as his own—lay within five miles of this very spot. He had to make certain, of course, and since he was here, it would be a simple matter of riding up to the ranch house and seeing who came to the door. Then he would know. It was almost dinner time, and the smoke from the chimney told him someone was home.

When he rode into the yard, several young children scattered like chicks before him, seeking refuge behind their mother, who appeared in the doorway.

Vance swept off his hat and bowed from his saddle. "Hello, Mrs. Rogers. I had no idea this was your home. I was exploring the countryside and when I saw your smoke I thought I'd see if I could beg a meal."

Hazel Rogers hesitated only a moment. She was alone with the children, and a woman alone had to be careful whom she invited in. Of course, Mr. Vance had always treated her with perfect respect—the time he had given her money for the doctor bill and the other time they had met at the store when he had given her children candy—and everyone knew he lived at the saloon with Rita Jordan. The idea that a man who slept with Rita Jordan might want Hazel was actually funny. Smiling at the thought, she said, "Howdy, Mr. Vance. Get down and come in. It isn't much since I wasn't expecting to feed a man, but you're very welcome."

Vance hesitated now. "I don't think your husband would be very happy if he found out you fed me, ma'am."

"He isn't likely to find out, Mr. Vance. He's in Fort Worth selling some cattle and won't be home for a week or more. Besides, we're obliged to you. Come on in and set."

He was totally unprepared for the interior of Hazel Rogers' home. The rundown condition of the buildings was about what he would have expected from a man like Rogers, but Hazel had so transformed the interior that it seemed like another world. Tapestries hid the rough walls and frilly curtains adorned the windows. An embroidered tablecloth covered a crude pine table and she had even made covers for the straight chairs. Everywhere he looked he saw evidence of her handiwork and creativity. Once again he tasted the nameless longing, smelled the magnolias. With effort he returned his concentration to the job at hand.

As he sat and ate of the simple food Hazel set before him, he casually inquired about the workings of the ranch. To his disgust he learned that Rogers owned the place outright. If there was one man Vance did not want to share the gold with, it was Rogers. He had been gone two weeks, would be gone a week longer, more probably two. If Vance could locate the gold and remove it before then . . . He asked about the size of the ranch, the area covered, what sort of terrain lay in different directions. Unfortunately, Hazel was not much help since she rarely left home and only then to go to town or to a neighbor's. She would be no help in locating the gold, but at least he had a week or two. If he did not find it by then, well . . . surely he could find it in a week.

Stella kept looking up from her sewing to watch Priscilla reading. She had not turned a page in at least fifteen minutes. Wonder what she's thinking? Wonder what happened in there with Dusty this evening? Priscilla was acting mighty coy. Stella smiled. *Mighty* coy.

Ruth broke the silence in the parlor. "Do you think it would be a good idea to ask Reverend Allen to come over and pray for Dusty's recovery?"

Stella thought it was a terrible idea and almost said so until Priscilla silenced her with a look.

"Oh, Ruth, what a marvelous idea. I'm sure Dusty would appreciate it very much," Priscilla said, giving Stella a warning glance. "Why don't you ride over and invite him for supper tomorrow night?"

Ruth flushed rosily at Priscilla's suggestion and agreed with alacrity. Later, when Ruth had gone to bed, Stella demanded, "Now just what was all that about?"

Priscilla looked up with abject innocence. "I'm merely concerned for Dusty's speedy recovery," she said.

Stella made a very rude noise. "He's not gonna be real grateful to you for this," she began, and then another thought occurred to her. "Is this by any chance part of your plan to get him jealous?"

"Hardly," Priscilla sniffed, not bothering to explain that she had already used Reverend Allen for that purpose, with very satisfactory results. "The fact is, in case you haven't noticed, Ruth is very fond of Reverend Allen, and I think that with a little encouragement, he might become equally fond of her."

"Reverend Allen?" Stella asked in amazement. "Oh, I knew about Ruthie likin' him, but him likin' her, that don't seem very likely."

"Then you may be in for a surprise," Priscilla warned her smugly.

Stella shook her head. "Too bad I don't believe in gamblin'! It'd be a pleasure takin' your money on this one," she teased.

"You'll see," Priscilla warned good-naturedly, and they left it at that.

Reverend Allen arrived shortly before supper the next day and promptly paid a call on the injured cowboy. Since Dusty had little use for preachers in general and even less use for a man who had proposed to Priscilla, their interview was understandably short.

Seeing the strange look on Reverend Allen's face as he emerged from the cabin, Priscilla could not resist an urge to see Dusty's reaction to the visit. She was in his room before she realized she had failed to think up an excuse for being there. At least Dusty was decent this time, having acquired one of George's nightshirts. But his expression was far from decent, and he was so angry, he did not seem to care why she had come. He only wanted to know one thing.

"Who sent for that jackass?" he demanded.

"I did!" she lied, offended by his attitude.

"Oh, I get it," he said knowingly. "You used me for an excuse to get your sweetheart here." It was an agonizing thought and why he tortured himself by expressing it was more than he could understand.

Furious, Priscilla could hardly control her voice. Hadn't she already set him straight on that point? "For your information, I asked him here because of Ruth."

"Ruthie?" he asked, completely puzzled. "Is somethin' wrong with Ruth?"

"Of course not! She . . . well, she happens to find Reverend Allen very attractive and . . ."

"Ruthie!" Dusty was incredulous. This was almost as bad as him coming to see Priscilla. "My God, you'd throw Ruth Steele away on that . . . that . . ."

"Jackass?" Priscilla suggested helpfully.

He glared at her, unable to believe anyone could have had such a stupid idea. Suddenly, Priscilla realized why he was so angry and that really rankled her.

"I know you think you're the official matchmaker for the Steele girls. It must be a shock to you to realize one of them can find a suitor without your help." He did not answer, so she continued. "I suppose you have someone all picked out for Ruth."

"Matter of fact, yes," he said belligerently, folding his arms across his chest.

"Who?" she demanded.

"Curly Yates."

"Curly Yates?" Now Priscilla was incredulous. "You can't believe Ben Steele would let his daughter marry an ordinary cowboy."

Dusty did not answer for a moment, and she could see his jaw muscles twitch as he fought for self-control. Then he spoke very slowly, as if explaining to someone of limited intelligence. "Curly ain't no ordinary cowboy. This minute he's trail boss, leadin' about three thousand head of cattle all the way to Kansas. When he gets back, he'll be the foreman here . . ."

"Foreman? But you're . . ." Priscilla began and then stopped. What had she been thinking? For the past twenty-four hours she had been living in a fool's paradise. Somehow she had assumed that because he had missed the drive, he would be staying on. Obviously, he had no intention of it. Something inside her turned over and she could hardly follow what he was continuing to say.

"When I'm gone, Ben'll need somebody knows how to run this place and it sure ain't gonna be George," he continued, not noticing Priscilla's reaction. "He's the sorriest hand you ever saw. An' it ain't gonna be that red-haired Bible-thumper! Curly, he can run this place as good as me, maybe better. Shoot, he could've left here a long time ago, got a foreman's job anywhere. Only reason he stuck was 'cause of Ruthie. He's been sweet on her since the first time he laid eyes on her. He's just been waitin' for her to grow up some."

"It's just . . . I thought . . ." Priscilla tried lamely.

"Ben Steele ain't no fool," he went on, ignoring her interruption. "He knows what Curly's worth to him, an'

336

he knows he'll need someone like him to boss the place. It just stands to reason that a son-in-law'll work harder than a hired hand."

"Of course. You're right, of course," Priscilla mumbled, trying to focus on Ruth's problem instead of her own. "At least Ruth should have a chance to decide for herself," she decided, regaining some of her composure. "You'd better warn Curly that he's got some competition, though," she continued sharply. "He's liable to come back and find she's married someone else." She left before he could answer.

Curly arrived late the next afternoon to report to Ben Steele that they would be leaving the following morning. Priscilla could see that he felt the importance of his new responsibility, and if before he seemed a carefree boy, now he seemed a man. She hoped Ruth noticed it, too. Dusty's arguments had convinced her that Curly was the right man for Ruth, after all. Indeed, it now seemed silly to pair her off with Reverend Allen, whom Priscilla herself had admitted was not much of a catch.

After his meeting with Ben, Curly paid Dusty a visit. "Howdy, pard," he greeted his friend. "How you doin'?"

"Fair to middlin'," Dusty replied.

Curly's grin was mischievous. "You should've stuck on that horse, boy. You're hurt worse'n he was."

"The hell you say? That horse ain't still alive?" Dusty demanded.

"Alive an' kickin'," Curly answered him with a chuckle. "I climbed down after him to fetch up your saddle, and damn if he didn't jump up and shake off and start friskin' around, good as new."

Dusty cursed Cyclone roundly for his failure to die in the fall, and when he was finished, he remembered

337

Priscilla's warning.

"Hey, pard," he said to Curly, "there's somethin' you gotta do before you leave. Grab up a chair an' I'll tell you."

Priscilla was sitting on the porch with Ruth, holding her a virtual captive until she saw Curly emerge from the cabin. If Dusty had done what she had told him to, then she would give Curly his chance. Taking Ruth by the hand, she fairly dragged the startled girl down the stairs. "Come here, Ruth. There's something I want to show you," she said, pulling her right into Curly's path. The three almost collided before Priscilla pretended to be surprised to see him.

"Why, Mr. Yates, hello! Congratulations on your new position." Curly removed his hat, somewhat embarrassed. "I know Mr. Steele has every confidence in you. Isn't that right, Ruth?"

Ruth sincerely, if shyly, agreed.

"Although I don't know how we'll manage around here without you while you're gone," Priscilla said. "We'll certainly miss him, won't we, Ruth?"

"Yes, we will," said Ruth. Ruth and Curly were looking at each other now. Curly looked determined; Ruth, puzzled at what she sensed but did not understand.

"Oh, will you excuse me? I need to check on Mr. Rhoades," Priscilla lied, stealing away from them. They did not even notice.

Priscilla heard Curly say, "I shore will miss *you*, Ruth."

Priscilla glanced over her shoulder. Ruth's cheeks were pink as she replied, "You will?" This was news to her, and very good news, too, it seemed.

Priscilla slipped into the cabin and went to the window

where she could watch unobserved. Dusty heard her come in.

"Who's there?" he called.

"It's Priscilla," she answered, never taking her eyes from the couple in the yard.

"What are you doin' out there?" he asked crossly.

"Spying on Ruth and Curly," she replied blandly.

"What are they doin'?" he asked eagerly.

"They're talking . . . now they're walking . . . looks like they're heading for . . . yes, they're walking down toward the river . . . Now they're out of sight." She walked into the bedroom where Dusty lay. "Your friend Curly is a fool," she announced.

"What are you talking about?" he asked, shifting uneasily under her angry glare.

"I'm talking about how he almost lost the woman he loves. Here he's loved her for—how long did you say?"

"Almost two years," he supplied reluctantly.

"Two years! And he never even let her know." Priscilla was furious. "He deserves to lose her. He might have come back to find her married to another man, never even guessing that he cared for her."

"He was scared she'd turn him down if he asked her too soon," Dusty tried to explain.

"So what if she did! There's nothing more attractive to a woman than a man who's in love with her. If Ruth had guessed that Curly loved her, why, she would have found him irresistible." Her temper made her bold. "You remember that, Dusty Rhoades." She turned on her heel and left, just barely stifling the urge to shake a confession out of him.

Dusty hated it when she was like that, her eyes blazing, her face all glowing, hands on her hips. Made him want to grab her and kiss her until she couldn't breathe, 'til she was helpless, and then he'd . . . Whew! He was sweating. Didn't do any good to think about things like that. He remembered what she'd said. He smiled to himself. Wonder what she'd say if she knew what *he* thought about *her*. Would she find him irresistible? He doubted it.

"You're very cruel," Ruth was saying, sitting on the split log bench down by the river.

"I am?" asked Curly, not at all certain whether that was good or bad.

"Yes, to tell me this when you'll be leaving tomorrow." She turned to him with eyes that said she thought him anything but cruel. "Now I'll be miserable for months until you get back."

Slowly, his face broke into a thrilling smile. Ruth thought he had never looked more handsome. "You'll really be miserable?" he asked, as if that were the best news he had ever heard.

Ruth smiled back, looking anything but miserable. "I'll be utterly and completely disconsolate"—a word she had read in a novel.

This *was* great news. He made a move and for an instant Ruth thought he would take her in his arms, but he held back, apparently unsure whether or not he should. She touched his face with her fingertips.

"How will I ever live through the next few months without you?" she asked, and he took her hand, pressing her fingers to his lips. Then they were kissing. Ruth had saved her first kiss for the man she was going to marry, and she spent it freely now, her first and many others.

When they paused for breath, Curly said, "When I get back, I'll have a question to ask you."

She looked at him with shining eyes. "You know what

my answer will be."

"You sure?" he asked uncertainly. "There ain't no one else?"

"What makes you think so?"

"Well, Dusty said the preacher . . ."

"The preacher! Dusty's crazy," Ruth declared, and at least she was sure that somebody was. It did seem crazy to have wanted Reverend Allen when all the time Curly . . . She shivered and hugged him tighter.

"Maybe we should tell your pa before I leave," he said.

"Oh, no!" said Ruth. "My sisters would tease me to death while you're gone. And if the boys found out, why, you wouldn't need to take a *remuda*. They'd ride you all the way to Dodge." She was right of course, so they decided to keep it a secret, never dreaming that everyone at the ranch had already guessed why they had wandered down to the river together. It was only a few days before one of the boys caught Curly writing a love letter on the trail.

A few days after Curly left, Dusty felt well enough to get out of bed. After a few more days of walking around his room, he began to exercise by walking around the ranch yard. In all this time, he had made no effort to engage Priscilla in conversation and had, in fact, avoided it. Priscilla decided to wait until his disposition improved, which she hoped would happen when he was able to get around better. One day, almost two weeks after his accident, she encountered him leaving the ranch yard. He was wearing the moccasins he used for walking and carrying one of Ben's walking sticks.

"Where are you going?" she asked politely.

"Down to the river," he said curtly, not quite meeting her eye, and half hoping she would go away, while his other half hoped she would not.

"May I go with you?" she asked, willing to accept the least encouragement.

"Suit yourself," he replied, slowly limping away. He wasn't about to invite her, but if she really wanted to come along, he wouldn't object, either.

Priscilla gave an exasperated sigh and planted her hands on her hips as she watched his laborious progress. If she were to suit herself, she decided, she'd snatch that walking stick out of his hand and do him severe bodily harm with it. She was of half a mind to say so, too, when he stopped and called back over his shoulder, "You comin' or not?" Who, she asked herself, could resist such a charming invitation? If he got too bad, she reasoned as she hurried to join him, she could always push him into the river.

He did not speak as they made their way across the ranch yard, and Priscilla, only too aware of how painful it was for him to walk, did not break the silence either as she slowed her pace to match his. When they reached the split log bench which Ruth and Curly had recently made such good use of, Dusty lowered himself carefully onto it, favoring his bad leg, and then, without looking up, reached into his pocket, pulled out a clean bandanna, and spread it out on the bench for her to sit on.

Priscilla hesitated only a moment before joining him on the bench. His courtesy, combined with his sullen silence, was a little disconcerting, but at least he seemed resigned to her presence. Dare she risk going a little further? Undecided, she took a moment to survey her surroundings. It was a lovely spot. The river here, too, was lined with wild fruit trees that had recently bloomed into glorious blossom, and the greening weeping willows swayed lazily in the gentle breeze that Priscilla now knew never stopped but only changed direction. Some romantic soul had placed the bench in a semi-secluded spot beneath a massive willow tree, thus providing the privacy so necessary to courting couples. Not that she and Dusty were courting, at least not yet. Anything was possible, though, and if he still had his mind set on leaving, she had better make the most of this opportunity. Perhaps if she started out slowly, testing his reactions. A little flirting, some gentle teasing, and the next thing they both knew, they'd be in each other's arms. It had happened so often in the past without any planning at all that Priscilla felt reasonably certain she could make it happen again. The thought sent an anticipatory quiver up the inside of her thighs and caused a strange contraction deep within her loins. Savoring her response, she cast about for something to say.

Dusty, meanwhile, was also trying to think of something to say in mounting irritation at his own stupidity. What on earth had he been thinking when he had invited her along? Instead of using his head, he'd been letting another organ entirely do his thinking for him, and while his head knew perfectly well how dangerous it was to be around her, that other part of him only remembered how warm and soft she felt closed all around him. It was enough to drive a man plumb out of his mind. But what a way to go, he thought, stealing a glance at the way her lush body filled out her simple calico dress. He almost jumped when she spoke.

"Men are certainly fortunate. I envy you, Mr. Rhoades," she said.

"What do you mean?" he asked suspiciously, not feeling the least bit fortunate.

"Well, your freedom. Men have so much more freedom than women. Take, for example, your plans to start your own ranch. All you have to do is climb on your horse and ride off until you find it," she explained, treating him to her look of wide-eyed admiration.

"You make it sound mighty easy," he said uneasily, not certain if she were teasing or not.

"Oh, it's hard work, of course. I realize that," she admitted, "but at least you have the opportunity to do it. If I wanted a ranch, I couldn't simply climb on a horse and ride off in search of one," she pointed out, maintaining her admiring look although he had not yet given her more than a passing glance.

He snorted. "Talk about easy, it's women got it easy," he replied bitterly. "All a woman's got to do is sit around and wait for some poor fella to propose to her. She wants a ranch, she waits 'til somebody with a ranch comes along."

"You make it sound mighty easy," she mimicked him, delighting in the bitterness she heard in his voice. "Suppose the right man doesn't ask?" she asked coyly.

For the first time he looked at her, full in the face, a hint of irony in his eyes. "*You* got no worries. The rate you're gettin' proposals, the right man's *bound* to come along," he told her, then he pulled his eyes away from her. Much as he liked looking at her, it was only inviting trouble. Having her so close was bad enough.

Priscilla stifled a groan. This conversation was not going at all the way she had planned. As gratifying as it was to know he did not like the idea of other men proposing to her, it got her no closer to having him propose himself, and might even prevent that very thing. She had better change the subject and fast.

344

"What's the name of that cattle that you like so well? Heifers?" she asked innocently.

A little disconcerted at the rapid change of topics, Dusty could only stare at her for a long moment, and then he laughed a little over her mistake and his own embarrassment. "No, it's Hereford," he corrected.

Cheered by the sound of his laughter, she gave him her most guileless smile. "What is it you like about them?"

Not bothering to ask himself why she would want to know a thing like that, he proceeded to explain to her how the Texas Longhorns—although admirably suited to life on a ranch and to long trail drives—were actually poor beef animals, their meat tough and stringy. Yes, she had noticed that. Herefords, on the other hand, were good meat animals. Now that fencing was beginning to catch on, he believed that the two types of cattle could be bred, under controlled conditions, to produce cattle with the best qualities of both. Priscilla listened, fascinated, as much because of his manner as because of the information. He spoke to her as an equal, without bantering or insulting or any of the little tricks he usually used to keep her at arm's length. In truth, he had forgotten the necessity for doing so. He was looking at her now, his voice serious and patient. He was looking right into her eyes, and she knew the power of those eyes. She had turned men into jelly with them. Confident of her ability to do so again, she turned them on him full force.

When he was finished with his speech about cattle, he stopped, seemingly unable to turn his gaze from hers. She had him now. With a coquettish smile, she asked softly, "Is it true you can't resist big brown eyes?"

Dusty heard her question but it seemed to come from a

great distance, and he had a hard time forming an answer, a hard time doing anything at all except watching the way those huge brown eyes were watching him, and then she tilted up her chin and all he could see were those sweet pink lips and they were parting in a smile, and then he was touching them, tasting them, and he forgot her question completely.

Priscilla surrendered willingly to his kiss, clinging to him with eager hands, curving herself to his embrace, but she was also mindful of the need to maintain control, to guide his passion into the proper channels. Once committed, she knew he would be honor bound to take her. But she must first get that commitment while she was still mistress of the situation, she warned herself, fighting the traitorous weakness that urged her to pull him down upon the grass. Turning her face, she offered him the secret place behind her ear to nibble on as she breathed out the words she thought might convince him. "What if I told you that you're the right man?"

It took a moment for Dusty's befuddled brain to register her question and another for him to make the connection with what they had been discussing before. He felt stupid, drugged, the way he always felt when she was in his arms, and he had a hard time forming a sensible answer. Even then, it wasn't too sensible. "I don't have a ranch," was all he could think of, knowing vaguely that that had something to do with who the right man for her was.

"That doesn't matter," she murmured, moving her lips back to his for a long, smoldering kiss.

That kiss was almost her undoing as her body seemed to slip beyond her control, her nerve ends sparking like tinder under his fiery touch. Her arms tightened around him, and he answered by crushing her to his chest, as if he would draw her inside of him, a possibility she found enticing, and so she enticed him back, sending silent messages with her hands and lips. He had no trouble at all interpreting those messages, so attuned were their bodies, and he began to stroke the breasts that nuzzled him so temptingly, drawing from her that purring moan he found so amazing and so irresistible. He never for a moment considered resistance, concentrating instead on moving aside the barriers to those roseate peaks that hardened obediently under his familiar encouragement. In another silent message, Priscilla pulled her lips from his, throwing her head back to offer him the smooth ivory of her throat. His lips blazed a trail down to the throbbing pulse and then continued on to encircle each creamy breast with a thousand searing kisses until her nipples burned like red-hot coals, and then he extinguished them in the warm, wet depths of his ravenous mouth. Priscilla laced her fingers into the soft, thick layers of his gleaming hair, forcing him to take more of her and he gladly obliged her, wanting only in that moment to bury himself in her yielding flesh.

Dusty began to send his own silent signals as one hand found the curve of her hip and then slid tantalizingly down her thigh. Priscilla responded, opening to his urgent stroking, welcoming the sweet invasion he promised with those magic fingers, but when he began to fumble with her skirt, she suddenly recalled her purpose. She must win his confession *before*, she *must*, she told herself, recalling what had happened the last time, and ruthlessly dragged her consciousness back from the world of sensation. "It doesn't matter if you don't have a ranch," she whispered breathlessly.

Dusty was still having trouble thinking, but he knew somehow that what she had said wasn't right. How could she not care that he didn't have a ranch when he knew that having a ranch was the most important thing? Why was she telling him he was the right man when he knew he wasn't? The answer came to him with such sudden ferocity that his passion was snuffed like a candle flame. He released Priscilla so quickly and so thoroughly that she fell quite ignominiously backward off the bench. Heedless of the pain in his hip, he leaped to his feet, rage at her treachery actually making him tremble. All she had wanted from him was a proposal, a proposal she could turn down and add to her list, to be recounted to the next poor sucker who came along. It would have been the perfect revenge. "Is that how you do it?" he demanded hoarsely.

Struggling to a sitting position on the grass while at the same time trying to get her feet down from the bench without completely exposing herself, Priscilla could only blink in surprise. "Do what?" she asked dazedly.

"Get men to propose to you. You look at 'em with them eyes of yours 'til they can't think straight an' next thing they know, they're on their knees. Well, it ain't gonna work with me, lady. Maybe you think just 'cause I love you . . ." He caught himself, too late. He would rather have died than let her know that, but unable to recall the words, he went on. "Well, you ain't hangin' my scalp on your belt!" he said in a strangely strangled voice, and limped away, leaving her sitting dumbfounded on the grass.

When she could think again, only one thought came:
He said he loved me!

When Old Man Rogers rode into town, it was almost
sundown. He had been drinking and felt like drinking
some more. He still had almost all the money he had made
from the sale of his cattle and he wanted to celebrate a
little before going home. Going home always depressed
him.

The Yellow Rose was crowded. A lot of strange
cowboys stood around, obviously men from passing
drives who had stopped in Rainbow for supplies. Several
of them were engaged in a poker game with Jason Vance.
Rogers bought a drink and went to watch the game, a
strange gleam in his eye.

Vance saw Rogers come in and the sight of the rancher
irritated him. For two weeks Vance had roamed the
Rogers' ranch searching for the spot where the gold was
hidden. He had the area almost pinpointed but as yet had
been unable to find it exactly. Now Rogers was back. It
would be dangerous if he were caught snooping or digging
on another man's property. Rogers would probably love
to have an excuse to shoot him. Vance felt the irritation
turn to anger, but as usual, his face betrayed nothing.

"Hey Vance, how about lettin' me in the game?"
Rogers taunted.

Vance smiled as if it were a joke, but one of the
cowboys at the table stood up and said, "Here, take my
place, mister. I already lost more'n I should have."
Before Vance could protest, Rogers had taken a seat.

Will, the bartender, appeared at Rogers's side.

"Excuse me, Rogers, but I'll hold your hardware until after the game." Reluctantly, Rogers turned over his gun.

"You get that sleeve gun of his, too. Don't forget who was the one got shot the last time," Rogers said.

Vance obliged by turning over his own gun, much to the surprise of all the strangers in the room. Swiftly, the story of Vance's shooting of Rogers made the whispered rounds.

The game began pleasantly enough. Vance recalled what Hazel Rogers had said about her husband being on a trip to sell cattle. For two weeks, Vance had ridden dusty or rain-soaked miles, and he was irritated. If he had enjoyed riding all over the country, he would have become a cowboy! Vance liked to be compensated for his labors and no one had compensated him for riding over Rogers's range. But Rogers had money, and Vance saw a way to get a little of his own back. Maybe more than a little.

As the play progressed, the other players began to drop out. Vance had been playing for several hours and had been winning, as was his custom with strangers, so he had a good stake. Before long the pots got too large for the cowboys, and with a joke or a groan, one by one they left the game until Rogers and Vance played alone. Vance purposely lost two hands. Once he folded holding two pair knowing full well that Rogers held only two queens and the other time he allowed Rogers to bluff him, knowing the rancher held nothing. Anyone could have seen the effect this had on Rogers. Obviously, the rancher wanted revenge on the gambler and saw a chance to beat him at his own game. With gleaming eyes and flushed cheeks he took up the hand Vance had dealt him.

Perspiration broke out on his forehead as he examined his cards.

After the initial betting, Vance inquired, "Cards?"

"I'll take one," Rogers replied unevenly.

Vance passed him a single card and no one in the room missed the gasp of surprise Rogers gave as he picked it up. "Dealer takes three," said Vance casually, as if he had not noticed, and dealt himself three cards.

The betting began, and a child could have seen how confident Rogers was. Vance tried to keep his raises conservative but Rogers soon had every last cent of his cattle money on the table. Vance required a loan from his employer to cover the bet.

"I'll call you, Rogers," Vance said coolly. The tension in the room was thick enough to cut. Not one man moved. Rogers smiled a slow smile and laid his cards down carefully. "Three twos, and two threes. Believe that's called a full house," Rogers gloated. The room was perfectly still, as if everyone had ceased even to breathe.

Jason Vance did not permit himself a display of emotion. As calmly as if he were playing for a two-dollar pot, he spread his cards. The silence became a murmur and the murmur became a roar. Rogers lurched to his feet, his face crimson, swearing loudly at the four aces that lay staring back at him.

"You damn card sharp! You cheated me!" Rogers bellowed, reaching instinctively for the gun which was not there. Friendly hands reached out to restrain him, calm him, but he shook them off.

Vance never batted an eye. "I'll give you a chance to get even, Rogers. How about one more hand, winner take all?"

"I got nothin' left!" snarled Rogers.

Vance considered a moment. "I've been wanting to take up ranching. Why not all this"—he gestured to the thousands of dollars of chips before him—"against your ranch."

For a moment Rogers stared, dumbfounded. A slow-witted man, he seemed to be laboring over the decision, but Vance, knowing more about human nature than most men, could see he was not even tempted by the proposition. He was, instead, trying to figure something out, a difficult process with his liquor-numbed brain. At last, he appeared to arrive at a conclusion. He stood up straight, adjusting his coat and squaring his shoulders in an almost comic attempt at dignity.

"Hell no, Vance," he sneered, and after retrieving his gun, he left, the room still silent as the batwing doors slapped behind him.

Later men would say that Vance simply shrugged and gathered up his winnings. No one had noticed the anger that flickered momentarily across his face. After buying a round of drinks for the house, Vance left the saloon. It was near closing and most assumed he simply went to bed. From her window, Rita watched him slip down the dark alley to the livery and then ride away into the night.

Old Man Rogers rode slowly, nursing his bottle. He was not really old, barely forty, but tonight he felt much older. He started when he heard the hoofbeats approaching, but then he laughed sardonically to himself. Guess I don't have to worry about no robbers tonight, he thought.

"Rogers, wait," the rider called and Rogers froze at the sound of that voice. Fury welled up in him as he turned his horse to face Vance.

"What you want, you low-down cheat?" he growled.

Vance ignored the slur. He had no intention of quarreling. He had a plan. The night was clear, and they sat close enough to see each other's faces in the moonlight.

"I have a proposition for you," Vance said. Rogers did not respond, so he went on. "Suppose I buy your ranch. I won a lot of money tonight, from others as well as from you. I could make you a good offer—not top dollar, but then the place is quite run down. Still, it would be enough to get you started someplace else."

Rogers sat for a moment staring, all the anger draining out of him, and then he began to laugh, chuckling at first and then surrendering to a full-fledged roar. He almost toppled from his horse, managing to catch himself before he actually fell, and, standing on shaky legs, he leaned against his horse and laughed some more.

Vance watched, uncomfortably, and then dismounted, not knowing what to say or how to deal with the situation. Finally, Rogers gained control over himself, and he turned to Vance, his face as hard as stone.

"You're slick, all right. I never woulda guessed until tonight, when you wanted my ranch. Who'd ever believe a tinhorn gambler would know? I'll just bet you didn't think *I* knew, did you?"

"Knew what?" Vance asked in perfect innocence.

"Don't bluff me, you lyin' thief," said Rogers. "I know why you want my ranch an' it ain't for the cattle on it, neither. You know there's somethin' there, somethin' worth a lot more'n cattle. Where'd you hear about it, Vance? Some old Mexican? Won't do you no good, though. You gotta have a map. The Mexican had a map. I seen it, more'n once. I was gonna guide him, 'cause I knew the country, but he up an' died on me, an' the map,

353

it just disappeared, but I knew where to look. It took a few years but I found the place. Then I got the money an' bought the land. No matter who finds it now, it's mine. All mine!" He fairly shouted these last words, and Vance, his frustration built up to the breaking point, could stand it no longer. He lunged at the rancher, grabbing at his throat to choke off those words.

Rogers was surprisingly agile and managed to break away, but he tried to swing a fist at Vance's face. Vance ducked the slowly thrown arm and struck several short blows to Rogers's midsection. They were clear of the horses, fighting back off the road. Rogers landed a few punches but his drunken condition combined with the beating he was taking made them ineffectual. Rogers staggered back a step and Vance caught him with a solid right to the chin that sounded in the dark stillness like a rifle shot. Slowly, it seemed, Rogers fell backward, back and back, falling long, long after he should have touched ground. Somehow, in the darkness, they had fought to the edge of the road where the ground fell away, not more than ten feet, but down to bare rocks. There Rogers struck with a muffled crash. Vance stood for a long time, chest heaving, fists clenched, listening. Listening for a groan, a movement. Nothing. Finally, he scrambled down the bank, feeling in the shadows for Rogers. There—a boot, a leg, a hand. Vance drew back swiftly. The hand was like ice. With unsteady fingers, he struck a match. The glow flickered off Rogers's eyes which stared, unseeing, at the stars. He gazed, transfixed, at the dead man until the match burned his fingers, and startled, he dropped it to the ground.

Panic surged in him. He had killed men before, better men than this, surely, but always with a gun. Always with

354

witnesses. Always with justification. Never with his hands. Never in the heat of passion. This was murder. Accidental, perhaps, but murder it would be in the eyes of decent citizens. He climbed clumsily back to the road. Finding his horse, he mounted and rode back toward town. As he rode, the cold sweat dried on his body. His heartbeat returned to normal. His panic subsided and his cool reason took control again. No one had seen him ride out of town. Even if someone had, he had no reason to follow Rogers. He had already won the man's money. Rogers had been drunk. Dozens of people could testify to that. More than likely, whoever found him would think it was a riding accident. Of course, it happened often enough. No one had any reason to suspect him. None at all.

When he got back to town, Vance was very careful to circle around and come in from the opposite side, in case some nosy old lady was watching. It was late and the town was dark. At the livery, Ol' Zeke was still snoring in the loft as he had been when Vance left. As he stole silently into his room, he permitted himself a smile. It was perfect. No one could possibly know. And now he had a new plan. This one was foolproof. In a few short weeks, perhaps only days, the gold would be his, and he would be heading east. Home.

In the next room, Rita struck a match to check the time. He had been gone quite a while, she noted, and had been sneaking back in the same way he had sneaked out. She idly wondered why, but she did not waste time puzzling about it. Sooner or later she would know why. She always knew everything, sooner or later.

*   *   *

Priscilla had spent a restless night, trying to decide what to do about Dusty. It seemed that she really had no problem. After all, she loved him and now she knew that he loved her. Nothing could be simpler, except for the fact that he could not or would not believe she loved him. Priscilla would never forget the look of outrage on his face when she had tried to get him to propose. Obviously, all the tactics she had used previously on men would be inappropriate. She needed a new approach, but the more she considered, the more muddled she became. What she needed was a change of scenery, something to get her mind off herself, clear out the cobwebs. Since it was Saturday, she decided to go for a long ride. Alone.

Dusty had made himself scarce ever since their encounter by the river the day before, and she saw no sign of him as she saddled Lady and rode out. Leaving word that she would be gone a while, she rode aimlessly, enjoying the view and the changing scenery. Before she was even aware of the direction she had taken, Priscilla realized that she was almost halfway to Hazel Rogers's house. Hazel would be delighted at a visit, and Priscilla decided she would enjoy talking to someone totally unrelated to her problem with Dusty.

Hazel *was* delighted and insisted that Priscilla eat with her and her children, since her husband had not yet returned from his trip. It was early afternoon and Priscilla was preparing to leave, when they heard the lone horseman approach. Hazel thought at first her husband had returned, but her children came rushing in, wide-eyed, to announce that the sheriff had come to call. Priscilla felt a cold chill as she watched Hazel's reaction to that announcement. Obviously shaken and expecting to hear that her husband had gotten himself into some serious difficulty, she braced herself and went out to meet Sheriff Winslow.

"Afternoon, Sheriff. Light an' set," she called.

"Afternoon, Miz Rogers," he replied. "Don't mind if I do."

He tried to appear casual, but Priscilla could plainly see that he brought bad news. Hazel sent the children outside, and when they were all seated, Sheriff Winslow began.

"Miz Rogers, I sure hate to have to tell you this, ma'am, but"—he paused, groping for words—"this mornin' some cowboys found your husband on the road between here an' town. Looks like he fell off his horse somehow an' . . ."

"He's dead?" Hazel asked, amazingly calm.

"Yes, ma'am, I'm sorry to say."

Hazel seemed almost relieved to find out he was dead instead of in jail, as she had feared. She put a shaky hand to her forehead, as if trying to get a grip on her thoughts. Then she remembered something. "Did you search him, Sheriff? He just got back from selling some cattle. He should have had a great deal of money."

Sheriff Winslow shifted uneasily in his chair. "He didn't have no money on him, ma'am."

For the first time Hazel showed strong emotion. "He must have been robbed, then! Someone must have killed him and robbed him!"

"No, ma'am, you see, before he started home last night, he got in a poker game at the Yellow Rose and lost every dime he had. I got dozens of witnesses to that. They also said he'd been drinkin' an' I guess that's what caused him the accident."

Hazel's face was white. "Thank you, Sheriff. You have

been very kind." She rose suddenly, went into her bedroom, and closed the door.

"I shore am glad you're here, ma'am," he said to Priscilla. "You think I ought to send over some other womenfolks?"

"Oh, yes," said Priscilla. "Could you get word to the Steeles? Tell them I'll be staying here. I'm sure Mrs. Wilson will want to come soon, also."

"I sure will, ma'am."

After the sheriff left, Priscilla went in to comfort Hazel. She mumbled a few consoling phrases to the weeping woman before Hazel looked up and said, "Please, Priscilla, don't make it worse! I feel like such a hypocrite. My husband is dead and all I can think of is what is going to become of us?"

"What do you mean?"

"That money John lost in the poker game was all we had. Oh, there might be a little left at the bank, enough to last a few weeks or months, but nothing else."

"You still have the ranch," Priscilla said.

"I can't run it alone, and I certainly can't pay any hands, now. I might round up a few hundred head of cattle to sell, but I couldn't even afford to feed the cowboys while they do it. I'm not even sure I can afford a funeral." Hazel began to weep again.

"Do you have any family?" Priscilla asked.

"Some cousins, back in Virginia, but I could never . . . Even if I could, they're poor people. They could never afford to take us in." She looked tragically out the window where her children played carelessly in the yard. "I'll have to sell the ranch, of course," she said half to herself, planning out loud. "But that might take months . . ."

Priscilla felt as if her blood had turned to fire. "You'll sell the ranch?" she asked eagerly.

"Of course," said Hazel, getting hold of herself.

"Hazel, if I . . . I mean, I think I know someone who might want to buy the ranch."

"Who?"

"Someone from Philadelphia," she said vaguely. "Would you sell, right away, for a fair price?"

Hazel's eyes lit up with hope. "Oh, yes! I don't have any idea what a fair price would be, though."

"Neither do I," Priscilla admitted, "but I . . . this person has a lot of money, so that doesn't matter. I'm sure George Wilson could handle the sale for you. He would make sure you were treated fairly."

"Oh, yes! Oh, Priscilla, do you know what that would mean? I could go to Richmond, open a shop like I used to have. I'd never have to depend on anyone's charity again." The sound of children's laughter suddenly sobered her. "I must tell the children about their father," she said. "Would you call them in?"

Chapter Twelve

Hazel insisted on a simple funeral the next day and asked only a few close friends to sit with her afterward. Priscilla managed to catch George Wilson alone in the Rogers' ranch yard.

"George, could I meet you at your office tomorrow afternoon after school? I have some business to discuss with you," she told him.

George smiled indulgently. He could not imagine what business the schoolteacher would have. "Why not just discuss it at home?" he asked.

Priscilla's serious look baffled him. "I'd rather not be overheard and"—she looked all around—"please don't tell anyone about our meeting, even Stella. Especially Stella."

"You may trust my discretion, Miss Bedford." He bowed, again amused by her seriousness.

Priscilla was afraid she might not get away that afternoon. She had told Stella she was going riding, but

Dusty spotted her. He always seemed to be skulking around the ranch yard nowadays, and Priscilla could not decide if it was so he could avoid her or spy on her. Today he was apparently spying, and he was curious because she was wearing her riding habit. Usually, she wore old clothes when she went riding for amusement.

"Where you goin' all dressed up like that?" he asked suspiciously as she saddled Lady.

"For a ride," she answered curtly. Since he had confessed his love to her but failed to stake any claims, Priscilla found his proprietary attitude a little ridiculous.

"Where to?" he insisted, knowing how foolish he must sound but unable to help himself.

She glared at him. "To town, if you must know. I have an errand."

He was not satisfied. "Why don't you get somebody to fetch you in a wagon?"

"Because I want to go alone!" she snapped. And I don't want everyone to know my business, she added mentally, especially you.

"*Ladies* don't ride to town alone," he announced.

So that was what was bothering him, she thought.

"An' they particularly don't ride into town on horseback."

"Well, this lady does," she replied, mounting herself. She spread her skirts demurely. Ever since that first impulsive ride on Lady, she had always been careful to ride sidesaddle when anyone could see her. "Good day, Mr. Rhoades." She forced him to give way to her as she rode out of the barn, leaving him fuming at her rebellion. On the way to town, she recalled what she had said to him about men having so much more freedom than women. Sadly, it was true.

As she rode down the main street of Rainbow to George Wilson's office, Priscilla began to feel uneasy. Perhaps people would think she was terribly brazen, but as she looked around, she felt somewhat relieved. The street was nearly deserted. She stopped in front of George's office and a sudden realization hit her. It would be most unladylike to jump off her horse in the middle of Main Street. She waited a moment to see if George would see her and come to her rescue, but he did not. Then she heard footsteps on the boardwalk and looked up. A familiar face smiled in recognition.

"Mr. Vance, how fortunate. Could I prevail upon you to help me down?" she asked.

Jason Vance stopped a moment, undecided, and then glancing around to make sure no one was near, he swiftly stepped over and lifted her down from her horse.

"Oh, thank you, sir," she smiled. "I'm afraid I have already scandalized the town by riding in unescorted. It would never do to fall flat on my face in the street, too!"

"Glad to be of service, ma'am," he smiled back. She was prettier than he remembered, her voice sweeter.

"I'm surprised to see you still here," she added. "Somehow I imagined you would not be in Rainbow very long."

"My business here took longer than I expected," he explained as they stepped up on the boardwalk to Wilson's office. "And I was offered a job, so I have stayed."

She looked at his black frock coat. "You are not a cowboy," she observed.

"No, I, ah"—she saw his cool reserve crack, just a bit, as if it pained him to admit it—"I'm working at the Yellow Rose. Well, if you'll excuse me, I'm late for an appointment," he ended abruptly, and, tipping his hat, he brushed past her without looking back.

Priscilla stood for a moment, puzzling. She had never been in a saloon and she could not imagine what sort of work a man like Vance would do there. Obviously, he had education and breeding. She would ask Stella later, when she thought of it. George had finally seen her and had come to escort her in.

"Well, young lady, how may I be of service to you?" George smiled when they were seated in his office.

Priscilla might have been irritated at his condescending attitude except that she knew she held the high card. She smiled sweetly back at him. "I have a business transaction that I would like you to handle for me."

"I would be delighted," he said.

"On one condition only, however," she warned. "You must keep this entire matter confidential. No one—absolutely no one—must find out. If you don't give me your word on that, I shall go to San Antonio to find another lawyer."

Intrigued, George became as serious as she. "Of course, you have my word."

Reaching into the canvas bag she carried, she pulled out a leather wallet containing various important-looking papers.

"I want to purchase the Rogers' ranch," she said, searching through the papers for the one she wanted. "Here is a draft from a bank in Philadelphia. I hope it will be adequate."

Stunned speechless, George took the draft. For a moment he stared at it, then looked at her, then back at the draft. "More than adequate. Far more. Priscilla, you're rich!"

She shrugged. "Well-to-do, perhaps. Hardly rich."

He shook his head. "Stella told me . . ." he muttered.

"It's difficult to fool Stella, but if I fooled you, perhaps I managed to fool everyone else."

"I realize it's none of my business, but why . . . ?"

"Why did I pretend to be poor? It wasn't that I wanted to. You'll probably think me silly. Perhaps I am. It's just that I wanted some excitement in my life. I wanted to go west. My father was quite ill for a long time before he died. I used to read to him to pass the time, and all he wanted to hear about was the West. I must have read everything in print on the subject, dime novels, scholarly tomes, everything. Then I saw Mr. Steele's advertisement. It seemed the perfect opportunity to go west and look around. If I didn't like it, I could always go back home." She smiled. "But I do like it, and now I want to stay."

George shook his head again. "You want to be a rancher?" he asked in disbelief. "Have you spoken to Hazel about this?"

"Yes. Poor Hazel is desperate, penniless. She must sell quickly. She wants to return to Virginia—that's where she's from—and open a sewing shop. It's been a dream of hers for a long time. But," she added quickly, "she doesn't know that I will be the one to buy the ranch. I told her I knew someone from Philadelphia whom I thought would buy it, that you would set a fair price and handle the sale for her."

"I will, certainly, but why all the secrecy?"

"I don't want Hazel to think it's an act of charity on my part and . . . well, I have other reasons for not wanting anyone else to know. I'll sign the power of attorney giving you the right to act in my behalf. That way, my name need not come up."

"Then no one else knows about this?"

"No one except you and me," she assured him.

George was thoughtful. "I know at least one other person who would be interested in the sale of the Old Rhoades property."

"He is the reason I don't want my name mentioned," Priscilla said simply.

"He'll be angry," he warned.

Priscilla could not help a smile. "He has been angry since the moment we met, as you well know."

George was still amazed, still trying to make sense of it all. "Do you know he's in love with you?"

Priscilla nodded. How well she knew that! "But he still intends to leave here as soon as possible, and alone."

George scowled. "Do you think that by buying the ranch you can keep him here?"

"Oh, no! I know that would be the one thing certain to drive him away forever. No, I'll work out my problems with Dusty Rhoades as best I can, if I can"—she laughed self-consciously—"and then, and only then will I tell him about the ranch. That's why it must be a secret."

"I'll do it, even though Stella will kill me when she does find out." They both laughed. "Now we must go to the bank and take care of this draft. Benson owes me some favors, so I think we can count on his discretion. You should probably threaten to take your money to San Antone, though, just in case."

Rita was waiting in her doorway at the top of the stairs when Vance got back to the saloon.

"A real gentleman, ain't you?" she asked.

"I beg your pardon, Mrs. Jordan," he said. Usually she was amused when he called her "Mrs. Jordan," but not now.

"I seen you helpin' that *lady* off her horse." Rita said the word "lady" as if it were a curse.

"She needed some assistance. I was glad to oblige," Vance told her blandly.

"I'll just bet! She knew you, though. She talked to you, smiled like you was old friends. Who is she?" Rita demanded.

Could Rita be jealous? It seemed unlikely, but Vance enjoyed seeing her so unsure of herself. "Oh, just a *lady* friend of mine." He put emphasis on "lady" and Rita's eyes flamed.

"Her name, Vance. Her name."

Vance demurred. "Priscilla Bedford. She's . . ."

"The schoolteacher!" Rita said triumphantly. Her face changed instantly and the anger or jealousy was gone. "So that's her. She's not so much," Rita said half to herself.

Vance hated to see his advantage slip away so quickly, so he tried to bring it back. "Oh, she's a great deal, I believe."

Rita's eyes blazed again. "That skinny, prissy, little . . . nothing! I'll bet she sleeps with all her clothes on. She wouldn't know the first thing to do in bed with a man. She'd prob'ly scream if one so much as touched her," Rita predicted vehemently.

"She's not skinny at all," said Vance. "I was in a better position to observe that than you, and I doubt if Priscilla ever screamed at anything in her life." Rita flared again when he used Priscilla's first name. "As for the other, well, I imagine that, with the right man, our little schoolteacher would be a very willing pupil.''

Rita made a strangled sound in her throat and moved as if to strike Vance. Then suddenly she checked herself and smiled smugly. ''You'll never be that man, Vance.''

Her words stung, far more than she had even intended, and it took all his self-control not to slap the smirk off her lovely face. Then his desire to wound her as she had wounded him brought forth a dim and distant memory. ''No,'' he replied brutally, ''but Dusty Rhoades might.''

Instantly, he knew that he had drawn blood. Rita was on him, tooth and claw, and only his quick reaction and superior strength saved him from being savaged by her nails. He shoved her violently, and she staggered back through the open door into her room. Turning in disgust, he would have left her then, except that her voice, shrill with anger, called after him, questioning his manhood in words he had never heard a woman use before. Using every ounce of self-control he possessed, Vance tried to stifle the unreasoning rage that welled up inside of him but failed. With a primitive roar, he lunged for her, instinctively slamming the door shut behind him.

His overpowering urge to throttle her quickly became something else entirely as his hands closed around the satiny skin of her throat. She must have seen the naked lust in his eyes because the momentary fear that had flickered across her face swiftly changed to rebellion as her struggles became more violent. In a flurry of arms and legs, Vance finally managed to force her down onto the bed, pinning her hands above her head with one hand, while with the other managing to pull open the wrapper she wore over a one-piece undergarment.

''I'll kill you for this, Vance,'' she gasped, breathless from her struggles, as he savagely ripped the delicate fabric from her body.

"You're welcome to try," he replied hoarsely, struggling with his trousers. Her cry of pain as he took her inflamed him to the point of frenzy, and he used her ruthlessly in a mindless rutting that ended in a wrenching spasm of release but brought no satisfaction.

He lay on her for a long time, his hand still imprisoning both of hers, his face buried in the curve of her shoulder, sucking air into his beleaguered lungs and along with it the musky, sweet, sensual smell of her body.

Vance fought down a wave of nausea as the realization of what he had done set in. Of all the evil things he had ever done, he had never forced a woman. Always he had prided himself on being a gentleman, and although he had used many who were willing, he had never used his strength to . . . He shuddered at the horror of it and then groaned in despair as he felt the surge in his loins. In spite of everything, he wanted her again.

Pulling back in disgust, he released his grip on her and began to rise, but her freed arms snaked up around his neck, holding him. "Don't stop, Vance," she breathed, and he looked down at her in amazement. The fury he had seen before was gone, replaced with a look of wonder and desire. Her green eyes sparkled up at him and her full lips parted in a sensual smile. "Don't stop," she whispered again, moving urgently against him, her hands compelling his face to meet hers.

He did not stop, and when he would have been gentle, Rita refused to allow him, churning her hips with maddening insistence until he was slamming into her with bruising, punishing force while she clawed at his clothes in a frantic attempt to feel his naked flesh pressed against hers. The touch of her tiny soft hands as they

369

moved over his back, his flanks, his buttocks, the sharp nails digging in with a strange mixture of pleasure and pain aroused him to an animal frenzy he had never known, and when he came it was with a cry of denial that he had been reduced to such a state.

With a sigh of revulsion, Vance pushed away from her and lay staring up at the ceiling, trying not to think of the way he had just behaved, but Rita's husky chuckle cut through the oblivion he had assigned himself to.

"What's the matter, Vance?" she taunted. "You scared you might've offended me? No need to worry about that," she assured him. "I ain't no fancy lady that needs to be gentled. Guess you forgot that." Rita's hands, meanwhile, were busy stripping off the remnants of her clothes and when she was finished, she went to work on Vance, brushing aside his feeble protests.

"I wasn't finished, Vance," she told him when he was naked, too. "A gentleman never leaves a *lady* unsatisfied, or didn't you know that?" she jeered as she grazed her fingers over his smooth chest and down, over his belly, teasing and tangling into the curling hairs that crowned his manhood.

"I . . . I can't," he insisted when he realized her intent, but she only laughed derisively, and lowered her face to show him that he could, oh, yes, he could indeed, and then he did. He took her again and again, heedless of the hours that passed, the darkening sky, the noises below as the saloon business picked up, and oblivious to the ribald remarks that Will was fielding about why both Rita and Vance failed to appear all evening. At long last they fell into an exhausted sleep, so sated that they both forgot Rita's preference for sleeping alone.

It was the last gray hour before dawn when Rita awoke.

A ripple of disgust went through her at the weight of Vance's arm across her waist and the feel of his naked body pressed against hers. He muttered a protest as she slipped cautiously from the bed, but to her great relief, he did not waken. At least he doesn't snore, she thought as she made her way to her wardrobe in the darkness and found another wrapper. Feeling her way, she found her rocking chair, turned to face the window, and she sat down, staring out of the dark room into the even darker night. Long hours she sat, watching with unseeing eyes as the dawn changed the world and a new day began. It was amazing, she thought, how she and Vance could hurt each other. It was almost instinctive. He had managed to cut her heart out, even in his ignorance, and she, it seemed, had returned the favor. She had feared his intelligence, and her fears had proven well grounded. She had thought to use sex as a distraction, but somehow it had just given him another weapon to use against her. It worked both ways, of course. She could use it against him, too, but it was not quite the same, just as his pain had not been quite the same earlier when they had flayed each other with words. His feelings for Miss Priscilla Bedford were quite different from hers for Dusty Rhoades. Vance might admire, even love the woman, but being the sort of man he was, he would never go beyond indulging in a few fantasies, while Rita would . . . well, that could not be helped. She would use the tools she had to protect herself. Even now the memory of Vance's words caused an ache deep down somewhere inside her, and she sat rocking, rocking and staring, her eyes burning with unshed tears, tears she would never shed, because she *could* never shed them. Rita Jordan had no tears. With pride she remembered the last time she had cried—at her father's graveside—but those were tears of relief, not sadness. Mattie had held her that day and soothed her, saying over and over how he was gone and would never hurt them again. Rita had sworn then that no man would ever hurt her again. What a fool she had been!

Rita Cade had been raised by her alcoholic father and a succession of Mexican or Indian women after her real mother had run off leaving her three-year-old daughter behind. Rita could understand why her mother had run off. Jacob Cade was a woman-beater, particularly vicious when drunk, and he was usually drunk. On occasion he beat Rita, but folks got testy when they saw a white girl walking around all battered up, so Cade tried to keep a woman around. Nobody much seemed to care if he saw a Mex or a squaw with a black eye or a busted jaw.

Some of these women ran off, as her mother had done, and two died. Rita had hated them all, hated their weakness. She had despised all creatures of her own sex until Mattie. Unlike the others, Mattie was white, but in a way, she was even lower than the squaws, because she had been a squaw. Mattie had been captured by the Comanches when she was a young bride, new to the frontier. Passed from brave to brave, and then from tribe to tribe, she had finally come into the hands of some fairly friendly Indians who allowed the Army to ransom her. If she had only known what that would mean, she might have stayed with the Indians.

Her husband and her family could not stand the thought of her being with the savages, but neither could they accept her back home. After all, she had been a plaything of those creatures. She was tainted, unclean. Her husband would not live with her; her family despised

372

her. A lot of people thought that a decent woman would kill herself before she would let an Indian touch her. The ones who thought that had never been taken captive, of course. They could not understand that the women on the frontier were survivors, and while many who were taken captive died, none died by her own hand. Mattie was a survivor. She had survived the Comanches and she had survived the white men, and she had survived Jacob Cade. He had only beaten her once before he took sick and died. Folks said his heart probably gave out from all that drinking.

Mattie stood dry eyed beside the grave, holding the weeping girl in her arms. She would love Rita as she would have loved her own child, and Rita loved her back, seeing in Mattie a strength no woman had ever shown her. For three years they lived together, eking out a living from Jacob's poor farm. Then, when Rita was sixteen, the drummer came.

Paul Williams was young and handsome in a flashy sort of way. Rita had never seen a man who always wore a clean white shirt and shaved everyday. Williams, on the other hand, had never seen an innocent young farm girl with such latent sex appeal. When he seduced her in the barn, he had expected an enjoyable experience, but even at that he was surprised. He had acted this scene with many young girls, but never had he encountered one whom he so much as wanted to see again. He begged Rita to go with him, to run off, to elope. Promising her fancy clothes and good times and marriage when he got the stake he was expecting, he convinced her.

Mattie must have known or at least suspected what would happen. Perhaps she knew Rita too well to stop her. Rita's only option was to marry a country boy and be a farmer's wife, and even at sixteen Rita Cade was showing herself unfit for such a dreary life. Mattie packed her a lunch and kissed her goodbye and watched her go as expressionless as the Indians who had taught her the secrets of life and death.

By the time Paul's buggy reached Dodge City, he was frightened. Rita had proven to be a very lively companion, more than equaling his demands at passion. He had bought her clothes and continued to promise they would be married. As incredible as it was, he had actually considered marrying her, at first. She had been so eager, so lustful, it seemed a sin to give her up, but now he was beginning to feel suffocated, devoured, trapped. Rita gave a lot, but she would always demand more than she gave, and Williams was beginning to believe he would not survive the relationship.

He spoke to her often of a big deal he had going with the Indian tribes and the government. Something to do with cattle, but he was always vague on details. He got her a room in a hotel and promised he would be back within a week. It was too dangerous to take her with him into Indian territory, so he gave her some money and promised to return, rich beyond her wildest dreams, to marry her. Rita was careful with the money but in two weeks it was gone, and she knew that Paul Williams was, too. At first she had been afraid that he had been killed by Indians and then she had been afraid that he had not been. Not that it mattered. What mattered was that she was a young girl alone in one of the wildest towns in the West. She must have money, and several men had already come around suggesting ways in which she could earn some. None of these men appealed to Rita, who had learned to be wary of men's promises.

Then some girls came to see her, girls not much older than she, and told her how she could make a good living. They took her to the dance house where they worked and presented her to Belle. Something about Belle reminded Rita of Mattie, for Belle was a survivor, too. Like Rita, she had learned early to distrust men and had made her own way. Now she owned one of the fanciest dance houses in town and she looked after her girls like a mother hen. She did not have cribs at her place of business, the sleazy cubbyholes where girls sold quick sex to drunken cowboys. If her girls wanted to entertain a gentleman for pay, they were free to do so, at their own quarters, which were nearby but separate. This distinction gave Belle's place an air of class and enabled her girls to demand top dollar. Not that they needed to do any whoring. They could earn as much in just one night of dancing and soliciting drinks as a cowboy earned in a month of punching cows.

Rita was a welcome addition to Belle's place of business. She enjoyed fleecing the cowboys of their summer's wages, teasing them, tempting them, and then refusing them. Oh, she gave in occasionally, to a high roller who could afford to buy a whole night with her, but few cowboys were willing to squander a month's pay for one girl for just one night, even if she *was* Rita Cade.

Rita saw Paul Williams once more. Quite by accident he came into the dance house one night, a little over a year after Rita had started there. She was charming to him, not even wanting to hear any excuses. He had done her a favor, she said, opened up a whole new world for her. She insisted that he spend the night with her, for old times' sake, no charge. As he left the next morning, shaking his head at his good fortune, Rita smiled and waved after him, saying to come back and see her whenever he was in town. Two days later, someone found him in an alley, dead, not a mark on him. The doctor said it was a real shame, a man so young to have a bad heart. A real pity.

When Vance awoke the next morning, stiff and sore from the activities of the previous night, he found himself alone in Rita's room. Spending only a moment recalling what had occurred between him and Rita, he rose, found his clothes, and beat a hasty retreat to his own room where he bathed and shaved and otherwise managed to make himself presentable. Over a late breakfast in the hotel dining room, he laid his plans. After last night, he decided, the sooner he got away from Rita Jordan, the better. What better way than to become a respectable rancher? He would be doing Mrs. Rogers a good turn, too, although when he thought about it, killing Rogers had probably been the biggest favor he could have performed for her. That decided, he lighted a cigar and made his way leisurely to George Wilson's office.

George was more than a little surprised to see Vance come in, but he was much too professional to let it show, and he gave the gambler a friendly greeting.

When they had covered the social amenities necessary to two men who considered themselves civilized, Vance finally got around to the reason why he had come.

"Wilson, I'm sure you've heard the story of how I won all of Roger's money the night he died," Vance began.

"I doubt there is a living soul around here who hasn't heard the story," George assured him.

"Ever since I heard about the . . . accident, I, well, I haven't been able to stop thinking about those poor children and Mrs. Rogers left with so little."

"It's a sin, the way that man neglected his family," George agreed, thinking he had guessed Vance's mission. "They'll never take charity, though."

"Certainly not. I knew that. What I had in mind was a little more practical. You see, I have been wanting to go into ranching for some time now. I had quite a sum of money saved for just that purpose and with the money I won from Rogers, I believe I have enough to make a reasonable offer for the property."

George leaned back and considered. No one had ever believed Vance wanted to be a rancher, and now, hearing it from the man's own lips, George was sure it was a lie. But why else would a man offer to buy a ranch? George could think of no reason.

"I'm sorry, Vance, but the ranch has already been sold," George said with manufactured regret.

"Sold? When? To whom?" Vance was incredulous. He could feel the ground slipping out from under him in a cold, sickening wave.

"A friend of mine from the East who had asked me to be on the lookout. As soon as I learned Hazel would sell, of course I closed the deal for my friend." George studied the gambler. He had expected disappointment, perhaps annoyance, but Vance was livid.

He could barely speak. "Yes, yes, of course," he mumbled and left without even saying goodbye. Vance stumbled across the street in a blind rage. Bursting into the saloon, he went behind the bar without so much as a word to Will and grabbed a bottle and a glass. Seating himself at a table, he began to drink, tossing off three quick ones and then, as the warmth stole over him, settling in to a slow, steady pace. He sat there all day and into the evening, and no one dared approach him. Many regular customers gave Will questioning looks, but Will could only shrug at the mystery. Rita came down, but if Vance saw her he gave no notice.

After closing, Vance walked, somewhat unsteadily, upstairs to his room, still carrying a half-filled bottle. Rita listened to him through the wall, consumed with curiosity. More than once she had heard him say how he never took a drink. Obviously, he was a surly drunk, but perhaps he was also a talkative one. If so, she could find out some things. She tapped on the wall between their rooms, the signal she used to call him to her bed.

"Go to hell!" he shouted through the thin partition.

More amused then angry, Rita went to his room, and finding the door unlocked, went in. Vance lay fully clothed on the bed, nursing his whiskey bottle. He seemed unaware of her presence. Solicitously, she went to him and removed his shoes, his tie, helped him off with his coat. He took no particular notice of her ministrations. Instead he seemed intent on something distant, a thought that he could not quite grasp. Then, suddenly, he began to curse someone. It took a moment for Rita to realize it was not she, but rather someone not present. She stood, quietly, and was rewarded by hearing the name Rogers. Why would he curse a dead man, especially one who had enriched Vance so well before his death? Rita sat down on the bed beside Vance and began to unbutton his shirt, murmuring sympathetically.

"What did poor old Rogers do, darling?" she asked.

He looked at her as if trying to place her, then he laughed hysterically. "Do? What did he do? He wouldn't sell me the ranch, that's what he did! And now somebody else bought it. I killed him for nothing!" He laughed again, but this time the laughter dissolved into drunken blubbering.

Rita might have been disgusted if she had not been so shocked. Vance had killed Rogers! She had seen him ride out that night and come sneaking back very late, but somehow she had never suspected that. For some reason, Vance wanted Rogers's ranch. Certainly not for the cattle. Why, then?

"Oh, darling, why in the world would you want an old ranch?" she cooed.

He swore violently again. "I don't want the ranch, you fool! It's the gold!"

"What gold is that?" she asked, afraid that at any moment he might realize she was pumping him. She need not have worried. His besotted brain could barely function.

"The Mexican gold!" He looked at her for a long moment as if measuring her intentions. "But don't worry, I'll find it. I've got the secret right here." He patted his stomach. "Right here." His voice trailed off and he began to snore softly.

Mystified, Rita stared down at him. She had heard countless stories of Mexican gold lost and buried all around but had never taken any of them seriously. Did Vance know of some particular cache? What secret could he have? It would have to be a clue of some kind that would enable him alone to find the gold, probably a map. He had patted his stomach. Could it be hidden on his body? Of course. Vance was not a trusting man. She began to undress him, going through each article of clothing as she removed it, but she found nothing. When

379

he lay naked, she went through his clothes again, more carefully. Still nothing. He had patted his stomach. If he had pointed to his head, Rita would have assumed that he had the secret memorized, but surely he had not swallowed it. Rita considered the matter a moment. Of course. It was so obvious. She removed the belt from his pants and found what she was looking for. The map was oddly impressive, although the landmarks meant nothing to her, but she deduced that Vance had somehow determined that the gold lay on Rogers's property. How ironic that it should be Dusty's old ranch. If only he still owned it. How sweet it would be to help Vance steal from him. Vance muttered in his sleep. Rita quickly replaced the map, put the belt back on the pants, and carefully hung them up with the rest of his clothes.

Returning to her room, Rita considered what she had learned. She now knew why Vance was in Rainbow. She also knew he had killed Rogers. Neither the gold nor the murder interested her, at least not at the moment, but she would file them away for future reference. She smiled. The next time Vance threw Dusty Rhoades in her face, she would have an answer.

Priscilla noted with satisfaction that Dusty had not met her eyes for five days. After he had shown disapproval of her ride to town, he had given her a wide berth. They sat at dinner every day with the family but they never spoke, and if he ever looked at her, she never caught him. He was running scared, she thought.

"Dusty," said George at dinner on the fifth day, "I have a job to offer you."

Dusty sat back, curious. His leg was much improved,

and he had been taking short rides but was still not ready for the herding of cattle. "Whatcha got in mind?"

"As you know, the Rogers' place has been sold to someone from the East." Dusty stiffened slightly and Priscilla regretted how much that fact hurt him. "The place is rather run down, and the new owner would like the buildings repaired before taking possession. Also," he paused for effect, "they are going to build a new house on the original site."

Priscilla watched Dusty's face as everyone else oh'ed and ah'ed over this announcement. It seemed frozen. "So?" he asked George.

"So, they have asked me to hire someone to oversee the work. We have some carpenters coming from Santone, and they've ordered one of those mail order house kits. It will be arriving soon. It should be quite impressive."

"I ain't no carpenter," Dusty declared. "I don't do nothin' can't be done from the back of a horse." Priscilla recalled how he had come out to fix the fence on a Sunday afternoon and had to cover a smile.

"Oh, I don't expect you to do any carpentry work, of course," George assured him. "I just need someone to make sure the workmen don't loaf and that everything that needs to be done gets done, that sort of thing. You'd only need to go over every few days or so. It would give you something to do. Ben has agreed to it."

There seemed no objection he could make and if he had reasons for not wanting to do the job, they were not reasons he cared to voice in company. "I reckon I'll do it," he said reluctantly.

"Good! The owner has authorized me to pay . . ."

Dusty looked up sharply. "I won't take pay. I'll do it

for . . . old times' sake," he said ironically, and he quickly rose and left the table while George tried to answer everyone's questions about the new house.

George had told everyone that a friend of his from back east had contacted him some time ago about purchasing a suitable ranch. George had agreed to keep his eyes open and had made a quick deal with Hazel for the property when the chance came. The Steele girls had wheedled and cajoled and threatened and cried, but George had kept his word and his secret, so no one yet knew the new owner's identity. Stella had even tried seduction, but to no avail. George had simply laughed and pointed out that with her fourth pregnancy becoming increasingly obvious, she would be better off trying to bribe him with a berry pie.

Hazel Rogers and her children left town that afternoon. No one had been hypocritical enough to continue to mourn John Rogers and so their leave-taking was a joyous occasion. With her new-found wealth, Hazel had purchased tickets for herself and the children on the stage to San Antonio where they would catch a train heading east. The excitement of anticipation had transformed Hazel until she was, Priscilla thought, almost pretty.

Priscilla and most of the Steeles came to town to see her off, and in the confusion Hazel managed to draw Priscilla aside for a private word. "Thank you, my dear friend, for everything," she told Priscilla, "and I hope you will be very happy at the Circle R."

Priscilla's surprise was genuine. "The Circle R? What do you mean?"

"I know that you're the one who bought the ranch," Hazel told her with a smile. "You really are a terrible liar, you know. You should practice if you ever expect to be any good at it," she teased.

Laughing, Priscilla hugged her friend. "I didn't do it for you. You have to believe that. I don't want you to think it was charity or anything. My motives were purely selfish," Priscilla assured her.

"Oh, I know what your motives were," Hazel said with a knowing look. "I hope you both find the happiness you deserve there."

There was no chance to reply to Hazel's outrageous statement since the rest of the Steeles were crowding around to deliver their own farewells, a fact for which Priscilla was very grateful. Her cheeks burned as she wondered silently just how many people knew about her and Dusty. It was a disconcerting thought.

Chapter Thirteen

It was obvious that Dusty took his new responsibilities seriously in the days that followed. He rode out early every day to his old home and came back late every evening looking as if he had done much more than supervise. Priscilla was consumed with curiosity to see how the house was coming, but she had to content herself with secondhand reports relayed through George. Apparently, things were going well, and after two weeks the house was basically finished.

That Saturday, Priscilla had gone down to the schoolhouse to bathe and wash her hair in privacy. After heating the water and filling the tub, she quickly stripped off her clothes, but just as she was stepping into the tub, she caught a glimpse of herself in the mirror. Putting aside her ingrained Victorian modesty, she walked slowly toward her own reflection, and for the first time since puberty, she gave her naked body a critical study. Her breasts, she decided as she watched the spring breeze caress her nipples to hardness, were adequate, neither too large nor too small. Just the right size to be fashionable but was that good or bad? It irritated her to realize that she suddenly did not care how fashionable her figure was but whether or not it was appealing to a certain pair of blue eyes. Even more irritating was the fact that she had no idea what men found appealing. Did they like large breasts or small? Certainly, they must like large ones or why would women who had not been "blessed" sew ruffles inside their bodices? But how large? And did different men have different preferences? Sighing with bewilderment, she put her hands on her waist, testing its slimness. It was tiny even without a corset, and she knew a certain cowboy whose calloused hands could almost span it. Tilting the mirror, she examined the lower half of her body. Her hips were nicely rounded, her legs long and shapely—not that it mattered, since no one ever saw more than her ankle—and her bottom, when she twisted around to examine it, was pleasingly plump and dimpled. Did men like plump behinds? Was that why bustles were so popular? Or did they not, and had bustles been designed to disguise a woman's true form? It was so confusing. Was there one particular thing about a woman's body that made a man look at it with that lustful gleam in his eye or was it everything all together or was it just that her body was so different from his? Not that Dusty ever looked at her that way any more, or at least not that she knew of. Of course, he had said that he loved her, and that probably meant that he still wanted her, but how could she be sure, especially when he took such pains to avoid her all the time. Did he secretly long to tear off her clothes and ravish her? A shiver coursed down her spine as her nipples once again tautened to stiff, pink peaks.

Feeling deliciously wicked, Priscilla fairly danced over to her bath and spent an inordinate amount of time lathering skin that seemed both softer and more sensitive than she had ever noticed before. When she had finished with her hair and the water had cooled to lukewarm, she finally emerged, wrapping her dripping hair in a towel and using another to briskly dry herself. She rubbed harder than she had ever felt necessary and soon her whole body glowed from the rough stimulation. A shimmer of a breeze teased the curtains and stole into the room to caress her most private parts with unseen hands. She fought down a desire to run outside stark naked and let the air and sunlight have their way with her. Dusty Rhoades had certainly awakened some very interesting emotions in her, she realized with a smile. Giggling at her own wantonness, Priscilla stepped into a pair of silk pantalettes and slipped on a matching silk camisole. The softness felt even more erotic against her strangely sensitized skin than the breeze had. Well, it wasn't like being naked, exactly, she reasoned, and besides, no one ever came down here on Saturday, and even if someone did, she would be able to hear him long before he could see her, and also, her hair would dry much more quickly in the sun. That decided, she snatched up a blanket and her brush and fairly ran outside to a secluded spot underneath the huge cottonwood trees.

She had been right. Her hair *did* dry very quickly, and as she sat, brushing it with long, slow strokes, she thought of Dusty. He had worked so hard on her house. What would he say if he knew it were hers? She winced at the thought. No, she could not tell him, not yet at least. Not until . . . until when? The time had to be right but what would have to happen to make it right? He had made love to her and he had confessed his love for her, but grudgingly, and that was not nearly enough. He still wanted to get as far away from her as fast as he could, and only fate—and a mean horse—had prevented him. Sooner or later he would get another opportunity or make one, and then he would be gone for good. What would keep him here? What would bind him to her with bonds he could not break? She had once thought that she could bind him with her body and then she had thought that if she could get him to confess his love, he would stay. Both theories had proven false, but she knew instinctively that there must be something that would keep him. If only she knew more about men, she sighed, as she lay back on the blanket to watch the sun filter through the leaves. Weary with her puzzling, she closed her eyes.

Dusty came riding into the ranch yard late that afternoon. Stella was standing on the porch, shading her eyes in the direction of the school.

"Somethin' wrong, Stella?" he asked.

She turned a worried face toward him. "Priscilla said she'd be up to the house a long time ago. I'm gettin' worried about her. Ain't like her not to come when she says."

"I'll ride down an' see what's keepin' her," Dusty offered, getting a little concerned himself.

Dusty dismounted beside the back door of the schoolhouse. Things were much too quiet for his liking, and he was just about to call out when he caught sight of the figure lying under the trees. He froze, forgetting for the moment even to breathe. Not that he had never seen her undressed before. He had seen her wearing even less, but it was not such a common sight that it failed to affect him. Desire shot through him like a flash fire that made the sweat break out all over his body, and his breath, when he remembered to breathe, came in an agonized gasp that was almost a moan. He knew that at any moment she would hear him or sense his presence and wake up, wake up and catch him staring at her like some drooling Peeping Tom, and yet he could not turn away. Even worse, the throbbing in his loins seemed to draw him toward her with an almost magnetic pull that he was powerless to resist. Stepping carefully so his spurs would not disturb her, he closed the distance between them, his eyes devouring her nearly naked body with a hunger all the more intense because he knew that at any second her eyes would open, and he would have to turn away.

She looked so sweet, so vulnerable lying there. He had forgotten how long and thick her hair was, spilling out around her now as he had imagined it would be when . . . And her skin, so white and delicate he could see the blue veins in her neck and the tiny pulse beating steadily at the base of her graceful throat; the even whiter silk that clung so lovingly to all the intimate curves of her body; the long, slender legs that emerged so enticingly from beneath the pantalettes and ended in such daintily perfect feet. Dusty watched, mesmerized, as her breasts came to life under his very gaze and hardened into little crests beneath their flimsy covering. Well he remembered how gently rounded her breasts were, how soft and warm her skin was under his hands and in his mouth. It had been a long time but not long enough that he had forgotten. Would there ever be enough time for that?

Sitting on his heels beside her now, his breath coming in such ragged gasps he was certain she must hear it, his blood pounding a primitive longing in his veins, he watched the slight rise and fall of her breasts, unaware that his hand had moved of its own accord to close over the lush mound.

Priscilla was having such a delicious dream. Dusty wanted her, wanted her so much that nothing else mattered, and he had told her so, in words that left no doubt as to his blatant need. Now he was staring down at her, his eyes like blue fire, so full of naked longing that her whole body yearned upward toward him. Her arms had already begun to move, to twine themselves around his neck, to pull his hard male lips down to her own pulsingly eager ones. He was beside her now, his arms around her, his mouth devouring hers, his rugged strength pressed against her yielding curves, his hands caressing, searing her sensitized flesh wherever they touched, burning her even through the silk that covered her. Her hands were busy, too, kneading and stroking the solid wall of his back and shoulders, while her legs tangled with his, sleek silk against abrasive denim, bare toes against cool leather. Their bodies melted together, two parts of one whole, naturally, gracefully blending into the choreography of pleasure that they had practiced in times past, hips straining against hips, hands searching, lips tasting, all in the fevered frenzy of mutual need. In the twilight world of slumber, Priscilla knew with the certainty of dreaming that she had discovered the solution to her dilemma. She would tell him. She must tell him. It was so simple. She moved her lips but no sound came out. She tried again and again, experiencing the frustration of one who sleeps and struggles to make that sleeping body perform, only to find it sluggish and unresponsive, while at the same time it responds to events inside the dream. Dusty's hungry mouth fastened onto the throbbing tip of her breast, his hands working magic down below, coaxing her to life, to passion, to all the many pleasures they had known together. With one mighty surge of will, she forced herself up and up, free of the somnolent bonds that held her until the words came tumbling from her throat, those secret words that were the answer to everything.

At the sound of her startled cry, Dusty's head came up, and blue eyes met brown in a morass of disoriented confusion. Her pliant body went rigid in his arms and the chocolate eyes that had been closed in what he had thought was passion now had opened in what he recognized with dismay as shock. And alarm, he realized with an agonized groan. Well, what had he expected? He had practically attacked her, knowing she was asleep. In the course of a few short minutes he had sunk from Peeping Tom to rapist. Mortified, he released her instantly and in the next second he was on his feet, his back turned.

"Didn't mean to scare you," he said, his voice unnaturally husky, his words stumbling over each other in nervous embarrassment. "Stella was worried about you. Sent me down to see if you was all right."

Priscilla gaped at his rigid back, trying with great difficulty to become completely awake. She had been asleep, that much her befuddled mind remembered, and dreaming, too, about Dusty, but some of that dream, at least, had been real. He had been kissing her in the dream, making love to her, and apparently he had been making love to her in real life, too, she surmised as she noticed how her breasts had spilled free of her chemise when she sat up, and how her nipples tingled as she drew the silk back over them, and how her loins ached with that familiar emptiness. If she had doubted before, she was now certain that he still wanted her. But there was something else, some other part of the dream, something very important she remembered, something she was going to say. She had been saying it or trying to when the sound of her own voice had awakened her, but for the life of her she could not remember what it was. "I . . . I must have fallen asleep," she stammered. "I was drying my hair." Scrambling to her feet, she snatched up the blanket, and feeling suddenly very exposed, began to cover herself with it until one look at Dusty's rigid stance convinced her that he would die before turning around. Now what was he all upset about? He *had* been upset, she remembered now, recalling the nervous way he had spoken to her. Was he still running scared as she had thought before? If so, that meant he was scared of *her*, that she had some power over him, and if she did . . . Oh, dear, she thought, suddenly realizing that she was standing there in her underwear. This was hardly the time or the place to be considering such things, and not knowing what else to do, she hurried into the schoolhouse. Hadn't he said that Stella was worried about her?

For the second time that day, Priscilla studied her reflection in the mirror, trying to see what he had seen when he looked at her. She did look different, somehow. Her eyes were brighter or something. Dusty Rhoades had a definite effect on her, and judging from the way he had been fumbling with the front of his pants, she had a pretty definite effect on him, too. She knew how to get to him now, too, or at least she would as soon as she

392

remembered what it had been, and when she did . . . She smiled at the newly seductive Priscilla in the mirror, feeling a very pleasant warmth invade her scantily clad body. "Dusty Rhoades," she whispered to herself, "you don't stand a chance."

The familiar creak of leather invaded her reverie, and she realized that he was mounting his horse, leaving— no, escaping from her. She ran to the window. Modestly, she stayed behind the curtain as she called out to him, "Wait, please! I'll only be a minute."

Reluctantly, Dusty dismounted. He was still too stirred up to even glance in her direction, so he stood, staring out into the distance for a while and then mechanically reached for his Bull Durham pouch and made a cigarette with fingers that trembled annoyingly. Good God, he must be crazy! What had possessed him to touch her like that, to kiss her, to . . . He hadn't known a peaceful night's sleep since he'd met her, and from the way he felt right now, tonight would be one of those nights where he lay awake all night in torment. The only alternative was to go ahead and finish what he'd started. Then he wouldn't have the physical pain any more, only the mental anguish to keep him awake. And if he made love to her one more time, and if it really did get better every time, like he was pretty sure it did, then how in the world would he ever get away from her? Groaning inwardly, he threw down his half-smoked cigarette and ground it viciously into the dirt. If he didn't get away from here soon . . .

"Here I am!" Priscilla sang out with a cheerfulness born of her new confidence. Her swift toilette had rendered her bewitchingly casual and faintly flushed, a combination Dusty found he could not observe for more than two consecutive seconds, but his hasty glance had told him everything he needed to know—that she was just as enticing dressed as she was undressed and that she did not seem at all upset about what had almost happened. Again. What on earth was wrong with her? Not that it mattered. He was upset enough for both of them. "Here, you ride. I'll walk," he offered gruffly.

Priscilla considered his offer for a moment and then, shaking her finger at him teasingly, she replied, "Oh, no, I know how you cowboys hate to walk. We can ride double." Stepping up to the stirrup, she waited expectantly for his assistance while she watched him try to think of an excuse to refuse to ride with her. Finally, with a sigh of defeat, he made a stirrup with his hands and bent over to give her a boost up. Smiling delightedly, Priscilla placed her hands on his shoulders with a caressing thoroughness that caused a sharp intake of breath on Dusty's part, and he propelled her into the saddle with unnecessary force. With obvious unwillingness, he swung himself up behind her, and holding the reins with exaggerated care to keep from touching her, he kicked the horse into motion.

Priscilla found it difficult to keep her seat, or at least pretended to, enjoying Dusty's annoyed grunts every time she brushed against him. The heat from his body and his nearness were affecting her, too, and she could not help but wish that he would lose control of himself and carry her off to some secluded spot and have his way with her. Unfortunately, he showed remarkable restraint and delivered her safe and sound to the ranch. He had never been so pleased to see a place in his life.

Priscilla found the Steele family in high spirits. A letter had come from their sister Sarah who lived over west of San Antonio. As usual, Stella would not permit it to be read until after supper. When Stella opened the letter, she found another envelope inside, addressed to Dusty, which she turned over to him. Then she read the one from Sarah. Their sister had nothing of great importance to say, but her letter was nevertheless a great diversion for the whole family. When Stella had finished and the others were asking her to repeat certain parts and discussing things she had said, Priscilla noticed Dusty unobtrusively open his missive. As he read, she saw his face turn grave and thoughtful. Carefully, he replaced it in his envelope and sat staring at nothing until Ruth remembered him.

"What did your letter say, Dusty?" she asked.

Starting, he tried to match everyone else's jovial mood. "Oh, Tim Kelly wants to offer me a job," he said with forced lightness.

Everyone demanded an explanation at one time, all except Priscilla, who felt suddenly cold.

"Seems Tim bought a herd from some fella down to Victoria. This fella's gonna drive it up to Santone and meet Tim there when Tim drives his own herd in. He's gonna hire some men there and send 'em up the trail." He paused, almost reluctant to tell the rest. "Wants me to boss the job for him." He looked around at all the staring faces. "Guess he figured I'd be in shape by now." He forced a smile but no one smiled back.

"When would you have to leave?" George asked.

"Accordin' to the letter, they should be in Santone in about two weeks."

For a long moment no one spoke or moved. Ruth broke the silence. "Are you going to do it?" she asked quietly.

"I'm gonna give it some thought," he answered. Then,

unable to look at their sad faces any longer, he rose and left the house.

Stella tried to recapture their earlier good humor, but Dusty's news weighed too heavily on everyone. Gradually, they all went about their own business, leaving Priscilla alone in the parlor, rocking a drowsy Matthew to sleep.

Priscilla's mind was in a turmoil. Two weeks! Less, because he would have to decide before then. If she wanted Dusty Rhoades, and she certainly did, then she would have to do something drastic, and soon. Cradling Stella's toddler more closely, she began to imagine a houseful of such children, all with red-gold hair and sky blue eyes. Crooning a half-forgotten lullaby, she began to make her plans and, as she rocked, she began to remember her dream and slowly, ever so slowly, the solution came back to her. It was faint at first, like a phantom trying to elude capture, but then it became more and more clear until at last she had it, and it was as simple as she had remembered, so simple that she had thought of everything else first. A secret smile curved her lips as she decided what she must do and vowed that, win or lose, she would never regret her choice.

Priscilla waited until it was completely dark, and then she suddenly remembered that she had to sleep down at the school since she had neglected to bring anything with her in the confusion of the afternoon. Leaving Matthew with his mother, she went out to ask Dusty to take her back down. She found him sitting on the corral fence, smoking.

"I forgot to bring my things with me this afternoon, so I'll have to go back to the school. Will you take me down?" she asked as guilelessly as possible.

Dusty sat for a long moment, watching her warily, absently fingering his cigarette. Then he cleared his throat. "Shore, I'll catch up some horses. Won't take a minute," he said a little less than enthusiastically.

"That's so much bother," she said. "Just saddle Lady. We can ride double again." She had almost added, Like we did this afternoon, but managed to restrain herself. She could see that he wanted to object, but more than that, he wanted to know what she had in mind. He was sure she had *something* in mind. He looked at her for another long moment then shrugged and reluctantly did as she had suggested.

Hoping against hope that he could deliver her safely to the schoolhouse without molesting her, Dusty swung up behind her on the mare and started them off into the night. She was wiggling again, just like this afternoon, brushing against him, shifting that round little bottom against his thighs. If she only knew what she was doing to him, she'd stop quick enough. Maybe he should tell her in no uncertain terms just what he wanted to do to her right now, he thought, before taking a long, steadying breath. The breath didn't help, though, because it filled his whole body with the scent of her, the smell of flowers and soap and that whatever-it-was that was uniquely Priscilla Bedford. Only barely managing to suppress a groan, Dusty was able to hold himself stiffly away from her tempting curves until they reached their destination, although he was certain she could hear the way his heart was trying to pound its way out of his chest and she could not miss the harsh irregularity of his breathing.

Gratefully, he dismounted outside her door, unable to suppress his sigh of relief. In the darkness, he missed her smile of triumph. Reaching up a hand to steady her, he was not quite prepared when she seemed to tumble from the saddle, but he somehow got his hands around her waist, that tiny waist, while she managed to clutch at his shoulders. She fell against him, smothering him with the sensation of her silky hair brushing his face and her full, round breasts pressing against his chest.

She uttered a startled, "Oh," as he steadied her, his large hands moving to cover her hips in the process. Still clinging to his shoulders, she regained her balance and looked up to meet his azure stare with eyes that glittered like a thousand stars. They stood that way for a long time, unable or unwilling to break the spell. Dusty looked down into her chocolate eyes as if trying to find the very bottom, knowing all the while that there was none. She felt so warm, so real under his hands, and she was looking at him like . . . like she looked when she wanted him to kiss her. She would raise her lips to him, just as she was raising her lips to him now, so sweet, so inviting, so . . .

He lowered his head slowly, so slowly, until he could taste her breath, until their lips were only a whisper apart, and then she ducked her head and twisted neatly out of his grasp. Shocked as he was, he did not miss the wicked grin she flashed him.

"Good night, Mr. Rhoades," she sang out as she waltzed toward the door. "Oh, please wait until I light the lamp. I just hate to go into a dark house. It's so frightening."

He stood there gaping until she slammed the door, and then he felt the cold fury flooding over him. The little tease! She knew his weakness and now she had found the perfect way to wreak revenge. Oh, he deserved it, he had to admit, but that didn't mean he would like it. He knew just how it would be. She would taunt him and tempt him and torment him but never give in again. He would never have a minute's peace. She would drive him crazy!

Mechanically, he pulled out the makings and tried to roll a smoke. He could roll one on the back of a moving horse, but he could not make one now. His unsteady fingers botched the job and in frustration, he dashed the mangled mess to the ground, cursing in a violent whisper.

There's nothing lower than a tease who'd lead a man on for nothing. Well, he'd show her. He'd take that job for Tim Kelly. In fact, he'd leave tomorrow. Go right to their ranch, and have a nice visit. Hadn't seen them in quite a spell. They'd be tickled to see him. That's what he'd do. Put a quick end to her little game. He'd show her.

Why in the hell was he still standing here? Oh, yes, she had asked him to wait until she lit the lamp. What was taking so long? He could hear her rustling around in there. Maybe she couldn't find a match. He waited, shifting his feet, restless. Wonder if something happened. What if somebody was inside? What if . . . ? He was just about to call out to her when she struck the match, and what he saw froze the words in his throat.

Priscilla stood naked, the lamplight making flickering shadows on the alabaster perfection of her body. He watched, mesmerized, as she lifted her arms and removed the pins from her hair, her full, ripe breasts rising and falling as she moved. With an eager reluctance he allowed his gaze to move downward, past her slim waist, her flat belly, her gently rounded hips and thighs, and then back up to the one dark spot in all that whiteness, the place where he could bury himself and be lost for all time. His eyes closed as the shock of desire went through him like a physical pain. When he looked again, she was gone.

Drawing a ragged breath, he stared at the now-empty window and considered his options. He could always ride away, pretend he had not seen her. Most men would call him a fool for that, but he knew it would be wise, oh, so wise, because he also knew that if he went in to her now, he would be bound to her as he had never been bound to another human being. It would be different this time, not just a quick tumble in answer to an overwhelming impulse. She was calling him to her bed and if he came, willingly, he would be making a commitment. She would own him, body and soul, and since she had had his heart for a long time now, he would have nothing left of himself at all. He would lose everything, just for the pleasure of touching her and tasting her and driving deep inside her and sharing with her that one sweet moment of ecstasy. All these thoughts flashed through his mind in an instant, but even as his reason was still urging escape, the aching, burning thing that was his body was moving toward the door.

His boots sounded unnaturally loud as he mounted the stairs. The door opened easily under his hand. Priscilla was sitting up in her bed, clutching the covers to her breast. Her eyes looked black in the lamplight, and they glittered like diamonds. Her chestnut hair spread over her shoulders like a glistening cape. He tried to read her expression, and, failing that, tried to speak some word to her, but no words came. With a self-consciousness he had not felt in years, he closed the door and made his way to her table where he laid his hat, and then he cautiously perched on one of her straight-backed chairs and pulled off his boots. Standing, he removed his vest and shirt, and when his hands moved to his belt buckle, he looked up once more. Would she watch him in the lamplight as he had watched her? Their eyes met and held for a moment, and then he removed the rest of his clothes under her admiring gaze.

He really was magnificent, she thought as she watched him moving in the lamplight. She had never seen a man's body before, never seen more of Dusty than a hurried glimpse. They had always been in a rush before, but not this time, and never again. This time she took care to study the way his broad shoulders gave way to a narrow waist and slim hips, how the red-gold fluff that furred his chest tapered to a point and then broadened again to crown his manhood and went on in a lighter fuzz down the well-muscled columns of his legs. Priscilla felt desire uncoil inside her and spiral up and out as she watched him lean over and blow out the light and then come toward her in the shadowy darkness.

She lay back against the pillow as she felt the bed sag under his weight, and fighting off one last small twinge of reluctance, she turned into his arms. Instead of the fiery burst of passion she had expected, he gathered her gently, almost reverently against him. Priscilla found her cheek pressed against his shoulder, and she breathed deeply of the essence of Dusty Rhoades. Sweat and tobacco and horse and leather and a faint muskiness that was his alone. She smiled slightly at the thought that she could probably find him in the dark, and curiosity got the better of her and she reached a tentative finger to touch the springy mat of red-gold hair on his chest that was tickling her nose. It was course and thick and exciting. Emboldened, she moved her hand to touch the skin beyond. It was soft, much softer than she had expected, much softer than the calloused hands that were now moving on her back, stroking her, arousing her. He was

401

soft, but hard, too, like satin stretched over steel, and he went still again as she allowed her fingers to explore his shoulder, both shoulders, any reluctance now forgotten in the wonder of discovery. He breathed her name as he found her lips in a kiss so sweet, so full of longing, that Priscilla felt she could hardly bear it. She answered that kiss with a longing of her own, and feeling her response, he pulled her to him with gentle strength, crushing her rounded breasts against the wall of his chest, molding her curves to his leanness, his hands now roving freely, discovering the uncharted expanse of skin that quivered under his touch.

Priscilla buried her fingers in the thickness of his hair, holding his face to hers in the kiss she never wanted to end. Her lips parted under his insistent tongue, and he gently explored the recesses of her mouth, greedily drinking in her sweetness, while his hands found the silken mounds of her breasts. Obediently, Priscilla arched herself to him as his thumbs moved insistently over her nipples, teasing them to hardness. When Dusty's mouth left hers, she uttered a cry of protest and sought to draw him back, but he chuckled as he pulled her clutching hands away. "I'll be back," he promised hoarsely as his lips trailed a path of fire down her throat, paused briefly at the throbbing pulse he encountered at its base, and then moved on to pay homage to the pebble-hard peaks his hands had produced. Priscilla moaned as his lips closed around one pink crest, teasing, tasting, suckling until she was writhing with pleasure and then moving on to the other.

Ruthlessly ignoring the clamoring of his own desire that demanded he take her swiftly, Dusty continued to arouse Priscilla in every way he knew, and he knew many. Having learned as a very young man, he had practiced over the years with more than one willing young miss. Not bad girls really, just girls more curious than cautious. Women seemed to sense that he knew how to pleasure them. Perhaps that was what drew them. He had never cared to analyze it. Only now was he genuinely glad that he knew how to love a woman as he felt Priscilla's body come alive under his touch. He would use this knowledge to bind her to him as he was bound to her, and never once did he think of the woman who had taught him how, so long ago.

Priscilla gasped as Dusty's hand moved lower, probing, caressing, seeking out her most secret places and producing those familiar ripples of pleasure in the process. If he had aroused her in times past, this time he inflamed her, maddened her, as his ravenous mouth slid lower, investigating the smooth plane of her belly, drawing a cry from her as his tongue dipped teasingly into her navel as if for one sweet drop of nectar and then moved on. Down one slender leg he went, caressing the inside of one trembling thigh, tasting the exquisitely tender flesh in the bend of her knee, discovering a sensitive spot on the curve of her ankle, pausing when her moaning told him to and then moving on, back up the other leg until he reached that precious apex and her restless hands demanded that he take her. Now.

She opened to him, welcoming him, cradling him with her arms, with her body as he slowly filled her, filled that aching void that her love for him created. "Oh, God, Pris . . ." he groaned as they lay motionless, their bodies joined, their souls mated in this final act of surrender.

Tears sprang to Priscilla's eyes at the beauty of it, and had she not known what came next, she would have been

tempted to lie there like that forever. "You love me
don't you?" she prodded, her hands holding him fas
against her.

"Yes, oh, yes," he rasped, unable to remember why i
had been a secret before.

"I love you, too," she whispered against his ear and
gloried as she felt the shock ripple through him.

He levered himself up on his elbows and squinted t
make out her face in the darkness. Had he heard right
Could it be true? "Pris? What . . ."

"I said, I love you," she interrupted softly, and befor
he could reply, she pulled his face back down to hers
When their lips met, all else was forgotten, words n
longer necessary. Their bodies moved in unison toward
common goal, arms and hands and legs and lips creating
harmony of pleasure as they strove toward the ultimat
satisfaction. Priscilla drifted into a world of sensatio
where only her body and his existed, and his only t
please hers. Intoxicated with the novelty of flesh agains
flesh wherever they touched, she could not get enough o
him, running her hands over hair-roughened flanks an
buttocks, wrapping her silken legs around his sinewy
ones, luxuriating in his virility, marveling at th
wonderful differences between them that caused such
awesome things to happen when they came together. An
awesome things were happening as he drove into her
again and again, and she eagerly met each lunge tha
brought them closer and closer. Priscilla felt the glov
that had been smoldering within her grow and spread like
molten lava, scorching all her limbs while at the same
time the source grew hotter still as each stroke stoked he
flickering core, igniting there a blaze that soon became a

holocaust, sweeping over her until its heat consumed her and she was no more.

When the flames at last flickered out, Dusty drew the sheet up over their rapidly cooling bodies and gently enfolded her in his arms. For a while they lay nestled together, Priscilla's head resting comfortably on his shoulder, her fingers tangling in and out of the springy hairs that matted his chest.

"I love you," she said softly, almost loathe to break the companionable silence.

Dusty sighed. Well, what had he thought, anyway? One time might have been an accident, but a woman like Priscilla Bedford would never keep coming back just for sex, would never keep subjecting herself to a man who treated her so cruelly if she didn't love him. He must have known it all along. He had just been too stubborn to admit it. Or too stupid. And she'd gone to a lot of trouble to prove it, too, he realized, remembering her elaborate seduction scene. "Couldn't you have just *told* me?" he chided playfully.

"I tried to tell you," she replied with exasperation, rising on one elbow so that she could see his face. "That day by the river. You got so mad, I thought you'd strangle me."

Dusty winced at the memory. "So that's what that was all about," he mused, wondering how he could have been so dense, and then he flashed her a sheepish grin. "Well, I know now," he informed her, and then they both laughed, the laughter of love and sharing and caring, and Priscilla snuggled back down into his arms, content.

"I guess you won't be leaving now," she guessed playfully, tracing a pattern around one flat, dark nipple.

Dusty flinched slightly from this first pinch of his new bondage. It was true, of course. He'd given up his freedom when he'd entered this room, but it still hurt a little to be reminded of it. "Well, one thing for shore, I'd better be leavin' *here*, right now," he said with forced lightness.

"Oh, no," Priscilla protested, but he silenced her with a finger on her lips.

"I can't stay here all night," he pointed out with ruthless logic. "I don't want folks talkin' about you," he argued, but the hurt in her eyes melted his resolve. "Here, lie down. I'll stay 'til you're sleepin'," he conceded. "And don't look at me like that. Shut your eyes!" he ordered with a feigned sternness that made her smile as she curled up beside him and fell asleep.

Priscilla awoke to someone pounding at her door. In a rush, the memory of last night came back to her, but before she could analyze her feelings, she heard Ruth's voice calling her. Of course, it was Sunday morning and they had come to fetch her to church. Quickly slipping on her nightdress, she hurried to the door.

"You sick or something?" Ruth asked, seeing Priscilla not dressed.

"I had a . . . a restless night and woke up with a sick headache. I think I'll stay in bed a while. I'm sure I'll be fine by the time you get back." Priscilla brushed off Ruth's offers to stay with her or get something for her head and convinced her to go on to church without her.

"I'll be down soon's we get back to check on you," Ruth promised. "Oh, here," she added as an afterthought, handing her a bouquet of wildflowers.

"What's this?" Priscilla asked bewildered.

"I don't know. Found 'em on your doorstep." Ruth

smiled mysteriously. "Must be from some secret admirer."

When Ruth had gone, Priscilla sat holding the flowers for a long time, for the first time realizing that nothing had really been settled between them. What would happen now? she wondered.

Chapter Fourteen

Priscilla was almost afraid to appear for dinner, wondering how she could sit across the table from Dusty and act as if nothing had happened. She need not have worried. When Ruth came back, she informed Priscilla that Dusty had gone over to the old Rogers' place and would not be back until the work there was finished, probably a few more days. At first Priscilla felt hurt, but then she realized that as far as Dusty was concerned, nothing had changed. All the reasons he had given her so long ago—on the day before his accident—for not taking a wife were still valid. He still had no home for her and no prospects of one in the near future. How could he know she did not need one? Of one thing she was certain: she must tell him about the ranch. He would be angry, perhaps hurt. It was possible that she might even lose him for good, but would he, could he really leave her, now? Yes, it was possible, but when she remembered their last night together, she doubted it.

Dusty managed to stretch the work at the ranch for three more days, but finally he had to dismiss the carpenters and head back to the Steele ranch and Priscilla. No matter how many times he went over it, he could find no answer. He had some money, would have more when Curly came back from selling his cattle, but not near enough to buy the kind of place that would be right for Priscilla. He knew how much money the new owner had spent on his old home, and he had nothing close to that amount. His only hope was to find some land to homestead. One of the carpenters had a brother in Arizona, had really talked it up. But that was across Texas and New Mexico, and that country was full of rustlers and other bad characters, cattle wars, and even renegade Apaches. He could go alone, of course, find a place and send for her. But that would take a year. At least. Could he stand to be separated from her for a year? It had only been three days now and already he was in physical pain. Would that pass or grow worse? And then there was that other possibility. Suppose Priscilla had a baby while he was gone? Odd, he had never considered that possibility with any other girl he had been with. Somehow it did not seem possible for a casual encounter to result in something so permanent, but it was different this time. There was something very permanent about this time. In any case, he could not simply leave, whatever his motives, whatever he might have planned before. That would put him in a class with Judd Slaughter. No, he had only one real choice. He would have to marry her and stay right here, set up housekeeping in the Steele's cabin, the same cabin where he had watched his mother sicken and die. The idea filled him with a nameless dread. How could she do this to him? She certainly knew that he would have to marry her, have to not only for convention but because he loved her. It was not as if he had not already, long ago, told her his prospects. What could have possessed her? Well, she had wanted it this way, and if she wanted him enough to do what she had done, she could have him. He would do the best he could by her, although God only knew what that might be. He would be a man. He would see her, somehow, tonight, and he would propose. And Priscilla thought he was *lucky* to be a man!

Dusty arrived at the ranch just in time to wash up for supper. At the table he gave a final report to George on the work at Priscilla's ranch. George seemed manifestly pleased and the girls asked a thousand questions.

"That friend of yours must have a big family, George, to need such a big house," Dusty commented.

George could not help a glance at Priscilla who had suddenly dropped her fork. "Not yet," he replied, "but I think they're expecting to."

Priscilla took advantage of a lull, later in the meal, to speak. "Dusty," she called down to him. It was the first time she had called him by his first name, and he fairly jumped at it. "Lady has a loose shoe," she said when he looked up at her. "Would you check it after supper?"

"Shore," he said as casually as he could. No one else seemed to notice anything unusual in the exchange.

Dusty expected Priscilla to meet him in the barn when he went to check on the mare, but she did not. As he had suspected, Lady did not have a loose shoe at all, but he waited to give Priscilla time to come. Then, giving up, he went out to find her lingering in the yard. She walked over to him as if casually inquiring after the mare. She was wearing a pretty little dress with flowers all over it and it hugged her in all the right places. Those brown eyes looked so huge and deep, and when he looked down into them, their expression stopped his heart. He had to jam his hands into his pockets to keep from grabbing hold of her.

Priscilla wanted so much to reach out to him, to feel those strong arms around her, but this was the wrong time and the wrong place for such things. She had something more important to consider. "Meet me at the bench by the river in a few minutes," she whispered. "I have something to tell you." Her heart was pounding, but she managed to at least look calm. This was it, then, the moment when she would discover just how much he really did love her, just how proud he really was and if that pride would prevent them from being happy.

He could only nod his assent. Something to tell him! What could she possibly have to tell him? His already strained imagination could only come up with one possibility. Dusty had no idea how quickly a woman could know that she was pregnant and it was certainly not a subject he could casually broach with anyone, but when he thought about it, remembering back to the first time, he realized she had had plenty of time to find out, if that was it. Well, he would not let her humiliate herself by begging him to make an honest woman out of her. He would simply propose before she could tell him. That's what he would do.

Waiting by the river, Priscilla paced nervously beside the split-log bench, oblivious to the natural beauty around her, concerned only with how best to tell him what must be told. The sound of hoofbeats startled her, and she had to smile when she saw that he had saddled Lady and ridden to their rendezvous. How like a cowboy, she thought. Western men were certainly different from eastern men. She had divined that when she was just a girl, standing among the stock pens at the Centennial Exposition. She had been won even then. She had only needed to meet *the* western man to make the dream complete. Now he stood before her, tall and strong, sober as a judge, befitting the moment. She thought her heart might burst with the love she felt for him. When he had dismounted, he started toward her and she met him halfway, stopping when she was at arm's length from him.

He wanted to take her in his arms, but something in her eyes held him back. "Pris, I . . ." he began, but she put her fingers to his lips to stop him.

"Wait, please, let me speak first," she said so urgently he could not refuse. Turning away nervously, she walked the few steps to the bench, sat down, and drew a deep breath. "I bought a ranch," she said quickly.

This was so different from what he had expected to hear that for a moment he did not comprehend her.

After several tries he managed to say, "A ranch? How could *you* buy a ranch?"

Her insides seemed to flutter; her fingers twisted together anxiously. Somehow this was more frightening than the night Judd Slaughter had attacked her. "Remember once I told you my father had left me some money? Well, it was actually quite a lot of money."

He reached back in his memory. What had she said about her father? Had she ever hinted he was wealthy? "You said your father was a printer," he accused.

"He was, at least he started out in life as a printer. He eventually became a publisher. He owned two newspapers, several magazines, a publishing house. We owned a home in town and one at the shore, as well as some other real estate holdings. Father also had interests in several businesses. In short, he was a wealthy man. I was his only heir." Priscilla gave Dusty a hasty, wary glance and then closed her eyes and braced herself for the explosion she was certain would come.

Dusty was dumbfounded. It took him a while to absorb this information. Then he remembered. "You said you bought a ranch. What . . . ?" And then he knew. The mystery was solved. "You bought *my* ranch!" he roared.

Priscilla jumped. Getting hold of herself, she said very distinctly, "I bought Hazel Rogers' ranch."

"You didn't even ask me!" he raged.

"I wasn't aware that I had to ask you if I could spend my own money to buy someone else's ranch," she said, slightly annoyed at his attitude. She had expected him to be mad, but now he was being unreasonable.

This checked his ranting, but he was still angry. He stared at her. She looked so small and innocent. How could she have done such an infamous deed?

She smiled sweetly and tried to look appealing. "Of course, I'll need someone to manage it for me," she said, hoping he would take the hint.

His eyes grew large with amazement. He looked at her as if he had never seen her before. Indeed, he was seeing a side of her he had not suspected existed. "You want to hire me to work at my own ranch?" Was that the reason she had seduced him? Did she just want a good foreman? Was that all he meant to her? he wondered wildly.

Now she was angry, too. He was, beyond doubt, the most impossible man alive. It was *not* his ranch. Why could he not see that? "Of course not!" she snapped. "I

414

thought we would be married."

She realized then that she had never yet seen him truly angry. His face turned almost purple, and he threw his hat to the ground and made a strange growling noise deep in his throat. "Now you've done it!" he gritted.

"Done, what?" she demanded in exasperation.

"You've gone and proposed. Dammit, Priscilla, you're positively unnatural. Don't you know it's the man who's supposed to do the askin'?" he raged.

"A person could die of old age waiting for you to ask!" she retorted. The words were out before she could think, and when she saw his face, she was not certain if they had done harm or good.

Instantly, his anger was gone. She could see he felt the guilt of her accusation. He knew he should have asked her long ago, months ago, after that very first time, but he had convinced himself that she didn't want him. After this last time, he could no longer pretend to believe that, and he should have come back the very next day begging her to have him, but he had been too proud. He turned his back, unable to face her, feeling the weight of her charge.

"I was *gonna* ask you . . ." he muttered, and he had been going to, too. Hadn't he decided that very thing, just minutes ago?

She jumped to her feet and went to him, tentatively placing a hand on his shoulder in an overwhelming need to reassure him. "I know you were. I know why you waited, that you were ashamed . . ." He stiffened at the word, and she withdrew her hand, clenching her fists in frustration. Why could she never do anything right with this man? Every time she opened her mouth, she made him furious. Every time she tried to placate him, she made him even madder. She could see it was foolish to continue until he cooled off. She checked an impulse to scream. Or to hit him. Shakily, she said, "If you still want me . . . I mean . . . think it over," she finished lamely and walked away. Once she turned to look back, half expecting he would be running after her, but he was still standing as she had left him. She went slowly back to the school to wait for him. It would be the longest wait of her life.

Dusty stood there a long time, trying to get control of his thoughts but without much success. Finally, he mounted Lady and went for a ride. He always thought better while he rode. When it got too dark to see, he reluctantly returned to the ranch, where he lay on his bunk, in the dark, staring up at the ceiling, his mind still a jumble.

At first he had cursed Priscilla for lying to him, but then he had grudgingly admitted that she had never lied. She had only failed to mention some things. If only he had known she was rich. He never would have . . . but she must have guessed that he would have avoided her like the plague. That was why she hadn't told him. And the business about the ranch! It still made his blood boil to think about it. She also must have known what his reaction would be to that. At least she had told him before letting him propose to her. He had to give her credit for that. If only he had known before he . . . He sat bolt upright on his bed. Now it was all clear to him! She had planned her . . . her *seduction*, yes, there was no other word for it, to trap him. She had him now, no matter what he thought about the ranch, no matter about anything. Telling him to think it over, as if he could think at all when he remembered her arms around him, her soft,

416

sweet lips, her eager flesh yielding to him. He had marveled at the fact that she had offered herself to him so boldly, so freely. He had known then that she was his, and his alone. And he was hers. No matter how many other women had come before, he knew that as long as she breathed, no other woman could ever tempt him again. He could not deny the sweetness of it, but it was bittersweet. He felt like a roped calf. Well, she might hogtie and brand him, but she would never castrate him. He would think of something, some way he could save his pride, come to her like a man. It was the middle of the night before he thought of a way.

Priscilla awoke with a start. The sunlight was streaming in, shining on her face. She was lying on her bed fully clothed and for a moment she could not recall why. Then it came to her. She had sat up late waiting for Dusty to come to her. When she could stay awake no longer, she had lain down expecting to hear him at her door at any moment, but he had not come, and she had fallen asleep. She fought off the wave of disappointment. He would never come to her in the middle of the night, she reasoned. He would come today. Probably as soon as school was out. Would she live until then? Without doubt. Could she forgive him for his foolish male pride? She would forgive him anything if he would take her in his arms and love her the way he had loved her that night. Thus resolved, she rose and began to change for school.

Ben Steele came to breakfast shaking his head. "I had the damnedest dream last night," he said.

"What was it, Daddy?" asked Ruth as she passed him a plate of eggs.

He chuckled. "It was about Dusty. I dreamed he came to me in the night, told me he was goin' to take his money out of the safe. Seems he was goin' somewheres, can't recall where or what fer, though. Strange. Where is the boy, anyways?" he asked, looking around.

No one else knew either.

"Ben junior, run out to the bunkhouse and find Dusty," Stella ordered. No one missed the hint of alarm in her voice.

Ben gave her a puzzled look. "You don't think . . ."

"George," Stella said to her husband, "check the safe."

George started to protest until he caught the look in Stella's eye, then he quickly left the room.

While everyone waited, Ruth asked anxiously, "He wouldn't leave like that, without telling anyone? In the middle of the night?" No one answered her.

After a seemingly endless interval, Ben junior came bursting in. "He ain't there! All his stuff's gone, too!" he told them eagerly.

George appeared, his face grave. "His money is gone, too."

Priscilla had noticed a strange reticence in her students all day. No, not all of them, just the Steeles. They would not meet her eye, and she had seen them whispering together outside during the lunch break. The afternoon dragged for her. She was expecting a visitor that day, and it was not the strained-looking Stella Wilson who did appear as soon as the children had gone.

Alarmed by Stella's expression, Priscilla rose to meet her, but Stella waved her back into her seat. She had to catch her breath since walking with her distended belly was becoming difficult.

"Stella, what is it?" Priscilla asked with apprehension.

"Dusty's gone," she said in the gentle voice generally reserved for deaths in the family.

A cold chill ran over Priscilla. "Gone? What do you mean, gone?" she demanded, unable to accept a statement of such finality.

"He packed up and rode out last night. Took the money Daddy was holding for him and some extra, too, against the sale of his cattle," Stella explained with brutal simplicity.

"Gone?" Priscilla's dazed mind could not quite comprehend. "Where could he have gone?"

"I was hopin' you could tell us that, honey," Stella said. "I know you talked to him yesterday. Did he say anything?"

Stella saw Priscilla's face go white. "No," Priscilla said quietly. "He didn't say anything, but I did." She looked up with tragic eyes. "I told him about the ranch."

Stella showed no surprise. "You told him that you were the one who bought the Rogers' place?"

Priscilla nodded. "You knew?" she asked incredulously.

"I suspected. What did he say?"

"Oh, Stella, he was furious! I've never seen him so angry. And when I suggested we get married . . ."

"You did that?" Stella cried. "No wonder! Good Lord!"

Priscilla began to cry, the tears flowing unheeded down her cheeks, her eyes staring in disbelief. "I've done it this time, haven't I? I've lost him for good," she guessed, her voice breaking.

Stella went to her, put her arms around her. "Oh, honey, it might not be so bad as we think. He did talk to Daddy before he left but Daddy was sound asleep and never did get waked up proper, so he don't rightly remember what Dusty said. He thinks he said he'd be back. At least he got that feelin'. Oh, honey, don't take on so. He took two horses with him, but he didn't take Lady. He'd never leave that horse if he wasn't comin' back."

Late that night, Dusty sat staring into the flame of his campfire. He was beginning to regret not waiting to say goodbye to Priscilla, although he had to admit it would probably not have been a good idea. He was still angry and seeing her again would have made it worse. Let her worry about him for a while. It would do her good. She was always so cocksure about everything, about him in particular. This would teach her not to take him for granted. She was so certain all she had to do was crook her little finger and he would jump into her bed or crawl to the altar . . . Well, the bed part was true enough, and he guessed the altar part was true, too, just as long as he did not have to *crawl*. Well, in a few days he would be where he was going and if everything went as planned, he would send a telegram. Besides, Ben knew where he was going and for what, more or less. Ben would tell Priscilla.

Priscilla never said another word about Dusty, and everyone was careful not to mention him when she was around. Her swollen eyes with the dark shadows under them spoke volumes, however. Stella began to suspect something deeper than simply a lover's quarrel.

420

At night Priscilla vacillated between fury and depression. She cursed herself for giving herself to a man so heartless that he would leave her without a word. Then she cursed herself for overplaying her hand and driving him away. She lost her appetite, and she felt nauseated all the time. Her head ached and her stomach ached, and she could not sleep. Worry, Stella said. Try not to think about it. Time heals all. Balderdash, thought Priscilla.

Then the telegram came. It was addressed to Ben. It said, "Business completed. Back by end of month. Tell everyone. Dusty."

And just who was "everyone," she wanted to know? The end of the month was a month away! What could take him so long to get back if he was finished with whatever business he had?

Priscilla no longer cried at night. Now she was just plain mad. It seemed to wear her down, carrying the anger inside her. Suddenly, her sleepless nights turned into nights in which she could not sleep enough. She found herself drooping in the afternoons as she listened to the children recite. She felt ill, although never quite ill enough to stay in bed. The nausea continued, although it never seemed to get worse. It just sat on her stomach, day after day, a constant reminder that all was not well.

The furniture that Priscilla had had freighted in from Philadelphia for her new home arrived. At first she refused to even go see it, but Stella preyed on her anger. Why should she let Dusty Rhoades rob her of the satisfaction that was rightfully hers? It worked. On Saturday, she and Stella rode out to meet the freight wagons and supervise the unloading. It was the first thing Priscilla had enjoyed in the month since Dusty had been gone. They both lamented the fact that Hazel Rogers was no longer around to make curtains for the new house.

At noon, Priscilla and Stella spread their picnic lunch on the newly dusted kitchen table. Smiling for the first time in many weeks, Priscilla picked up her sandwich and froze. The nausea hit her in a wave, and feeling the gorge rise in her throat, she bolted out the back door. Leaning over the back porch railing, she retched and retched until her stomach was completely empty. Stella helped her back inside to the parlor and took her to the sofa where she lay down, pale and trembling.

She smiled weakly at Stella. "That's been coming for a long time. I guess all that worry finally got to me."

"You felt sick for a while?" Stella asked, deeply concerned.

"Yes, weeks. I never actually vomited before, though. Funny, now I feel hungry . . . famished!" Priscilla laughed self-consciously.

"Sit still. I'll bring you somethin'," Stella said and returned to the kitchen. In a few short minutes she had transferred their picnic to the front room. She watched Priscilla eat with great interest. "You have anything else wrong with you? I mean, any other aches or pains?" she asked thoughtfully.

Priscilla considered a moment, then shook her head. Then she laughed. "Well, there's something, but it could hardly be related to a stomach disorder."

"What is it?"

"Well," Priscilla looked around and lowered her voice in case the freighters might be near. "My breasts are sore."

Stella's head jerked back. Priscilla laughed again and said, "See, I told you it wasn't related."

Stella looked at her closely. "You must be expectin'

your monthly soon."

Priscilla considered. That must be it, she thought. She was certainly due. When? She thought back. When had she menstruated last? Certainly not since . . . it hit her like lightening. The sandwich slipped from her fingers, and she felt the blood rush from her head. No! It was impossible! Yet it was not impossible. She had been fine before, after those other times. In fact, she had somehow never given a thought to getting pregnant before, and her flow had come each time, right on schedule. Each time, that is, until this last time. How many weeks had it been? Five, exactly, she calculated. Her last flow had been weeks before that. The nausea, the weariness, her sore breasts, it all made sense now. Do not look at Stella, she told herself. Stella will know. She can read minds. She will know everything.

Stella already knew. "Honey," she said gently, taking Priscilla's hands. "Is there any way . . . I mean . . . you're in a family way, aren't you?"

Once more Priscilla was weeping on Stella's shoulder. How many times had Dusty Rhoades made her cry like this? No man had ever caused her to cry a single tear. Now she wanted to die. She was not even sure she still wanted him, not after the way he had treated her, and now this! Stella, it seemed, was outraged. Priscilla could hear her mumbling incoherently.

"I'll kill that Dusty Rhoades. Why, when I get through with him, they'll carry him out in a handbasket!" Stella was saying.

With a jolt, Priscilla realized that Stella thought she had been seduced and abandoned. As logical as that conclusion was, Priscilla's pride would not allow her to let her friend believe it. "It wasn't his fault," she sniffed.

"I made him . . . do it."

"Oh," Stella said sarcastically, "I guess you held a gun to his head."

"No," Priscilla admitted, "but I did make it . . . very easy for him." The memory of her boldness brought the color to her face. Her shame forced her to turn away from Stella.

Stella could not help a grin. "So that's how it was. Well, I guess you're not the first woman thought she could trap a man that way. It's not a bad idea either, if it works. I used it myself."

"You!" Priscilla gasped, her head whipping back around to stare at Stella in disbelief.

"Had to," Stella affirmed. "George had some fool idea he wasn't good enough for me."

"George, not good enough?" Priscilla could hardly imagine the dapper George Wilson ever being unsure of himself.

"You gotta know the story," said Stella, glad to ease Priscilla away from her current problem. "See, when George first come here, he was a cowboy, ridin' the grubline. You might've heard folks say how terrible a hand George is. Well, it's true. He couldn't hold no kinda job, he was so bad. Thing was, everybody liked him, and they just couldn't stand to send him away. Daddy really took a shine to him. First man we ever had on the place who'd been to college. Daddy had a lot of respect for a fella with education who didn't let it go to his head, if you know what I mean. Daddy wanted him to stay, but even though all the boys tried real hard to teach him, he just never could get the hang of bein' a cowboy. Too much of a city boy, I reckon. Meantime, I'd fallen for him, head over heels, and he was kinda sweet on me, too. I was quite a looker back then. Well, Daddy had found out, somehow, that George had studied law, an' he was tryin' to convince George that Rainbow needed a lawyer. George wasn't too sure. Guess he thought Daddy was just bein' kind. To make a long story short, I . . . ah . . . let him take advantage of me. 'Course, I was luckier than you, 'cause I didn't get caught.''

Priscilla's problems came back to her in a rush. "What am I going to do?" she groaned.

"Well, one thing for sure, you're gonna have a baby. An' if Dusty Rhoades wants to live to be any older, you're gonna get married," Stella declared.

"Oh, he mustn't know," Priscilla cried. "At least not until I see him, find out where he's been and why, and . . . if he still wants me." Priscilla sat up straighter, determination in her voice. "And if I still want him. If I don't, well, then I won't tell him at all. I'll simply go back east, someplace where no one knows me," she decided.

Stella frowned at the glint in her friend's eye. She knew that Priscilla meant every word.

Rita looked down at Vance in disgust. "You're not much use to me like that, Vance."

He looked up from where he lay on the bed through bleary eyes. He had not shaved or changed his clothes in days. He held a half-empty bottle of whiskey. It was not yet noon. "Well, my dear, if you'll help me get my pants off, I'll do my best," he offered sardonically.

Rita grabbed the bottle and threw it across the room where it smashed to the floor. "How long you gonna stay drunk?" she demanded. "It's been a month or more since you found out Hazel Rogers sold the ranch to someone else. Aren't you even gonna try to get the gold any more?"

Even half drunk, Vance realized the significance of what she had said. He had never told her about his attempt to buy the ranch and to his knowledge, he had never told her about the gold, either. She smiled at his shocked expression.

"Glad you ain't as drunk as you look," she said, crossing her arms triumphantly.

"How did you . . . ?" he began.

"Some you told me. Most I just figured out. It don't matter. What matters is I found out somethin' last night might interest you." She grinned her feline grin.

Vance pushed himself up on one elbow and shook his head in an attempt to clear it. "What is it?" he managed to ask.

"I found out who bought the ranch," she said smugly. "You'll be dee-lighted when you hear."

"Well?" he said when it became obvious she would not volunteer the information.

"Your *lady* friend, Miss Prissy Bedford." Rita thoroughly enjoyed the effect this had on Vance. "Just think, Vance. Maybe you can get the gold and the girl, too!" she goaded.

Vance swung at her, but she dodged him easily, laughing. "From what I hear," Rita continued, "school'll be over this Friday so she should be moving out to the new house. Maybe you should call on her, real polite. You could ask her to let you snoop around her place 'til you find that treasure. She's so well-bred, she'll prob'ly say that's fine with her." Rita's sardonic laughter echoed in the room long after she left.

Once alone, Vance sat straight up. His head was aching, but he was already thinking, trying to plan. First thing, he would sober up. Then a trip to the barber. When he was himself, he would be able to think of a plan. Maybe he *would* call on Miss Bedford.

Priscilla felt drained. All week she had been drilling her students on their recitations for the last day of school. They would each say a "piece" for their parents who were all coming tomorrow. Today had been the final rehearsal and all had gone well, but Priscilla's heart had not really been in it. At least it had given her something to occupy her mind. After tomorrow she would have nothing to think about but herself, and the prospect was not a happy one. She was sitting at her desk in the empty classroom when she heard the heavy footsteps on the porch.

Dusty had first gone to the new house, half expecting to find her in residence. Peering in the windows, he had seen the fancy furnishings like something out of a picture book, but he did not need to be told that no one lived there yet. Now he stood at the door of the school. He felt like a kid on Christmas morning. Dusty had played this scene a thousand times in his mind on the trail back from North Texas: He would walk in, Priscilla would see him, break into an adoring smile, and rush into his arms. After that, the scene ended in various delightful ways, but the beginning was always the same. He paused in the doorway while she looked up. Finding it too difficult to wait for her to come to him, he strode down the aisle toward her as she slowly rose to her feet. He was grinning from ear to ear. She looked pale, a little sickly, he thought. She had been worried about him! That was good! But wait, she wasn't smiling. That was not good! She was putting her hands on her hips. And scowling. His grin began to fade.

"Where the hell have you been?" she demanded, her fury shocking him almost as much as her language.

He stopped dead. This was all wrong! What was the matter with her? Here he was home after being gone more than a month, and she was mad! Why, she should be grateful he had come back at all. He glared back at her. "You told me to think it over!"

"Think it over? You've been gone over a month!" she shrilled, amazed at her own vehemence.

"I think slow," he yelled back, then caught himself. If things were going wrong, he wasn't helping any by being sarcastic. "I had some business," he said, controlling his voice.

"What sort of business?" she asked coldly, crossing her arms in silent challenge.

"Didn't Ben tell you?" he asked uncertainly.

Priscilla tried to control her anger. Getting angry would not get her the explanation she desired. "Ben never was really awake when you talked to him," she explained with careful patience. "All he could remember was that you said you were leaving and were taking your money. We thought you had gone for good."

Dusty thumbed back his hat. "I'll be damned," he murmured. No wonder she was mad! Suddenly remembering, he reached in his vest pocket and pulled out a crumpled piece of paper. "This is the business," he said as he offered it to her.

She snatched it from him and examined it. It was a bill of sale for one hundred head of Hereford cattle, signed by

W. S. Ikard. It took Priscilla a few moments to realize the significance of it. "You went to . . . to . . ."she faltered.

"To Henrietta," he supplied.

"And bought these Herefords?" He nodded. "Why?" she asked stupidly.

He rubbed the back of his neck. Why, indeed? He was wondering that himself, now. "So that," he explained carefully, "if some rich lady rancher wanted me to marry her, I'd have the cattle that would make her herd the best damn one in Texas. It's sort of a dowry." He grinned sheepishly, embarrassed.

Priscilla looked down at the paper again and then back at Dusty. She began to realize that he had *not* left her, that it was just an effort to save his foolish male pride, that he had planned to come back to her all the time. With bells on. And Hereford cattle, of all things. Almost against her will, the anger drained out of her. "You . . . you . . . I don't know whether to kiss you or kill you!" she wailed.

"Kiss me first," he suggested, and she did. As usual, one kiss led to another as they rediscovered the delights of being together again, but long before Priscilla had sufficiently refreshed her memories of him, he broke away and scooped her up in his arms.

With a startled squeal, Priscilla hastily threw her arms around his neck and clung as he carried her away. "Where are you taking me?" she demanded breathlessly.

He grinned mysteriously. "Someplace flat," he replied, and before she could respond to that obscure explanation, he plunked her down in the middle of her bed, dusted off his hands, and then sat down beside her to remove his boots.

Scrambling to a sitting position, Priscilla tried to look outraged while at the same time experiencing a very familiar excitement at the thought that he was going to make love to her. "What do you think you're doing?" she demanded indignantly.

He threw an exaggerated leer over his shoulder as he removed his shirt. "Take off that dress and you'll find out," he suggested.

"You certainly have your nerve," she blustered, nevertheless flushing faintly at his proposal. "Do you think you can . . ."

"Hush up, woman!" he commanded sternly. "I'll think you're not happy to see me!"

"I'm not!" she lied, responding to a perverse desire to provoke him. "Why should I be? You leave here without a word . . ."

"I told Ben where I was going," he reminded her.

"Without a word to *me*," she corrected.

Dusty heaved an exasperated sigh. "Now suppose I *had* told you where I was goin'. Would you have let me go peacefully? Wouldn't you have tried to stop me? Maybe even have made fun of me?" he coaxed her.

Priscilla made a disgusted face. He was right, of course. They would have had a jim-dandy of a fight over that one. "You could have written," she pouted.

"I sent a telegram!" he grated.

"To Ben! Not one word to me!" she whined.

Dusty lifted his eyes heavenward for a moment as if for strength and then rubbed the back of his neck wearily. "If I *had* sent you a telegram, how long do you think it would have been before everybody in the county knew about it? Would you have wanted everybody wondering why I was sending you telegrams? Maybe even asking you why?"

"No," she admitted reluctantly. "But you could have . . ."

"I should have written!" he confessed, lifting his hands in surrender. "Now, will you forgive me and take that dress off, or do I have to tear it off you?" he asked menacingly.

Priscilla giggled and then lowered her eyes provocatively. "I'll take it off," she said with false meekness, "but maybe you could help me a little . . . Oh!" she cried as he lunged for her, punishing her with the most delicious kisses. It was a punishment she accepted willingly and returned eagerly, and soon he had indeed helped her remove her dress and almost everything else, but when he reached for the tie to her pantalettes, she slapped his hands away. "Oh, no, you don't," she cautioned playfully. "You'll tear them like you did before."

"I did?" he asked, drawing back in frank amazement. "When did I do that?" he added, watching closely as she slipped the delicate silk down over her shapely hips.

"Once, when you were in a hurry," she said coyly. "Now are you going to take off those pants or do I have to tear them off of you?" she asked, imitating his threatening tone, and then she blushed, uncertain as to how he would react to such brazenness.

Dusty threw back his head and laughed delightedly. "I'd like to see *that*!" he proclaimed, wrestling out of his stiff new jeans with great difficulty.

Then they were in each other's arms, legs intertwined, lips fused in a kiss of reunion that reaffirmed the vows made before and gave promise of many more to come. Hands explored, seeking and finding remembered de-

431

lights. Priscilla nuzzled her tingling breasts into the springy thatch that covered his broad chest, thrilling to the prickly sensation and to his moan of response as he clasped her to him. She could feel the evidence of his desire hot and hard between them, and she knew the moist, gaping emptiness, the taut, aching desire to have him once again.

"No, not yet," he protested feebly as her hands and legs and lips urged him into her. "You're not ready yet," he gasped.

But she was, ready, ready, ready, and he sank into the dark, welcoming depths of her, lost for all time in the cushioning warmth of her body, hardly aware of the love words he whispered or the promises he made. At that moment he would have promised anything she demanded, but she demanded nothing. She only gave and received in turn those luscious sensations that grew and grew, gathering, building, until her frail body could hold them no longer and they burst forth in brilliance, cascading over and around their coupled bodies like showered sparks from some massive conflagration.

When the last of the tremors died away, Dusty rolled over on his back carrying Priscilla with him, and she nestled across his chest with a contented sigh. After a long moment of cozy snuggling, Dusty made a thoughtful sound. "Well, now," he drawled, "that was almost as good as I remembered." At first he thought she was going to let him get away with it, but just when he began to grin complacently, he yelped in pain as she sank her tiny white teeth into his shoulder. In the wrestling match that followed, Dusty allowed her to pin him to the bed, only because he so thoroughly enjoyed feeling the silken length of her pressed against him.

Imprisoning his two huge hands with her tiny ones, intoxicated with the knowledge that she held his overwhelming power in check with her fragile weight and feeling the reckless terror of the lady who rode the tiger, she taunted, "*Almost* as good?"

"Wellll," he conceded, "*as* good." But when she lowered her mouth to his other shoulder and bared her teeth, he cringed in mock horror and relented frantically. "Better! Better!"

Priscilla raised her head and studied his face critically, as if looking for signs of dissembling, and she saw those beloved features change in a matter of seconds from playfulness to passion as he whispered, "The best," and effortlessly broke her hold on him. In the next second she found their positions reversed, his glorious weight crushing her to the mattress, his mouth wet and warm on hers. It was a kiss of promise, but a promise that would be kept later, she discovered, as he drew back and ordered, "Now get some clothes on. We've got some business to attend to."

"Business?" she asked stupidly, her mind unable to make such a sudden change.

"I bought you some cattle. I want you to see them," he told her blithely, freeing her from his overpowering grip and sitting up to find his own clothes.

"Cattle? You want to go look at cows?" she asked incredulously, rising up on her elbows. "When we could be . . ." She let her voice trail off suggestively.

"Miss Bedford! I'm shocked!" he said, and he looked it, too. So much so that she giggled. "Anyway," he added reasonably, "these are not just cows. They are Herefords. I went to a lot of trouble to get them for you, and the least you can do is put your clothes on to go see

433

them. Of course, I'd be glad to take you just the way you are," he offered just before dodging the pillow she heaved in his direction. "Besides, we can't do anything else right now, anyway," he added with a sad and meaningful glance downward that made her giggle again.

This time it was Priscilla's turn to dodge a pillow, but between teasing and tickling, they both managed to get dressed in a remarkably short time. Priscilla had to sneak up to the ranch and spirit Lady away because, as Dusty pointed out, if anyone saw him or found out where she was going, they would never get away. Luckily, everyone at the Steele's seemed to be occupied elsewhere and since most of the men were away on the cattle drive, Priscilla made her escape undetected.

On the ride out to Priscilla's new ranch, Dusty taught her the fine art of kissing while on horseback, and had they not been in such a hurry, they might not have made it at all. When they arrived, Dusty proudly displayed the white-faced cattle that he had penned in the new corrals temporarily until he could put up some fencing out on the range for them. When he began to explain in some detail how he planned to breed them with the Longhorns, Priscilla cut him off the best way she knew, with a very exciting kiss, and demanded that he let her show him how she had decorated the house.

He had already looked in the parlor windows, and he felt a little strange going into the elegantly furnished rooms, but Priscilla's eager enthusiasm quickly overcame his reluctance. After all, he reasoned, this was going to be his home now. He might as well get used to it, he added mentally, while at the same time wondering how he could get used to Chinese vases and Oriental rugs. Only now was he beginning to get a true picture of just

434

how wealthy Priscilla really was. That was also something he would have to get used to.

By the time they reached the master bedroom, Dusty had just about decided that he could get used to anything as long as Priscilla was involved, and he playfully suggested that they put the enormous four-poster bed to use. Giggling like a schoolgirl, Priscilla dodged his embrace and dashed out of the house, easily outdistancing him since he was hampered by his high-heeled boots. She had intended to hide in the shadows of the porch and ambush him when he came out, but she stopped dead when she saw the two men standing in the yard.

They were both staring, grinning at Priscilla's and then at Dusty's behavior as he came clumping out onto the porch. Dusty immediately assumed his old foreman's dignity, straightening his vest and clearing his throat. "Miss Bedford, these are the two hands I hired in Henrietta to help bring back the herd." He gestured toward a tall, lanky cowboy. "This here's Shorty, and that's the Count. This is Miss Bedford, the owner I told you about."

Priscilla smiled graciously. "How do you do?" Obviously, Shorty was struck dumb, but the Count, a small, wiry young man with a carefully waxed moustache, swept off his hat and bowed from the waist.

"*Enchanté*, mademoiselle," he said.

"*Merci beaucoups*, monsieur," Priscilla replied and, continuing to speak in perfect French, inquired, "Are you really French? Are you really a Count?"

"*Oui*," he replied, "I am really French, but alas, I am but a poor peasant. The cowboys, they make a joke when they call me a Count."

Priscilla laughed. She had spent several summers in

435

France, and this cowboy's accent gave him away to her as a nobleman. How on earth had he ended up in Texas? she wondered. The Count shot a glance at Shorty and then asked, very politely, still in French, "Dear lady, would you settle a question for me?"

Wary of cowboys and their tricks, Priscilla rolled her eyes. "Let me guess. You have made a bet with Shorty about something."

He gestured apologetically. "My friend here, he thought you would be a dried up old maid. I, of course, being French, expected you to be a lovely young woman, as you so obviously are."

Priscilla laughed again and said, still in French, "So you win. What is the question?"

"I also felt that, judging from Monsieur Rhoades's careful toilette this afternoon that he would be proposing to you soon, if he had not already done so."

Priscilla glanced at Dusty who was quite perturbed over this conversation he could not understand, especially since his name had been mentioned. "He did not tell you about us?" she asked, still in French.

"No, he said only that we would bring the cattle to this ranch which was owned by a Miss Bedford."

Priscilla smiled mischievously. "You are correct, Count. Mr. Rhoades and I are going to be married on Saturday."

The Count grinned expansively. Walking swiftly up onto the porch, he took her hand and kissed it, murmuring his heartfelt congratulations. She heard a startled sound from Dusty's direction as the Count turned on his heel and retreated, dragging Shorty along with him.

"What was that all about?" Dusty demanded, his face

turning an alarming shade of purple.

Priscilla turned a beaming smile on him. "He was congratulating me."

"For what?" he gritted, uncertain as to whether hand kissing was an insult or not.

"I told him that you and I are getting married on Saturday," she announced gleefully.

"Saturday! That's day after tomorrow!" Dusty protested, the alarming color draining very suddenly from his face.

"Well, I can't get married *tomorrow*. I already have plans," she replied sweetly.

Chapter Fifteen

Priscilla's last day as the schoolteacher went very well. All the parents were duly impressed with the progress their offspring had made, and all regretted that Priscilla would no longer be teaching since she was going to be a rancher. After the furniture arrived, she had been unable to keep her secret any longer, and everyone knew all about her now, or at least almost all. She mentioned her forthcoming marriage to only one other person outside the Steele family, and that was Reverend Allen, who was suitably surprised.

"M . . . Miss Bedford!" he exclaimed. "You're going to marry *Mr. Rhoades*?" The incredulity in his voice made Priscilla smile.

"That's right," she assured him, completely unabashed. "And as I promised you before, I am now seeking your professional services. We'd like to be married tomorrow at about 3:00, if that would be convenient."

"I . . . yes . . . I mean, certainly, but such haste! I mean, don't you want to take some time to plan something fancy? A lady such as yourself deserves a little pomp and circumstance for such a major event in her life. At least allow us a few days to suitably decorate the church . . ."

Priscilla suspected that Reverend Allen was picturing himself as master of revelries at this momentous event and greatly enjoying the prospect, enjoying it far more than she and Dusty would. "I'm sorry to disappoint you," she interrupted, a slight smirk curving her mouth, "but we both want just a simple ceremony with no fuss, and we won't be using the church at all. We thought we would be married in the Steele's parlor."

Reverend Allen looked so crestfallen that she was almost tempted to reconsider her plans, but he bore up valiantly under his disappointment and promised her a beautiful and moving ceremony in any case. Then he excused himself to find and have a word with the prospective groom, a scene Priscilla was glad she would not have to witness.

Priscilla and Dusty had no further time in which to be alone, since the Steele women needed Priscilla's guidance in planning the wedding supper and in decorating the parlor for the ceremony. Ruth loudly lamented the fact that they had no time in which to make a white wedding gown, but since Priscilla would have felt rather hypocritical wearing white under the circumstances, she was just as glad. Everyone enjoyed exchanging knowing looks when Ruth announced that when *she* got married, she would have a white dress *and* a veil.

That night Priscilla slept with Ruth, at Ruth's insistence, and so Dusty had no opportunity to sneak into her room for even so much as a good-night kiss. Consequently, neither of them slept very well that night and both were up early, anxious for the day to be over so that they could, at last, be alone again.

The wedding was a very intimate affair with just the members of the Steele family present along with Shorty and the Count. George and Ruth stood up with them, Stella declining because of her rotund stomach, and Ben gave the bride away.

As she helped Priscilla dress, Stella inquired, "Did you tell Dusty about the . . . you know?"

Priscilla smiled. "No, I'm going to wait until later. I want him to know that he married me because he wanted to, not because he had to." Stella nodded, understanding the wisdom of such a move.

Surprisingly, Priscilla felt totally calm when she came into the parlor. She was wearing a pale yellow muslin gown that she had deemed too fragile and light-colored for western life but which satisfied Ruth's slightly lowered standards for a wedding gown. Her face was lightly flushed, partly from suddenly becoming the center of attention and partly from the very ardent look Dusty was giving her. Dusty, in turn, appeared to be fairly nervous, and his face was a trifle pale, but those bluer-than-blue eyes were saying, "Wait until tonight."

Reverend Allen kept his word to Priscilla and made the ceremony as beautiful as mere words could, while at the same time acceding to Dusty's wishes to make it as brief as possible. It seemed to Priscilla that the few minutes it took to unite them were both the longest and the shortest period of time she had ever lived through, and when Dusty bent, very solemnly, to brush her lips with his own when Reverend Allen pronounced them man and wife, she knew that she must be the happiest woman alive.

In honor of the occasion, Stella relaxed her rules about alcoholic beverages and allowed George to propose a champagne toast to the newlyweds. A little later everyone sat down to the fanciest meal anyone could remember Maria's having prepared, and at long last, after much well wishing and jesting, Dusty and Priscilla were allowed to make their escape.

Priscilla had insisted on postponing their wedding trip for a few months until things at the ranch were in order. She knew Dusty had plans to fence in the new cattle and hold a proper roundup to see how much restocking they would have to do. Another reason was her recurrent morning sickness. She did not want to travel until that had passed.

Stella tactfully suggested that Shorty and the Count take a few days off and see the town of Rainbow. They gratefully rode off to bend their elbows at the Yellow Rose. Dusty and Priscilla rode out to their ranch alone.

Dusty insisted that Priscilla wait until he had unhitched the horses from the buggy they had borrowed from the Steele's so that he could carry her over the threshold. Laughing and pretending to stagger under her weight, he carried her into the darkened house. After setting her down, it took him a moment to strike a match and light a lamp, an action that brought memories of another time and place to Priscilla's mind. When Dusty turned back to his bride, he surprised a look of uncertainty on her face.

Smiling gently, he hurried to reassure her, placing his hands on the soft curves of her shoulders. "Don't look so nervous, wife. It's not like you don't know what happens next," he teased, but his attempt at humor backfired.

442

Priscilla stiffened and turned away from his grasp. "What is it, Pris? What's wrong?" he asked, the concern evident in his voice.

Priscilla closed her eyes and took a shaky breath. Until a moment ago, she had not been aware of carrying any guilt for what had happened between them before. She had, in times past, felt humiliated and used, angry and hurt, but never guilty. Had it been because she had never planned it before, because it had just happened? Perhaps, but she had certainly planned what had happened that night at the schoolhouse and now . . . Now they were married, man and wife, their right to be together sanctified by God, legalized by men, and suddenly that earlier night seemed wrong somehow. And what must Dusty think? Men had funny ideas about their wives, wanted them to be perfect ladies, but she had behaved like a wanton, seducing him shamelessly. Oh, he had married her, but then he had never really proposed, not in so many words. She had railroaded him into it, and he had felt an obligation. "Pris?" his voice was insistent now, cutting into her thoughts. "What's wrong?"

"This. Us. Here together, tonight. It isn't right," she explained lamely.

"What isn't right?" he demanded, turning her again to face him, his hands holding her shoulders more tightly this time.

"I mean . . . this should be our first time together. What happened before shouldn't have happened. You probably think . . ." She had almost said, I'm a whore, but managed to stop herself, acutely embarrassed and equally ashamed. The training of a lifetime could not be discarded very easily, she had discovered.

Dusty gave an exasperated sigh. "*What* do I think?"

443

he insisted.

Priscilla could not meet his piercing blue stare so she lowered her gaze to watch her hands that were nervously twisting together. "You . . . well, you can't have much respect for me . . . after I let you . . ." She could feel the heat rising in her face as Dusty gave another impatient sigh.

"I was there, too, remember? Every single time," he pointed out. "Do you respect me?"

She looked up, startled. He was perfectly serious. "Of course," she replied.

"Then why shouldn't I respect you?"

Priscilla was amazed. "It's different for a man!"

"Is it?" he asked.

She bridled. "Of course it is! You know it is!"

"Look," he explained patiently, "if it's all right for a man to make love but not for a woman, then who is he supposed to do it with?" She opened her mouth to reply, but he did not give her a chance. "Don't say whores, because that's not the same thing at all. Maybe you're right. Maybe we should have waited until we were married, but if it was wrong, then it's a mistake we're both guilty of, not just you or you more than me. Equal. Understand?" Priscilla nodded, wanting to believe him, glad at least that he believed himself. "Besides," he added with a mischievous grin, "I'm not sure it wasn't a good idea."

"*What* was a good idea?" Priscilla asked suspiciously.

"You know. A little tryout before making it legal. I mean, you don't buy a horse until you've ridden it . . ."

Priscilla's cry of outrage was accompanied by a blow from her fist that bounced ineffectually off his broad chest, but after a few seconds of righteous indignation, she joined him in a fit of laughter that left them weak and teary eyed. Then, before Priscilla knew what was happening, Dusty had ducked down and hoisted her over one shoulder. Heedless of her shrieks of protest, he carried her off into the darkened house.

"Put me down," she cried with all the dignity she could muster while upside down, and very soon found herself dumped unceremoniously onto the center of the large bed Dusty had previously admired. He was standing over her, hands on narrow hips, long legs spread in a lordly stance, a look of artificial sternness on his handsome face.

"Take off your clothes, woman. I'm demanding my husbandly rights," he ordered as he began to strip out of the black broadcloth suit and stiffly starched white shirt he had purchased only the day before in honor of the occasion of his wedding.

Priscilla watched in stunned amazement for a while until he got down to unbuttoning his pants, and then she flashed him the same wicked grin she had used on him once before. "Don't you want to go outside and watch through the window?" she asked provocatively.

She watched with great curiosity as his expression changed from surprised to pleased to lustful in a few swift seconds. "I think," he replied, his voice thick with desire, "that I'd like to watch you close up, this time." The look of naked longing in his eyes caused something deep inside her to contract in a spasm of response. Her dark eyes never left his as she slowly slipped off her shoes and stockings and then stood up to remove the rest of her clothing piece by careful piece, the lamp from the front room casting just enough light to illuminate the scene. Then, as she had done before, she removed the pins that held her hair, noticing with great curiosity how ragged Dusty's breathing had become and how a vein in his neck seemed to be throbbing.

When at last she shook her hair free around her shoulders, he came to her, enfolding her naked body in a bone-crushing embrace, his kiss hungry and demanding, her response no less so. When he had ravaged her lips, leaving her breathless, his mouth moved on, scorching her throat with searing kisses and then her shoulders, until she was moaning softly. Next he covered her breasts, already swollen and tingling, teasing and nipping until her tender nipples stood erect to his ravenous mouth. Priscilla cried out his name as his tongue traced patterns on the sensitive peaks, her hands roaming restlessly over the sleek strength of his back and shoulders. Lowering himself to his knees, he proceeded to kiss the quivering flesh of her belly and thighs, finding at last the core of her desire. Priscilla cried out as his tongue enticed her most sensitive spot, and in a few more moments, her weakened knees gave way and she allowed him to lay her gently across the bed. Never ceasing his caresses, his hands roamed freely over the rest of her, exploring every curve and hollow until Priscilla thought she would go mad with wanting him, but he ignored her pleas and continued kissing her until she could stand it no longer, and she surrendered to the waves of ecstasy that shuddered out from the very depths of her being.

Slowly, the room came back into focus as Priscilla's senses turned outward from her sated body. Dusty still knelt on the floor, his cheek now resting against the smooth plane of her abdomen. Why had he not taken her? The question burned in her mind but her strangely lazy lips could only form one word. "Dusty?" she asked, her real question unspoken but conveyed.

He lifted his head to study her love-softened expression for a moment before rising to remove the rest of his clothing. If she had been concerned that he did not want her, the sight of his arousal stilled her fears. Then he was moving her, centering her on the bed and lowering himself onto her willing body. "Oh, darlin'," he groaned as he joined their bodies, "it feels so good."

Hardly had Priscilla had time to enclose him in her embrace than she felt him shudder and heard his male outcry of need and fulfillment. Marveling, she simply held him, gently stroking the body that she found she now loved as well as the man inside it as she listened to his rasping breath return to normal. At last he levered himself up onto his elbows, holding most of his weight off of her, but maintaining their union. He gave her a wry grin. "Do you have any idea how many times I've dreamed about this the past few weeks?"

Priscilla's smile answered his own. "I think so," she teased.

He sighed. "I wanted you so much. I knew I'd never last. That's why I . . . did what I did to you first, so you wouldn't feel cheated."

Priscilla felt anything but cheated and she felt her heart swelling with new depths of emotion. How could she possibly have thought she loved Dusty Rhoades before, when she knew him so little? Knew him, that was the key. Now she really knew him, and she marveled at the knowledge. "I love you so much," she whispered, sad that mere words could not adequately describe her new-found feelings.

He did not seem to mind the inadequacy as his mouth met hers in a devouring kiss that blocked all rational thought from her mind. It was only when she felt the quickening of renewed desire that she realized he was moving within her again. She had already begun an instinctive response to his primitive urgings when she managed to gasp, "Again?"

"Yes, darlin', oh, yes," he murmured against the satin of her skin as their bodies began to move in unison in that mysterious dance of love, ever the same, yet ever different. This time he told her what she did to him when she moved beneath him in uninhibited response. This time he told her how he loved to hear the sound she made when he made her happy. This time he told her how soft her skin was, how her breasts came alive under his touch, and how perfectly wonderful he found her in every way. Each declaration seemed to touch a chord within her that raised her passion one tone higher and then one tone higher still in a crescendo of sensation, swelling and pulsing until every nerve end sang in glorious harmony, and she cried out his name with every breath, until her breath and all else ceased in that timeless instant before her world exploded.

It was much later, as they lay entwined in the twilight between passion and sleep, that Priscilla realized she had a question about her new husband, a question she was not certain she wanted answered and yet felt compelled to ask. She lifted her face to watch his reaction. "You must have known a lot of women before me," she stated, too cowardly to ask outright.

His eyebrows shot up in surprise and then he gave her a teasing smile. "I don't know about that, and I'm sure I'd remember something that important." Suddenly, she realized that since he had come back, he no longer spoke to her in his standard cowboy drawl. The knowledge that he was no longer holding back from her, hiding his true self, gave her courage to probe more deeply.

"Well," she insisted, "you must have known at least one." She noticed he held his breath a moment and then let it out in a deep sigh. He realized now what she was getting at. She was curious about his skill as a lover.

"Then there was someone?" she prodded.

"It was a long time ago," he said, his voice expressionless. "A *long* time ago."

"Why didn't you marry her?" she wanted to know, curious as to why he had felt no sense of duty toward this girl.

"She wasn't the kind of girl you marry," he replied.

"Did you love her?" Priscilla held her breath for the answer.

"I was just a kid. I thought so, but . . ." He considered. "No, I never loved her. Not the way I love you."

Touched, Priscilla kissed him tenderly. She was wondering if this would be the right moment to tell him about the baby. Then she saw he was grinning. "What's so funny?" she demanded.

"Well, there *was* another woman in my life you should know about," he said.

"Who?" she asked, suddenly suspicious.

"Stella."

"Stella! She said there was never anything between you two," Priscilla insisted, certain now he was teasing.

"Well, it wasn't much, but"—he pretended to be reluctant to admit it—"I did kiss her once."

"When?" Priscilla was delighted.

"Oh, we were about fourteen, fifteen, I guess. I grabbed her in the barn one day."

"What did she do?"

"She blacked my eye," he said indignantly, as if still outraged by such a humiliation. "That's when I decided not to marry one of the Steele girls."

Priscilla dissolved into gales of laughter and soon the whole bed was shaking as Dusty joined her. For a moment Priscilla wondered if it wasn't indecent to be so happy and so much in love, and then Dusty was kissing her again. He was playful at first but soon became more insistent, and she could feel his growing desire against her thigh. She pulled away to get a good look at his face, and the bold brightness of his eyes convinced her that he did indeed want her again. "How . . . how many times . . . can we . . . do this?" she asked between kisses.

He paused a moment as if to consider and then smiled provocatively down at her. "I don't know," he replied honestly. "Why don't we find out?"

Any reply she might have managed was swallowed up by his next kiss.

Vance was so delighted at the effect his news would have on Rita that he could almost forget how much it complicated his own plans. He had been chafing under the knowledge that Rita knew his secret. This might almost make up for it. He found Rita in her room where she had been all evening. She had not seen the two new cowboys, the tall, skinny one called Shorty or the small, elegant one they called the Count. Nor had she heard the interesting story they had to tell.

Rita was annoyed that Vance came in without knocking, but she forgot to mention it when she saw the grin on his face. "Well, now, don't you look like the cat who swallowed the cream."

"I just heard something that might interest you," he replied with studied nonchalance.

"An' what might that be?" she asked sarcastically.

"Dusty Rhoades is back." He savored the look of relief that flashed across her face. She covered it well.

"Where was he?" she asked, her voice sounding strained.

"Seems he went up to Henrietta and bought some rather unusual cattle. I forget the name of the breed." He paused for effect. "He delivered them to Miss Bedford's ranch."

"She's restocking the ranch," Rita said aloud but to herself. "She sent him for the stock."

"I don't think so," Vance disagreed. "She did not know about it. I believe he meant it to be a surprise, sort of a wedding present."

"Wedding present? She gettin' married?" Rita asked, too sharply.

"She *got* married, this morning." He paused, watching her closely. "She married your very dear friend, Dusty Rhoades."

The strangest sound that Vance had ever heard came out of Rita's mouth. Almost an animalistic cry of agony, it set the hair all over his body on end. Afterward he could never name the emotion that sound expressed. Rita became like a wild thing, clawing at her hair, her clothes, throwing everything she could lay hands on in a blind, raging fury. Vance let himself out as quickly as he could, although her anger seemed not to be directed at him at all, but at someone not present. Dusty Rhoades, of course. What could he have done to her? Vance wondered for the thousandth time as he retreated to the safety of his room.

Much later in the light of day, her fury spent, Rita could again think rationally. She cursed herself for such a horrible display of emotion, but how could she have guessed that the news would hit her so hard? Of course, she had expected him to marry someone, sooner or later, but she had expected a decent length of courtship first, some warning. That would have given her time to plan and organize, and she almost certainly would have prevented the wedding. She had fully intended that no woman would ever have him. From what Will had told her this morning, everyone thought that they had been secretly engaged for some time and were only waiting until Dusty got back with the mysterious cattle. The fact that he had personally overseen the construction of the new house and the repairs to the other buildings seemed proof of this theory.

Dusty Rhoades had pulled a fast one on her, but he would not get away with it. Changing her clothes for something suited to an afternoon buggy ride and securing a rig from Ol' Zeke at the Livery, she rode out into the pleasant Sunday afternoon sunshine.

Priscilla awoke the next morning to find a pleasant warmth at her back. It was only after she had wriggled herself into it more comfortably that she realized it was shaking. Suddenly wide awake, she flipped over instantly to discover her husband trembling with silent laughter. "What's so funny?" she demanded, more than a little disconcerted at finding a man in her bed for the first time ever when she woke up, and then finding him laughing.

"I really like the way you snuggled up to me with your little bottom," he said, forcing down his laughter but unable to suppress his delighted grin. "Did I ever tell you what a cute bottom you have?" he added, reaching around to caress the object of his admiration.

"No, you did not," she replied, trying to sound indignant while at the same time her body was melting under his touch.

"Well, you do," he told her, "but as nice as it is, and as nice as the rest of you is, too, I'm afraid I'm not going to be able to do anything about it until I've had some breakfast."

"Oh, no!" Priscilla cried, jerking out of his arms and sitting up abruptly.

"What's the matter?" he asked, sitting up beside her, so alarmed that he forgot to even admire the way her lovely breasts bobbed from her hasty action.

"I can't cook!" she said in complete dismay. "I've never made anything but biscuits, and you know how they turned out. And stop laughing or I'll make some and make you eat them!" she threatened her convulsed husband.

"I . . . I'm . . . sorry . . . darlin' . . ." he gasped, holding his side. "It's just . . . I thought . . . never mind. Lucky for you—and me—I know how to cook. It won't be fancy but at least we won't starve while you're learning. Guess I'd better get some clothes on," he supposed, rolling to his feet with an agonized groan. "It's a crime, you know, to make a man cook his own breakfast after the way I worked last night. Was it five or six times? I lost count," he told her with a wicked grin.

Priscilla gasped at his impudence. "What about me?" she demanded. "I was there, too," and she had the very pleasant aches to prove it.

"Of course you were there, darlin'," he told her kindly. "I couldn't have done it without you, but after all, I did all the work." He skillfully dodged the pillow she

453

threw, chuckling at her outrage. "Now get some clothes on unless you want your first cooking lesson in the raw," he cautioned just before he ducked again.

It was quite late when they finally finished eating, and Priscilla had vowed silently that the first thing she was going to do was to hire a cook. Dusty was a patient teacher, but Priscilla found it too humiliating to be taught to cook by her husband. Shooing Dusty out of the kitchen after their breakfast to smoke on the porch, she proceeded to clean up the dishes. At least she was not completely useless, she thought. She was almost finished with her task when she heard Dusty call.

"Hey, Pris, we got company."

Priscilla was annoyed. Who would have the gall to come calling on them the day after their wedding? Not even bothering to remove her apron, she went out onto the front porch to see who it could be. Dusty stood on the top step, squinting in the noonday sun at the approaching ball of dust. Soon they could make out a buggy and then a woman driving it. At last Priscilla could see well enough to know that she did not recognize the visitor.

"Now, what in the hell does she want?" Dusty muttered through clenched teeth.

"Who is it?" she asked, a small knot of apprehension forming in the pit of her stomach.

"Rita Jordan," he spat out.

For a moment Priscilla could not place the name and then she remembered. The woman from the saloon. "Do you know her?" Priscilla asked and instantly regretted it. Surely every man within a hundred miles must know her.

"I know her," he said evenly, but Priscilla could see the back of his neck was red with anger.

Priscilla stepped down beside him, instinctively

forming a united front against this intruder. Rita stopped the horses as close to the steps as possible. She was smiling, but Priscilla could see the woman was not happy.

"What do you want?" Dusty demanded.

Rita feigned offense. "Is that any way to talk to an old friend? I just heard about the weddin', an' I come to congratulate you." She looked Priscilla over rudely. "An' to get a look at the bride." Rita seemed to consider Priscilla for a moment. "Kinda skinny, but that don't always mean nothin'." She smiled her evil smile again and turned to Dusty. "Is she as good between the sheets as I am?"

Priscilla almost gasped. This creature had as much as admitted to having slept with Dusty. Suddenly, Priscilla realized that he was not denying it. She looked at her husband. His face was turning purple, the cords on his neck stood out like ridges, his fists were clenched as if preparing to do this person physical harm. She examined his face. What did she see there? Anger, even hatred, but to her relief, she saw no guilt. Perhaps at some time he *had* been with this woman, but not since he had known her. On that Priscilla would have staked her life. When, then? His words of last night came back to her: "Someone . . . a long time ago . . . not the kind of girl you marry . . ." All this flashed through her mind in an instant, and then she was sure.

Rita turned her attention back to Priscilla, fully expecting her to either faint or go into hysterics. "Didn't he tell you about us, honey?" she asked condescendingly.

Far from feeling either faint or hysterical, Priscilla lifted her chin, squared her shoulders, and forced her face into a smile. "Of course he told me all about you," she said coolly. "He also told me how long ago it was and . . . how very little it meant to him."

Rita could not have been more shocked if Priscilla had pulled out a gun and shot her. She might know a lot about men, but obviously she knew nothing about her own sex, failing to credit them with even the nerve that she herself possessed. Muttering a curse at Priscilla, Rita struck the horses and rolled swiftly away in a cloud of dust.

Dusty and Priscilla watched in silence as she disappeared from view. Feeling a sudden urge to be alone with her thoughts, she said, "My dishwater is getting cold," and went back inside the house.

By the time she finished the last of the dishes, Dusty had come back inside also. Priscilla heard him enter the kitchen and sit down at the table. Taking two clean cups, she went to the table and poured what was left of the breakfast coffee for them and sat down opposite him.

Dusty watched her and then passed a hand over his face, as if to wipe off the last vestige of anger. Priscilla noted that he could look her in the eye. He had done nothing he was ashamed of.

"You were great out there," he said, his eyes showing his increased respect for her.

She waved his compliment away. Then she laid her hand on his across the table. "That . . . that . . . she came out here to hurt us," she said, voicing the conclusion she had just reached. "She deliberately tried to put something between us. I honestly think she thought that she could ruin our marriage. Why would she do that?"

She could see that it was something he did not want to talk about. He squeezed her hand as if for courage. Almost to himself he said, "So long ago. Let's see . . . it'll be seven years this fall. It's hard to believe it could still matter to her." Then as if remembering he was not alone, he looked up into her eyes. "I'd better start at the beginning, so you'll understand.

"It was the summer I turned eighteen. Ben finally persuaded Ma to let me go up the trail. I guess she could see if she didn't let me, I'd run off and do it anyway, and she figured I'd at least be safe with Mr. Sims to look after me. Mr. Sims was Ben's foreman then, and Ma trusted him. They took me along as wrangler—that means I took care of the horses. The boys were mighty hard on me, what with me being the youngest one. They must've pulled every trick in the book on me. I guess they figured by the time I got to Wichita, I'd earned my manhood. That's when they thought up the best—or the worst—trick of all." Dusty sighed and Priscilla could see he hated to tell the rest. "They all chipped in to pay someone to . . . be nice to me."

"And Rita Jordan was that someone," Priscilla guessed.

Dusty nodded. "You gotta understand. She looked different then. Not hard and ugly like she does now."

Well, that was something, Priscilla thought. Not many men would call Rita Jordan ugly.

"She worked at a Dance House. The boys took me there and she kinda sidled up to me and started flirting. After a while, she asked me to see her home. Well, she did what she was hired to do, but honest, Pris, I was so green, I thought she did it because she liked me. I never dreamed she'd take money for it, she looked so young and sweet." He gestured helplessly.

"Then what happened?" Priscilla prompted him.

"She . . . she told me to come back to see her, in the

afternoon when she was off work. It was a bad year for cattle and it took over a week for Sims to find a buyer." He looked guiltily away. "I went back every day. When it finally came time for us to leave . . . well, somehow— and for the life of me, I still can't figure out how—she got me to propose to her."

How, indeed, wondered Priscilla. She guessed that might explain his reluctance with her. "Why would she want to marry a penniless cowboy?"

Dusty looked away again. "I lied to her. I made out like we still owned the old ranch. I even let her think the herd we'd brought in was mine, that Sims was teaching me the cattle business." Priscilla nodded her understanding. "Well, I went to Mr. Sims—he was holding most of my pay for Ma—and told him I needed some money for a wedding ring. Sims was no fool and it didn't take him long to get the whole story from the boys. At first I wouldn't believe it, but then I had to. I wanted to go to her, tell her just what I thought of her, but Sims wouldn't let me. Guess he was afraid she'd win me over again. Anyway, he went himself. From what he said, he found her standing on the porch with her bag in her hand." He stopped again, searching Priscilla's face for any trace of condemnation. He found none. "That was the last I saw of her until she came here a few years back."

"What happened when you saw her here the first time?" Priscilla asked, her suspicions newly aroused.

"It was the funniest thing. We'd heard that a woman had bought the saloon, so a bunch of us went to get a look at her. Of course I knew her right off, and I could tell she knew me, too, only she never let on. I steered clear of her after that."

"Didn't you ever wonder why she came here?"

Dusty shrugged. "I thought about it, sure. It just seemed . . . I don't know . . . conceited to think she'd come here because of me. I just put it down to coincidence. Besides, all this time, until today, she never even let on she knew I was alive."

Priscilla sighed. "I have a feeling she knew very well you were alive. You know the old saying, 'Hell hath no fury like a woman scorned'. I'm afraid we haven't seen the last of her, either."

Jason Vance was reading a week-old San Antonio newspaper on the sidewalk in front of the saloon when he saw Rita drive back into town. He had not even been aware that she was gone and from the look on her face, he had a pretty good idea where she had been. Only one person could arouse such wrath in Rita Jordan. He followed her as she stormed into the saloon.

"Where in the hell have you been?" he demanded.

She cursed him violently and told him it was none of his business, but he grabbed her arm, making her wince with pain.

"You went to see Rhoades, didn't you?" he accused.

"Yes," she hissed, wrenching her arm loose.

"You little fool! Just what did you hope to accomplish by that?"

She glared at him. Vance shook his head in wonder. "Did you have some crazy idea you could break up their marriage?" From Rita's expression he knew he had guessed correctly. "Did you actually believe *she* would be jealous of *you*?" Vance began to laugh until Rita struck him a stinging blow on the face. He watched as she disappeared up the stairs.

Once in her room, Rita stripped off her traveling clothes and donned a dressing gown. She still could not believe how calmly that little ninny had taken the news that she and Dusty had been lovers. Nor could she believe he had told such a thing to his wife. Still trembling with rage, she sat down in her rocker by the window to collect her wits. She may have failed this time, but she would not do so again. Ultimately, she would pay him back for the hurt and humiliation she had endured. She thought back to that fateful autumn, when Dusty Rhoades had ridden into Wichita with the last of the drives for that year.

Rita Cade was already sick of her life at the Dance House and the crude, awkward cowboys who paid each night for the privilege of pawing her and stomping on her feet. It was still easy to earn vast amounts of money by simply dancing, but Rita was no fool. She could see the sleazy shacks down by the tracks where girls not much older than she had had to set up business because they were too sick or too ugly to work at a place like Belle's. Once fresh and young like Rita, they had succumbed to consumption, the great killer of prostitutes, or the other diseases one did not speak of in polite society. The late hours in the smoke-filled halls had robbed them of their youth, and now they lay in lice-infested beds, waiting for any man who came along with a dollar in his pocket. Rita wanted out.

Rita would never forget the day Belle had called her to her office. Belle was still laughing at the proposition the two cowboys had made, when Rita walked in. The men had hooted and yelled when they saw her, proclaiming her perfect for their purpose. Rita had been intrigued by their plan for seducing their young friend. It would provide a challenging relief from the boring sameness of her nights at the Dance House.

Dusty Rhoades was nothing like she had expected. Tall and handsome, he was far from the gawky bumpkin his friends had made him out. She had no trouble in getting him to dance. In fact he seemed quite taken with her and succeeded in charming her completely. Rita began to doubt his innocence until the call came for the cowboys to buy drinks for their partners. Dusty was visibly shocked that such a sweet young girl would be drinking whiskey. She hastily explained that it was only tea, and that in reality the girls were forbidden to drink liquor while working. It was just another way to separate the poor cowboys from their summer's wages. He was satisfied with this explanation and he claimed her for another dance. Ordinarily, the girls were only allowed to dance twice with the same man. That kept anyone from becoming too possessive, and Belle had several burly bouncers lounging around to enforce the rule, but they had all been alerted to Rita's assignment, so they allowed Dusty as many dances as he wished. This was not many since, as Rita had been warned, he was not carrying much money, the trail boss having withheld most of his pay so he would not squander it.

After several dances, Rita asked him to walk with her to her room to change her dress, since she had accidentally spilled something on it. Rita lived in a small house that she shared with two other girls. Once inside, she insisted he accompany her into her bedroom, joking that if she left him in the parlor, one of the other girls might come in and steal him. The room was small, containing only the bed, a bureau, a screen, and one straight-backed chair. Dusty perched uncomfortably on the chair as Rita slipped behind the screen.

Rita could see that while he was obviously excited to be in her room, he was also uneasy and nervous, but he continued to make conversation. Amazingly enough, Rita found him delightful to talk to. His nervousness became pure terror when she stepped from behind the screen wearing a silk wrapper and quite obviously nothing else. He made a half-hearted offer to leave, but she assured him his presence was completely welcome. They talked some more, with Rita sitting up on her bed, resting her tired legs. Then she asked him if he would rub her feet—they got so sore from all that dancing. By now he was only too willing, and when her wrapper slipped open to reveal most of her legs, she had no trouble at all getting him to join her on the bed.

She pretended just enough knowledge to get them through pleasantly. When it was over, he was contrite, apologetic, convinced he had ruined her. He tried to leave lest he harm her reputation, but she convinced him to stay. She had been paid for the whole night, and besides, she wanted him to stay.

The next morning he had asked if he might see her again, call on her as if they were courting. The idea was so novel, Rita could not resist. She was, after all, only seventeen. She told him to come in the afternoon when she did not have to work. That was an easy time for him to get away from the herd since all the other men wanted to be off at night to take advantage of the attractions of Wichita. Mr. Sims had not seemed overly concerned either, thinking the boy could not get in much trouble in broad daylight.

That first afternoon Rita confessed her sad story of the father who beat her and the lover who betrayed her.

Dusty had been so outraged, so eager to avenge her honor, that Rita almost regretted having to tell him that the drummer was dead. Then she had taken him to bed and shown him things that both delighted and amazed him, things that made the afternoon hours fly by.

Mr. Sims could find no cattle buyers, so Dusty came every day for a week. They spent delicious autumn afternoons in Rita's bed alternating the throes of passion with quiet conversation in which he told her all about his life in Texas, his ranch, his mother, his friends in Rainbow, his adventures on the cattle drive. Lovingly, he described his home on the banks of the Clear Fork River, and Rita could imagine herself strolling along its banks with him. Each day the vision became clearer and each night at the Dance House became longer, more unbearable.

At last Dusty had come, and she did not need to be told to know he was leaving. It seemed to her that he was her last hope for a normal life, the kind of life she had never known. No matter that she would find it unbearably dull after a month. She wanted it anyway, and Rita knew how to get her way with men. That afternoon was the most exciting Dusty Rhoades would ever know, and when he headed back to camp, he was an engaged man.

He had promised to return in time to take her to supper, and then they would be married. Rita was watching for him on the porch when that hateful Sims rode up. She knew the type, the self-righteous hypocrite. Probably had a mistress in every town along the trail but thought she was not good enough for a lousy cowboy. He had made her a speech on how she had led a good boy astray and should be ashamed of herself. He called her a cheap hussy. She replied tartly that she was not cheap, that she got more for one night than he did in a week. Then she had cursed him as he rode off in disgust. It had taken her years to pay him back for that, but she had paid him, and she would pay Dusty Rhoades, too. Oh, she could have killed him or had him killed long ago as she had the others, but that was too quick, too painless. Besides, he must know why it was happening and that she was responsible. That would take careful planning.

Vance interrupted her thoughts. She glanced up at him as he came into her room. She could see he was angry with her, but she did not particularly care. He pulled up a chair beside her.

"You know what you've done, don't you?" he asked.

"No, what have I done?" she replied indifferently.

"You've ruined any chance we had of getting the gold away from them discreetly."

"We!" Rita inquired. "Since when did you include me in your little treasure hunt?"

"Since you forced me to, my dear," he said. "I had a fairly workable plan, too, but you've spoiled any chance we might have had to carry it out. Now they'll be suspicious, on guard. No one, least of all you or me, will be able to con them. We will have to think of something else." Vance eyed her thoughtfully. "Just think, my dear, how angry Rhoades will be when he discovers you have taken a fortune in gold from under his very nose. That should more than repay you for a broken heart."

Rita's eyes flashed at him for a moment, but then she smiled an evil smile. "Make your plans, Vance. I'll do whatever you say, just so long as I see Dusty Rhoades miserable."

Chapter Sixteen

As was his habit when in town, George Wilson was taking his noon meal at the hotel. He was pleased to see Sheriff Winslow come in and motioned for the sheriff to join him.

After they had exchanged pleasantries, the sheriff remarked, "Heard you had a weddin' out your way."

"Yes," George replied. "It came as a surprise to most folks, but some of us have seen it coming for a long time."

"Hurts to lose our schoolteacher so quick like, but I don't reckon she would've been around long anyways, with her bein' so well fixed an' all."

George smiled. He had no intention of revealing Priscilla's financial situation to the gossipy sheriff so he changed the subject. "It was just fortunate for Mrs. Rogers that we were able to find a buyer so quickly for her place. Of course, she had another offer on it, too, just a few days after selling it to Miss Bedford, er, Mrs. Rhoades, I should say."

"Oh, yeah, an' who was that?" asked the sheriff, perking up.

George shook his head, as if he still could not believe it himself. "Jason Vance, of all people. He said he felt guilty because he had won all of Rogers's money, and he wanted to help out the widow."

Sheriff Winslow mulled over this new information. It jogged his memory and came together with another piece of information filed there. "Funny thing," he mused. "That night Rogers died, Vance tried to get him to bet his ranch on a hand of poker against all the money Vance had won."

"Sounds like Vance was mighty interested in Rogers's ranch," George commented, more to make polite conversation than for any other reason.

Sheriff Winslow murmured agreement and then turned the conversation to other matters, but he did not forget what George Wilson had told him. He turned the facts over in his mind, examining them from every angle, comparing them with other facts he knew, and something that had been troubling him. The doc had asked the sheriff if Rogers had been in a fight the day he died, since he had found some unexplained bruises on the dead man's body. So far, the sheriff had been unable to account for those bruises. Also, he had never quite been able to figure out how and why Rogers would have fallen just where he had. By the time he had gotten out to take a look at the spot, the ground had been too trampled up to tell anything from the tracks.

Winslow was a slow thinker, but he was not dumb. He knew that everything about Rogers's death did not quite gel, but he would not quit until it did. Now he had a new lead. He had half suspected that Rogers had had a fight with someone but could not think of a reason for it. Now, it seemed that someone had been very interested in Rogers's property. But why? Winslow suspected he knew someone who could answer that question. After lunch he went for a stroll around town.

He found Zeke sleeping in the shade, his chair tipped back against the wall.

"Sure, I recollect somethin' about Rogers's place," said Zeke, rubbing his whiskered chin after getting fully awake. "He used to brag on how there was some kinda gold buried out there. Leastways, I think that was it. Mebbe it was a gold mine, though. I ain't fer shore on that. It was just some ramblin' he'd do when he'd got on the outside of too much red likker."

"Thanks, Zeke," said Sheriff Winslow, flipping him a two-bit piece.

"Always glad to oblige, Sheriff," chuckled Zeke.

Usually, Winslow avoided the saloon whenever possible. Something about Rita Jordan got under his skin and it was not the usual thing. He could not deny that he found her attractive. What man would not? But something else—he could not say just what—made him think more of a deadly rattlesnake than a beautiful woman when he looked at her. Today, however, he would overlook his prejudices. He had business at the Yellow Rose.

Jason Vance was playing solitaire in the empty saloon. He greeted the sheriff in his usual reserved manner. They chatted over the weather and business and the town in general.

"Hasn't been much for me to do lately," lamented the

467

sheriff. "Biggest thing to happen around here in six months was Rogers gettin' killed." His eyes were on Vance's face, but Vance betrayed nothing.

"And that was an accident," Vance commented.

Sheriff Winslow pretended to contemplate this for a moment. "That's what folks think, all right. Me, I got my doubts."

Vance was obviously interested now. "Really, Sheriff? What makes you think it wasn't an accident?"

"Oh, a lot of things that I ain't at liberty to discuss for now." He paused as if finished and then added, almost as an afterthought, "An' of course, there was the gold."

A less astute man than Winslow might have missed Vance's slight reaction to that comment.

"Gold?" Vance asked casually. "What gold?"

"Oh, everybody's heard Rogers brag on how he had gold on his place," he said offhandedly. "Well, reckon I'd better mosey along. Don't want folks sayin' the sheriff spends the whole afternoon settin' in the saloon."

Vance sat motionless for a long time after Winslow left. He had underestimated the sheriff. That could be a fatal error. Vance knew the sheriff was on the scent of Rogers's killer and sooner or later he would find someone who had seen Vance ride out of town that night. It might take him a while, but Winslow would not quit. Vance knew the type. He cursed himself for being so stupid as to actually attack Rogers. If only he had been able to find the gold, he would have been long gone. Vance's hands played solitaire through the long afternoon, but his mind was working on one final, desperate plan to get him the gold and make his escape. It was so obvious he wondered that it had not occurred to him before. There was at least

468

one person who could take him right to the spot, and Rita could help.

That evening, Dusty and Priscilla sat on their front porch, enjoying their third and last night of solitude. Tomorrow, Shorty and the Count would return and the business of the ranch would begin in earnest.

Priscilla turned lazily to Dusty. "What's your real name?" she asked.

He winced. "I was wondering when you'd get around to that. It's Phillip."

She smiled. "Why, that's a wonderful name. You aren't ashamed of it, are you?"

"Not exactly ashamed. I'm just not overly fond of it."

"I see," said Priscilla thoughtfully. "I was wondering if, for example, we had a son, would you want him named for you?"

He took her hand in the gathering darkness, and she could hear the emotion in his voice as he said, "If you give me a son someday, you can name him anything you like."

She had an overwhelming desire to kiss him, but she knew if she did, her chance to tell him would be gone. She sighed as if relieved. "That's good to know, since I calculate our son should be making his appearance this winter."

For a long moment he did not speak or move. He sat staring at her face in the shadows. "Our son?" he said at last.

"Yes, or our daughter. Of course, we won't know for certain until it's born, but it will definitely be here before spring."

"You . . . you're going to have a baby?" he asked stupidly.

"Yes, my darling, that's what we have been talking about." She smiled tenderly at his beloved face.

"How? When? How do you know? Are you sure?" he stammered.

Priscilla laughed, delighted. "I'm sure. Stella and I figured it out just a few days before you got back. As to how and when, it must have been that night at the school . . ."

"You didn't tell me," he accused, suddenly aware of a very important fact. "Before the wedding, I mean."

She sobered instantly. "I did not want you to marry me because you had to. I would have wondered the rest of my life if you had really wanted to."

"I oughta spank you! Keeping it a secret!" He stared at her in wonder and indignation for a moment and then said, awed, "A baby."

"You may now kiss the mother of your child," she said sweetly. "And then you may take her to bed."

If she had expected a violent burst of passion, she would have been disappointed, because when he took her hands and drew her to her feet, his kiss was so gentle and tender that it brought tears to her eyes. Then he picked her up as if she were made of glass and carried her to the big four-poster bed where he set her down with infinite care. Sitting down beside her, he simply stared at her as if trying to memorize every feature, every curve, every pore of her lovely face. "Oh, Pris, I love you so," he whispered and then heaved an exasperated sigh. "No, that isn't right. I more than love you. I . . . adore you. I worship you. I . . . there just aren't words to describe the way I feel about you."

Priscilla blinked and one crystal tear slid out the corner of her eye. "I know," she told him, remembering their wedding night when she, too, had been unable to find words adequate to tell him how she felt. She reached up one hand and lovingly traced the contours of his face.

"You must have been scared to death," he suddenly decided, remembering certain facts about their separation. "When you found out about the baby, I mean. Not knowing where I was or even for shore if I was coming back. What would you have done if I hadn't come back?" he asked, the pain he felt on her behalf twisting his handsome face.

Priscilla shook her head, unwilling to consider such a thing at such a perfect moment. "You did come back," she said simply. "That's all that matters. That, and the fact that you love me and our child, and that we love you. You've made me very happy. And besides," she added impishly, "I was too busy being mad at you for leaving to even think about being scared."

For once he did not rise to her bait but only shook his head in wonder. "You're quite a woman, Mrs. Rhoades. I wonder what I ever did to deserve you."

"You know perfectly well what you did," she informed him, growing a little impatient with all this cherishing. Although she was certainly enjoying it, she was hoping for a little less talk and a little more action. "If you take those pants off, I'll even let you do it again."

His sky-blue eyes widened in shock for a moment, and then his face cracked into a huge grin. "I'll be damned," he muttered just before he began to remove his clothes. Halfway, though, he paused. "I don't want to hurt the baby," he said, a worried frown creasing his forehead.

Priscilla could not help her gurgle of laughter. "If we haven't hurt the baby yet," she pointed out, "I think he

471

must be pretty safe."

His frown deepened. "You should have told me before. I might have done something . . ."

"It's all right," she reassured him with some impatience. "Stella told me, and she should know!"

He grinned sheepishly. "I guess she should," he allowed and hastily finished undressing. In a few more minutes they were both naked, but Dusty still could not bring himself to make mad, passionate love to her. Instead he began a slow, langorous worship of her body. Starting at her lips, he worked his way down to her toes, covering every inch of her with tiny, adoring kisses until she burned, without and within, with a fever so intense she thought she might die of it. When he finally came to her in answer to her broken pleas, it was as a supplicant seeking entry into a holy shrine. She accepted his homage as a benevolent goddess granting him her consummate favors, and they moved together in adoration, each of the other, savoring the glory that was theirs alone. Instead of the fiery flash that usually crowned their lovemaking, she felt this time a golden glow that not only released the heat of their passion but seemed to fuse them, heart and soul, into one splendid entity.

Afterward they lay for a long time, basking in the warmth their love had created, hands idly stroking, lips leaving sweet, moist trails on already damp skin. Before Priscilla was even aware that he had shifted, Dusty planted a large, wet kiss on the still-flat plane of her abdomen and then raised his head and spoke into her navel. "Well, Phillip Alexander Rhoades the third, I hope we didn't disturb you," he said rather loudly, in case his son might not be able to hear, buried so deeply in his mother's body.

Priscilla's jaw dropped in surprise at the sight of her enormous husband speaking into her stomach to a baby whose existence she had barely had time to consider. Now that feeble life had a name, courtesy of its father, and a family, and it was no longer just an "it," a disturbing presence which might or might not cause insurmountable problems. Rather, it was their child, a real person, the fruit of their love, and suddenly Priscilla was laughing and crying at the same time, and Dusty was holding her, not knowing whether to comfort her or rejoice with her, but holding her nevertheless, and so they passed the last night of their brief honeymoon in joyous abandon, unaware of the evil that was closing in on them.

The next morning, Shorty and the Count arrived, and Dusty promptly sent them out to dig holes for fence posts. They grumbled loudly at this assignment, but since Dusty had already warned them before they hired on that this would be part of the job, they did not refuse. Both had worked with the Hereford cattle long enough to believe that what Dusty predicted for them was true.

Dusty himself had a mysterious errand to run. Taking the wagon, he refused to tell Priscilla where he was going, and he was unsure when he would return. As much as she hated to see him drive away, she did have things to do in her new home. She was alone when she heard her visitors arrive.

Dusty was whistling as he drove along. He could hardly wait to get home. Home! He could remember a time not very long ago when he was certain that he had nothing. Now he had everything a man could want, and a baby on top of it all. Priscilla would be so pleased when she saw

473

what he was bringing her. He had completely forgotten about it until she had told him about the baby. It was a trunk his mother had left him. Inside were some keepsakes that had been hers but also some baby items that his mother had instructed him were for his own children. He could hardly wait to see Priscilla's face.

He was later than he had planned. It had only taken a short time to locate the trunk and load it, but the Steeles had invited him to eat with them. As much as he wanted to hurry back to Priscilla, the temptation to eat at the Steele's table as an honored guest instead of as a hired hand was too much. Now it was the middle of the afternoon. Rounding the bend, he was startled to see a strange wagon in the yard. Stranger still was the fact that Priscilla did not come to meet him. He unhitched the wagon and cared for the horses and still no sign of life from the house. He walked warily to the front door.

What he saw when he entered his home was so astounding that at first he did not think to feel alarmed. That gambler with a Winchester pointed at Priscilla. It could not really be happening. Then he heard a familiar laugh and, turning, saw those hate-filled green eyes, and suddenly his blood ran cold. It was real, all right, and he would have to use every ounce of intelligence he had to get them out of it.

"What the hell's goin' on here?" he demanded.

Jason Vance smiled, somewhat apologetically, Priscilla thought. "If you will be so kind as to remove your gunbelt and have a seat over there by your lovely wife, I will be glad to answer your question."

Dusty gave brief thought to drawing the gun he had for some inexplicable reason donned that morning, but the chance that Vance would fire at Priscilla was too great.

474

Reluctantly, he unbuckled his gunbelt. Rita snatched it from him and buckled it around her own hips.

When Dusty was seated, Vance began his explanations. "You see, Mr. Rhoades, there is a large amount of gold buried on your property. I believe you know where it is. I would like you to help me find it."

Dusty looked in astonishment at each of the people in the room. Priscilla was clearly as surprised as he. Rita seemed to almost gloat and Vance simply smiled his enigmatic smile. "Is that what this is all about?" he asked unbelieving. "Don't you think if there was gold here and I knew where it was, I would have got it long ago?"

"Oh, you know where it is, all right. You just don't know that you know. You see," Vance began, but Dusty broke in.

"Are you talkin' about some Spanish gold, a payroll or something like that? Buried back about fifty years ago?" Vance nodded. Dusty shook his head in disgust. "That gold ain't here," he declared.

"You seem mighty sure of yourself, cowboy," Rita snapped.

Dusty ignored her. "I *know* it ain't here, an' I'll tell you *how* I know. Then I'll give you about ten seconds to apologize to my wife and get the hell out of here."

Vance seemed more intrigued than anything else. "I'm listening," he said.

"Back when I lived here before—it was during the war and my Pa was off fightin'—some Mexicans showed up one day. They was well dressed, real prosperous lookin'. They told my Ma they was lookin' for something they thought was buried on our property. Said it belonged to the government of Mexico. Asked for permission to look around. They even paid us some money—gold pesos—

for the privilege. So they looked. I was just a kid so they didn't pay me much mind. I hung around a lot and heard that what they was huntin' was buried gold. Had a map and everything. Only thing, the landmarks on the map were wrong somehow. The map was a copy or something and not the original. Anyhow, they never could find anything. They even asked me some questions, showed me the map and everything, but I couldn't make heads or tails out of it. Finally, they got to fightin' among themselves and give up. You see, Vance, if they couldn't find it, how'd you expect to?"

Vance considered a moment. With his left hand, he reached into his inside coat pocket and pulled out a yellowed paper. "Because I have this. Would you be kind enough to look at it?"

Dusty took the offered map and unfolded it with a look of profound disgust. He glanced over it quickly, and for an instant a flicker of recognition passed over his face. He covered it well, but they had all seen it. Shrugging with elaborate casualness, he tried to hand the map back to Vance. "Don't mean a thing to me."

"On the contrary, Rhoades, it means a great deal to you," Vance said.

"He knows!" Rita insisted. "He knows just where it is!"

"If I did, I'd never take you to it," Dusty said icily.

"Your courage is commendable," Vance said. "Indeed, I am sure you would die before leading me or Mrs. Jordan to the gold, but you have forgotten one thing."

"What's that?"

"*Mrs.* Rhoades," Vance replied with elaborate casualness. "I can't believe you would allow her to die for such a trivial thing."

476

Dusty glared at the gambler with narrowed eyes. "You're low, Vance, but I don't think you're low enough to kill a woman."

"I am glad to say that you are correct. However, the same cannot be said for my companion." Vance gestured to Rita. "It seems that for some reason, unknown to me, Mrs. Jordan harbors a grudge against you. I am sure she would like nothing better than to—what shall I say—see you single again?"

One look at Rita confirmed Vance's statement. Priscilla felt her blood turn to ice as she looked into those catlike eyes. She turned back to Dusty and could see how difficult it was for him to control his temper. His neck and ears were bright red.

"All right, Vance. You win. I don't know about the rest of the map, but I can take you to the tree, the one with the turtle carved on it," Dusty admitted grudgingly.

Vance's whole body jerked forward. "That's exactly where the treasure's buried. You know where it is?"

"I know that tree. If you say that's the place, I'll take you there."

"Believe me, Rhoades, that's all I want. Once I have the gold, you and Mrs. Rhoades will have nothing to fear. Rita and I will be on our way." He looked to Rita for confirmation. She nodded reluctantly.

"Let's go then," Dusty said. "The women go with us."

"There's no reason for them to sit around in the hot sun while we dig," Vance said reasonably. "It may take hours. They'll be much more comfortable here. When we're finished, we'll come back here, I'll take Rita, and we'll go."

Dusty looked at Priscilla. He could see how much the strain was telling on her, and he knew she was not strong because of the baby. She probably should *not* sit out in the sun. Priscilla met his eyes. "Go ahead," she said. "I'll be fine."

"Pack us a bait of grub, Pris. No tellin' how long we'll be," he told her gruffly. Rita followed Priscilla to the kitchen while Vance followed Dusty to the barn for the tools they would need.

When the men had been gone only a few minutes, Priscilla began to regret her decision to stay behind. The prospect of sitting there staring at Rita Jordan for hours was appalling.

"Do you mind if I do my chores?" Priscilla asked. "It will help pass the time."

Rita smiled evilly. "Nothin' I'd like better than to see what a lady does around the house. Go ahead."

Rita followed her as she busied herself around the house, inventing little things to keep her hands busy and her eyes from the hands of the clock which moved with agonizing slowness. From time to time, Rita made a comment.

"I was married once. 'Course it wasn't long enough for me to really get the hang of it. In fact, it wasn't no longer than you've been married." Another time she commented, "Don't seem like it'd be much fun to be married. Same chores every day. Same man every night." Priscilla bit her tongue. She refused to give this woman the satisfaction of arguing with her.

At last the shadows lengthened in the yard and the sun went down.

"Ain't you gonna fix no supper?" Rita demanded.

The thought of food almost made Priscilla gag. "I'm not very hungry," she answered through clenched teeth.

"Well, I am. Fix somethin'," Rita said.

Unwilling to admit her lack of cooking skills, Priscilla proceeded to the kitchen where she heated some leftovers for Rita, who wolfed them down. The smell of the food aggravated Priscilla's morning sickness, and it was only sheer force of will and pride that kept her from vomiting.

"Ain't you gonna eat nothin'?" Rita asked.

"No," said Priscilla. "That is, I might have a cup of tea." She thought perhaps that would settle her stomach.

"I'll fix it," offered Rita. "I could use some tea myself." Priscilla was too amazed to protest.

When Rita set the tea before her, she accepted it gratefully. As Priscilla sat cautiously sipping the steaming brew, Rita began to talk. For a moment, Priscilla was overcome by the incongruity of it—here she was, this woman's prisoner and yet they were chatting over a cup of tea. That feeling passed into horror, however, as she listened to the story Rita told.

"When I was a kid, my old man used to beat me. He liked to beat up women. Always kept a woman around, just for that. He beat one woman too many, though. Mattie, she wouldn't stand it, so she killed him. Don't look so shocked. He had it comin'. She poisoned him. It was a trick she learned from the Indians, a slow-workin' poison. A couple days, you keel over. Your heart just quits. Nobody ever knew. It's a good trick to know. You never can tell when you'll meet a man who needs killin'. I've met a few. There was one, the one who made me a whore. They found him in an alley. Another fella"—Rita's face turned dark with hatred—"the self-righteous hypocrite. It was his fault that . . . But you said you knew all about that." Rita paused as if mulling over past injustices. "I was married. Did I tell you? Three days.

479

They made nasty jokes when they found Sam Jordan dead in my bed. Said I'd killed him. I did all right, but not the way they thought. Then I come here an' Franklin, that old fool, don't have sense enough to sell out when he's got the chance. I don't give second chances." Rita smiled, knowingly. "You finished with that tea, yet?" Priscilla nodded dumbly, numb from the horrors she was hearing. Rita nodded her approval.

Priscilla struggled to find her voice. "Are you going to kill Dusty, too?"

Rita laughed. "If I was, I woulda done it long ago. No, that's too easy. I want him to suffer for what he did to me. I ain't gonna kill *him*. I'm gonna do something that'll make him hurt the rest of his life. I'm gonna kill *you!*"

It took a moment for the truth to sink in, and Priscilla looked down in horror at her empty cup and then back at Rita.

"That's right, honey," Rita said, almost solicitously. "In about two days, you'll just drop dead. By then you'll be glad, 'cause it won't be no fun at all watchin' your darlin' Dusty moon over you."

Priscilla opened her mouth to protest but before she could, a familiar feeling clutched at her stomach, and she bolted for the door. Leaning over the porch rail, she wretched as she had there once before until her empty stomach could only heave. At last she turned, weak and trembling, to face Rita, who stood outlined in the door, a look of total shock on her face. For a long time, neither moved.

Priscilla's brain at last began to function, and her first thought was that the poison was gone, no longer in her body. She might not die, would not die, and Rita had confessed murder to her. At that instant she saw the light of realization in Rita's eyes also.

Suddenly unsure, Rita began looking about, as if she might find some means of escape. Then her hand touched Dusty's gun, still strapped to her hip. Fumbling, she drew it just as Priscilla lunged. They fell together, half in, half out of the doorway. Priscilla's hand clutched at the gun as Rita fought desperately to turn it toward her. The mass of struggling arms and legs thrashed wildly, hampered by the doorway, until suddenly a shot rang out, and both bodies lay still.

Jason Vance paused for a moment to wipe the sweat from his brow and ease his aching back. Physical labor was not his game and the blisters on his hands were giving him a painful reminder of that. He glanced up to where he had tied Rhoades to a tree for a well-earned rest and wondered how long he should let the cowboy sit there before forcing him back to work. Meanwhile, he felt it necessary to dig himself. It was already dark and he was using the light of several lanterns he had had the foresight to bring. Rhoades seemed to be dozing, and Vance's eyes strayed up the tree to which he was tied. It was there, all right, no doubt about it—visible even in the darkness. The crude carving of a land turtle—the symbol for treasure buried in the direction in which the head pointed. The head pointed directly toward the hole in which Vance stood. Of course, the terrapin also stood for death, defeat, and destruction, facts which Vance had chosen to ignore. The gambler cursed and Rhoades started awake.

"Find it yet?" Dusty asked innocently.

"No, damn you," Vance growled, climbing out of the

hole. He picked up the map again and held it to the light. Looking up, he squinted into the darkness and looked back at the map. "I don't get it. It just doesn't fit."

"I told you. That's probably the same map them Mexicans had. That's why they never found this tree. You can't argue that ain't the markin' shown on the map."

Vance nodded grudgingly. "We should have hit it by now, though. The map says it's buried the depth of a shovel handle. We're down more than six feet already."

Rhoades grinned. "Maybe somebody got here first."

Vance almost struck him, but remembering the digging to be done, he restrained himself and instead untied Rhoades and ordered him back to work.

Dusty had been digging for a few minutes when he stopped, having seen something of interest. While Vance was busy rolling a cigarette, Dusty quickly stooped down and picked it up. Glancing at it in the poor light, he quickly dropped it into his vest pocket but not before Vance had seen him.

"What was that?" the gambler demanded, jumping to his feet.

"What was what?" asked Dusty innocently.

"Don't get smart. The thing you put in your pocket."

Reluctantly, Dusty pulled out the object and passed it up to Vance. He could see the gambler's eyes gleam even in the shadows as he examined the coin. Scraping the dirt off of it, he saw it was a square 'Dobe dollar, the old gold coin used by the Spanish. Surely it had been part of the treasure.

"This proves we're in the right place," he proclaimed excitedly, as if Dusty should share his enthusiasm.

The cowboy leaned lazily on the shovel. "Or it *was* the

right place." When Vance looked at him quizzically, he continued. "Way I figure, this was the place, all right. That coin proves it. But it ain't here now. You said yourself we should've hit it by now."

Vance was about to protest when two shots rang out in the darkness. They were far away but unmistakable.

"What was that?" Vance asked.

"Sounded like gunshots to me," drawled Dusty.

Vance eyed him suspiciously. "Two shots fired close together. That's a distress signal."

"Mebbe somebody's in trouble."

"Or maybe somebody's looking for you." Vance doused the lanterns, and they waited in the darkness for a long time. Dusty sat down in the hole and rolled a smoke. Vance cursed when he struck the match but it was probably not visible to anyone but him. Finally, Vance sat down, too. At long last, two more shots rang out, closer this time. "It's somebody looking for you, all right," Vance decided. "I wonder what happened to Rita? I should have guessed Priscilla would outsmart her."

Dusty cringed. He was not at all sure that that was what had happened. He was fairly certain, however, that the shots were fired for him. He need only get Vance's gun and fire off even one round to bring the searchers. Waiting, he watched the gambler carefully.

Vance hit his palm with his fist. He was remembering the curious sheriff. The lawman would know for certain that he had killed Rogers when he found out about this treasure hunt. Suddenly it seemed more important to be free than to be rich. Besides, he still had the money he had won in the poker game. That was plenty to make a fresh start, and Rhoades was probably right. Someone else had already gotten the gold. It just was not here.

"Get up out of that hole," he called to Dusty.

Dusty started to climb out, lost his footing, and fell. "Mind givin' me a hand? It's hard to see what you're doin' down here."

Without thinking, in the interest of speed, Vance reached a hand down to the cowboy. Dusty pulled with a jerk and Vance toppled over into the hole. In an instant Dusty was on him, pounding with his fists. Instinctively, Vance grappled, trying to rise, to get in a good punch, but he was pinned too closely, hampered by the steep sides of the ditch. The fight was over in seconds. Vance lay stunned and motionless. Dusty pulled the gambler's gun from its holster and quickly began to climb. He was halfway to the surface when he heard a loud explosion in his head and a thousand stars flashed before his eyes. He clawed upward, frantically trying to cling to consciousness, but it was hopeless. He slumped backward, senseless, into the broken earth.

Vance stood for a moment, the shovel still poised in his hands, in case Dusty stirred, but he did not. Vance grinned with satisfaction as he retrieved his gun. More than once that trick had worked for him. He had learned early that in a brawl, the last man on his feet usually walked away with the table stakes, so he had learned to play possum until the more enthusiastic of the fighters had knocked each other out. It was a good trick. Vance climbed out of the hole and got some rope from the wagon. He had just finished tying Dusty when the cowboy came to.

Dusty shook his head to clear it. It took a minute to figure out where he was and why. It all came back when he saw Vance standing over him.

"What are you gonna do, Vance?"

"Well," he replied, again climbing from the hole, "I am *not* going to kill you. Not that I have any reservations about doing so, you understand, but because a shot would attract too much attention. Also, I would rather not have a posse of outraged citizens with ropes on my trail. I will be leaving now. I'm taking my saddle horse, and I'm going to drive off the wagon team. I figure that by the time you work yourself loose and walk back to the ranch, I will have a fairly good start."

"I'll come after you, Vance," Dusty promised through clenched teeth.

Vance shrugged. "You're welcome to, but I am hoping that that lovely wife of yours will convince you how foolish it would be. As for myself, I doubt a team of wild horses could keep me from her bed for a single night. I'm sure she will persuade you to be reasonable." He thought for a moment and then said, as if to himself, "You've got the real treasure on this ranch, Rhoades. You'd be a fool to leave her."

Dusty cursed, but Vance ignored him. Finally, Dusty remembered another matter of business. "What about Rita? Ain't you goin' back for her?"

Vance actually laughed. "Of course not. I never had any intention of going back for her. Would you?"

Dusty had no answer for that. Vance was casting about for anything he might need to take with him. He picked up the map and looked at it for a second, then laughed again, bitterly. "Shall I leave you the map, Rhoades? As a reminder? Tell you what. If you'll tell me why it is that Rita hates you so much, I'll make you a present of it."

Dusty simply glared up at the gambler.

Vance shrugged again. "Of course, a gentleman never tells." He flung the map from him and it floated down into Dusty's face as he walked to find his horse in the darkness.

Dawn was graying the sky as Dusty limped into sight of the ranch. Lights were burning in every window, it seemed, and the yard was full of wagons and horses. With mounting dread, he recognized one of the Steele's wagons, the doctor's buggy, and the sheriff's horse. With leaden feet, he walked the last few hundred yards to the house.

As he approached the porch, a woman's rounded figure appeared at the door. It could only be Stella. "He's back! It's Dusty," she cried, hurrying out to meet him. Taking his hands, she quickly looked over his dirty clothes, his sweat-stained face. "You all right?" she asked eagerly.

He nodded wearily. "Where is she?"

Stella hesitated a moment. "Inside," she answered.

Dusty's hands tightened on hers. "Is she all right?"

Stella's eyes were tragic. "Yes, but . . ."

"Is she all right?" he demanded again.

"She ain't hurt but . . ."

"But what?" he asked, terrified to hear the answer.

Stella spoke as gently as she could. "She ain't in her right mind. Somethin' happened." Dusty had already pushed by her. Brushing past George, the sheriff, and the doc, he stormed into the house, his eyes searching every corner for Priscilla. Stella's voice rose behind him. "Rita Jordan's dead."

He stopped and turned back. Stella caught up with him. Breathlessly, she explained. "Your hands came in after supper. They found Rita dead, out by the back door. Shot. Priscilla was here, still holdin' the gun, just rockin' an' starin'. They couldn't get nothin' out of her. The Count stayed with her while Shorty fetched us an' then went to town fer doc an' the sheriff.''

Dusty looked up to see the doctor who had come in behind Stella. ''She doesn't seem to be physically harmed but—''

Stella interrupted, ''Nothin' she says makes no sense. We asked her what happened an' she says Rita tried to kill her. We asked where you were an' she says diggin' for gold. Honey, I made her a cup a tea and she flung it across the room screamin' how it was poison!''

''Where is she?'' he asked once again.

Stella pointed toward the bedroom, and he slowly walked over and carefully opened the door. Priscilla lay on the bed, pale as death. His heart lurched when he saw the powder burn on the front of her dress. It had been that close. He called her name.

She stirred and sat up, looking around like a lost child. He called her name again. With a cry of recognition, she reached out for him. He hurried to her side and they clung to each other. Suddenly, she pushed him away. ''You're all right?''

He nodded. ''You?''

Priscilla's eyes were unnaturally large. ''She's dead.''

''I know.''

''She tried to kill me.'' He nodded encouragement and slowly, painfully the story came out. He held her as she sobbed out the last of it, his face grim. When she was finished, she looked up. ''Vance?'' she inquired.

''Gone,'' he replied and held her again. At last he stirred. ''I'd better tell the others what happened. They think you're crazy, all that talk about gold and poison.''

She clutched at him anxiously. ''First, send the doctor

in. There's something I have to know."

She told the doctor about the poison.

"If it worked like she said," he commented, "I doubt that you had it in you long enough to do any harm."

"Doctor, I . . . that is, I'm going to have a baby. Do you think . . . ?"

The doctor's eyes were kind. "How far along are you?"

Priscilla flushed, conscious that she had only been married for three days. "About six weeks."

He patted her hand. "You'll have to do worse than that to shock me. You having any bleeding?" She shook her head. "I doubt the poison would have hurt anything. The shock might cause some problems but you stay in bed a few days. Likely everything will be fine. I better send Sheriff Winslow in. He's almighty curious about what's been goin' on here."

Stella and George stood by as Dusty told both his story and Priscilla's to the lawman. "Vance had some sort of treasure map. It was buried Spanish gold, I think," he explained. "He and Rita Jordan showed up here yesterday and threatened to kill Pris if I didn't take him to the spot where the treasure was. I guess he figured I would recognize the landmarks and he was right. I took him out, and we dug a hole but didn't find any gold. He got scared when he heard the shots—I guess that was folks looking for me?" His friends nodded and he continued. "He tied me up, ran off the horses and high-tailed it. He had left Rita Jordan here to guard Pris. The woman must have been a little crazy. She told Pris how she'd poisoned all these men, even Franklin when he wouldn't sell out to her. She used some kind of Injun poison. Then she told Pris that she'd poisoned her. Luckily, Pris got sick and threw it all up. Then Rita tried to shoot her, and they fought over the gun. You can figure out the rest."

It was, Priscilla realized with some surprise, the honest truth that he had told, but without any embarrassing references to his past affair with Rita.

"Why d'you suppose she tried to poison you, Mrs. Rhoades?" asked Winslow.

Priscilla cast about for some explanation that would not betray their secret. "She was jealous, I guess," she said lamely.

"Jealous?" The sheriff was mystified.

"You gotta be a woman to understand, Sheriff," Stella explained helpfully. "A woman like that would just naturally hate a lady like Priscilla. She wasn't in her right mind, either. She must've thought in some crazy way that Priscilla was a threat to her. I don't guess she really needed a *good* reason. Seems like she just poisoned anybody she had a mind to."

The sheriff nodded. He was mentally making plans to telegraph word for area lawmen to be on the lookout for Vance. Someone needed to ask him some questions about Rogers's death. Meanwhile, he decided not to tell anyone his suspicions. No use upsetting Mrs. Rhoades any more right now. "Reckon we better head on out. You folks have had more'n enough company fer one day."

Later, Priscilla sat on her bed eating breakfast from a tray that Dusty had brought her. The golden sunlight streaming through the window gave the lie to the nightmare of the preceding day. Dusty sat in a chair beside the bed, his eyes never leaving her. Occasionally, she looked up at him and smiled.

"Penny for your thoughts," she asked.

"I was just thinking how scared I was when I got back

489

to the ranch. It might've been you instead of her."

She nodded solemnly. "At least Mr. Vance didn't hurt you."

Dusty smiled grimly and touched the lump on the side of his head.

"Well, he didn't hurt you much," she conceded. "He might have killed you. I guess he wasn't really a bad person. Not like her."

Dusty did not share her opinion, but he decided not to argue. She ate for a while longer.

"Poor Mr. Vance," she commented.

"Poor?" he asked, amazed.

"All that looking, for months, and not even to find the gold in the end. I almost feel sorry for him."

Dusty snorted. She ignored him and then said, almost to herself, "I wonder who did get the gold."

"Nobody, I reckon."

"Nobody? But you said it was gone," she accused. He had told her the whole story in detail after everyone else had left.

"I said we didn't find it. That's 'cause we were digging in the wrong place," he told her blandly.

Priscilla's eyes were wide with amazement. "But the turtle, carved on the tree, just like the map . . ."

Dusty grinned slowly. "You remember the story I told Vance, about the Mexicans?" She nodded. "Well, there's more I didn't tell him." She leaned forward, eagerly. "See, a couple years later, after the Mexes left and Pa came home, I found that tree, the one with the turtle carved on it. We were having a roundup and Pa had sent me out to rustle firewood. The tree had been lightning-struck and was rotten. It was pure luck I happened to see the carving at all." He stopped.

"Didn't you tell anyone?" she demanded.

"I told Pa. He just laughed. Said the only treasure we had on the place was the cattle. That's what would make us rich. He was busy with the roundup and all, but I made him promise he'd help me look for it when he got back from the drive. He never got back," he told her simply.

Priscilla nodded. After a moment she asked, "Did you ever tell your mother?"

"Yeah, well . . . you had to know her. She was real peculiar about money. She said if the Good Lord wanted us rich, we'd earn it. Thought it was pagan to go diggin' around looking for gold, especially if it belonged to someone else. She would probably have given it back to the Mexicans if we had found it."

"So you never even looked for it?" she asked incredulously.

"I looked some. I dug around a little. That's where I found my lucky gold piece," he told her.

"That square coin I saw!" Priscilla cried. "That was the coin you tricked Vance with!" she realized. "It really was part of the treasure. But how did the turtle get carved on the other tree?"

"I carved it there. You gotta remember, I was just a kid. I was thinking if those Mexicans ever came back, I'd fool them. I reckon it was a good idea," he grinned boyishly.

She looked at him with wonder and her eyes held the same gleam he had seen in Vance's when he had looked at the coin. "Then the gold's still out there," she said.

He looked at her with disapproval. He got up and removed the tray from her lap. Then he knelt down beside the bed and took her hand in both of his. He looked at her with eyes more serious than she had ever seen

491

them. "Look, honey," he said. "Don't *you* start. We don't need any gold. We're rich enough." His voice became hoarse with emotion. "We got this place. We've got each other."

With her free hand she touched his hair, and he buried his face in her lap. Vance had been right, he knew. A man would be a fool to go after gold when he had her.

Priscilla looked down at him. The sunlight caught his hair and she could see the golden flecks. He was right. They *were* rich. And he was the treasure. "Love me," she whispered.

His head came up. He wasn't certain he had heard her right. "What . . . ?"

"I said, love me. Love me now." She needed him, needed to feel him inside of her, needed his love to wash away the horrors that had come between them.

Her dark eyes glittered with desire, and Dusty's response was instinctive, but his good judgment held him back. "You shouldn't," he cautioned. "Doc said . . ."

"That I should stay in bed," she supplied. "I'm not going to get out of bed. Please," she begged, drawing his face to hers.

The touch of her lips drew all resistance from him, and he followed her willingly when she tugged him down onto the bed. The fragile fabric of the nightdress Stella had helped her change into was no barrier to his seeking hands, and Priscilla impatiently pulled open the buttons of his shirt, longing for the warmth, the strength of him. Soon they were free of all restraints, their bodies intertwined, their lips whispering the secret words that only lovers know. Priscilla cried out in ecstasy when his power filled her, and Dusty had the oddest sensation that she was drawing more than just his seed from him as she

492

seemed to absorb the very essence of his life into her depths. When they both lay sated and panting, Dusty very tenderly brushed the damp chestnut curls from her forehead and left a very chaste kiss in that newly bared spot. "Did I hurt you?" he asked, a worried frown creasing his own broad forehead.

Priscilla's arms tightened around him. "You could never hurt me," she declared with certainty as she clung to him with greedy hands.

He knew that was a lie, a lie of love, but nevertheless a lie. He had hurt her badly, cruelly, in the past, but she was partly right: he could never hurt her again. "You're so precious to me," he told her softly.

She looked at his face, her eyes filled with love. "When I came here, I was looking for something. Just like Jason Vance, I knew there was a treasure here, and I found it when I found you."

"Oh, no," he denied, unwilling to accept such a tribute. "You're the treasure. Even Vance said so before he left. He was pretty worthless, but he was right about that."

Priscilla heaved an exaggerated sigh. "Do you realize that we have been arguing ever since the moment we met and we're *still* arguing?"

Dusty thought this over and then grinned wickedly. "We didn't have one single argument during the last three days," he pointed out.

She giggled. "I guess we were too busy doing other things," she said, running one hand up his thigh provocatively.

"Oh, no, you don't," he warned sternly, removing her hand from its dangerous position. "You've been 'busy' enough for today. It's time we both got a little rest.

Neither of us got much sleep last night." Settling her more comfortably on his shoulder, he snuggled down and was quickly sound asleep.

Too keyed up to sleep so quickly, Priscilla watched the face she loved soften in sleep. He was wrong, she decided. They both were. They were not the treasure. No, it was something much bigger, much more important that was so valuable, and that was their love. Their love was the real treasure in Rainbow. Along with that they had each other, their child, the ranch—everything anyone could possibly want.

And somewhere out there was all that gold . . .

MORE RAPTUROUS READING

WINDSWEPT PASSION (1484, $3.75)
By Sonya T. Pelton
The wild, wordly pirate swept young, innocent Cathelen into an endless wave of ecstasy, then left with the morning tide. Though bound to another, the lovely blonde would turn one night of love into a lifetime of raging WINDSWEPT PASSION.

BITTERSWEET BONDAGE (1368, $3.75)
by Sonya T. Pelton
In sultry, tropical Morocco, Rosette would forget the man who had broken her heart. And forget she did in the tantalizing embrace of mysterious, magnetic Mark — who knew he'd always keep her in BITTERSWEET BONDAGE.

AWAKE SAVAGE HEART (1279, $3.75)
by Sonya T. Pelton
Though Daniel craved tantalizing Tammi, marriage was the farthest thing from his mind. But only Tammi could match the flames of his desire when she seductively whispered, AWAKE SAVAGE HEART.

THE CAPTAIN'S VIXEN (1257, $3.50)
by Wanda Owen
No one had ever resisted Captain Lance Edward's masculine magnetism — no one but the luscious, jet-haired Elise. He vowed to possess her, for she had bewitched him, forever destining him to be entranced by THE CAPTAIN'S VIXEN!

TEXAS WILDFIRE (1337, $3.75)
by Wanda Owen
When Amanda's innocent blue eyes began haunting Tony's days, and her full, sensuous lips taunting his nights, he knew he had to take her and satisfy his desire. He would show her what happened when she teased a Texas man — never dreaming he'd be caught in the flames of her love!

Available wherever paperbacks are sold, or order direct from the Publisher. Send cover price plus 50¢ per copy for mailing and handling to Zebra Books, 475 Park Avenue South, New York, N.Y. 10016. DO NOT SEND CASH.